Besieged...

Payback is a bitch—and Phoebe McKinn is just the she-wolf for the job.

Phoebe was a child when she witnessed powerful politicians slaughter her pack and family. She's hungered for revenge ever since. She probably won't survive her quest, and her death will accomplish the government's goal of annihilating all shifters, but she's vowed to take the assassins down with her.

Werewolf secret agent Parker Rowe is anxious to return home after an undercover gig, but his plans are derailed when he prevents a mugging. Turns out the victim isn't just any female—she's his fated mate.

Meeting Parker shocks Phoebe. She believed she was the last living werewolf. The crone who raised her shared what shifter knowledge she had, but most of Phoebe's heritage and Parker's expectations of her are a mystery to Phoebe. Not the sex—she enjoys that—but she can't risk being distracted from seeking justice for her family.

Parker reluctantly puts his life on hold so he can protect Phoebe and help her with her mission—but can he convince her that survival is the best revenge?

TROPES/THEMES/CHARACTERS: Werewolves, fated mates (but not insta-love), shifters, vampires, witches, supernatural, paranormal, politicians, attempted genocide, revenge.

MJ COMPTON

Each book in the trilogy is a standalone romance, but because of the overarching story, the books are best read in order.

Besieged by the Moon

Service for Sanctuary Book 3

MJ Compton

Comptonplations Publishing

To the victims of the COVID-19 Pandemic.

May you rest in peace.

Acknowledgements

To my original publisher (Soul Mate Publishing) and editors Debby Gilbert and Char Chaffin for their endless patience while I wrestled with this manuscript.

The Purples, always and forever for listening to me whine: Carol Lombardo, Christine Wenger, Gayle Callen, and Kris Fletcher.

CNYRW Saturday Morning Critique—thanks to all who showed up and gave me such great feedback. Special thanks to Ron Bagliere for sharing his elevator knowledge.

Jim Callen and Christine Wenger for their gun expertise.

My Facebook family, fans, and friends for telling me what they'd smell while walking on a summer night.

My husband Steve, who told me when we got married that he didn't expect dinner on the table every night and has kept his word.

Contents

Chapter 1

PHOEBE MCKINN KNEW SHE'D made a mistake when she found herself out past sundown on the night of the new moon. New moons brought bad things. The darkness not only increased her vulnerability but also abetted the criminal.

Walking from the bus station to the most exclusive neighborhood in Warwick, Minnesota might not be the smartest thing she'd ever done. Yes, she carried her quarterstaff, so she wasn't totally unarmed, but shifting would always be her best weapon. Besides, she needed to know...

The metro bus stop sat only two blocks from the entrance to the gated community. Waiting in the kiosk should have been safe enough given the neighborhood, but tonight a gang of young men congregated nearby. Their catcalls didn't bother her—no self-respecting werewolf paid attention to cats or other paranormal creatures—but this night, when she couldn't shift, not even in self-defense, she mentally kicked herself for not heading straight to the youth hostel she'd located online. She had no business scoping out the exclusive Elysian Estates...yet.

The hoodlums lurked as if they could sniff her vulnerability. Not that she couldn't take her harassers. She was strong. Werewolf strong. Her quarterstaff gave her an advantage.

"Hey, bitch!"

If only they knew being called 'bitch' wasn't an insult in her world.

A few whistles pierced the darkness.

The gauntlet began.

Phoebe held her head high. Her strength surpassed the standard issue non-lycan female. Males bent on teaching a female her place ought to be something she could handle without breaking a sweat. On any other night.

"Smile, bitch!"

She bared her teeth, but it didn't have the same effect as when she traveled four-legged. She kept walking, every sense focused on her surroundings: the scent of freshly turned soil; crickets counting out the next day's temperature; the late summer evening chill brushing her skin; the moonless sky.

There. Footsteps behind her.

"You ignoring me? I don't like being ignored."

His cohorts laughed.

A few yards separated her from the bus stop, clearly marked by light puddling from the streetlamp. She didn't know what time the next bus would be coming through. Waiting for it would be the same as inviting the young men to continue harassing her. She'd have to locate another kiosk. She didn't mind. Her muscles begged to move after long hours already spent on the bus to Warwick.

Except someone emerged from the shadows onto the sidewalk in front of her.

Phoebe stopped. Light and dark played on the thin young man's face, distorting his features.

"Come on, bitch. Be nice to us, and we'll be nice to you."

The males surrounded her, a tightening ring of beasts on the prowl. On any other night, she could shift and be done with these yakked-up hairballs.

She refused to surrender to the fear nipping at her. Terror cast its own aura. She would not give these bottom dwellers the satisfaction.

She clutched her quarterstaff with both hands.

The ring tightened around her, preparing to go in for the kill. Someone caught her arm. "How about a kiss?"

Phoebe wrenched free, but a second, a third, a fourth hand grabbed her. Touched her with callused fingers. Someone's hangnail scraped her wrist.

The oak quarterstaff cracked against a forearm, followed by a shriek. Not hers.

And they stank. Her head filled with the stench of unwashed bodies, rotting teeth, clothes desperately needing soap and water. Garlic sausage haunted someone's breath.

"Be friendly, and we won't hurt you," a disembodied voice promised. As if honor bound these creatures. Sure enough, something grabbed her breast.

Phoebe screamed and swung her weapon. She hadn't trained in mob control.

A foul-tasting hand clamped over her mouth. She bit down hard enough to draw blood, which might have satisfied her rage in other circumstances, but not tonight.

Someone yanked her denim jacket down her arms, disabling her hands. "Toss the stick," a rough voice commanded. Someone else wrung her breast hard enough to squeeze tears from her eyes. She tried to kick. Scream. Flail her way free of her jacket.

Fabric hissed as it separated. The slash seared her thigh. The roar in her head muted the filth spewing from her attackers' mouths.

Except not all the cries were filth. Surprise. Shock. Fear. Phoebe opened her eyes—not realizing she'd scrunched them shut—in time to see a tall, dark-haired man swing his fist at Sausage Breath's jaw.

She heard the smack and crunch as knuckles met flesh and bone. Catcalls turned to whimpers. Several attackers ran into the darkness which spawned them. At least two sprawled in crumpled splendor on the sidewalk.

She snatched up her quarterstaff and sniffed the air. Her rescuer's scent filled her head. She recognized his aroma, although she hadn't been caressed by it in years: the earthy spice of werewolf blood. A fellow homo lupus rescued her.

She scented more than werewolf on her rescuer. Instinct tingled in her blood. Unfamiliar, but undeniable. She knew. Her kind always knew.

He kicked the bodies lying on the concrete before straightening and looking at her. His eyes glittered like smoky quartz. Dark hair clung to his cheeks. He shook his head, and the fine strands flew off his face, leaving only shadows to define its contours.

Giddy delight urged her to rush to him, but she held back. "Oh. It's you. It's about time you showed up." A lifetime ago her grandmother told her a female waited her entire life to meet her mate.

"Your leg," he replied as he approached her.

His voice. Oh, Goddess, his voice created the male version of a siren's song.

She limped toward him, using the quarterstaff as a cane, but he held up his hand. "You're bleeding."

Blood loss would explain the wet sensation on her leg and the queasiness roiling in her stomach. "I think one of them used a knife."

He scooped her off her feet, tossed her over his shoulder, and headed back in the direction from which he came.

"Um, excuse me?" She tried to keep the quarterstaff off his body.

"I need to get your pants off—"

Well, then. He was rushing things, but she didn't mind.

"—so I can look at your leg."

Oh. That. "Are you a doctor or something?"

"Something."

"It's only a scratch." Her thigh throbbed. "I'm starting to heal. I can think of better things to do when my pants are gone."

"Not subtle, are you?"

She appreciated her view of a fabulous male butt working his jeans. "Why waste time? We both know we're mates. Let's get the marking done so we can get on with the other things we have to do."

Maybe the way her head bounced around upset her world view. Wonky. Fading in and out. Swirling. Sparkling. Something was desperately wrong with this scenario.

Corbie, her foster mother, claimed male blood left their brains, flooded their penises, and prevented rational thought. Lycan or sapien, men were the same when it came to sex. Then why was Phoebe the one plagued with lightheadedness?

"We don't even know each other's names," her future mate pointed out.

"I'm Phoebe."

"Parker Rowe, Loup Garou, Colorado."

"You're a long way from home, Parker Rowe. Looking for me?" *Please, please be looking for me. Phoebe Rowe. The perfect name for me. Oh, Goddess, any name will do. Even one from Loup Garou.*

"Actually," he said, "no."

Ancient Ones. Parker deposited his mate in the front seat of his borrowed pickup truck. The overhead dome light illuminated the cab only enough for him to determine the shallow knife wound on Phoebe's thigh had started healing. In a few more minutes, she'd be well enough for him to claim her. No drama. No angst. Unlike his closest associates, his would be an uncomplicated mating. Phoebe was lycan. She acknowledged him as her mate.

He could mark her, then they could start for Loup Garou in the morning. Mating wouldn't interfere with his plans.

"I don't want my first time to be in the front seat of a truck." She clutched a stick as if it were a weapon.

She'd answered a question he didn't want to ask. His female indulged in no pre-mating sex experiments with sapiens. Not all modern she-wolves cared about lycan conventions.

No, he wouldn't claim her in another lobo's pickup.

He'd drive Phoebe to Ethan's house, where he'd be better able to treat her wound and access Selena's herbal remedies.

He could mark her, then they'd hit the road. He planned to be back in Loup Garou with time to spare before starting the next class in his paramedic training. He'd missed too much time by being sent to Minnesota on a pointless mission.

He jammed the key into the ignition and twisted. "Anything else I should know?"

"I'm nervous about this. Sapien females say intercourse hurts the first time."

"It's my responsibility to make sure I don't hurt you," he replied. He put the truck in drive and pulled away from the curb. Where could he find the traditional mating offering of berries this late at night? "It's my duty to make sure you're happy. How can you be happy if I hurt you?"

"I'm going to hold you to that. Oh, and keep in mind, I'm allergic to strawberries."

She must have been reading his mind.

"I didn't know werewolves could have food allergies." To his knowledge, alcohol was the only lycan allergen. The homo lupus couldn't consume many foods sapiens considered normal: chocolate; grapes in any form; artificial sweeteners were deadly. You'd never find a werewolf living a millennial lifestyle because avocado toast was poison. Death sentences, not allergies.

"How's your pain right now?"

One shoulder rose. "No pain. Itching, so I'm healing."

"I still want to check it. Did you see what he used to cut you?"

"A box cutter or a knife. I'm not sure which. He was fast. I should have been faster."

Strange, unfamiliar emotion rose in him. Fierce. Protective. "Why were you out alone, tonight of all nights?"

"I'm new in town. I'm looking for..." She stopped, as if she'd revealed too much.

As if her reply answered his question.

He scanned the dark streets around him. A traffic light a few blocks ahead spilled red like blood onto the pavement. "Where are you from?"

"Tennessee."

"You're a long way from home for a single female." Although he'd tried for neutrality in his tone, he winced because he failed. He couldn't help his hard wiring.

"Yeah," she admitted. "I'm not a fan of double standards. I can take care of myself."

Her take on how they'd met differed from his. He'd seen a female being attacked, and being a nice guy, he'd stopped to help. He'd rescued her.

"If you say so. You mentioned you were looking for something. Trouble?" He glanced at the stick resting against her thigh. "A weapon?"

"No, I'm trying to track down a rumor I heard."

"Your mate is exiled in Minnesota?"

"Ha. What do you mean, 'exiled'?"

He knew evasiveness when he heard it, even if mating fever played havoc in his brain. "What are you looking for? Maybe I can help."

She didn't answer for several moments.

"Hello?"

"You're not from around here, so I doubt you would know anything about...where the youth hostel is." The passing streetlights backlit her profile. "Explain this exile thing to me."

It seemed Phoebe was good at deflecting.

Maybe if he answered her question, she would answer his. "I'm an emergency medical technician. My alpha sent me to help with something." Except he couldn't help. Only the Ancient Ones could raise the dead. "It didn't work out. What's your story?"

"If I told you, I'd have to kill you."

She spoke lightly, as befitted the tone of the joke, but Parker's gut insisted Phoebe wasn't kidding.

He turned onto the thoroughfare leading to Ethan's neighborhood. "I'm tough."

"I'm tougher."

Her arrogance amused him. "I picked up on that."

Her heated glare seared him.

"You don't need to be sarcastic. Those jerks caught me off guard."

"I have no doubt. So why were you outside Elysian Estates?" The gated community wasn't on any chamber of commerce list of places to visit.

"Why were you?"

"I'm on my way home after helping friends move into their new apartment."

"In Elysian Estates? You must have impressive friends."

She seemed to know a lot about the exclusive community. Too much for casual interest.

"Depends on your point of view. I'm staying with the local pack alpha. Erik Wolfe's daughter."

Phoebe waited a beat before responding. "A female alpha?"

"Only because she's Erik Wolfe's daughter."

Erik Wolfe was a legend among lycans. He'd been in the Pentagon on September eleventh. He'd lost his life while honoring the service for sanctuary treaties.

Phoebe didn't react. How could she not know the name Erik Wolfe?

"You're staying with this female?" Phoebe's stillness pleased him. Another female might have squirmed or fidgeted. Even wounded, Phoebe remained as still as a wolf waiting for prey.

"Yeah. Her mate, Ethan, is my colleague. His family originally came from around here." Vague enough without being evasive.

"Really?" Softly asked, but with keen interest. "He's Varulv exiled to Colorado?"

"Not exactly." Ethan's story wasn't Parker's to tell.

"So you're staying with him, not her."

A fine distinction, but one that might matter to a mate. "Right. Ethan bought the house they live in, so technically it is his."

Phoebe's silence lasted two blocks. "I heard all the lycans in the area were gone."

"A few Varulv survived." Parker would never forget the stench of rotting bodies. Never be able to unsee the corpse of a child who'd tried to hide in the same bush Parker puked on. Sights and smells shouldn't bother him, but the Ulvskog massacre would upset anyone with a soul.

"There's a dozen or so, mostly living in Ulvskog. Because Ethan mated with Selena, our alpha sent a contingent here to help with...things."

"What things?"

Parker noted the vampires who once guarded the corner of Oak and Ash Streets hadn't returned. *Thank the Ancient Ones.* "Things Selena needed done for her pack." Ethan's business was not Parker's to share.

He pulled to the curb in front of Ethan's orange house.

"This is where you're staying?" She eyed the house as if she didn't trust it.

"Until tomorrow," he said. "I'm going home tomorrow."

"Oh. Before you go, can you drive me to the bus station to pick up my backpack? I left it in a locker so I wouldn't be encumbered on the new moon."

Her logic made sense. What would have happened with the thugs if she'd been weighted with luggage?

"We can pick it up on our way." Dakota could stop at the bus station on the way to the airport, where Parker planned to rent a vehicle to drive home.

"Excuse me? On our way where?"

"Home."

"Colorado? I don't think so."

Maybe his mating wasn't going to be as smooth as he'd thought.

"I just got here. I have things to do. You can go on ahead."

As if he would leave his mate behind in a place where their kind risked their lives by breathing. "You're coming with me."

A mated female joined her male's pack. Selena and Ethan were an exception due to Selena being her pack's alpha and Ethan's own alpha heritage.

"Let's not argue." Phoebe's tone turned sultry. "Don't we have other plans tonight?"

"Oh, we do," he assured her. He unclasped his seat belt.

For all his inward pissing and moaning about being sent to Minnesota on a fool's errand, the Ancient Ones knew what they were doing. No drama. No soul searching. No secrets. A plain, old-fashioned mating between two consenting lycans. After witnessing everything his pack mates suffered, he'd wondered if marking a female was worth the trouble.

Chapter 2

So much for the youth hostel.

She didn't want to stay there anyway. The other pitfalls from meeting Parker? He could put serious kinks in her plans. He needed to stop prying into her business. Maybe the marking thing could wait. Especially if Parker considered hauling her off to Colorado when she was so close...

Meeting Parker's friends didn't make her to-do list, either. Especially an alpha. Phoebe didn't know lycan protocols. Coming to Warwick probably violated half a dozen courtesies.

Memories of the life torn away from her as a child clutched her soul. She recognized what Parker's scent meant. She understood in her DNA what he expected, yet her neediness for Parker stunned her. She half wanted him to throw her over his shoulder and saunter into the house, a male staking his claim.

What was wrong with her? How could she even imagine such a scenario?

"Can you walk?"

"I'm fine." Her wound had stopped itching.

She opened the door as Parker arrived to assist her. She started to slide out, but Parker caught her. He smelled nice. She wanted to sink her teeth into him and taste.

Her leg twinged when she put her weight on it, so she leaned heavily on her quarterstaff.

Parker steadied her. "Maybe you're not as healed as you thought."

He kept his arm around her waist as she limped toward the house that glowed like an October Hunter's Moon on this late August evening.

"I'm surprised you aren't healing faster." He inserted a key into the lock. "I'll have to check when we get inside and the light is better."

"Does checking involve removing my leggings?" The idea more than appealed.

"Yes."

Maybe she expected too much. She knew the ecstasy of a shift. She anticipated the thrill of a kill. She believed she would never mate, and learning she'd been wrong delighted her. Parker's casual attitude didn't seem to match her own enthusiasm.

"Hello," Parker called out as he led her down a dark hallway. A fishy scent lingered in the air. "Britt and Dakota are moved. I'm beat."

"Wait a minute," a female called out. "Who's with you?"

Parker muttered something before replying. "My mate. I'll introduce you later."

Laughter followed his announcement. "Don't hurt her!" a male shouted. "And make sure she's happy."

Phoebe wondered if she should be embarrassed.

"Sapien or lupine?" the female asked, her voice growing louder.

"Scat." Parker tightened his hand on Phoebe's waist. "Lupine."

"Then I should know her." The female spoke from a doorway, where light from the room behind her backlit her silhouette.

"She's injured," Parker bit out. "I need to tend to her wound."

"Let me get my bag." The female started toward them.

"I'm fine." Phoebe's words came out rough. Phlegmy.

"You're not fine," Parker growled at the same time he pinched her waist.

"I'm Selena Wolfe Calhoun." The female ignored Parker. "Alpha of the Varulv. And you are?"

"Phoebe from Tennessee."

Selena loomed over her, as if to intimidate her.

"My mate is wounded," Parker repeated, his hand remaining firmly on her waist.

"How?"

"She ran into some thugs right after she got here."

Parker's evasiveness told Phoebe he didn't want the alpha she-wolf to know his business.

"The new moon is a bad night for a female to be out alone."

"Good thing I was there." Parker nudged Phoebe forward. "Now, if you'll excuse us—"

"But I haven't excused you. Phoebe? What's your pack?"

"One from Tennessee. You've probably never heard of it."

"Try me."

Phoebe should have anticipated the question. She should have developed a plausible tale, close enough to the truth to be believable.

"Okay. I confess. I didn't grow up in a pack." She lowered her chin and stared at Selena. "I'm a foundling."

"A foundling?" Selena's sharp tone betrayed her disbelief.

"My foster mother called me a survivor."

Selena's alpha brain couldn't be slow or dense. How long would it take her to connect the dots?

A tall, dark-haired male joined them. "What's going on?" he asked, as he massaged Selena's nape.

Phoebe froze. She couldn't swallow. He reminded her of—

"What's wrong?" Parker must have felt her body tense. "Is your wound bothering you?"

"Do I know you?" the other male asked. Phoebe couldn't speak.

"This is my mate. Phoebe." A threat edged Parker's tone. As if he could read her mind. Or as if he, too, sensed the...vibrations between Phoebe and the other male, mistaking the vibrations for something sexual.

The other male stared at Phoebe. "I'm Ethan Calhoun, mated to Selena."

Pure Loup Garou blood didn't flow through Ethan's veins. Maybe Parker believed his buddy Ethan was merely another French-American werewolf, but Ethan lived a lie.

Parker tightened his grip on Phoebe's waist. "I need to tend to my mate."

Selena's mouth widened in a mocking smile. "Phoebe and I can bond later."

"I can't wait," Phoebe lied. How had someone as mundane as Selena Wolfe ended up with someone like Ethan Calhoun?

Parker released Phoebe's waist to open a door. Steep stairs vanished into the darkness below.

"Think you can manage?" His low, intimate tone sent shivers through her body.

"What's down there?"

"Sleeping quarters. The handrail is sturdy."

"I have my quarterstaff." The stick disguised a multi- purpose tool. "I'll be fine."

She would always be fine. Survival depended on nothing less.

The narrow stairwell meant she needed to follow Parker down the steep passage. Each step strengthened her leg. The wound stung like fire ants swarming her thigh, but she knew the burn meant healing.

By the time she made it to the basement, her entire body, not only her wound, itched. Her skin could no longer contain her want. Her need. Her lust. The cool, rational part of her brain assumed mating fever caused the symptoms. For the first time in her life she didn't want to be rational. She wanted to be shocking. She wanted to be free from the shackling constraints of other people's expectations. If she couldn't let loose with her mate…

Parker's arm slid around her waist again. His touch drove her crazy. "How are you doing?"

"Great," she replied. "I think taking the stairs accelerated the healing process."

He quirked a brow at her. "I never heard of such a thing."

"Okay, maybe it's your touch making me hotter. I mean better." Her tongue slipped, but she refused to be embarrassed for admitting her mate's touch did things to her body.

"Hotter and better, huh?" He guided her toward the far end of the open space.

"What are you going to do about it?"

"What do you want me to do?"

"Don't they teach single lobos about mating where you come from?" Because she sure as shit didn't know.

He narrowed his eyes, as if he understood the insult. "We depend on instinct."

She studied the room. A few single cots lined one wall. A couple double mattresses carpeted the cold concrete floor. The front seat of the truck might have been better.

So far, mating disappointed her.

She'd waited long enough. Time to take the initiative. She twisted away from his half-hearted embrace and tossed her quarterstaff into a corner. Her jacket followed. Static crackled in the short tufts of her hair as she whipped off her t-shirt.

"What—are you hurt?" Parker pushed aside her arm, as he took in her bound breasts. "Why are you bandaged?"

She laughed, low and throaty. "I'm fine. They get in my way."

In more ways than one, but she didn't want to go there. Not tonight. She started unwinding the cloth. "Want to help?" Sapien males were fascinated by what they called her rack. Maybe her apparent lack caused Parker's insipid reaction to her.

"You squish them on purpose?" he asked. "Mashing them can't be good for them."

"Why don't you check them out?" she offered. She wanted his touch. She ached for him to drag his fingers across her bare skin. If he didn't place his hands on her body soon, she would have to hurt him.

"You're my mate," she reminded him, resenting he needed reminding. "You're supposed to want to touch me. Is there a problem?"

His Adam's apple bobbed in his throat. One heartbeat passed. Then a second.

"Ohh-kay." She dropped the binding cloth to the floor, then snatched up her discarded shirt. "I guess I don't understand mating as much as I thought I did. My bad. I thought there would be more...passion. More emotion."

"You're trying to goad me into hurting you," he growled.

"I'm trying to goad you into marking me. I figured touching you might give you a clue. But if you're not interested, you're not interested."

The zipper on his jeans told a different story.

Parker snatched her shirt from her hand and threw it atop the binding material. "Don't you know you're supposed to massage my ego? Marking is traumatic for males."

"I've never heard that." She crossed her arms over her breasts.

"Performance anxiety," he grumbled.

"I have nothing to judge you by, so what's the problem?" She inched closer to him and stretched her hand toward his chest.

He brushed against the finger she poised to trace his nipples, which were hard, pointed, and visible beneath his loose-fitting shirt. "No problem."

BIG PROBLEM. SEVERAL PROBLEMS. Two were on Phoebe's chest. Breasts. Big breasts. Parker didn't know where to start. How to start.

The third big problem tightened his jeans and grew with every beat of his heart. Based on the way his fly threatened to burst from straining to contain his still-growing cock, tiny Phoebe might have a problem accepting him into her body. A big problem.

She touched him. Her fingers brushed his chest. His nipples. Intense sensation shot straight to his groin. Little blood remained in his brain. Maybe lack of oxygen prevented him from figuring out how to start. Maybe he should follow her lead.

He used his forefinger to trace her aureole. The soft flesh tightened. Puckered.

Phoebe's breath whistled through her teeth.

He took his touch further and lightly pinched the tip of her breast.

She seemed to like that, too.

He slid his arm around her waist and pulled her onto a mattress. He cushioned her fall, then rolled to his side to face her. She smelled wonderful, like...like...a good mate should smell. With her breasts cradled in his lucky palms, he nuzzled her neck.

"Mmm."

The soft sounds Phoebe made assured him he was doing better.

Thinking turned to static from lack of blood in his brain. Instinct took over. Instinct, cause, and effect. If he did this, she responded with that. Nip the cord on the side of her neck, and she writhed. Based on her increased heart rate and respiration, along with her delicious fragrance, she liked being nipped. Nibbled. Licked. Sucked. He found her mating spot.

Her luscious breasts kept his hands busy as he nibbled his way down the side of her neck. He drew a nipple into his mouth. A burst of mating scent rewarded him.

The female drove him out of his mind.

He fumbled for the fastening on her pants. Didn't find one. The black stretchy material clung to her like a second skin. He didn't have the time or the patience to search for an opening. He cupped her crotch and discovered dampness seeping through the material. Not urine. Phoebe-needs- fucking juice.

He curled his fingers into the cloth and tugged. The fabric stretched. A second yank with a touch more mating fever behind it did the trick. He flung the garment to the floor. She wore no underwear. He laid her bare for his exploration. His plundering. His pleasure.

She'd been busy. She'd managed to unbutton his waistband and unzip his fly without him being aware she'd done so. Her tiny, hot hand slid into his briefs.

His breathing turned to groans. He thrust against her hand, lost in the physical sensations.

"Hey." She wrapped her fingers around him. "Save that for me."

How did she have the focus to speak?

Her. Right. He used his fingers to foreshadow what he planned to do with his penis. Her vagina was wet. Tight, but lubricated enough for one finger. He inserted a second one, stretching the passageway he knew could accommodate the birth of a child after months of hormonal preparation. He didn't have months. He needed to be inside her now.

Ancient Ones, don't let me hurt Phoebe.

Numbness, except where Phoebe touched him, settled in his body. A vampire could sneak up behind him and bite him on the neck and he wouldn't notice. He wouldn't even smell the creature because his mate's scent and her arousal filled his head.

He inserted a third finger into her vagina. He needed to be gentle when he didn't want to be gentle. When he needed to ravish her.

He rolled her onto her back. Her legs splayed; he crawled between them. "I don't want to hurt you," he muttered against her ear, then nipped the lobe.

"I'm tougher than I look." Her tongue darted to his throat.

He jumped when she licked a particular area. He'd never heard males had mating spots, but she'd found something that increased his need to thrust inside her. He fumbled as he positioned himself. Lust banished his sense of direction, his sense of anything except the need to possess this female.

She recoiled as he pushed.

"Do you want me to stop?" His voice mimicked gravel rolling about in his throat.

"No." She dug her fingers deeper into his shoulders.

He retained enough sense to say, "I'm not supposed to be hurting you. If I start, I might not be able to stop."

"Stop talking and do it." *Whatever the she-wolf wants.*

He hurt her; he knew it as well as he knew his own name, but Ancient Ones, she felt good. So good.

Phoebe clung to him. Didn't fight him. Accepted him. Other than her breath rasping against his ear, she didn't make a sound. Not a whimper or a sigh, much less a moan.

She clutched him, like moss grew on rocks. She moved in sync with him, a good sign for their future.

His brain shut down.

WHAT'S ALL THE FUSS about? Phoebe wondered as Parker panted over her. Yes, the moment when he'd first thrust into her was nice, might have even made her happy but she was ready to move on.

Parker withdrew so she could roll until she assumed the traditional marking position on her hands and knees.

No need to talk or explain. They moved in tandem, instinct controlling their bodies while her mind considered how this wrinkle in her agenda, this mating, might change how she approached her reason for being in Warwick. She didn't travel to Minnesota to mate. A mate might mess up everything.

She was so preoccupied with her thoughts, she didn't expect Parker's bite. He clamped his teeth on her marking spot. All rational thought fled her brain. The world went white. Her physical body vanished, or so it seemed, existing only on a plane surpassing the ecstasy of shifting.

The fuss made sense.

Parker collapsed, rolling to the side. He flung his top leg over her hip. His hot breath stirred the hair on her nape.

She was mated. No going back now. She was stuck with this male until she died.

She didn't have a choice. Mating happened at the whim of the Goddess. Corbie should have considered Phoebe's lack of a mate in Tennessee didn't mean one didn't exist. Didn't mean Phoebe could be with anyone else. Corbie should have understood why...

"So, you're a doctor? My mother will be thrilled," Phoebe lied.

"I'm an EMT, working toward being a paramedic. Big difference." Vibrations from his voice rumbled against her back.

"They have schools to teach lycan medicine? Doctors and nurses?"

"I'm not a doctor, and no, I don't think schools for werewolf medical professionals exist." He rubbed his penis against her bottom. "Homo lupus and homo sapien are close enough in physiology that I can adapt my knowledge to help my pack."

He didn't ask her a thing about herself. She didn't mind. The fewer lies between them, the easier life would be.

"So, you don't want to play doctor?" She waggled her hips.

He didn't react. Maybe he didn't know the sapien joke. Being raised with sapiens contained many perils, including sexual.

Corbie's grandson had taught her all about sexual peril.

"No, I'm an EMT," he repeated. "Long way from being a doctor."

"You don't want to examine me? See if I'm hurt?" She tried to sound playful or seductive.

"I hurt you?" He sat up. "Why didn't you say something?"

"You didn't hurt me." She swallowed a sigh. "I was being frivolous."

Focus, Corbie would say. Stop being distracted by the unimportant. How silly to have believed mating was important.

"What?"

"The important thing is we're mated. You've marked me. We are one in the Goddess's eyes."

"The Goddess?"

She rummaged through ancient memories. "The Creator, then."

"Creator?" Suspicion darkened his words. "What's your pack again?"

Ah. At last nonsexual her mattered. "I never said," she admitted. "An obscure pack in Tennessee."

"We're all from obscure packs."

"I've heard of yours," she countered. "Loup Garou from Colorado. First pack to immigrate from Europe. They brew the poison otherwise known as Moonsinger Beer. Toke Lobo and the Pack, mandatory favorite band of every lycan in America, whether or not they like country music, is Loup Garou's native son. How am I doing?"

"You don't like Toke Lobo?"

"Music is frivolous. I'm destined for more important things." Goddess, she sounded like a prig. One with a stick firmly embedded up her backside.

"So, you're the serious type." He lay next to her and pressed his burgeoning erection against her buttocks. "I guess I'm going to have to change your mind about music. Country music. Toke Lobo."

"Why? Is he a relative?"

"No. He's my boss."

Phoebe bolted upright. "What?"

"I work for Toke Lobo and the Pack. He's also my alpha." Parker's steady gaze did nothing to reassure her.

Goddess. What sort of crap did she land in? "You're in a band?"

"I'm an EMT, remember? I travel with the band."

This could be a disaster. She hoped she kept her facial expression in the neutral range. "Toke Lobo and the Pack are here?" Her voice squeaked.

"No. But Ethan, the lobo who owns this house, plays steel guitar for the band."

Damn. The last thing she needed was a famous musician entangled in her life. She needed stealth and solitude, not an entourage.

"Why does Ethan own a house so far from Loup Garou?"

"His mate is here. I know females usually leave their packs to live with the male's pack, but there are extenuating circumstances." Parker nudged her hip with his cock. His fully erect cock. "Ethan's love life bores me. I prefer to concentrate on my own."

He pushed into her, groaned, then said, "You feel so good."

"You, too." She sought something to brace her body to absorb his thrusts, but the thin mattress offered nothing but the rough concrete basement floor and wall. Exhaustion plagued her. Traveling from Tennessee by bus had not been a positive experience.

How rude would it be if she fell asleep as he...

She could sleep here. Safely sleep. She'd worry about her backpack later.

Parker might be a monkey wrench in her plans, but a pack provided cover. Provided...sanctuary.

He stilled. His breathing evened, and his heartbeat, his chest pressed against her back, slowed.

Her stomach rumbled. She couldn't remember the last time she'd eaten.

"Sounds like you're hungry." Parker rolled away from her. "Let's get dressed and find you some food."

She examined her leggings. The cut on her thigh had healed but Parker had finished destroying the garment in his haste. "I have a problem."

"Maybe Selena has something you can borrow," Parker suggested.

Selena was a giant compared to Phoebe.

"I could use one of your shirts as a dress," she countered. She preferred wearing Parker's clothes.

"I don't have many clothes with me. I packed light to come to Minnesota."

"It's only for a few hours." She'd packed light, too, bringing only what would fit in a backpack.

"All right." Still reluctant.

Phoebe placed her hands on her hips and glared at him. "You put your cock inside me, but you can't lend me a shirt for a few hours?"

His face darkened. He pulled a shirt the same color as his complexion—wine red—from a canvas duffel in the corner and tossed it at her.

She caught it, simpering, "Thank you."

"I hope you like fish." Parker pulled on his jeans. "Or hot dishes. Selena has been experimenting with weird concoctions."

"Local fish?" Phoebe toyed with her quarterstaff.

"Oh yeah. The Varulv and Limmikin—"

She froze. "What did you say?"

Parker turned and stared at her unbound breasts. "Hmm?"

"Varulv?" Her voice cracked.

"Selena's pack. She's the alpha. This is their territory. They subsist ninety-eight percent on fish from the local lakes."

As if I give a damn about fish. "Varulv and who?"

Parker got a clue. He raised his gaze from her boobs to her eyes. "Limmikin?"

The lump in Phoebe's throat wouldn't let her speak.

"Native shifters." Parker studied her, as if trying to read her mind. "Not many know about them. I didn't. Ethan didn't know he was Limmikin until recently, although he's half, through his father."

She couldn't swallow. Couldn't breathe.

"Ethan's grandfather kept his background a secret because a local politician tried to eliminate the pack. Are you okay?"

She was wheezing. She'd practiced endlessly not to react when startled, but Parker's revelation blindsided her.

"Sit and put your head between your knees." He followed the words with action, pushing her onto a cot, then placing his hand on her nape.

Her mind raced, a contrast to the slow, deep breathing she used to calm herself. Steady herself. She'd overreacted.

The dizziness passed. She could swallow. She lifted her head. "Thanks," she croaked.

"What set you off?" Parker's smoky quartz eyes gleamed in the murky light.

Phoebe's stomach growled. "Tired and hungry, I guess. I'm ready to gnaw off my own arm."

Both were true. After putting food in her belly and taking a power nap, she'd be good to go. Her reconnaissance plan needed to change with the new intel she'd been given, but her survival continued to depend on her ability to adapt.

"Then let's find you some food."

Chapter 3

Phoebe followed Parker up the steep stairs.

"I need to introduce you to whoever else is around," he muttered as they entered the hall. "Come on."

An ancient female sat with Ethan and Selena in the front room.

"Old Olivia, this is my mate, Phoebe." Parker kept his hand on Phoebe's lower back.

"Welcome." The old she-wolf's scrutiny unnerved Phoebe. "I'm Olivia Hagtorn. Where have you been hiding?"

Phoebe tightened her grip on her quarterstaff. "I beg your pardon?"

"Where have you and your family been hiding?" Olivia repeated.

"She claims she doesn't have a family." Selena's stare was not welcoming. "She claims she's a foundling."

Selena irritated the snot out of Phoebe.

"She's Limmikin," the old she-wolf declared. "Can't you see it on her?"

Phoebe cringed. Some words were never meant to be spoken, yet the Varulv and Loup Garou tossed them around like beads at a Mardi Gras parade.

"Limmikin?" Ethan shot to his feet. His dark eyes seemed to drill into her soul. "Who are you?"

She raised her quarterstaff across her chest as Parker dashed in front of her, creating a barrier between her and the other lobo.

His action annoyed her. She could defend herself. "My name is Phoebe, and I'm a foundling from Tennessee."

"Here." Ethan gestured at the sofa. His gaze never left her face. "Sit next to Selena."

"I'm fine." Phoebe's voice sounded natural, despite an ache in the back of her throat. Calm. Talking wasn't as difficult as she'd anticipated. She sidled next to Parker. "I've been on a bus for a long time. I need to stretch my legs."

"I thought you were wounded." Selena's scrutiny might have unnerved a sapien female.

Parker glared at Selena. "She's healed. She's as lycan as you or me."

"I never said she wasn't."

"Then what's your problem?"

Parker's belligerence confused Phoebe.

"I'm better now," she told Selena. "Thank you for your hospitality. I've been on a bus forever, so a regular bed is a blessing."

Corbie taught her well. Selena seemed appeased by the conciliatory words.

Phoebe touched Parker's elbow with her free hand. "I'm hungry," she reminded him. A good mate would feed her.

"We're not finished here." Selena's tone held a warning. "There's plenty of fish in the fridge. You can eat here."

"I want to know about Limmikin," Ethan added. "My grandfather is going to want to know about Limmikin. He's the Limmikin pack alpha."

Phoebe's quarterstaff fell from her hand and bounced on the floor. The ache in her throat sharpened. The room shimmered. "Pack?"

"Right now, there's you, me, my father, and my grandfather."

I belong to a pack?

She curled her fingers deeper into Parker's elbow.

He shot her a dark look as he hooked his arm around her waist.

She could be a silly female and faint, or she could warrior up and face down the hostility in the room.

"I'm a foundling," she repeated. She would not deviate from her story. "My foster mother found me wandering in the woods when I was about eight."

Eight years, two months, four days.

"My first name is the only thing I remembered."

Never tell, her grandmother warned as she shoved Phoebe out the back door. *Limmikin is our secret.*

Phoebe slipped from Parker's grasp and picked up her quarterstaff. "I'm from Tennessee." She straightened her spine, her weapon firmly in her grasp. "My name is Phoebe."

She tilted her head so she could look Parker in the eye. "I'm a hungry Phoebe whose mate has promised to feed her. And unless it's catfish, I'm not in the mood for fins."

"I'M NOT IN THE mood for fish either," Parker admitted to Phoebe as they stood outside Ethan's house. He never wanted to see walleye on his plate again. "I hate to keep borrowing Ethan's truck."

Phoebe lifted one shoulder. "Walking doesn't bother me."

"I heard there's a diner not too far from here."

"A diner is fine. I'm not finicky."

"I figured the fish comment was more a ploy to leave than anything else." He clasped her elbow and headed toward Mooney's. "You sure your leg is okay?"

"I'm healed. The miracle of DNA."

Yet she kept the long, smooth length of wood at her side, as if she didn't trust her leg to support her slight weight.

"Why do you carry a stick?"

"It's a quarterstaff. A weapon. A female needs to protect herself."

"Like you did a couple hours ago?" He couldn't help reminding her he'd rescued her from the thugs outside Elysian Estates.

"The new moon weakens me more than it weakens you because I'm female and more susceptible to the moon's whims."

He'd never heard such a thing. Werewolves in Tennessee must be an odd bunch. Maybe Selena and the other Varulv ways were different from the Loup Garou habits, but in inconsequential ways. Regional ways. So far, Phoebe's differences proved to be downright strange.

They had the rest of their lives to excavate each other's foibles.

"Why a big stick?" He wanted to learn how Phoebe ticked so he could cherish her.

"It's my weapon of choice. I wanted to be an archer but bow and arrows are tough to carry when you're four-legged. My options were limited to spear or quarterstaff."

"An archer, huh?"

"I'm good," she said. "But I need to be sensible."

"And a stick is sensible?"

"I can carry a quarterstaff in my mouth."

Okay. Her explanation made sense. "Do you have a name for your staff?"

Phoebe stumbled. "I beg your pardon?"

"It's not polite to beg. Do you have a name for your staff?"

"A name?"

"You know. Excalibur, or Betsy, like Davy Crockett's gun. You've heard of Davy Crockett, right?"

"I'm from Tennessee. Of course, I've heard of Davy Crockett. What does he have to do with my quarterstaff?"

"I wondered if you named your weapon."

"No."

"You should. How about Jeeves?"

"That's stupid."

Parker didn't think it was stupid. She referred to the stick as her staff. Jeeves was a butler's name in the old movies he'd watched while on the road with the band. Butlers were staff. Jeeves made sense.

Another block passed before Parker spoke again. "So you're Limmikin?"

As her mate, he deserved an explanation, but Phoebe kept going, slightly swinging Jeeves.

Maybe if he told her what he knew, she would open up. "Ethan's grandfather escaped with his mate to Loup Garou in Colorado," he explained. "They were the only survivors of a...purge, like the one in Ulvskog a month or so ago."

"Ulvskog?"

"Selena's village."

"When you say purge, you mean massacre, don't you?"

She spoke the word without inflection, as if the ugliness couldn't touch her.

"I'm not a delicate flower, unable to cope with the cruel world, Parker. I know more about the world's cruelty than you can imagine."

"All right. A massacre." He couldn't be blamed for wanting to shield his mate.

"I'm not surprised massacres are still going on."

"You know about the purges?" Parker tightened his clasp on her elbow.

"Here? Not until you told me. How many escaped?"

"The first time? Only two I know about. Hatch and his mate. This time, a dozen or so Varulv survived."

Phoebe stopped. "Hatch?"

"Ethan's grandfather. Old Olivia calls him something else. His Limmikin name."

"Hache-Hi? I remember stories—" Phoebe broke off.

"So you are Limmikin."

She scanned the shadows around them, Jeeves now in both hands, across her body.

He wanted to assure her they'd driven off the vampires; that boogeymen no longer existed. He sniffed the air to be sure: the scent of grilling meat from the diner; freshly cut grass. No vamp.

She replied in a hoarse whisper. "There are things we don't, we can't, say."

"The world is asleep except for us."

Phoebe shook her head.

Parker hooked her arm again and resumed walking. "A few months ago, Ethan came to Warwick on a mission. Within days, someone gunned down most of the Varulv pack. Slaughtered them. Ethan told me the automatic weapons cut Selena's grandfather in half. I can't imagine finding a loved one so brutally slain. Selena is one tough she-wolf."

MOONEY'S SAT RIGHT WHERE Dakota promised it would. A diner. Nothing fancy. Nothing modern. A bright spot in the darkness. Perfect for him and Phoebe.

He held the door for his mate.

The place was empty, and they were quickly led to a sticky booth. Phoebe sprawled across her seat, as if its cleanliness meant nothing. Rancid grease perfumed everything. She ordered without opening the menu. "Steak as rare as you're legally allowed to serve. No fries. No dressing on the salad. Water, minimal ice."

The same meal Parker planned to order.

"Why are you in Warwick?" he asked, as he realigned the salt and pepper shakers.

"Chasing a rumor." She blinked sleepily at him.

He tried to envision her face across a meal from him for years to come. His imagination wasn't good enough.

"What, no candles?" she asked in a teasing voice, after their waitress brought their water.

"What are you talking about? The electricity isn't out." Learning how this female's mind worked was proving to be a chore.

Phoebe studied the ceiling, as if checking the lights. "It's a joke, Parker. Our first meal together. According to movies and TV, we should be dining by candlelight."

"Oh."

"You don't have a romantic bone in your body, do you?" she asked. "You're an EMT. I suppose you have to be pragmatic."

She made being sensible sound bad. Somebody needed to keep all their paws in reality.

He started rearranging the sweetener packets on the table by color.

She'd deflected him away from what he wanted to know.

"You'd heard of Ethan's grandfather before tonight?" Parker tried again.

"I think...things happen for a reason...like my inexplicable urge to come to Warwick. To be outside Elysian Estates tonight. If I ignored the urge, we wouldn't have met."

"You wouldn't have been attacked." At least she counted mating as a good thing. He still hadn't made up his mind.

"If I hadn't been attacked, you couldn't rescue me."

Another skillful deflection.

The waitress interrupted to tell them their meals would be out shortly.

"About Hatch," Parker prompted, once the waitress departed.

Phoebe stilled. Her eyes glazed, as if they were seeing something beyond the sticky red vinyl and world-weary employees of Mooney's Diner. "I heard a story. A fairy tale. I'm having a difficult time accepting a legend is real. The story scared me so much I couldn't sleep for weeks after my granny—"

"Your granny? I thought you were a foundling."

She lifted her water to her mouth. Sipped. "I was eight when I lost my...way. I had a granny. I do recall snatches of my childhood. How do you think I knew you were my mate?"

Her knuckles were white as she set the water glass on the table. She flexed her fingers, then pushed the ketchup bottle toward him. "This could use wiping down."

"What?"

"You seem obsessed with the condiments on the table. I thought you might want to wipe down the ketchup bottle."

Parker leaned forward until he was in her face. "You are so full of baloney your eyes ought to be pink."

"I am Limmikin." She seemed to choke on the word. "My ancestors' blood still flows in my veins and will flow in our offspring's veins. Is that what you want to know?"

Parker snapped his mouth shut. He'd hoped she'd deny Old Olivia's diagnosis.

"Until today, I thought I was the only one of my kind."

He couldn't help blurting, "But you knew about Hatch."

"Hache-Hi is a legend. A story told by grannies when putting the children to bed. He represents victory over prejudice, power rising from bloodshed. He isn't real."

"Hatch Calhoun is very much alive."

"I'm still an endangered species."

The chilling phrase explained something bothering him. "That's why you were looking at Ethan as if he were a god or something. The male who should be your mate."

Oh, he didn't mean to confess his insecurity.

Her eyes widened and her jaw dropped. "You're jealous?" Her voice squeaked. "I was stunned. I haven't seen another Limmikin since I was eight."

"Why?"

"Because massacres aren't limited to Minnesota."

Chapter 4

Parker stared at her as if she'd sprouted a second head, four additional legs, and wings. "Are you saying you survived a massacre?"

Phoebe managed to keep her expression bland. She would never be able to forget the shrieks, her younger brothers crying, the smell of blood, of feces and urine from the dead, the bodies rotting in the humid Tennessee summer. Sometimes, even fifteen years later, she could taste gunpowder when stressed. Like now.

"I'm saying the Goddess has miraculous plans for me. For us. She brought me my mate, who is connected to others of my kind."

Her death might be closer than she wanted to admit. She swallowed the thought.

"You didn't answer my question."

Parker needed to know the truth. Why not sooner than later?

Because she wasn't ready. This night brought too many shocks to her brain.

The waitress arrived with their salads and steaks. Saved by the bowl.

"Enough about me." Phoebe pulled her plate closer. Her stomach rumbled in response to the aroma of rare beef. "Tell me about Parker Rowe."

"You know everything there is to know." He picked up his knife. "I'm an EMT for my pack. I tour with Toke Lobo and his band. I'm heading back to Colorado to get my paramedic certification."

"What's the difference between an EMT and a paramedic?" She didn't care, but she didn't want him picking at her brain.

"A paramedic has more specialized training."

"Then you're not a doctor." She cut her steak into bite- sized chunks.

"Not even close."

He didn't inquire about her profession. Good thing because ninja, assassin, and stealth fighter all sounded silly, especially since she couldn't claim them. Yet. His obsession with her roots bothered her because he seemed to care more about the long-ago past than moving forward.

Their forks chinked against their plates, loud in the silence between them as they ate.

"I don't cook much." A safe topic to break the awkwardness.

"My mom can probably teach you. A neighbor is teaching Selena."

Phoebe paused, fork in midair. "Seriously? Selena is an alpha, yes? Cooking should be the last thing she focuses on."

"Dakota's mate, Britt, can't cook either. What is it with females nowadays? Domesticity isn't good enough for you? At least Selena is trying."

As if she knew who Dakota and his mate were. "I'm too busy to learn domestic skills right now. Maybe later."

He popped a chunk of steak into his mouth. "Selena is alpha and a healer. She does stuff with herbs. She's not too busy."

Phoebe sipped her water to wash down her annoyance. "Well, bless her heart." She fought the urge to grit her teeth. "I'm glad you told me. I'm not prepared to integrate with the local packs, so I'm having a difficult time quantifying my current situation."

"Your current situation? You're a mated female. What is there to quantify? Lone wolf?"

He was lucky she didn't smack his head with her quarterstaff. "Something like that."

PARKER STUDIED THE FEMALE he'd marked. What had the Ancient Ones done to him? She attacked her salad as if she suffered from a bellyache and craved fresh greens to soothe it.

"I take it you have plans." He swirled a chuck of meat in the dark pink juices puddled on his plate.

She popped a cucumber slice into her mouth. "I need to retrieve my backpack from the bus station."

Another evasive answer.

"I'm at your service." Tomorrow. On the way to the airport to rent a car to drive back to Colorado.

She picked up her glass and sucked an ice cube into her mouth, giving him strange ideas. He squirmed.

She grinned, then crunched down on the ice. His eyes widened; his lips parted.

Another awkward silence. Then she yawned. "Forgive me. I didn't dare sleep on the bus."

Parker didn't get her meaning. He slept on the band bus all the time when Toke Lobo and the Pack toured. Sleeping on the bus was second nature. He said as much to Phoebe.

"Oh, it's a female thing. Sleeping in public isn't safe for a solitary female. Too many predators. Besides, your band bus was private." She speared another cucumber slice.

He hated cucumbers. "Do you want my cukes?"

"Please. Thanks. You don't think about personal safety the way I do because you're not female." She spoke in a matter-of-fact tone. She stretched across the table and jabbed her fork into the cucumber slices he'd pushed aside. "Nor would it occur to you to force yourself on one."

Her assumption he was an honorable lobo placated him.

"I'm glad we ran into each other on my first night in town." Phoebe bit into the cucumber. "I was figuring out what to do when the thugs jumped me."

"I'm glad we ran into each other, too. What were you doing hanging around Elysian Estates?"

"Familiarizing myself with the neighborhood. I thought this late at night, given the neighborhood's reputation, I could explore without attracting attention."

Something about her words didn't sit well with him. "Why would you need to explore Elysian Estates?"

Phoebe lowered her chin, her tiny triangular face dominated by her large eyes. "My arrival in Warwick isn't random. I wouldn't have chosen to come to a place frozen over half the year."

"But you're descended from the Limmikin, who are from frozen Minnesota."

"Can anyone help where our ancestors lived? Your ancestors chose to leave Europe. Mine were driven from Minnesota. The hostility alone is enough to make me paranoid."

"Yet you came. Why the focus on Elysian Estates?" The free-fall sensation in his gut hinted at an answer he wasn't going to like.

Her fork clattered into her salad bowl. "All right. I'll tell you. I don't know if you're aware, but there's a movement—"

"The Limmikin don't have treaties," he interrupted. He was so damn sick of treaty talk and even sicker of the Peters family's congressional dynasty. "The Peters problem has been resolved."

Phoebe blinked. "What?"

"The Peters problem. You know, Congressman Peters and his two vamp-scat-sucking sons."

Technically, the problem still existed, and Parker hadn't been directly involved.

"I don't know what you're talking about."

Could he have misread the situation? "Forget what I said. Let's start over, before I rudely interrupted you. There's a movement to do what?"

"No." Her chin sank lower until it hovered above her chest.

Parker had a great view of her forehead. Her large, dark, liquid eyes fixed on him with an unnerving steadiness.

"Explain," she ordered.

"You first."

"This isn't a child's game, Doc. Tell me what you meant."

"The movement to abandon the service for sanctuary treaties is why I'm in Minnesota." Not precisely the truth, but not a lie. "Congressman Bryant Peters used lycan services for years but did an about-face on the treaties. He killed himself before he could be brought back around."

Her brow wrinkled. "I remember hearing about his suicide. Wasn't there a sex scandal involved?"

"He called himself the Sexorcist on his dark web site. He exploited underage girls." Parker choked on the words. Forced sex was so far out of a lycan's mindset, many didn't comprehend the concept. He had a difficult time himself.

"And you didn't kill him?" She sounded offended.

"He shot himself when threatened with exposure." Selena and Ethan had witnessed the congressman's death.

She fell silent, as if mulling his words. When she spoke again, he wasn't sure if she was talking to him or merely thinking aloud. "Seems there's more than one thing going on. I wonder if they're related."

A scary thought. "I shared my story with you."

Her pensive gaze turned...mischievous. "You showed me yours so you want me to show you mine?"

Now what was she blathering about?

The grin faded as quickly as it arrived. "Never mind. Bad joke."

He decided to follow her advice. "If you're not here to deal with the Peters family treachery, why did you come to Warwick?"

"Maybe to find you. Or to locate the Limmikin alpha."

Maybe she thought her evasiveness was cute or clever, but Parker had had enough. "I don't think starting our lives together with secrets is a good idea."

"If I told you, I'd have to kill you, and that's an even worse way to start our mated life."

Her tone was light, breezy even, but Parker didn't think she was joking.

"You started to tell me about a movement, and I rudely interrupted you. I would like to know what you were going to tell me." He used as placating a tone as he could manage.

She lifted her chin a fraction. "I didn't come to Minnesota so much as I'm tracking someone who will."

"Someone at Elysian Estates?"

She picked up her glass and brought it to her mouth, her eyes wide as she gauged his reaction.

Parker wracked his brain. Politics didn't interest him, so Ethan's mission bored him. He remembered something about a visiting politician. Richard Tuttle, if he recalled correctly. United States Senator from Tennessee. He also knew the Peters congressional dynasty funded attempts to eradicate the werewolf population. The Peters family lived in Elysian Estates. He'd helped Ethan rescue Dakota and his mate Britt from there, one night a few weeks ago. A party had gone sour when Connor Peters tried to kidnap Britt.

"A politician or a vampire?"

Vampire?

"Ha, ha. The Doc does have a sense of humor." She stabbed her fork into another bite of steak.

"I have a perfectly fine sense of humor." He speared a ring of red onion. "I'm not joking about the vampires. Britt Towne ashed one in Elysian Estates a few weeks ago."

"Who is Britt Towne and what does 'ashed' mean?"

"Britt is Dakota's mate. Dakota drives bus for Toke Lobo and the Pack when they tour. When you neutralize a vampire's undead state, they burst like a vacuum cleaner bag full of icy dirt and ash."

"Didn't you tell me you're an EMT, not a fantasy author? Mom is going to be so disappointed."

"How can you have a mother if you're a foundling?"

Phoebe stared at him a moment, then pushed away her plate, her steak half-eaten. "So much for your sense of humor. If I have to explain the joke, it won't be funny."

"It's not funny now." He would get the hang of her. Eventually. Hopefully. "Explain to me about your mother."

"It's a sapien joke. I guess you haven't spent much time around sapiens."

"I spent years on the road with Toke Lobo and the Pack. Who do you think populated the bars they played in?"

"I don't think about trivial things." Her light tone belied the bludgeoning words.

"Doesn't being your mate count for something?"

Her shoulders stiffened.

Point to me.

"We have different communication methods. We're in our getting to know each other phase." More evasion.

"I can't get to know you if you keep confusing me," he explained.

She visibly relaxed. "You're right. I apologize. What have I said to confuse you?"

"Your mother."

"Every sapien mother wants her daughter to marry a doctor, or so the story goes. Therefore, my mother will be disappointed you're an author, not a doctor." As if her mother would ever know.

"I'm not a doctor or an author. I'm an EMT." The distinctions weren't difficult to grasp.

"Hey, Doc, close enough. And I'll show you mine if you'll show me yours is something nasty sapien boys say to girls. It's a sex thing."

Rage, as red as his dead sister's jacket, blotted his vision. He clenched his knife in his fist. "How do you know about sapien sex things?"

"Because I lived with sapiens from an early age who taught me sapien males have many tricks to be sexually abusive."

Parker's stomach slowly unknotted. His vision cleared. "Seriously?" He knew Congressman Bryant Peters and his oldest son raped Selena when she was a teenager.

"Seriously. Anything else? I have an irreverent sense of humor. I'm working on being less frivolous."

He shoved his plate to the middle of the table, his meal mostly untouched. He couldn't eat now even if he were hungry. "Why would you think I would abuse you sexually?"

She turned away from him, hiding her face. "I would never think you were abusive. I was teasing you. Flirting. never meant to dishonor you. Besides, I could never deny you."

"Yes, you can." Not all males understood the consequences of ignoring a female's wishes. If not for Selena's confession, he would not be enlightened. "All you need to do is say no."

She tilted her head. Maybe she was listening to the vibes in the room or something. "Okay. The same goes for you."

He couldn't imagine a scenario where he wouldn't want to have sex with this female. Even now, he was ready again. "Thank you." A lame response, but the best he could do. "Are you ready to head back to Ethan's house?"

"I'm done with my meal, but I don't know if I'll ever be ready to face your friends."

Chapter 5

The light night air was a welcome contrast to Tennessee's heavy, humidity-laden summer nights. Nothing weighed her down, not even the awkwardness of her mating with Parker.

"Is your wound bothering you?" Parker asked, as if she hadn't already used her injured leg.

"My wound isn't why I'm dawdling," she admitted. "Your friend's mate gives off negativity. I'm not in the mood to deal with attitude. She's not the boss of me."

Parker tensed. "Well, you and Ethan were giving off some strange vibes."

"You thought they were strange?" Phoebe's voice rose half an octave. "Try standing on our paws."

"I still don't understand."

Phoebe studied the overhead sky. Too much disruptive city light dimmed the stars. "He reminded me of...someone. I don't want to talk about it."

They continued without speaking, their footfalls scuffing on the uneven sidewalks. Most houses they passed were dark. Here a backyard light puddled; there late-night TV illuminated a window with a pale bluish glow. Early Christmas lights twinkled on the eaves of another dwelling. Dog droppings scented the air.

They rounded onto Ethan's street. Ash, according to the street sign. Phoebe noted there were two houses on the block. The other glittered in the feeble beams of the corner streetlamp.

"Help me. Please."

Parker stopped. "Did you hear that?"

Phoebe tilted her head to get a better sense where the plea came from.

"Please. Somebody."

"Over there." She pointed to the sparkly purple house. "Helga," Parker muttered. He sprinted toward the house. Phoebe followed.

"Helga?" he called out. "It's Parker Rowe, Ethan's friend. Are you okay?"

"I fell," came the weak reply.

He tried the doorknob. Locked. "I'm going to have to break down your door."

"Wait." Phoebe wouldn't want anyone breaking down Corbie's door when there might be other options. "What about a back door or a window?"

She tested a front window. A moment later she opened the door for Parker.

He rushed past her to the occupant sprawled on the living room floor. "What happened?"

Phoebe's nose prickled at the familiar scent of burnt sage clinging to the air in the stuffy, overheated room. She left the window open to air out the place.

"The batteries in my TV remote are dead, and I haven't had a chance to get to the store," an old woman whined, as Parker knelt next to her. "I went to turn on the TV and fell. I hate getting old."

"What time?" "Before six."

"I'm sorry we didn't hear you when we got home." Parker clasped the old lady's wrist and looked at his watch. "Did you lose consciousness?"

"Maybe."

"Are you in any pain?"

"My leg hurts."

"Phoebe, call 9-1-1," Parker barked.

Phoebe shed her paralysis. If Parker wanted 9-1-1, the old woman had to be sapien, yet Phoebe's senses told her Helga was...more.

Her quarterstaff clattered to the floor as Phoebe pulled out her phone. "What's the address?" She couldn't direct an ambulance to the house twinkling like a midnight sky, across the street from the harvest moon house.

"Forty-one Ash Street," Helga provided. Phoebe made the call.

"Who are you?" Helga asked, after Phoebe disconnected.

"She's my mate," Parker replied, as if Phoebe couldn't answer herself.

"Phoebe from Tennessee."

"Phoebe Rowe," Parker corrected, as he ran his hands along Helga's leg.

Helga yelped, then said, "You're a shifter."

"Yes, ma'am."

Phoebe needed to do something. Something useful. She wanted to tuck this frail female away from the world to keep her safe. She knelt on Helga's other side and took the old woman's hand in hers. "Can I get you something to drink? You must be dehydrated from being here all night."

"She can't have anything to drink," Parker said. "If they need to operate on her leg, she shouldn't have anything in her stomach."

"Operate?" Helga spoke in a faint voice.

"Your leg is broken. They may need to repair it with pins."

"Pins?"

"Screws."

Phoebe patted Helga's hand. "Parker is giving you the worst-case scenario."

"No, I'm not. I'm being realistic." He sounded annoyed. "Don't sugar coat anything. Helga's tough. She staked vampires a few weeks ago."

Phoebe studied the woman anew. "Really?"

"They infested the street," Helga said.

"Nasty battle," Parker added. "Helga rocked the night. She's resilient."

Helga squirmed, then winced and grew paler. "I hope you're right. At my age, the body turns traitorous."

Distant sirens serenaded the night.

"Take a few deep breaths," Phoebe suggested. Although her lycan body healed quickly, Corbie had taught her a thing or two about pain management.

Helga's hand was thin; her skin dry and papery. She squeezed Phoebe's fingers, and despite her fragile appearance, Helga's strong grip reminded Phoebe of Corbie's hand. Granny's hand.

Maybe talking would keep Helga's mind off her pain. "Tell me about staking vampires."

"Only on the night we cleaned the bloodsuckers out of the neighborhood." Helga's crepey eyelids fluttered. "We had a good night. Olivia and I may not have been able to shift like the others, but we were useful. I miss being useful."

"Yes." Parker stood at the window, surveying the street. "You were. You were magnificent."

"Poof. That's the sound a vampire makes when it explodes."

"Poof," Parker echoed.

"What's going to happen to my house?"

Phoebe squeezed Helga's fingers. "Nothing. Your friends across the street will keep an eye on it for you."

"I want you to stay here. Promise me you will."

Phoebe stilled. "You don't know me. I could be a thief or an assassin." Moreover, she didn't want to be bound by a promise to a stranger when it might conflict with her vow to her ancestors.

I'M NEVER GOING TO escape Warwick.

Helga's injury overrode Parker's need to go home.

"Do you have any family we should call?"

Phoebe and Helga's clasped hands bothered him.

"There's no one." Helga sounded sad. "My daughter died."

Parker had heard the story. Congressman Bryant Peters, in Helga's words, fucked her daughter to death.

Speaking of fucking, if Helga offered a guest room with a real bed, he'd be willing to stay in Warwick an extra night or two. The mattresses on the floor at Ethan's house weren't kind to a lobo's back. Besides, he needed privacy with a mate. Worrying about someone else showing up in the basement probably held him back with Phoebe. Or maybe she'd held back.

The instantaneous bonding between his mate and Ethan's weird neighbor irked him. He ought to be the one holding Helga's hand, comforting her until the ambulance arrived. Instead, he opened the door for the sapien EMTs to enter.

Identifying himself as a fellow emergency medical technician visiting from out of state, he gave them his quick assessment of Helga's condition, then let them go to work. Horning in on their jobs would have been rude.

"Where are you taking her?" he asked. Not that he knew his way around Warwick. But Selena and Britt did. They could take responsibility once Parker and Phoebe hit the road.

"Warwick General."

Phoebe retrieved Jeeves, then slipped out the door, as silent and unobtrusive as a shadow. They'd communicated without words, a freaky sensation. She seemed to read his thoughts. He'd witnessed mating in action before, but never understood all the subtleties.

Someone needed to deal with the bureaucracy. The paperwork. Insurance companies. Parker had no experience with the sapien establishment. He'd gladly turn over responsibility for Helga to Selena and Ethan. They were the alphas.

Phoebe returned with Selena as the ambulance doors closed.

"How did you find her?" Selena asked

"We heard her as we were coming back from the diner," Parker replied.

Selena frowned. "How could we have not heard her earlier?"

"Helga is elderly. Weak," Phoebe offered. "Ethan and I were distracted when we arrived. We didn't hear her until we were in front of the house."

"She's in good shape," Parker added. "Broken leg, not a compound fracture. The worst thing going for her is her age."

The ambulance pulled away from the curb, lights flashing, siren silent.

"She's not young." Selena sounded worried as the ambulance raced up the street.

"Will she be okay at a sapien hospital?" Parker asked, hoping Selena could shed some light on Helga's genus.

"I hope so. I don't know any more about her than you do."

"She's sapien," Phoebe interjected. "With something else."

Selena stared at Phoebe. "How do you know?"

Parker prepared to defend his mate.

Phoebe didn't need his help. "It's a gift, I guess She's...enhanced. Maybe her witchery gives her talents beyond a normal sapien."

Selena bristled. "Wiccan is a religion, not sorcery."

"I'm familiar with Wicca. I know a few Wiccans back home. My guess is Helga is a crone. A wise woman. A crone rescued me. Raised me."

"What?" Parker and Selena asked at the same time.

"Wiccan beliefs are based in the truths of the Goddess. Growing up in a coven instead of a pack isn't a big stretch."

Every word she spoke made him wonder what the Ancient Ones had joined to him.

"Maybe Helga sensed a...connection to me when she offered us her house," Phoebe continued.

"What?" Selena's hands rested on her hips, and her eyes were as wide as her gaping mouth.

"Helga asked us to stay here, keep an eye on things," Parker hastened to explain. His truth took a different spin than Phoebe's statement. "It's only for a night. We're heading to Colorado. Remember?"

Selena closed her mouth. Her jaw pulsed as she gritted her teeth.

"Why don't you grab Ethan's truck keys, and I'll drive us to the hospital," Parker suggested. "They're taking her to Warwick General. Do you know where it is?"

"Not really." Selena's brittle tone betrayed her irritation. "I don't drive, and riding messes up my sense of direction."

"Maybe I should call Dakota." The Ancient Ones gifted the professional bus driver with an infallible sense of direction.

"Yes, we want to see Helga," Phoebe said, "And we will. But there's nothing to see yet, until she's admitted, x-rayed, possibly even operated on."

"You're right." Parker with his sapien medical background, should have pointed out the obvious. "But Helga may need help getting admitted, unless her insurance information is on file."

"Right." Phoebe perused the cluttered room.

Parker thought she was leaving when she strode across the room, but instead, she opened a door next to the front door. A closet. A hint of stale perspiration escaped into the living room.

"Don't go poking around," Selena cautioned.

"I'm not," Phoebe replied, as she vanished into the closet's dark depths.

Fifteen seconds later, she emerged, holding a black bag. "I'll bet Helga keeps her insurance card in her wallet."

She extended the bag to Selena. "You're her friend. You check."

Good strategy on Phoebe's part, Parker thought. Acknowledging Selena's role as alpha without saying so.

Selena snatched the bag from Phoebe. "I can't believe she hauls all the stuff around," she muttered as she pawed through the contents. She withdrew a wallet. "Maybe we should get Britt to help admit Helga."

Britt, Dakota's sapien mate, was also Selena's best friend.

Selena pulled out a card. "Gammel. Helga Gammel. Funny. I never knew her last name before."

"I'm familiar with the process." Phoebe spoke softly. "I'd like to help. Helga reminds me of my foster mother."

"The Wiccan crone."

Selena didn't need to be so sarcastic.

Parker started toward Phoebe, his instinct to protect his mate, even from an alpha, too strong to deny.

Phoebe's tiny shoulders squared. "Yes. Corbie, who happens to be a Wiccan crone."

"Fine. Knock yourself out." Selena turned to Parker. "Call Dakota for a ride."

Only the sound of the windows rattling in their frames followed Selena out the door.

"Just a guess, but your friend is new to being alpha, isn't she?" Phoebe sounded more amused than annoyed.

"Was slamming the door on her way out your first clue?" he asked, as he pulled out his phone to make the call. He'd never seen Selena behave like a brat before. "Her husband is my colleague. I barely know her."

Chapter 6

Hospital smells assaulted Phoebe as soon as she and Parker entered the building. Couldn't sapiens detect the poisons polluting the air? She gripped her quarterstaff tighter. The security guard tried to prevent her from entering with the stick, but she used it as a cane and faked a limp.

They tracked Helga to a curtained cubicle in the emergency department.

"There you are," Phoebe greeted Helga, finding the woman's gray color against the white sheets concerning. Even her bright blue eyes seemed faded.

"Here I am," Helga agreed in a weak voice. "What kept you?"

"We were waiting for Parker's friend, the bus driver." Meeting Dakota Towne had been an interesting experience.

"They want to operate on my leg, like Parker predicted."

"I didn't predict," he muttered. "I diagnosed."

"I couldn't remember your contact information. Phoebe, you're a good niece, but you didn't give me your new phone number."

Parker lifted a clipboard chained to the foot of the bed.

Phoebe propped her quarterstaff against the bed and took Helga's thin, icy cold hand in hers.

"She got your name right," Parker said. "Phoebe Rowe."

"She's not senile." Phoebe smiled at the second crone who'd adopted her. She could play along. "The pain is confusing her. Right, Aunt Helga?"

"Right. I'm terrible with numbers anyway, and you keep changing yours."

Since Phoebe used a disposable phone, her number changed according to her gut. How had Helga known?

"Maybe Parker should leave his phone number," Phoebe suggested.

He didn't argue, but took the pen chained to the clipboard and scrawled something on the paper.

He was clearly a rules-follower. Well, she'd have to work around his foibles.

"They're going to operate on me tomorrow," Helga fretted.

"Then why are you still in emergency? I'll see about having you moved." Parker left the room.

Helga squeezed Phoebe's hand. "You got yourself a good one."

"I'm glad you think so." Phoebe wasn't so sure.

"You'll stay in my house? Protect it?"

"Where else would I stay except with my favorite aunt?" Phoebe leaned forward and kissed Helga's cheek. Cold. Thin. Dry.

"One of the two houses on the charmed block." Helga dropped Phoebe's hand to pluck at the sheet covering her.

"Charmed? Because they're painted like the Harvest Moon and the Milky Way?" What else could an orange house across from a sparkly dark purple house be called?

Helga rolled her eyes. "Ash Street. The cross streets are Oak and Hawthorn."

"The sacred triad works with addresses?" *What an interesting theory.*

"It works against vampires. Poof." Helga's thin lips twisted into a smile. "But not their factotum."

"Well, it sounds as though you sent them to their coffins, so I'm not going to worry about them. Other supernatural beings don't concern me as much as sapiens do."

Vampires didn't concern Phoebe. She wasn't even sure she believed in them.

"Factotum," Helga repeated in a whisper. "They're listening."

Phoebe opened her mouth to ask Helga what she meant when the curtain clanked aside and someone wearing a white lab coat shuffled in.

"Tell my niece what's going on." Helga resumed whining.

Phoebe braced herself for a barrage of medical gobbledygook.

"She broke her leg. It's a clean break. Due to her age, we're going to operate and screw in a metal bar to hold the bone in place until it heals."

Phoebe tuned out the rest. Parker, with his medical expertise, should be the one taking notes on the care and feeding of old sapien women.

She no sooner thought Parker's name when he reappeared. "This is my...spouse," Phoebe told the doctor. "He is an EMT, so you should talk to him."

"He's not on the consent form." White Lab Coat frowned as he scanned Helga's paperwork.

"Then give me the form, and I'll add him." Helga's persnickety old woman act vanished. Clearly her helplessness manifested only when she needed it.

"When are you operating?" Phoebe asked while Helga's pen scratched on the clipboard. "Helga mentioned something about tomorrow?"

"Tomorrow morning," White Lab Coat confirmed. "The surgeon is unavailable today."

"Why isn't she in a room?" Parker asked.

"Paperwork."

"How long do you think it will take?"

"I'm not in administration. Do you have any other medical questions?"

"No," the two females spoke in unison.

"I guess not," Parker followed up.

White Lab Coat left.

"Helga, would you have a problem if Dakota ran us to the bus station to pick up Phoebe's luggage?" Parker asked.

"You're going to abandon me?" Helga resumed cranky old lady mode.

"I need to get my backpack from the bus station, and Parker's friend is still here with his vehicle. We'll return shortly. I need something to wear besides Parker's shirts."

"HELGA IS A CHARACTER." Parker boosted Phoebe into the SUV's back seat. His hand lingered on her backside. Too bad they were on Helga duty.

"I think she's frightened." Phoebe settled herself behind Dakota.

"Helga's a great old lady," Dakota said. "You should have seen her staking vampires. Where am I going again?"

"Bus station, then the airport so I can rent a vehicle." Parker hated being dependent, which he'd been ever since arriving in Warwick.

Several "in two miles, four hundred feet, turn left, turn rights" from Dakota's GPS later, he pulled into the bus station parking lot.

"You have arrived at your destination," Dakota's phone announced.

"I'll be right back." Phoebe grabbed Jeeves and bounded from the vehicle before Dakota could park.

Parker unlatched his seat belt and bolted from the SUV after her. If not for her unique scent, he would have lost her in the throng. The masses swallowed her petite figure. Who knew the bus station would be so busy before dawn?

Phoebe was fast. Ethan was the only other person Parker ever saw move as quickly. If they were in a race against each other, Parker would put his money on Phoebe. Meanwhile, Parker tried to dodge the people lumbering in his way. Overhead televisions droned, adding to the cacophony.

Phoebe's delicate natural aroma kept him from losing her in the crowd. He followed the strand through the labyrinth until he located the room where storage lockers lined the walls.

Phoebe stood in front of a secure-looking unit and dialed the combination lock. "You didn't need to follow me." She didn't divert her eyes from her task.

"DNA overrides common sense."

"There's your sense of humor again."

"What's that supposed to mean?"

"We aren't amused by the same things, Doc." She opened the locker and pulled out a black backpack. "I need to return the lock."

"Your luggage is one backpack?"

"Yeah." She slung an arm through a strap.

She traveled lighter than he did, and he'd learned to be an efficient packer from his time on the road with Toke Lobo's band.

The backpack's weight pulled the fabric of Phoebe's shirt tight against her breasts. Why hadn't she bound them? "Use both straps." He didn't intend to growl, but the suggestion emerged as one.

She lowered her chin. "Excuse me?"

"I can see every bump on your nipples, and while I am fond of them, I don't want anyone else developing a need to get acquainted with them."

"Oh." She did as he asked, which only made the situation worse.

He looked around before grabbing the cloth and yanking it away from her body.

"You're going to be a good mate," Phoebe murmured.

"I already am." He shouldn't have to defend his qualities to his female.

"Yes. You are."

Did she mean it?

"Give me the backpack." He could resolve two issues with one gesture.

She slipped the straps from her shoulders. "You don't need to be so grumpy."

He couldn't wear the pack unless he adjusted the straps to accommodate his height, so he carried it. It weighed nothing.

They were heading toward the counter so she could return the padlock when she stopped. The flow of disembarking passengers slowed to a trickle. Only the incessant chatter of the overhead televisions disturbed the quiet lobby.

Yet Phoebe didn't move. She stared at a TV where a solemn young man told viewers, "Senator Richard Tuttle from Tennessee arrived in Warwick, Minnesota last night."

The video cut to someone shoving a microphone into the senator's face as he made his way through an airport lobby. "What brings you back to Warwick?"

Parker barely heard Phoebe's whispered response. "I saw you."

TUTTLE IS IN TOWN.

Phoebe couldn't shake her excitement as she changed her clothes. She'd guessed correctly. Her plan might work.

Parker waited for her on Helga's front stoop.

"Selena and Old Olivia are at the hospital. Selena texted Helga's room number to me." Parker eyed Phoebe's body, his face folding into a frown. "You look like a ninja."

"Thank you." She raised her quarterstaff in a mock salute.

"It wasn't a compliment. What are you up to?"

"Visiting Helga at the hospital." She headed for Parker's rental, another oversized SUV she'd need help climbing into. Another control mechanism.

Phoebe did not want to be at the hospital all day. She had things to do. But first she needed to figure out how to ditch Parker. Too bad they didn't have time for a quickie before returning to the hospital. Sex might discombobulate him enough to make slipping away easier.

They found Helga in her room. She dozed, as did Olivia Hagtorn, who was stretched out in a recliner. Selena sat in the visitor's chair, scrolling through her phone.

"Oh." Selena tucked her phone into her pocket. "Helga wondered why Phoebe left."

Selena's neutral tone belied the resentment behind the words.

"Are they medicating her?" Parker scanned her chart. "Okay," he muttered. "Okay."

"What's up, Doc?" Phoebe asked.

Parker lifted his gaze from the paperwork to her. "She's on some fairly strong meds, so she might sleep between now and her surgery in the morning. She's scheduled at ten. When she's not asleep, she'll probably be groggy and disoriented."

A too-long day threatened to grow longer. Phoebe swallowed her impatience.

"You don't need to stick around," Olivia mumbled from her corner. "Selena can call Ethan to come get you. I'll stay. It's not as if I have a village to rebuild or a mission to accomplish."

Phoebe's lungs froze. How did the old female know?

"I'm not rebuilding a village," Selena snapped. "I have a pack to do the heavy lifting. Restin Garnier is overseeing the work. Parker is supposed to rejoin him."

"Parker has his own wheels now and is supposed to be heading back to Loup Garou this morning," Parker reminded her.

Phoebe turned to Parker. "What?" He couldn't be serious. Helga needed them. Besides, she had Tuttle in her sights.

"I thought you were helping Restin in Ulvskog." Although Selena spoke in a neutral tone, any lycan worth her DNA could hear the tension she tried to hide.

"Not happening. I'm mated now. I'm taking Phoebe back to Loup Garou, where we will live happily ever after."

Sounded like a great plan to Phoebe...once she eliminated Tuttle.

"I wish you'd stay for Helga's sake," Selena said. "She's a sweet woman, and she's lonely."

"I'm staying. I can't desert my aunt." Phoebe dared Parker to contradict her.

He could go to Colorado on his own, freeing her to do what she needed to do. She could join him...after.

Parker growled. "We'll discuss it later."

"You could go to Ulvskog and help while I stay in Warwick with Helga."

"He doesn't like my village. No one from Loup Garou does. They're not used to real trees." Sarcasm dripped from every syllable Selena spoke.

"We believe in the sky," Parker retorted. "We like the moon shining down on us in every phase and believe we shouldn't have to hunt her down when we need her."

"Children, behave." Olivia gave them a look perfected by generations of lycan grannies.

Phoebe remembered it well.

"Don't disturb Helga. Didn't Dakota mention a steak house Britt introduced him to? Maybe you three need to put some red meat in your bellies and calm down."

Chapter 7

Phoebe's virtues, Parker decided, suited him much better than Selena's would. Selena had been cranky on the ride to the restaurant, expecting Parker to ignore traffic laws because they were late meeting Ethan. Then she stopped to greet a few people sitting at a table by the door. By the time they made it to their table, Parker had gained a whole new appreciation for Phoebe's silences.

"How's Helga?" Ethan asked.

"Holding her own." Parker answered before anyone else could. "They're putting pins in her leg tomorrow. She'll be in the hospital for at least a week while the physical therapists work with her. When she goes home, she'll need someone there twenty-four-seven."

Hint, hint.

"I heard she claimed Phoebe's her niece." Ethan's lazy expression hinted at a different agenda, one omitting responsibility for his elderly neighbor.

"Yes." Phoebe's clipped response barely made a sibilant "s". "I don't mind. She reminds me of my foster mother. She asked Parker and me to keep an eye on her house in her absence."

"Not a bad plan. Your own place will give you some privacy." Ethan winked.

"So will driving home to Colorado." Parker remained firm.

"We didn't have any privacy," Selena reminded Ethan.

"Because we sheltered your pack when they needed a place to stay."

Since most of the Varulv had been slaughtered, including Selena's alpha grandfather, housing the survivors had landed on her shoulders.

Parker sensed he wasn't going to win this one. He'd be spending more time in Warwick. He studied the other restaurant patrons.

The clientele consisted of a mix of business and casual diners. Necktie wearers sat at tables next to t-shirts. In the far corner, a lone woman accompanied two men, one of whom looked familiar. The female emitted strong unhappy vibes. Nearby, several men in dark suits who weren't eating eyed everyone in the restaurant.

Jeeves tottered to the floor. Phoebe's eyes were enormous in her waxen face. Even her usually pink lips were barely darker than her complexion.

Parker went on high alert. He retrieved Jeeves and handed it to Phoebe. Her fist tightened on the stick.

"What's wrong?" he asked as quietly as he could.

"Nothing." She sounded stiff, her voice cracking from not being able to bend with the words.

Parker smelled the falsehood.

One of the suits' gaze caught on Phoebe. His face went ashen.

The older man at the next table glowered at Phoebe, infuriating Parker. *Who is glaring at my mate with such loathing and fear?*

"You know those people?" He jerked his head toward the offending males.

"Not really."

He barely heard her above the restaurant din.

"I think the old guy is Senator Tuttle." Ethan spoke marginally louder.

"Yes." Phoebe barely breathed the word.

"You know the Tuttles?"

"No." She propped Jeeves against the table next to her and picked up the menu, which fluttered like leaves being battered by rain until she inhaled deeply and closed her eyes. The shaking stopped.

A smile curved her lips and her eyes opened. "We lived in the same town for a while. Like Ethan and Elysian Estates are in the same city."

Which didn't explain her reaction.

"Do you want to leave?" Parker asked. "There are other restaurants."

"No. You promised me the best steak in town."

He'd made no such statement but didn't contradict her.

"I've always heard great things about this place." Selena lived in Warwick the longest, so she should know. "Apparently the political machine has heard the same rumors. The female is Nola Peters."

"Slumming it among the unwashed masses?" Phoebe's light tone betrayed nothing. She never lifted her eyes from the menu. The others couldn't see her face, but Parker could.

Her faux calm hid a deep, boiling anger.

He couldn't enjoy his meal with his mate so upset. No matter how skillfully Phoebe hid her angst, he sensed it. If the Tuttles were in town, offering support to the lecherous Peters family, Parker questioned their morals. And their connection to his mate.

"The Tuttles are not good people." Phoebe continued to read the menu as if was a New York Times best seller.

"They didn't try anything funny with you, did they?"

"Funny?"

"Sexual," he ground out between clenched teeth.

She laid the menu on the table and stared at him. Color returned to her face.

He should have chosen a better time and place to ask. Ethan and Selena seemed frozen.

Yeah. He should have waited.

"If they had," Phoebe replied, her voice soft but every word concise and clearly articulated, "I would have killed them."

"As you should." Selena's quiet tone belied the fury of the words. "I did."

"Congratulations." Phoebe's shoulders relaxed. "You have no idea how...liberating it is for you to not judge me."

"Then what is going on between you and the Tuttles?" Parker pressed.

Phoebe picked up the menu again. "The top sirloin looks good."

Here we go again. "What's going on with you and the Tuttles?"

Phoebe sighed as if expending great patience in dealing with him. "I don't want to discuss this here."

"Tough." His mated male obligation gene defied her pigheadedness.

"You have to promise you won't overreact."

Not scattin' likely.

She studied his face, then closed the menu and replaced it on the table. "Later."

Selena echoed Phoebe's action. "You're right. I'm going to order the top sirloin, too."

Ethan caught Parker's eye and shook his head, as if warning Parker not to force the issue. "Top sirloin? I was thinking about a t-bone. Then I'd have a bone to gnaw later."

Parker took the hint.

Once their meals arrived, Ethan started talking about his frustration with the lack of progress in his mission. The congressman he'd come to Warwick to negotiate with blew out his brains. Then Ethan helped kill the sons who'd been named interim congressmen. The local political party didn't know how to proceed until a special election could be held. No sitting congressman with whom to negotiate marooned Ethan in Minnesota.

"But you're not planning to return to Loup Garou," Parker pointed out.

"I have a life I'd like to begin with my mate in Ulvskog."

"So do it." Parker had his own agenda. "Have Britt or someone call you when the political mess here gets straightened out. It's not as if Ulvskog is across the country." He flipped the cucumber slices from his salad into Phoebe's bowl.

Phoebe speared one and bit into it.

"Cute," Selena said. "I wouldn't have considered cucumbers."

"What?" Parker asked.

"Botanically speaking, cucumbers are a berry."

Plants were Selena's forte. If she claimed cucumbers were berries, who was he to argue? Especially since he'd now fulfilled his mating obligation by gifting his mate with berries.

Phoebe went rigid next to him. Cucumbers insulted her?

Parker followed the line of her gaze. The Tuttle party was preparing to leave.

Phoebe clasped Jeeves, which worried Parker. Why would she need a weapon in a restaurant?

The dark suits at the table next to Tuttle's preceded the Tuttle party from the dining room.

Security detail. Parker should have known when they didn't eat.

Senator Tuttle stumbled when he saw Phoebe. His ruddy complexion waned ever so slightly.

Parker's gaze flicked between the senator and Phoebe, who lowered her chin and stared at Tuttle.

Tuttle immediately averted his eyes as if Phoebe didn't exist at all.

His younger clone glared at her.

Parker contained himself until the Tuttles vacated the premises. "What was that about?"

Phoebe picked up her water glass and sipped. "Senator Tuttle has a contract out on me."

Chapter 8

Parker, Phoebe decided, needed to chill. All his angst couldn't be good for his health.

"He what?" The hoarseness in his voice as he tried to whisper strained her control.

"Put a contract out on me. He wants me dead." She spoke matter-of-factly, not wanting Parker to know how frightened she'd been. How scared she remained. She focused on her success. She continued to outsmart and evade the senator.

All conversation ceased as the server arrived to ask about their meals.

Parker's face turned the same color as the inside of her steak. "You can't make an accusation without an explanation," he said after the server left.

Phoebe popped a chunk of meat into her mouth and chewed. Swallowed. "It's no big deal. The first time, he used a stupid redneck. I dealt with it. He's in prison."

"Good for you." Selena continued eating, unlike Parker and Ethan. They stared at Phoebe, a tsunami of cold waves rolling off them that might have chilled another female.

"Why?" Parker sounded as if he were choking. He clutched a section of the tablecloth. Poked a thumb through the fabric.

"Can you breathe?" Phoebe asked. "Do you need the Heimlich?"

"No, I need answers."

"Then don't snarl." She sliced off another lump of beef.

"Maybe," Ethan interjected, "this isn't the time or place for this discussion."

"I agree. I wouldn't have mentioned it if we hadn't run into Tuttle." Phoebe sopped more steak juice. "I'm surprised he frequents a place like this. Back home, only the five-star exclusive restaurants are good enough for his gold-plated palate."

Parker's complexion darkened even more.

"Hey." Phoebe dropped her fork and covered Parker's fist with her hand. His behavior worried her. "We'll talk later if it matters so much to you. But you need to calm down and eat. I don't want you having a stroke. Try inhaling deeply for a count of eight, holding for a count of eight, then exhaling slowly for a count of eight."

His mouth worked as if he wanted to speak, but nothing emerged.

Maybe a punch to the solar plexus would restart his breathing.

"Are you trying to make me a widow before I have a chance to be your mate?"

He didn't answer.

"Okay." She dropped his hand and scraped her chair away from the table. "Heimlich, here we come."

"Let me." Ethan, too, pushed away from his meal. "I'm bigger and stronger."

Phoebe held out her hand, palm up, as if to say, he's all yours. If Ethan wanted to alpha up on her, fine. Somebody needed to get Parker breathing again.

"I'm not choking," Parker rasped out. "I'm outraged."

"You're a male." Selena's mild tone removed some sting. "You're having a difficult time thinking your female is capable."

Selena's comment annoyed Phoebe, but she bit back a sharp response and smiled. *Always smile*, Corbie told her. *Smiling disarms people.*

"I'm flattered you're outraged on my behalf," she told Parker. "But if it's going to make you sick, we need to come up with a better solution."

There. Public support instead of humiliation.

Phoebe scooted closer to the table and replaced her hand on Parker's. "I don't mean to get you all worked up. I have a learning curve."

He drew in a deep breath, expanding his chest. His color receded. He pulled his hand from hers.

The rejection sliced her. She swallowed her hurt, but it stuck in her throat like a lodged chunk of meat. Her appetite fled.

She'd known she couldn't tell him everything. She didn't know how to relate to a male in a loving manner or with kindness. She never wanted to hurt Parker or make him worry. Her life hadn't prepared her to mate.

She would never fit into the lycan world. Corbie did the best she could, finding sapien ways for Phoebe to master lycan urges. She found teachers for Phoebe when she couldn't dissuade her from her innate need for revenge. But there were two things neither Phoebe nor Corbie considered. The lycan mating instinct, and what lay beyond Senator Tuttle's death.

Parker couldn't swallow another bite. The steak on his plate tasted great until Phoebe's announcement. Now other things filled his mouth: sand, bitter herbs, disappointment, and confusion.

The most powerful man in the U.S. government put a murder contract out on his mate. Or so Phoebe claimed.

He could hide her in Loup Garou, where his pack could protect her, where he could protect her. If not for Phoebe's promise to Helga, they could be on their way within the hour. He'd gone behind Restin's back to beg for Tokarz's permission to leave. Permission granted. He shouldn't be stuck in Minnesota because his new mate made reckless promises made more reckless by attempts on her life.

Yet Tuttle's threat seemed to have no more effect on her than storm clouds had on a full moon.

Phoebe ceased eating after her confession. He wanted to yell at Ethan and Selena to hurry, but yelling at them, with their alpha arrogance wouldn't do any good. They would do as they wanted, including lingering over their lunches.

At least Ethan picked up the tab, although he took his sweet time about paying.

Then Selena and Ethan stopped to socialize with the same two men Selena chatted with on the way in. Selena bared her teeth. "My elderly neighbor fell this morning. We'll be tag teaming her at the hospital for the next couple of days. In case you're looking for us. If you have more questions. You know the drill."

Finally.

"Phoebe and I will do the hospital shift later," Parker told Ethan as the couples split up in the parking lot. "Helga shouldn't have too many visitors at one time."

Phoebe didn't speak. She clutched a white paper sack holding her and Parker's uneaten meals in one hand and Jeeves in the other.

Jeeves. How effective a weapon could a stick be? Even a Kevlar stick couldn't stop a bullet.

He'd seen her in action last night. Or lack of action since he needed to rescue her. Her weapon didn't impress him.

Parker contained himself until they were on the main thoroughfare. "Do you have something you want to tell me?"

Phoebe stared out the window, as if fascinated by the fast-food and other franchises lining the street. "No, but I have a question. Are we going back to Helga's to have sex?"

Parker nearly choked. "Probably," he admitted. "But mating is only one reason I didn't want to go directly back to the hospital. I want to know more about what's going on between you and Tuttle."

"Oh."

He glanced at her but saw only the back of her head. A second peek revealed the reflection of her blank expression in the window. "Aren't you going to answer my question?"

"I'm waiting for you to ask one. Another one."

He banged a fist on the steering wheel. She was driving him mad. "Why does Senator Tuttle have a contract out on you?"

"You shouldn't grind your teeth. It's bad for them."

"You know, your evasiveness isn't as cute as you think it is."

She turned away from the scenery. "It's automatic self- defense. I grew up immersed in sapien culture, not lycan. My foster mother taught me to...pass as sapien."

Oh, scat. "You're not in a sapien situation now. I'm lycan, like you, and I'm your mate. You have to talk to me. I need to know if you're in danger so I can protect you."

Maybe he should have added cherished to his speech but cherishing this female might be beyond his capabilities. If not for the sex, could he possibly resent being shackled to her until one of them died?

He didn't want her to die. He certainly didn't want Tuttle to kill her.

"Concentrate on your driving." She delivered the advice in a soft, gentle tone. "Discussing my history with Tuttle now will only distract you."

He fumed as they left the main roads for the forest of streets leading to the houses on Ash. Phoebe's hard- headedness rivaled his sister's.

Phoebe produced a key to unlock Helga's front door. "I took it from Helga's purse before I gave it to Selena," she explained.

Helga's house smelled funny, like stale incense and rotting fruit. He ought to open a window to air out the place.

He followed Phoebe to the kitchen, where she stowed their doggy bags in the refrigerator.

"Are you ready to talk now?" Not his most civil tone. Phoebe brought out every negative lycan stereotype in him.

"Yes." She squared her shoulders and turned to face him. "I don't know how to be a mate, so this is all my fault. I apologize and beg your patience."

He hadn't expected to be blindsided by meekness from her "I'm new to being mated, too," he reminded her.

"But you have an advantage I don't." Her chin lowered, which made her eyes appear wider.

He sensed a con coming.

"Maybe we should sit down. Get comfortable." Her husky voice deepened.

Typical Phoebe con job. But he trailed her to Helga's fussy front room. Scraps of lace dripped from the arms and backs of the chairs and sofa and protected the wooden side tables from being scraped by the accumulated clutter. Breakable clutter, a wolf-in-china-shop cliché come to life.

Phoebe perched on one end of a floral-print sofa and patted the cushion next to her. As much as his brain suggested he avoid proximity, other body parts ruled. He sat beside her. The sofa proved more comfortable than it looked.

Jeeves remained within her grasp.

"I need to tell you about me." Phoebe stared at a spot on the wall. "I don't know my status—alpha, omega, or anything between. My name is Phoebe. I don't know my birth surname. My foster mother called me McKinn. She claimed it would keep the memory of my family and my pack alive." Phoebe's voice lacked inflection or emotion.

"She found me in the woods. She came to visit my granny. Instead she found...the aftermath of other visitors. Tuttle's Troopers."

"Tuttle's Troopers?" He'd never heard of such a group, but he instinctively knew their purpose. He'd smelled the aftereffects of their visits in Ulvskog.

"The name his...vigilantes are known as among the victimized."

Yeah. He figured as much. His stomach knotted.

"My memories are spotty. Some, I'm not even sure are memories, but maybe things I conjured from Corbie's questions. I was eight, so...a blur due to trauma."

Parker had been ten when his life went to human hell.

Phoebe swallowed hard. Her pale complexion lost another shade or two. "My parents, grandparents, and younger brothers were home on the night of the new moon. Corbie theorized the lack of moonlight saved me."

Her eyes glazed over, as if she looked inward at her memories instead of how her words affected him. Her voice went from its usual soft, minor key to a droning singsong. A disconnect, circumventing emotional shading.

"At eight, the moon phase didn't matter to me. It did to my parents, though."

She paused to inhale deeply. Her bound breasts rose, paused as she held the air in her lungs, then lowered as she slowly released the breath, the way she'd recommended to him at the restaurant. Nothing else on her body moved.

He sensed her emotions, though she worked at bypassing them.

Her words grew softer, closer to a whisper than spoken communication. "I heard guns. The loud noises frightened me. Frightened my brothers. My mother screamed for us to hide. My brothers were too young to know to be quiet."

Ancient Ones. The churning in his gut unknotted his stomach. Maybe not finishing his steak had been a good thing.

Phoebe's attention snapped to the present. To Parker. Homed in on him like a laser pinpointing a target. "I climbed a tree."

She broke off. Her throat muscles worked as she swallowed. "This is difficult for me to discuss, even with you."

He took her hand. Her fingers were wadded into her palm, creating a fist. An icy fist.

"I witnessed Tuttle's Troopers murder my parents and brothers. Neighbors. Everyone I knew. The life I knew."

He knew what witnessing a sibling's death could do to a soul. What she described surpassed even his horror. He squeezed Phoebe's hand, trying to thaw her icy fingers.

"Ever since that night, my life has been a secret. Hidden. Not in shame, but in preparation."

"Preparation for what?" His words emerged in guttural fragments because emotion thickened his throat.

"Senator Richard Tuttle must pay."

"You said he put a contract out on you."

That was the first thing her mate had to say after hearing she'd survived a massacre? Right. As Corbie would say, she could find sympathy in the dictionary between shit and syphilis.

Phoebe suppressed the impulse to grab her quarterstaff and wreak serious damage on Parker.

Instead, she said, "I know his deepest secret."

"Does he know you? By sight?" Parker pressed.

She wrenched her hand free and jumped off the sofa. Reliving the night her world ended always triggered strange and crazy emotions. Why should sharing her worst nightmare with the male chosen for her by the Goddess ease the pain?

"Not until recently."

Parker in no way indicated he wanted to comfort her.

Well, she didn't need anything from him. Time to remind him.

"You admire Selena's toughness because she found her grandfather's mutilated corpse. Well, I witnessed my father, my mother, my grandparents, my brothers being mutilated." Every ounce of willpower she possessed went into keeping her voice steady.

She turned her back on Parker. Stalked to the window. Peering at the empty street through a gap in the curtain reminded her of peeking through the leaves of the tree in which she'd hidden.

"Did I tell you I climbed a tree to escape? My father used to joke I was more feline than lupus." Her voice cracked. "The joke was on him."

"Phoebe." Parker's hand on her shoulder startled her. He'd left the sofa and come to stand behind her without her being aware. The murky memories mired her physical senses.

"I didn't wet my pants like my youngest brother did." She couldn't stop. Parker had pressed the start button. She couldn't pause until the story concluded. "I focused on becoming one with the tree. A hunter instead of the hunted. Did your family play hunting games with you? Someday you will hunt with the pack, so you must learn stalking skills?"

Parker slid his hand down her torso until he found her waist.

"I saw it all. I witnessed every bullet. Heard every slur and sneer and snicker." The rotten-egg reek of spewed bullets.

She hit the fast-forward button.

"I stayed in the tree until the smell..." She would never get the stench out of her head. The molecules or whatever were embedded in her nostrils, her sinuses, tainting everything.

Parker wrapped both arms around her and pulled her against his solid body.

"I hid in a cave where we used to play." She'd shut down all her senses but her hearing. Concentrated on the cave's darkest corner, where she cowered. Focused on becoming one with the darkness, letting the darkness absorb her until they were the same thing.

No one found her for three days. Three days in which she turned her thirst and hunger into darkness. Three days to remold the core of what Phoebe had been as a child into her future identity.

"I am the only survivor. The last of my kind."

Her confession crouched between them, creating a barrier she didn't know how to breech.

"So now you know. I am a foundling. I didn't grow up in a pack and have only rudimentary lycan instincts. Corbie did the best she could. She knew some shifter stuff from being friends with my granny."

She wanted me to marry her grandson.

Parker's embrace tightened, tempting her to steady herself against him. She couldn't, though. She could never relax. The ugly duckling always needed to be alert on the pond.

"I'm not surprised you're so tense all the time," he murmured, his breath hot against her ear. "A shifter growing up sapien. Ancient Ones, it's a miracle you survived at all."

Maybe she had imparted a glimmer of what drove her to Parker.

"You're my miracle mate." He lowered his face to her neck and nuzzled her mating spot, which annoyed her as much as it aroused her.

"Corbie did everything she could to help me. Taught me how to meditate so I could deal with my more violent tendencies. Adolescence and the shift were...challenging for her. For us both."

And Dustin. The mistake she'd wanted to make but didn't. The boy who professed to love her; who tried to seduce her; who created the need for her to learn sapien self- defense skills. Dustin had set her on her current path.

Her rejection of him caused her rift with Corbie.

"Why did you say Tuttle has a contract out on you?"

She did owe Parker an explanation. "He knows I'm alive."

"He knows you're a lycan? How?"

"He knows I survived his...purge. Isn't purge the word you used?" She couldn't go any further.

"How?"

Because she'd blundered. Made a grave error in judgment. By the time she figured out what she'd done, too much time had passed to rectify the mistake.

No more true confessions. They tired her. Parker presented her with the perfect diversion.

Phoebe rubbed against Parker. Due to the difference in their heights, her bottom missed ground zero by several inches. Parker still understood her intent. His body screamed, *Go for it!* The few remaining functioning brain cells cautioned him: *Beware!*

"You haven't answered my question."

"Which one?" She seemed to melt into him like candle wax.

His focus faded as more blood rushed south.

What if I bend her over, pull down her leggings, and mounted her right here, in front of the window?

Maybe once the newness wore off, he'd retain more control. More capacity for thinking about something other than how his penis enjoyed being buried deep inside this female. Phoebe wouldn't be able to use his body against him. Tonight, her actions betrayed her plan to distract him with sex. Pleasure had nothing to do with her motivation. Until he built up his immunity to the mating instinct, she could manipulate him and probably would. Anything to avoid telling him what she didn't want him to know.

The female used a real talent for shifting his focus.

"Are you trying to seduce me?" Her low, throaty chuckle caressed his libido. "What's up, Doc? Don't answer. Let me guess. You are."

"Let's take this someplace else. Someplace not in view of the neighborhood in broad daylight." He slid his hands from her breasts to the waistband of her leggings.

"Think we can make it to the guest room?"

Chapter 9

THEY DIDN'T MAKE IT to Helga's guest room the first time. Parker mounted Phoebe on the living room floor. The second time she wrapped her legs around his waist as he tried to knock the pictures from the wall in Helga's short, narrow hallway.

The third time, they made it to the bed. By the time they located the guest room where they'd stowed their belongings, Parker destroyed a second pair of leggings. He tossed her onto the bed, yanked her turtleneck over her head, and shredded her binding cloth.

He fell on her bare breasts like a starving infant.

Beds, Phoebe discovered, didn't make the act any different. She enjoyed fucking, especially when Parker worked her marking spot, but sex didn't distract her. Except when she climaxed. Orgasms were great, but something seemed...missing.

The best part about sex was she'd found a way to manipulate Parker. To distract him and keep him occupied. The less he knew about her activities, the safer he would be.

She needed to finish her task alone.

She rested on her side. Parker spooned against her back. He gave off heat like a Beltane bonfire.

Parker's fingers toyed with one of her nipples. She lay on his arm, but she didn't immobilize him. "How does Tuttle know you survived?"

His question surprised her. Why didn't he ask her if she'd enjoyed herself, or discuss going back to the hospital for Helga or what she wanted for supper? The possibilities were endless. No. He homed in on the one thing she didn't want to discuss.

"I've relived enough past traumas for the time being." If she couldn't be open with her mate, she couldn't be honest with anyone. Survival in the sapien world depended on her secrets.

"I'm on to you, you know."

Phoebe wiggled her butt against him. "Doc, are you trying to give me a hard time? I think you gave me three this afternoon."

"You might be able to temporarily distract me with sex, but I'm not a stupid lobo."

"I never thought you were. You're an EMT who's going for paramedic training. That takes brains. I could never be smart enough to study medicine."

"About the paramedic training." He pinched her nipple. "I need to get back to Colorado before the next session starts."

"Go." *Please.* "I'll join you when Aunt Helga has recuperated."

"I'm not leaving you here alone."

"I won't be alone. I'll be with more of my kind than I have in the past fifteen years. It'll be a party. You should trust me because they're your friends."

"Mating means staying together. At least at first. Rand and Hatch are here without their mates, but they've been mated for years."

Another name she didn't recognize. "Who is Rand?"

"Ethan's father. Hatch's son."

"So there are three other Limmikin in addition to me?" A slow thrill rolled through her.

"Four, counting Hatch's mate."

"Ethan is only half Limmikin? And his father is here?"

"Rand and Hatch are both helping rebuild Ulvskog."

"Selena's ancestral village, right? So I'll be safe here, with your Limmikin friends. You can go back to Colorado and your paramedic training."

"You're not going to get rid of me." Parker rolled onto his back, bringing her with him, until she sprawled across his body. The rough hair on his chest abraded her skin. "I like sex. A lot."

"I know," she assured him. "I'm smart, too. Not like you're smart, but in my own way."

He cupped her butt cheeks and squeezed. "You're supposed to like sex a lot, too. You're supposed to be happy."

Phoebe peered into his smoky quartz eyes. "I am happy. You make me happy in ways I can't explain. I never thought I would find other werewolves, much less a mate." She drew her forefinger down the side of his face. "Much less a handsome mate. Not to mention smart. Someone who wants to do something with his life. You make me giddy."

Maybe she laid it on a bit thick, but every word was true.

"Why did you become an EMT? To travel with Toke Lobo?"

The light in his eyes dimmed. His expression grew solemn. Her mate kept secrets, too. She could see him weighing every word before he spoke it.

"Our kind doesn't have adequate medical care. We tend to rely solely on folk lore and the old ways. Old Olivia is a healer, and her ways are rooted in generations. Homeopathic medicine. There is nothing wrong with the old ways, but the sapiens and their medicine have other concepts to offer."

He never explained why he chose to become a modern medicine man.

"If I could become a doctor, I would, but the moon limits me," he added.

Oh, Goddess, she knew his helplessness against the moon. She could relate to lunar limitations on many levels.

"You would make a wonderful doctor. You have great instincts."

She yawned and burrowed closer to the pillow beneath her head. "I need a nap before we visit Helga. My natural sleep patterns have always fought sapien daylight schedules."

"I get it. The adjustment to daylight life is always annoying. We needed to in Ulvskog because construction is easier in daylight. The paramedic training is daytime, too. I'll help you ease into changing your circadian clock."

Annoyance flared. "You know, for once in my life I'd like to be the one who doesn't have to change her ways. I want to be a she-wolf living in a pack without having to accommodate the sapien world."

"You're the one who made promises to Helga, not me."

PHOEBE OPENED HER EYES and panicked. *Where am I?*

Then she scented her mate. Parker. The past twenty-four hours clicked into place. Arriving in Warwick. Thugs. Parker. Mating twisting her agenda. Too much crap weighing her down.

Not Parker or the mating, but everything packaged with him. Packs. Protocols. Touchy alphas and injured neighbors.

Phoebe's long nap recharged her. Parker sprawled beside her in the frilly bed in Helga's furbelowed guest room. A breeze ruffled the curtains through the open window. Darkness cloaked the room.

Night, her milieu.

Not wanting to waken Parker, she eased from the bed. She snatched her clothes from the floor. She needed some alone time, and she hadn't been alone since meeting him. Even pack creatures needed time to meditate.

Pinkish orange light from the streetlights filtered through Helga's curtains, illuminating the living room enough for Phoebe to comfortably move through the obstacle course.

Helga owned so much...stuff. Too many possessions could suffocate a female. Phoebe much preferred the starkness of the house across the street. Many sapien problems lay in their inability to breathe. Breath was life.

Corbie's house, where Phoebe grew up, had been cluttered but not like Helga's. Not like the hoardings of an unhappy old woman.

Phoebe made her way to the kitchen, where she paused to pull on her leggings and shirt. The hinges on the back door were silent as she opened it.

Light pollution didn't invade Helga's backyard. The only illumination came from the lightning bugs flickering in the low hedge marking the boundaries and from the overhead stars. Dew dampened the grass beneath Phoebe's bare feet. A skunk left its calling card somewhere down the street.

Phoebe didn't have a yoga mat, so she plopped onto the dew-covered grass. Better to become one with the Earth, she told herself, even though she'd soaked her butt. Arranging her legs in the lotus position, she settled in to meditate.

She studied the sky until she found Vega, shining brightly overhead, and focused on its light. Meditation should settle her. *Empty your mind. Forget the discomfort of your wet ass. Your hunger. How you have to grovel at Selena Wolfe Calhoun's paws. Breathe. Focus on the cool air brushing the rims of your nostrils.*

A dog barked. A motorcycle roared past the house.

Ignore the distractions. Release. Push your breath from your body, taking negativity with it.

Her left calf cramped. "Shit!" She tried to straighten her leg, but the muscles wouldn't cooperate.

"Are you okay?" Parker's silhouette shadowed the door. His naked silhouette.

"Yes," she gritted. Her leg tried to curl into itself.

He scurried toward her. "What's wrong?"

"Cramp." She tried to work the stone-hard muscle.

Maybe if she could get up and walk it off...

Parker's feet left shadows in the dew as he crossed the yard. He squatted next to her. "Let me."

His fingers were lean and long. Strong. They dug deep into her calf, creating a different, better pain. "That's some charlie-horse."

Chills raced through her. She clenched her teeth so hard she feared she might break them. She'd never experienced such intense pain.

Parker used both hands to reshape the muscle. His fingers dug deep. "You're probably dehydrated. You didn't drink much today. What color was your urine the last time you went?"

She leaned back on her elbows to put space between them, even though he still massaged her leg. "I didn't look. But you're right. It's been a strange day."

As if she spoke about personal matters with strangers every day. Mating didn't make Parker any less a stranger. Barely twenty-four hours had passed since he rescued her from the thugs outside Elysian Estates. Now he was rubbing her leg and asking about the color of her piss.

The spasm eased. She straightened her ankle. Her shivering slowed. "Thank you."

He continued manipulating her calf.

She started to pull away from him when another spasm struck. She gasped.

"I've got you." Parker didn't pause in his counterattack.

Several agonizing minutes later, the cramp was only a sore memory.

Parker stood and extended his hand. "Need help getting up?"

She grasped his hand, and he pulled her to her feet. "I was trying to meditate. I missed this morning."

"You meditate every day?" His arm went around her waist, as if he expected to prop her up in case the cramp returned.

"I try."

"Why?"

"Calming my mind helps my focus. Corbie thought learning to meditate would help control my...lycan traits."

"Makes sense. Does it help?" He held the kitchen door.

"Mostly, I think. Sometimes. Meditating didn't keep the full moon at bay, though."

"What did you do?"

"A lot of field trips and camping."

She didn't have the words to explain something she herself didn't grasp. She'd heard other girls, sapien females, discuss menstruation, and at first, she thought getting a period meant turning into a beast, which terrified her. Corbie explained the fundamental difference between Phoebe and the sapien females with whom she went to school. The conversation cemented Phoebe's outsider status. She was alone in the world, the only one of her kind remaining. An endangered species.

Parker closed and locked the door behind him. "I'm hungry."

"We have our lunch leftovers," Phoebe reminded him. "Let me change, then I'll throw the food in the microwave."

She didn't mention his nudity.

Parker followed her into the bedroom, where he unplugged his phone from the charger and checked for messages. "Ethan texted a while ago, asking us to join them for supper."

Phoebe draped her wet leggings over a chair back. "So?"

"He texted again an hour later and told us not to come."

"Selena has banished us. My heart is broken." Phoebe didn't bother to hide her sarcasm.

"You wish. The cops are looking for you."

"They are?" Phoebe kept her tone as cool as the dew coating Helga's grass.

"Any idea why?"

"None, unless I got picked up on security cameras outside Elysian Estates last night. You've been with me every moment since we met." *Suffocating me with togetherness.*

"What about before?"

She resented the implication. "Before what?"

"Between the bus station and Elysian Estates."

"I hiked." Her jaw ached from clenching her teeth. "Why were you at Elysian Estates?"

Enough was enough. She stalked out of the bedroom. "I don't answer to you any more than I answer to Selena."

He stomped after her. "Would you prefer answering to the cops?"

"I was attacked outside Elysian Estates. You witnessed it. Maybe security cameras caught the ambush. The cops could be looking for you as well as me." She could have driven Toke Lobo's tour bus fleet through her argument.

She made her way to the kitchen and opened the refrigerator door, even though her appetite had fled.

"Why are you giving us a difficult time for trying to help you?" Parker stood in the doorway.

"I'm not. I don't know what you want from me." She snatched the white paper bag containing The Steak Out leftovers.

"The truth!"

She lowered her voice as she slammed the refrigerator door. The stuff Helga stored on top of the appliance rattled. "I told you the truth. I got off the bus, walked to Elysian Estates, where thugs attacked me and you rescued and fucked me."

Her blunt statement didn't seem to faze him. "Then you have nothing to hide."

"I have nothing to hide." Except from the thought police.

Parker's phone vibrated, the buzz loud in the quiet following her assertion. The screen illuminated his face as he read the text message.

She opened and closed cupboard doors until she found plates. She pulled out two. Tremors wracked her body, and her legs still ached from the cramps.

"Okay. Selena wants us to stay put. And quiet. She thinks her house is being watched. The local guys mentioned something about feds being involved. Ethan's getting in touch with our FBI contact."

Phoebe's legs gave way. She hit the floor with a thud and stared up at Parker. "What? What FBI contact?"

Parker dropped his phone as he knelt next to her. "What happened? Are you all right? Are the cramps back?"

"What FBI contact?"

"Luke Thibodaux, Toke Lobo's drummer, has a side gig with the FBI's computer sex crimes division. Maybe you should drink some water." Parker climbed to his feet and repeated Phoebe's earlier cupboard door routine.

Why is Toke Lobo's drummer moonlighting with the FBI's sex crime division?

"You guys think texting is secure?"

"Luke has a secure land line." Parker found a glass and carried it to the sink.

"How secure is it when someone calls on a cell phone?" She didn't trust technology. Yeah, she used cell phones, but she didn't trust the things. She changed phones every month. He didn't answer, as if he couldn't do more than one thing at a time and filling a glass with water from the faucet took all his attention. She tried to focus on how...sweet he was being. How he tried to take care of her.

He squatted next to her and handed her the glass. "Drink it all."

Drinking was easier than arguing. The tepid water quenched her thirst. He'd nailed his diagnosis.

Barely a day gone by and he'd shaken up her life so much, she no longer recognized it. Her focus drifted from her past to her future, a future in which she'd never before believed. Having now caught glimmers, burying the past became crucial. The future promised so much better.

But burying the past meant burying Senator Richard Tuttle. Warwick, Minnesota might be her last opportunity.

Chapter 10

"SHALL WE HIT MOONEY'S for breakfast before we check in at the hospital?"

Phoebe stopped toweling her wet-from-her-morning- shower head and stared at Parker. "Hospital?"

"Helga's surgery is this morning."

"Oh. Right. I have to be there, don't I?"

"You're her next of kin." Sarcasm dripped from every syllable he spoke.

"I had nothing to do with what she did, and you know it. Did you check with Selena to see if we can leave the house?" Phoebe could give as good as she got. She dropped the towel and pulled on her leggings.

"Yeah. We're good to go."

If not for his SUV, Phoebe would have found a way to ditch her interfering mate. She had so much to do before she could assume the life he wanted with her. Tasks she needed to accomplish. Alone.

Alone would protect him.

Thank the Goddess he'd finished talking. She'd already told him too much. He might start fitting pieces together in problem-creating ways.

They didn't speak on the way to the hospital, which Phoebe appreciated. She didn't have to worry about what words to use without lying to him.

Parker brought along a book to read while they awaited word on Helga's surgery. Based on the title, she assumed he planned to study for his paramedic classes.

Selena and Olivia arrived as Parker and Phoebe were settling in. There were too many others in the waiting room for Selena to create a scene.

Phoebe propped her quarterstaff against her chair and settled into her zone. Outside distractions couldn't penetrate. Thinking and planning were good. She'd prefer doing daylight reconnaissance at Elysian Estates, where she speculated Tuttle was staying. According to her research, the Tuttle and Peters families went way back.

"Phoebe McKinn?"

Her name being spoken aloud jerked her from her reverie.

She blinked. Stared up at two vaguely familiar looking men, one of whom was unnaturally tall. Oh, yeah. Selena's friends from the Steak Out.

Parker slammed his book shut and stood. "What do you want with her?"

There were moments when a mate came in handy, especially one still freshly in the throes of mating fever.

The shorter man answered. "We'd like a few moments of your time, ma'am."

Selena crossed the waiting room before Phoebe could answer. "Detective Clerkin, Anderson. What brings you to the hospital?"

"Like we told you last night, we have a few questions we'd like to ask Ms. McKinn."

Oh. The cops about whom Ethan texted.

"She's Mrs. Rowe, now." Parker corrected him. "Can I see some identification?"

The shorter man reached into his pocket. Phoebe glimpsed his sidearm. He pulled out a leather case and flipped it open. The badge confirmed her suspicion. Mickey Clerkin, Warwick City Police Detective, first class.

Phoebe's gut tightened. She could handle this. "I'll be happy to speak with you."

She had nothing to hide. Yet. At least not from these two officials. She rose from her chair with all the grace she could muster, comforted by her quarterstaff's smooth wood against her palm. Calm was the key. Calm meant control.

Parker planted his hand on her lower back and nudged her to follow the tall detective.

Selena joined the parade.

"The next room on the left is a meeting room we can use," Clerkin said from behind them.

Tall Cop pulled open the door, revealing a cramped room containing a round table and several chairs. A bare window looked out on a brick wall.

"We tried to contact Ms. McKinn last night," the tall man said. "I'm Detective Anderson, by the way. What's with the stick?"

Okay, she did have something to hide. "I have a bad knee."

Parker pulled out a chair for her. She sat. He remained standing behind her.

"Mrs. Rowe recently arrived in Warwick." Selena claimed the chair next to Phoebe. "What could you possibly need to speak to her about?"

Why was Selena butting in?

The detectives must have wondered, too. "I'm sorry, Ms. Calhoun, but are you an attorney?" Detective Clerkin asked. He and his partner sat across from Phoebe.

"No, but I need to know if she needs one."

Parker pressed Phoebe's shoulder before she could ask why, a signal to let Selena speak for her.

Clerkin focused on Phoebe. "When did you arrive in Warwick?"

"Two nights ago."

"Why are you here?"

This is America, where anyone can travel anywhere they want within its borders.

"I'm visiting my foster mother's aunt. Helga Gammel. She fell, you know, and is being operated on right now." Phoebe shook her head. "Thankfully, I happened to be here when it happened. My foster mother is extremely upset."

"You're married now?"

Parker squeezed her shoulder again. "Yes."

"Do you have some identification?"

"Nothing with my married name on it. We're newlyweds. Parker is here for work. When we decide where we're going to live, I'll have it updated." The truth always worked best.

"Do you have proof of your marriage?"

"You crossed the line," Parker growled.

The detective backtracked. "We received a tip that one Phoebe McKinn is in Warwick in order to inflect bodily harm to a visiting dignitary."

Phoebe pushed away from the table, stood, and spread her arms. "Look at me. Do I look as if I could do bodily harm to anyone? Besides, why would I want to harm my cousin?"

Everyone at the table looked confused. They hadn't heard anything yet.

She purposely deepened her natural drawl as she reclaimed her seat. Parker's hands once more rested on her shoulders. "You're talking about Selena's husband, Ethan, right? My cousin? I mean, Ethan's in Toke Lobo and the Pack, but I wouldn't think celebrity classifies him as a dignitary."

"Your cousin? I thought you're here to visit your stepmother's aunt."

"Foster mother," Phoebe corrected. "Yes. Aunt Helga. We're all so worried. Broken bones at her age can be a real challenge. Mamma Corbie is beside herself worrying."

Clerkin frowned. "But Ethan Calhoun is your cousin? I'm trying to get this straight."

"Right. Ethan isn't my first cousin, or even a second cousin, but we're cousins." She beamed. "He's the famous one in the family."

"How does your husband fit in?"

"None of your business," Parker snapped.

Phoebe covered his hand with hers. "It's okay, honey." She stretched her mouth into a wide smile for the detectives. "Love at first sight. Cousin Ethan has been telling me forever about his friend Parker. He was right."

"Aren't we getting off track here?" Selena's dry tone meant business. "The last I knew, visiting Minnesota isn't even a misdemeanor."

Detective Clerkin acted as if the weight of the world on his shoulders prevented him from being as tall as his partner. "We received an anonymous tip claiming Phoebe McKinn intends to harm Senator Richard Tuttle, who is visiting our local congressman's grieving family."

Phoebe propped her quarterstaff against the table, then stood. Parker must have read her mind because he inched back. "I'm asking you again. Do I look like I could inflict bodily harm on anyone?"

Use the weapons you have. Your size will work in your favor.

"The security cameras outside Elysian Estates show you were there last night." Anderson tag-teamed her.

Security cameras. Check. Good to know. "When did sightseeing become illegal?"

"At ten o'clock at night?"

"The sky was beautiful. I'd been cooped up on a bus for hours. Do I need to pay a tariff on rarified air or something?"

"The security tapes showed you were accosted."

"You mean attacked by a gang? Who knows what would have happened if Parker hadn't met me." Phoebe sank to her seat again, and Parker resumed his pose behind her, hands on her shoulders.

"Someone is concerned enough about your presence in Warwick—at the same time as the senator—to warn us," Clerkin repeated.

"I'm sure the Senator and I have been in the same city numerous times. We're both from Soddy-Daisy. Coincidence?"

"This is ridiculous," Selena snapped. "The poor girl came to visit her aunt, who she found on the floor with a broken leg, and who is now in the hospital having her bones screwed together. Now you guys are hassling her. You're not the best welcoming committee around, you know."

"We have enough trouble with our own politicians without adding an out-of-state senator to the Warwick missing politician black hole," Anderson said.

"Am I missing something?" Phoebe asked.

"He means our local congressman put a bullet in his brain immediately after Ethan and I visited him. And I do mean immediately." Selena didn't seem to mind filling Phoebe in. "Then his oldest son disappeared after harassing me at home. And the second son has also vanished. He left most of his blood in Britt's bed."

"Who's Britt?"

Parker squeezed Phoebe's shoulder. "Dakota's wife. You met him yesterday."

"Oh. I guess I can see why the authorities are concerned something might happen to a visiting senator." Phoebe forced sincerity. "In Tennessee, we vote 'em out of office. Much more civilized."

"We take all warnings seriously."

Pompous cop speak.

"Even from cowards who are afraid to put their faces, behind their accusations?" Phoebe fluttered her eyelashes at the detectives.

"What do you know about Senator Richard Tuttle?"

Phoebe willed Parker and Selena not to repeat the slip she'd made at the restaurant the previous day.

"We're both from Soddy-Daisy. Our neighborhoods don't border each other, like Ethan and Selena's neighborhood doesn't border Elysian Estates."

"This interview is over." Selena climbed to her feet.

Parker tapped Phoebe's shoulder, so she followed suit as she automatically grasped her quarterstaff.

The detectives also stood. "We'll be keeping an eye on you."

"Good. Maybe I'll feel safe again. Last night's encounter scared me."

Chapter 11

Helga's complexion matched the dingy hospital sheets, and only the slight lumps in the blanket covering her revealed a body at all. Although Phoebe had never seen Helga other than injured, she thought her bogus aunt appeared thinner. Her dry, flaky skin sagged.

She's dehydrated.

Yes, tubes pumped fluids into her, machines monitored her blood pressure, her heart rate, and modern medicine only knew what else, but what about her water intake? Parker might be better qualified to judge Helga's condition, but Phoebe knew all about hydration. Dehydration could have been behind Helga's fall.

"Her color is good," Parker murmured. He cupped Phoebe's elbow.

Good? For fog, maybe. Not a sapien female.

"Considering everything," he amended, as if he knew Phoebe disagreed.

"She looks dehydrated to me."

"Yeah. Sometimes it happens. We'll keep an eye on her once we get her home."

Helga's lips twitched.

"She's going to wake up powerfully thirsty," he continued. I'll see if I can find some ice chips."

"Ice chips?"

"To wet her lips and tongue. Not enough to swallow, though, because she'll vomit if she has anything in her stomach right now."

"Oh."

Parker took off, leaving Phoebe alone with Helga.

Phoebe studied the woman's face. Her crinkled eyelids fluttered. Twitched. Popped open. The normally vivid blue eyes were clouded, as if a storm brewed inside her. Her tongue flicked between her cracked lips. "Water." The gruff voice didn't resemble Helga's at all.

"Parker went to get you some ice."

Helga's eyes closed again.

Phoebe placed her hand over Helga's cold one. "Your surgery was successful. The social worker is going to give us instructions on your care so we can get you home as quickly as possible."

The eyelids twitched again. "Don't do it."

The words were crisp. Precise. Not spoken like a woman battling her way out of general anesthesia, but from some deeper, unearthly place.

Phoebe's stomach clenched.

"Martyrs only create more followers." Helga shifted restlessly, as if trapped in a nightmare. "Promise me you won't turn him into a martyr."

Oh. That. How did Helga know?

Phoebe couldn't make such a promise. She knew the risks. She might not survive. She accepted the possibility. The probability.

Her younger brothers' cries still echoed in her dreams.

The taste of gunpowder still tainted her meals.

"If you won't promise your aunt, promise me." Parker entered the room carrying a paper cup. He used a paper towel to pluck an ice chip from the cup and gently ran the frozen water over Helga's lips.

Helga muttered something.

"I don't even know what she's talking about." A lie, and Parker probably knew it.

From the look he gave her, he didn't appreciate it, either.

"Neither of you is the boss of me," Phoebe said after watching Parker ply Helga's lips with ice for several moments.

Parker's hand faltered before he resumed his task. "Don't we mean anything to you?"

She burrowed into her psyche to find an unoffensive answer. "Symbolically, yes. But I don't know either one of you, and you don't know me."

"We won't have a chance if you go through with your plan and you're caught."

DUSTIN HOLLOWAY WAS GOING to pay. The words rhymed. Maybe she could write lyrics and sell a song to Ethan for Toke Lobo to use. The Ballad of Dustin Holloway, the horny little asshole who would betray anyone because he couldn't get laid.

The thought dogged Phoebe during Helga's surgery, while she sat with her alleged aunt post-surgery, and even when she and Parker took a dinner break.

Every once in a while, she caught a glint in Parker's eyes, assuring her he'd be prying into her business again. Later. When he could safely speak. Back at Helga's, or, Goddess forbid, at a command performance with Selena and Ethan.

Well, she needed to know things, too. Later.

"I'm not going to Selena's," Phoebe declared as she flopped onto Helga's sofa. "I'm exhausted."

Parker plopped next to her. "I'm don't want to go either. It's been a long day."

"Too long." She never thought she'd be happy to see Helga's ugly floral furniture again.

"And you and I need to clear the air."

"We sure do." The best defense was a good offence. "Why did Selena stick her nose in my business with the cops at the hospital this morning?"

"She's alpha."

"Alpha is only a concept for me, and she's not my alpha. Or yours, either."

"She's alpha of the pack living in this territory."

"I thought you said Minnesota is Limmikin territory. Which means I have more rights here than Selena, even if she is mated to a half-Limmikin male."

"The Limmikin were strictly forest-dwellers. The Varulv split their time between the woods and Warwick."

"Your pack nonsense is confusing and ridiculous." Phoebe couldn't imagine having to live with strictures beyond the ones imposed by her DNA. Growing up in the coven meant she'd lived in the sapien world. The ruling class.

Even protecting her virginity had been easier. Some sapien circles valued virtue as much as lycans did. Sex was why Dustin turned into a jerk. Now Parker needed a tedious explanation because Dustin brought in the cops.

"My foster mother's grandson works security for Senator Tuttle." She blurted out before she lost her nerve. "I saw him at the restaurant yesterday."

Parker froze. His Adam's apple bobbed in his throat as he swallowed.

"I didn't spot him on TV at the bus station, so I didn't know he'd come to Warwick with the senator. We grew up together. We were friends. At least, I thought we were."

"What happened?"

"We went steady in high school."

Parker's tone grew dangerous. "And?"

"He wanted more from me than I wanted to give him. Corbie drilled into me about how lycan females should only be with their mates. You know. Sexually. So even though I figured I'd never find my mate, I shouldn't be with Dustin. Then Corbie decided we were mates."

"His name is Dustin?"

"Yeah. He didn't handle my rejection well. And because we grew up in the same house, he knew about my true nature."

"He ratted your survival out to Senator Tuttle."

"The only reason I haven't killed Dustin is because Corbie loves him. Corbie saved me. Did her best by me. I couldn't repay her by killing her only blood relative."

"If you'd been raised properly, killing him wouldn't be an issue." Parker's tone turned brutal. "Did he molest you?"

"Nope. Whenever he tried to touch me in ways I didn't like, I smacked him with my quarterstaff."

"Not hard enough."

"Hard enough to make him tattle to Tuttle."

"I see why you think there's a contract to kill you." Parker's paralysis vanished. His leg jittered as if motorized. His thumbs and forefingers rubbed each other hard enough to wear off the skin.

"No hitmen have shown up on my doorstep recently."

"They know you're here now, though."

"They both saw me at the restaurant. If I had to guess, I'd say Dustin called in the tip to the local cops."

"You're probably right." He pulled out his phone. "We need to let Selena know."

Phoebe snatched it from his hand. "We don't need to do anything except stay alert."

"When one lycan has trouble, the packs pull together." He took the phone from her. "Selena is the alpha of this area. We need to let her know."

"Fine." Phoebe stood. "You tell her. I'd better meditate into calm before I use my quarterstaff on you."

Phoebe wished she knew how to make Parker angry enough to stalk off and brood. To leave her alone. She didn't want him around while she meditated. His presence disturbed her calm.

She turned to face the hiding moon. Turned her back on her mate. He threw everything off kilter.

Velvety ribbons of mist twined in the trees at the rear of Helga's yard. The heavy air warned of a storm. The night should have been cool, but leftover heat from the day further weighted the atmosphere.

A sign, Phoebe thought. An omen.

She settled on the damp grass for a short meditation session. The neighborhood skunk made his rounds and let everyone know about his bad mood. She placed her quarterstaff next to her. The meditation would purify her. Many tasks needed to be accomplished this night. She'd sloughed off enough.

PARKER ALLOWED PHOEBE HALF an hour before he peered into Helga's backyard to check on her. He stood in the doorway. Her unique aroma lingered, trapped by the humidity, and unfazed by skunk, but he didn't see Phoebe. He settled his mind and searched the shadows. Nothing. Then he closed his eyes to better hear her breath, her heart. Dogs in the next neighborhood barked. Someone's television blared into the night. No Phoebe.

She'd given him the slip.

He tamped down his fury. He should have foreseen her escape. He strode onto the lawn and identified the spot where she'd sat, then eyeballed the tiny stains her footprints left in the dew.

He didn't have a choice. Luckily, the humidity trapped scents and didn't allow them to disperse, so following her trail was easy.

She knew a little about Warwick now. She'd acclimated.

Did she choose to go to the hospital or Elysian Estates?

He started to follow her scent, but his feet tangled in something. He stumbled. He picked up debris. Except it turned out to be clothing. Tiny, black clothing. Phoebe's. No body heat remained in the fabric, which meant she must have shifted shortly after he'd left her to meditate. A quick scan of the ground around her clothes confirmed Jeeves was missing, too.

She'd taken off on her own and left him with no choice but to follow her.

The fact she'd shifted at all confirmed something else.

She wasn't pregnant.

IF ONLY SHE DIDN'T have to carry her quarterstaff in her mouth. One day she would figure out a better way to keep it with her at all times, but for now, she clamped the wood between her teeth and trotted toward her destination. If anyone noticed her, hopefully they'd mistake her for a dog.

Avoiding the gang accosting her on her first night in Warwick would have been easier in her four-legged form. An animal garnered more respect than a female.

Her lycan form easily traveled the distance between Elysian Estates and Ash Street. She possessed a better sense of everything now, even knew what scent she needed to track once she squeezed her way into the gated community. The Goddess may have tested her, but Phoebe prevailed.

The need for revenge couldn't be meditated out of her DNA. Corbie never understood rage wasn't something Phoebe chose.

Phoebe's nose picked up a bouquet of odors, some pleasant, some not so nice. None belonged to those she sought. They weren't the types to jog, even on Elysian Estates' private roads. Any exercise would be in a personal gym in their home. The challenge would be finding out which mansion belonged to the Peters family. Phoebe didn't know their vehicles' scents. She would have to sniff her way around until she located their residence.

If Dustin happened to be there, finding the estate would be as easy as shifting on the full moon.

Running into the whole gang at the restaurant had been a gift.

As Phoebe discerned her first night in town, there were no motion detector lights on the gated community's perimeter. The residents assumed their fence and shrubbery would keep them secure.

They didn't factor a werewolf burrowing into the enclosure. The security cameras would see only a canine with a stick in its mouth.

Once inside, she discovered a lack of cover, except by the hedge. The clustered trees weren't substantial enough to hide anything. The shadows they cast were their best function, but only two nights after the new moon, the lack of ambient light prevented them from being genuinely useful.

The low landscaping, however, could have been custom-made for a slinking wolf.

The individual properties boasted decorative shrubbery and motion detector lights. The light sensors were fixed about two feet above the ground to prevent random squirrels or raccoons from running up the electric bill or causing undo alarm. A surprising lack of smaller creatures cavorted through the lawns. Or anywhere. She sniffed a rabbit. Skunks were probably forbidden.

Odors were always sharper on a humid night. A sliver of moon cast no light as it waxed away from newness. Dark and aromatic, the perfect night for hunting—

No. For scouting. Scouting led to making plans, plans led to action. She knew what her outcome needed to be but she would decide the strategy. Since she'd arrived in Warwick, her options increased every day.

Learning Elysian Estates' convoluted layout, where narrow roads twisted leisurely amid meticulous landscaping, challenged her. Since no house was in sight of another, no nosy neighbors could spy on her.

She sniffed around for an hour but found no trace of those she sought. She'd investigate one last residence before heading back to Parker. To Helga's house, she amended.

She followed a hedge lining a sinuous curve of a driveway she wouldn't want to plow come winter.

The reek hit her like an electric fence or an invisible wall. The stench should have made her vomit; only her rigid self-control prevented her from leaving behind such easy DNA. Her sense of direction faltered. She slunk away from the evil aura as quickly as she could.

What in the Goddess's name smelled so horrible?

Once away from the stench, she didn't dawdle in making her way back to the spot through which she'd entered the community.

Where she ran smack into Parker. She didn't scent him before seeing him because her nose still cowered from the putrid odor. Her quarterstaff fell from her mouth.

"Nice night for a stroll." He held out her clothes. "Although you might want to shower before you get dressed. You stink like vampire."

Phoebe's head jerked. Vampires? Vampires smell that bad?

She should have known. Her DNA should have warned her.

Instead of shifting, Phoebe picked up her quarterstaff in her mouth and started trotting toward Ash Street.

Parker fell in beside her. "You couldn't tell me where you were going?"

She couldn't decide if he sounded more hurt or angry.

He shouldn't be either.

"Didn't it occur to you I'd be worried?"

His state of mind didn't matter. Couldn't matter. Her goal remained her only priority.

"I guess not," he continued. "I don't know what you think you were doing inside Elysian Estates tonight, but the vampires now have your scent."

Vampires couldn't possibly smell her. Nothing penetrated their stench. She needed to warn Parker and the others that vampires thrived, despite their claim.

Her teeth tightened on her quarterstaff. She hadn't come to Minnesota to appease an accidental mate and his pack.

They padded toward Helga's house.

Parker seethed as he strolled beside his stink-covered mate. Steam ought to be spewing from his ears and other orifices. His crazy, certifiably mad mate had no business skulking around Elysian Estates. She knew the Peters family played host to Senator Tuttle. Stalking him proved her insanity.

At least she couldn't argue with him while in four-legged form.

As much as she frustrated him, they were mates. The female the Ancient Ones chose for him. Why did they give him another hard-headed female? If not for her promise to Helga, he would whisk Phoebe back to Loup Garou where she couldn't get into trouble. Where he could keep her safe. "I don't think you should go into Helga's house smelling the way you do. Maybe I should hose you off in the back yard first."

Phoebe's lips curled. Her teeth flashed.

"We can do it in your current form. You don't need to be naked human," he assured her.

The low rumble coming from her chest in no way resembled laughter.

"We can't abuse Helga's hospitality by bringing vampire stink into her home. Or didn't your foster mother teach you basic etiquette?" He didn't try to hide his contempt. Phoebe wore him out with her half-answers and annoying deflections.

PHOEBE FOUND BEING HOSED off in the back yard to be more enjoyable than it sounded. Concentrated water pressure hit the points where her joints might be sore in the morning. And yeah, she didn't realize how much bad odor she'd picked up before leaving, until the stench bonded to the water and sloughed off into the grass.

She wasn't polluting Helga's house, only her lawn. Phoebe hoped the tainted water wouldn't kill the grass.

Drying off involved shaking the water from her pelt followed by shifting. The heat from transforming from four to two legs completed the drying process.

Shaking off her residual guilt for eluding her mate should have been as easy as shaking off the water, but she couldn't. She half expected Parker to jump her right there in the back yard, but instead, he handed her the clothes she'd discarded earlier in the evening. He didn't speak.

Corbie couldn't have warned Phoebe about mating nuances because Corbie didn't have the honor or the privilege of a fated soulmate. She'd been mistress of her destiny.

Phoebe didn't bother getting dressed. Parker would have her naked as soon as they were inside.

Except he didn't touch her. Odd.

She crossed the kitchen and opened the refrigerator door. The cool air countered the nighttime mugginess. She plucked a water bottle from the top shelf and unscrewed the top. The door swung closed on its own.

"That's it?" Parker broke the quiet with a cracked voice.

"What's it?" she countered.

"No excuse? No warped logic? You merely take off without alerting me? Didn't it occur to you I might worry?"

"I'm not used to asking anyone's permission to do anything."

She finished off the water. She'd probably have to get up in the middle of the night to pee, giving Parker yet another reason to jump her bones.

He stood across the kitchen from her, leaning against the counter, arms crossed over his chest. Disapproval leaked off him in waves. He didn't want her. His rejection hurt. Scratch that. He didn't want her body; he wanted her words. He wanted her mind. What made him believe mating meant he could possess her very being?

"Don't you wonder why the senator from Tennessee is spending such a long time in Minnesota?" she asked.

"I don't care," he replied. "You exposed yourself to vampires tonight. Doesn't the risk mean anything to you?"

"Well, first off, I've never encountered vampire stink before. I plead ignorance." She decided to throw him a bone. "I should have guessed because you told me vampires plagued the town."

Yeah. Vampires gave her more stuff she needed to think about. Mates and vampires: her need to destroy Tuttle grew more complicated by the day.

"Why did you go skulking around Elysian Estates?" Parker sulked like a toddler.

"Tuttle and his son are the Peters' houseguests. They reside in Elysian Estates." Why did she need to repeat something he knew?

"Then you should have asked for help. Dakota and I could have gone with you."

"Dakota? Why would I need a bus driver to figure out where the Peters house is?"

"Because he and Britt were there a few weeks ago. They were inside the house. Britt met the Senator and his son." He didn't need to grit his teeth. "I helped Ethan extract them."

"I didn't know."

"I know. You're so intent on doing what you want, you forget you're a pack animal."

She froze. Goosebumps rose on her arms and neck. "I haven't been conditioned to be part of a pack." Even her words were stiff, as if they'd turned to ice.

"It's not conditioning. It's genetic. It's who you are. You are lycan. You can't keep a secret from your pack."

"I have no pack." How could he have forgotten her past?

"You're Loup Garou now, whether you want to be or not."

Instinct and duty played tug-o-war inside her. The innate truth in Parker's accusation niggled at her conscience.

Too much to think about. Too much on top of a too- long day. She needed a quick orgasm to relax her and sleep. She tilted her head to the left, exposing her mating spot. She sucked on her index finger, then used the wet digit to stroke the place on her neck where Parker marked her. Heat shot straight to her female bits. She thrust her breasts slightly forward.

Parker audibly swallowed. Shadows hid his lower body, and not even her keen lycan vision could make out details. Based on the increase in his heart rate and breathing, being angry didn't affect his arousal.

She said nothing, but sauntered toward the guest room, hips swaying.

Parker would follow. He had no choice.

Chapter 12

"I NEED TO STRETCH my legs." Phoebe stood, quarterstaff in hand. The waiting room, with its tasteful beiges and other shades of light brown, depressed her. She'd dozed on and off for an hour or so. No matter what time they arrived at the hospital for Helga-duty, she was in physical therapy. So they waited.

Now Phoebe needed to move. Needed to pay attention to the tingling in her mind. She couldn't focus while sitting with Parker, who triggered a craving for sex. Selena only asked to be bitch-slapped, and Olivia Hagtorn spooked the crap out of her.

Ever since the night she slipped off to explore Elysian Estates, Parker hadn't let her out of his sight. He woke when she woke. She would start howling if she didn't create solitude soon.

"I'll come with you." Parker climbed to his feet and stretched. His spine cracked.

"I need to be alone." Maybe she could have been more tactful, but she sincerely required a place where she could gather her thoughts uninterrupted. A haven away from hospital smells. An escape from Selena's unspoken disapproval.

Phoebe sauntered away from the waiting area, swinging her quarterstaff.

The lights were too bright and the tile floor too shiny. The halls reverberated with the clacking footsteps of people scurrying like rats in a maze.

She focused on her third eye. Except, as usual, she couldn't find it. Corbie despaired over Phoebe's lack of second sight. But Phoebe didn't need a sapien tool like a third eye because lycans possessed perfectly good, useful senses. She didn't need magic to find her way out of the hospital. Exit signs helped.

Except she found herself in the emergency area again. She headed toward the outside doors when a familiar voice stopped her.

"My father is injured. He needs to be seen now." Rick Tuttle. She'd know his voice anywhere.

"I'll need his insurance information."

He had health insurance, courtesy of the United States government, unlike thousands of his constituents, including Phoebe.

"Do you know who my father is?"

"Sir, that's what I'm trying to find out."

No Dustin in the cluster of dark-suited men who milled off to one side. Maybe she was about to get a break.

Phoebe hugged the wall. There were no shadows to absorb her. HIPAA laws or not, the emergency center didn't offer much patient privacy.

Junior Tuttle lowered his voice, but Phoebe's lycan ears had no problem overhearing. "My father is Senator Richard Tuttle."

"Do you have ID for him? I also need his insurance information."

One of the senator's entourage took over from Junior. The senator himself was nowhere to be seen.

Maybe a hangnail required hospitalization. Or a pimple needing popping.

Nola Peters, in beige slacks and a black-and-beige print top, placed her perfectly manicured fingers on Junior's arm. She spoke so softly even Phoebe, focusing her hearing, couldn't eavesdrop.

Junior shook off Nola's touch. She retreated, her face a mask of cool indifference. But Phoebe glimpsed, for a second, pain.

After hearing Parker's version of Congressman Peters and Sons, Nola's display surprised Phoebe.

You're getting weak, bitch. Nola Peters is nothing unless she's the means to accomplishing your mission. Don't be sorry for her.

Phoebe resented her lack of numbness. She blamed Parker. He'd fractured the compartment labeled Emotion. Everything leaked from the crack, even empathy for a woman she should find contemptible.

Forget Nola Peters. She was ancillary to Tuttle and his son. Maybe the fates were on her side. Events happened for a reason. Phoebe found her mate living across the street from a crone who needed assistance. Who fell and required hospitalization. For some reason—the fates adopting Phoebe—Helga claimed Phoebe as her niece, her only family, which gave Phoebe carte blanche for being in the hospital. Phoebe not only had the right to be on the premises, she had an obligation. And now the fates dropped the senator neatly into a bed in the same facility.

What could possibly be more convenient?

PARKER FOUND PHOEBE OUTSIDE the main hospital doors, sitting in a lotus position on a stone wall containing red flowers and other decorative plants. Her eyes were closed. Both middle fingers formed circles with her thumbs, the heels of her hands resting on her thighs.

The sun glinted off her hair, creating rainbows in shades of blues and greens. She looked more like a painting than a flesh and blood female.

Except for Jeeves resting across her lap.

Her fingers straightened. She brought her palms together and drew them to her chest.

Ah. She'd been meditating, not napping. Still, her redirected awareness left her vulnerable.

He sat next to her on the retaining wall. "You shouldn't zone out, not in public. It isn't safe."

"And sunlight can cause skin cancer. Life isn't safe."

An image of a young Phoebe, cowering in the back of a dark cave while sapien males roamed the forest shooting at any moving target, sickened him. Yeah, Phoebe had a point. She would have a lot in common with the Varulv rebuilding Ulvskog. Maybe he should take her there and introduce her around.

He needed to do something with her.

"There's been a kink in my plans," she said. "It still amazes me when seemingly disparate situations come together in new, unforeseen ways."

He waited for her to explain.

She did not. "What's the word on Helga? Is she out of PT yet?"

"No. She has a lot to learn before they'll release her. She's going to need round-the-clock care."

"It's a good thing you haven't gone back to Loup Garou yet. Your medical training will come in handy. Why were you looking for me when I told you I wanted to be alone?"

Her con couldn't appease him or induce guilt. He'd lost one hard-headed female when he was a kid. He refused to lose another. "You're my mate, and some things you say concern me."

"You're sweet." Phoebe patted his thigh.

"You don't need to insult me." Lobos, even omega lobos, weren't supposed to be sweet.

"I didn't mean it as an insult. In the world where I grew up, too much togetherness led to trouble. I've told you before. Pack ways are foreign to me."

"Yours are to me, too, and I grew up in a traditional pack." He hated defending his instincts.

"I'm not your standard she-wolf."

No kidding.

"I won't apologize for being who and what I am. The reasons are valid."

"I'm not questioning your rightness or wrongness."

Phoebe unfurled her legs. Jeeves landed on the wall next to her. Her feet dangled above the sidewalk. "There's been a kink in my agenda. I need to rethink my strategy."

"Maybe I can help. You know, the mated thing and all." If he helped, he'd be able to keep an eye on her. He'd have her back and could intervene if she needed him, whether or not she wanted his assistance.

Her chin lowered. Her eyes widened, their darkness stained red by the sun. "Thank you. I appreciate your offer."

But she didn't agree to accept his assistance. He'd have to make sure she did.

"I suppose we should check on Aunt Helga's progress." She stretched her legs as if preparing to hop from her perch.

"Selena said she'd text me."

"Maybe it's good for Selena's ego I left."

"Probably." Selena could be prickly.

"I'm going to tell you something." Phoebe's abrupt change of topic surprised him. Usually she merely deflected. "You may hear it on the news soon enough."

As if anyone in Ethan's house listened to the news.

They'd depended on Helga for updates on current events. "You can't tell anyone I know this. I'm trusting you, as my mate."

More drama. All her half-informative pronouncements were nothing but drama. A need for attention.

Her voice dropped to less than a whisper. "Senator Tuttle is being treated in the Emergency Room as we speak."

He twisted to face her. "What?" He couldn't possibly have heard her correctly.

"Senator Tuttle is in the ER. Junior Tuttle is making a scene. Imagine a United States senator getting upset because he was asked for his insurance card."

Only the most rigid self-control kept Parker from choking.

"If the senator is admitted, I think visiting my aunt is going to be a whole lot more productive."

"What are you going to do? Sneak into his room after lights out and smother him?"

"Maybe. Thanks for the idea."

Maybe Phoebe didn't appreciate sarcasm. "Can you ever have a discussion without being enigmatic?"

She stared at him like a panther stalking its prey.

The pose irked him further. "Okay, I get it. You spent the past fifteen years passing for sapien. In the lycan world, being vague and pretending to be wise is annoying."

He hopped off the wall. "I'll let you get back to your meditation. I'll be with Helga."

How dare Parker mock me?

Phoebe resisted the urge to follow him and give him a good knock on the head with her quarterstaff.

So much for trustworthy mate material. She'd always known she'd be alone when exacting her revenge on Tuttle, except for ten seconds of hoping her mate might be an ally. After hearing her life story, she'd wished Parker would be as anxious as she to see the senator pay for his crimes. The reality check shouldn't hurt, but it did.

On the positive side, all kinds of accidents could happen in a hospital.

The photocopy of her Tennessee non-driver ID, stuck to her chest, gave her access to visit her alleged aunt. If she happened to learn her senator was in the same facility, why shouldn't she, one of his constituents, stop by his room? He worked for her, a fact for which he might need a reminder.

She gripped her quarterstaff. She would be delighted to prod his memory. Demonstrate the true meaning behind the phrase knock some sense into him.

Maybe she could find some way to poison him. Something slow acting and painful, maybe starting out with physical paralysis so she could explain in detail how he would suffer. Except paralysis wouldn't let him experience pain, and he needed to hurt.

She eyed a discarded cigarette butt half-buried in the dirt around the flowers. Another dozen butts and she could concoct a beautifully lethal topical nicotine poison.

Today's lesson: Always keep your mind open to new possibilities. Possibilities. Always possibilities.

PARKER FOUND SELENA AND Old Olivia where he'd left them: waiting for Helga's physical therapy to end.

"Where's Phoebe?" Selena's question accused him of not being able to control his mate. As if Selena allowed Ethan any say over her actions.

"She's busy." Parker dropped into a chair across from the muted television and stared at the screen.

Footage of Senator Tuttle interrupted the game show. Parker aimed the remote. Audio blared until he lowered the volume.

"Senator Richard Tuttle, who is in Warwick to jumpstart the search for late Congressman Bryant Peters' missing sons, is being treated at a local hospital for an undisclosed injury."

Ancient Ones. How did Phoebe know?

"I wonder what happened to Tuttle?" Selena peered at the television.

"He must be here," Old Olivia added. "General is the only hospital in the area."

Should he betray his previous knowledge and Phoebe along with it, or did he tut-tut and say nothing else?

Tut-tut.

"Phoebe's going to be interested." Old Olivia studied Parker, not the television.

"Maybe."

"Maybe?" Selena took up Old Olivia's position. "Didn't she follow Tuttle here from Tennessee?"

"No. Phoebe came first."

"How did she know Tuttle would be in Warwick?"

"Because all he's done is talk about the shameful way the investigation to locate his good friend's missing sons has been mishandled. As if Tennesseans give a howl." Phoebe stood in the doorway.

Parker hadn't heard her arrive. Her boots muffled her footfalls.

She crossed the room and dropped into a chair in the corner, as far away from the other females as possible. "He's in Minnesota to reactivate the Peters investigation. After all, Junior is engaged to Nola Peters, who is greatly distressed by her brothers' unknown whereabouts."

"Someone has to be," Selena said. "Tuttle is not to be trusted."

"I don't trust any politician." Selena's expression mirrored Phoebe's.

"Your cop friends—"

"Not mine," Selena interrupted. "Britt's. She went to high school with them."

"The joys of small-town living," Phoebe murmured.

"You have an odd definition of joy."

"I take my pleasures where I can get them. Like Tuttle being hospitalized." Phoebe wouldn't be sidetracked. "Your cop friends can't be too happy to have their competence questioned. Maybe we can help them."

Oh, no. Parker wanted as far away from the investigation into the Peters brothers' vanishing act as possible.

Selena eyed Phoebe as if trying to read her mind.

"This isn't the time or place for this discussion," Parker reminded the females.

"Tonight then," Selena said. "My place. Dinner."

Chapter 13

"I don't want to have dinner with Selena, Ethan, and their Scooby gang." Phoebe perched on the edge of the bed in Helga's guest room. She hated the constant company of people she didn't know and always having to be on guard not to betray too much.

Fresh from his shower, Parker dripped water across the room. He couldn't have used a towel? Not that she didn't admire the view...

"You don't have a choice. We don't have a choice." Parker smoothed back his wet hair. It flopped forward again as he rifled through the clothes in his duffel. "It was your idea."

The view improved. He was one well-put-together lobo.

"My idea?" How did he come up with his absurdities?

Parker pulled the badly wrinkled trillium-red colored shirt, the one she'd borrowed her first day in Warwick, from the tangle. For someone who supposedly spent time on the road, Parker lacked packing skills.

Someone was going to have to do laundry soon. *Probably me because I'm the female.* She hoped Helga hid machines in her basement. Laundromats weren't on Phoebe's list of favorite places.

Naked Parker gave her other ideas. Better ideas. Ideas not involving clothes at all.

"We're not going to disrespect the local pack alpha." Parker pulled on his boxers, concealing the scenery. "Besides, you suggested we help the local cops locate the Peters brothers."

Phrased that way, the missing men sounded like a boy band.

"Fine. You go, then." She had things she could do, such as visit Senator Tuttle in the hospital or track down Dustin and give him a poke or two with her quarterstaff.

Or laundry.

If Parker wanted her to attend Selena's gathering, he'd have to hoist her over his shoulder and carry her across the street.

Twenty minutes later, that's what he did. She should have protested harder, whacked him with her quarterstaff or grabbed his privates, but if he wanted to make an entrance to prove his top wolf status in their mating, fine. Goddess, he smelled so good...

Phoebe hadn't met several people who were present. Selena introduced her best friend, Britt, who happened to be mated to Dakota.

When Parker deposited her in the living room, her anger at being coerced into this gathering vanished.

Two males stood by the far window. Two unfamiliar males, but males she knew nonetheless. The ache in her heart expanded. Her own father and grandfather, had they survived, would resemble these males. Tears dampened her eyes, clung to her lashes.

Here was her alpha. Not Selena with the chip on her shoulder, but the tall man with his years, joys, and sorrows etched on his face. Iron-gray streaked his black hair. His dark eyes fixed on her and widened.

She knew his name without being told: Hache-Hi, hero of her childhood legends. She scrambled off the sofa where Parker dumped her and scurried across the room to greet him.

Do I bow? Curtsy?

In the end, she merely held out her hand. "I am a foundling called Phoebe McKinn. I remember my granny's stories about you, Hache-Hi."

The sharp dark eyes fixed on her. His gaze plunged into her soul and read her darkest secrets. "Hatch." His voice was as rough as the palm grasping her hand. "I haven't been Hache-Hi in several generations."

She bowed her head to acknowledge his wishes.

"Look me in the eye, girl," Hache-Hi—Hatch— commanded. "Where are you from?"

Meeting him eye to eye sent a thrill through her. "Tennessee. Politicians massacred my pack about fifteen years ago."

"Do you remember anything?"

"Not much. I was young."

"You and I have much in common. You should be proud you survived."

The other male turned out to be Ethan's father, another full-blooded Limmikin named Rand.

Phoebe wasn't alone in the world. Still an endangered species, but not alone.

"You remind me of my grandfather," she told Hatch. "To look at. So please excuse any rudeness in my stares. And Rand, you are so like my father..." Her voice broke. She leaned on her quarterstaff because the muscles in her legs threatened to abandon her.

"You are like my mate when she was younger," Hatch told her. "So my stares are as rude as yours."

Parker joined them, slipping an arm around her waist. She leaned into his strength, grateful he'd seen her weakness. Grateful he'd hauled her across the street. She'd thank him later.

"Great. We've gotten the sentiment out of the way. Now can we get down to business?" Selena leaned against one side of the doorjamb.

Ethan echoed her position on the other side, two gargoyles standing guard. "Supper won't be ready for a bit, so we have time to talk."

Olivia hobbled to the sofa. Hatch sat next to her, as befitted their elder status. Phoebe folded herself into the lotus position at Hatch's feet. Parker joined her.

Selena focused on Phoebe. "I need to know what you think you're doing."

PHOEBE LOWERED HER CHIN and stared at Selena.

"We need all the facts before we can move forward. Maybe you think being secretive is cute or attractive, but frankly it's mostly annoying," Selena continued.

Not even an eyelash fluttered. Phoebe might as well have been a statue. Parker heard her heart beating, heard the whoosh of her respiration, but Selena's insult didn't affect her at all.

Maybe presence was missing in their intimate moments. She always seemed to want him, but when she had him, he sensed an absence. Oh, she climaxed easily enough, fulfilling his obligation to ensure her happiness, but she didn't respond to him. Any male who happened to be her mate could bring her to orgasm. Parker wanted more from her.

Starting now, against Selena. "Phoebe isn't familiar with pack ways."

He might be mistaken, but Phoebe's dark gaze seemed to soften, like dirt in the rain.

Selena's nose rose. "Ignorance doesn't mean—"

"Don't judge something you don't understand." He didn't care if he was rude or not.

"I suppose you do." Selena's sarcasm didn't go unnoted.

"No, I don't. But I'm trying to keep an open mind." Phoebe's hand crept to his thigh. His inner thigh. He swallowed hard. "What I'm saying is what you or I would think is enigmatic or mysterious may be a coping mechanism. Imagine shifting the first time surrounded by sapiens instead of your pack."

The right corner of Phoebe's mouth twitched.

"The woman who raised her needed to distill discipline in her so she could live among sapiens."

"You make me sound like a cyborg." Phoebe's low voice pierced the silence in the room, despite the motorcycle racing up Hawthorn Street. She squeezed Parker's thigh. All the saliva in his mouth dried.

He wanted nothing more than to toss Phoebe over his shoulder again and storm across the street to Helga's house. Hearing someone else bad-mouthing his female infuriated him, even though Phoebe annoyed the scat out of him. Selena's alpha status didn't matter.

Hatch shook his head at Selena. He'd been alpha of the Limmikin as long as Selena led the Varulv. "Parker makes good points. Maybe they should leave town. We could use their help in Ulvskog."

No. Leaving meant going home. Loup Garou.

"What an excellent idea." Selena sounded relieved.

"I'm off Ulvskog duty." Parker wanted to make his status crystal clear. "I have my alpha's permission to return to Colorado in order to attend classes for my paramedic certification."

"Yet you are here." Selena's nasty smile added to his irritation.

"My mate made a promise to the crone across the street. I honor my mate so her promise is also my promise." Parker dug in his heels. He refused to return to the dank forest, looking over his shoulder for Bigfoot.

"I can't leave." Phoebe's lips curved into a serene expression. Her hand left Parker's thigh to rest on the floor next to Jeeves. "My aunt needs me, and I need Parker's expertise when it comes to her recuperation."

"She's not your aunt." Selena's tone matched her faux smile.

"But I'm the one to whom she'll be released." A faint trace of smugness crept into Phoebe's voice. "Britt, did I hear you make homeopathic skin care products? I would like to consult with you about the cremes and lotions Aunt Helga will require. She's dehydrated, if I'm reading her skin correctly."

Britt seemed surprised to be included in the conversation. She sat on the sofa, squashed between Old Olivia and the arm, where Dakota perched. "Water. Make sure she's drinking enough. And yeah, I have some hydrating cream that will work wonders on her."

The corners of Phoebe's mouth lifted, as if manipulated by a puppeteer. "Thank you. I do worry about my aunt."

"Ethan and I can care for Helga," Selena snapped. "We've been keeping an eye on her since we moved here."

"And yet Helga claimed me as her niece."

Fury—maybe jealousy—glittered in Selena's eyes.

Yeah, she'd grown up without a mother, but Old Olivia cared for her. Phoebe had a crone, like Helga.

Parker understood Phoebe's need. He tried to explain. "Helga is like Phoebe's foster mother—a crone. Can't you respect her feelings?"

"Parker said the wisest thing I've heard here tonight." Old Olivia shifted in her seat. "Explain your foster mother to us."

Phoebe braced herself before looking Hatch in the eye and relating the Tennessee version of a Limmikin massacre.

"Tuttle has to die." Selena didn't hesitate to react.

"He's not the only one." Phoebe launched into an abbreviated account of her foster brother's treachery.

"What can we do to help?" Hatch wanted to know.

"We need a specific plan," Selena advised. "You're not alone anymore. You have a pack, and this pack has experience in dealing with political betrayal."

PHOEBE WENT AS STILL as she could. *My hearing must be on the fritz.* Or else her longing to belong overruled her common sense.

She'd shared her story, as unemotionally as she could.

Each telling seemed to lessen the trauma.

She'd picked up on how Britt, Dakota's mate, had been Selena's college roommate; on how Olivia had been mated to Hatch's brother. Their lives were interwoven in ways Phoebe would never experience.

She'd ended up entwined with Dustin Holloway and Senator Richard Tuttle. She couldn't escape her past.

Now this group of friends and family—this pack—with no connection to her wanted to help her extract payment from Tuttle and Dustin.

"You're not in this alone anymore," Hatch assured her.

"I did some four-legged reconnaissance at Elysian Estates a few nights ago. I ran into something weird."

"Vampires," Parker interrupted. "She stunk so bad, I needed to hose her off before she could come inside."

"Vampires?" Everyone asked at once.

Right. This group had tightened their bonds while staking vampires.

"Where?" Selena asked.

"I don't know. The last house I nosed around while searching for Tuttle or Dustin's scent. I never found them."

"Vampires," Dakota muttered as he started pacing the perimeter of the room.

Ethan pursed his lips and narrowed his eyes. "Is it possible Elysian Estates is their sanctuary? The place they congregate to sleep in the day and get their orders?"

"Inside Elysian Estates?" Britt's face folded into a scowl. "I don't see how. I was there not too long ago."

"We established you can't smell vampires," Ethan retorted. "The night we were there, I smelled only the one you staked. Dakota, you were there for a while. What did you smell?"

"Nothing until Britt's kill. Oh, and when I found Judd's body outside the hedge, there were definite notes of Eau de Undead."

"What I smelled slammed me like a wall of stench," Phoebe explained.

Parker backed her up. "She reeked something awful. As bad as the night we fought them."

"New recruits? We put a serious dent in their forces." Selena stared at a spot on the wall as if reading something there. "It bears looking into. Dakota, you know where the Peters estate is. You can check the grounds out, see if the smell is coming from there or somewhere else."

Britt protested, but Dakota nodded.

"I'll go with him," Ethan offered.

"Tuttle is mine. He's in the same hospital as Helga. I heard him being admitted this morning." Phoebe wanted no confusion about Tuttle's fate. She didn't give a damn about vampires. They were alpha Selena's problem.

"Yeah?" Selena's interest renewed. "Any idea why?"

"I didn't get a chance to investigate."

"Okay, you and Parker focus on finding out why the Senator is in the hospital. Should be easy enough since you're visiting your sick aunt." Selena delegated effortlessly.

"I want Dustin duty." Parker stretched his legs and draped an arm across Phoebe's shoulder.

She resisted the urge to huddle into its protection, maybe touch him more intimately. Later. She could show her appreciation later.

"He betrayed the trust of both his grandmother and my mate." Parker continued to fume. "He doesn't deserve to live."

"What's in it for him?" Britt's eyes left her pacing mate and fixed on Phoebe.

"He wants to hurt me because I wouldn't put out. Sapien guy stuff."

Britt snickered. "I know a lot of sapien guys, and blue balls may play into his reasons, but there has to be more."

"Are you saying my mate isn't worthy of inspiring an insatiable need for revenge?" Parker growled.

"I would never be stupid enough to insult her," Britt replied. "I'm saying sapien males don't get the depth of emotion tied up in mating."

"Sapien males obsess," Phoebe reminded Britt.

Britt hooted. "And lycan males don't? What world have you been living in?"

"The sapien world." Phoebe kept her tone cool.

"Sapien males stalk. Not all, but there are many who won't take no for an answer. You were needier, requiring more of his grandmother's attention," Britt offered. "He likely misread her actions as her loving you best and thought being your boyfriend, your lover could reclaim his grandmother's attention for himself."

"Dustin had plenty of Corbie's attention. He always complained about her nosing around in his business."

Phoebe never discussed Dustin with anyone. She didn't understand the give and take or how Selena could be such a bully, but still offer her help, and delegate others to help. Other than the gangs of mean girls in high school, she didn't know how to deal with a pack.

Something chimed.

"Supper's ready," Selena announced.

By the time they'd finished eating and talking over various scenarios for dealing with Dustin's betrayal and Senator Tuttle's perfidy, Parker was too tired to deal with a mate.

But Phoebe stared at him, her dark eyes luminous, lips curved in a come-hither smile. She stuck her forefinger in her mouth, then slowly withdrew it.

Sweat broke out on Parker's forehead. In his armpits and the channel of his spine.

With her finger fully exposed, glistening with her saliva, she brought her hand to her neck. To her mating spot. Using only her finger, she caressed the point where he'd marked her.

His penis stirred.

She sauntered from the room, hips swaying in silent invitation.

The other males stared at him.

"She's insatiable. What can I tell you?" He thought his explanation made sense.

"You must not be making her happy enough." Ethan snickered.

"She's in heat." Old Olivia sounded annoyed.

Parker jerked. "What?"

"She's in heat. In season. Her human cycle has synced with the moon cycle. Her body craves pregnancy. I'm surprised you don't smell it on her."

Parker clambered to his feet. In heat. The Ancient Ones wanted them to breed. No time to waste. A female's estrus didn't last long. He hurried after her.

Chapter 14

Quiet now, after non-quiet hours doing his damnedest to impregnate his mate.

Parker snuggled closer to Phoebe, who sprawled in the middle of the bed. Sex scented the heavy, sweltering air. The sheets were as limp as his penis.

He buried his nose against Phoebe's neck and sniffed. Maybe. Or maybe wishful thinking on his part. He'd scented pregnancy only once: when Toke Lobo knocked up his mate on the night he'd claimed her. His sapien mate. Before telling her about being a werewolf. Ugly scene.

Parker licked Phoebe's mating spot. She didn't stir. He worked his mouth down to one tender, pink nipple. Only the nipple responded. He drew the tightening bud into his mouth and gently suckled. In a few short months, he'd be sharing her breasts with his child. Did Phoebe taste different this morning than she had last night?

He wanted her pregnant for so many reasons. Every lycan male wanted babies. Mate and offspring were the key to a happy life.

Mated and expecting. Parker needed to let his parents know. He should have called them after he claimed Phoebe, but there never seemed to be enough time. They would be thrilled, especially since so many lobos of his generation mated outside the genus. Like Tokarz, the pack alpha, and the members of Toke Lobo and the Pack. Parker and Ethan were the only ones blessed with mates who didn't require explanations. His offspring wouldn't be limited to shifting on the full moon.

Phoebe would have to abandon her vendetta against Senator Tuttle. She needed to let the males handle her revenge. She, being an ideal lycan female, would do everything possible to safeguard the babe growing within her. Pregnant meant he could whisk Phoebe off to Loup Garou the moment he could locate someone—preferably Selena and Old Olivia—to take over Helga's home care.

Parker abandoned Phoebe's breast in order to nip his way to her belly. Her ribs were visible. Her thinness concerned him. She needed to eat better while gestating. In a year, her soft, unmarred skin would sport the stripes of carrying a child. He sniffed, hoping to catch a whiff of growing infant. He lapped at her navel.

"What are you doing?" Her hoarse voice hinted at having screamed in passion all night. A lie. She'd participated, but silently.

"I didn't mean to wake you." His lip vibrated against the concave area between her ribs and hip bones.

"How am I supposed to sleep with you licking me?" She sounded cranky.

"Relax and enjoy," Parker suggested. "We don't need to be at the hospital for a while yet."

"Aren't you ever nocturnal?"

"I was up all night," he reminded her. "You were there."

"All the more reason to sleep while we can," she grumbled. "What's gotten into you?"

Wasn't fatigue a symptom of pregnancy? Building a baby required incredible amounts of energy. Pregnancy exhausted females because the fetus drained the mother-host of what it needed to survive. To thrive. Like a parasite, but better.

Going forward, his Phoebe needed extra special care.

SEVERAL HOURS LATER, PARKER woke with a sense his life was turning to scat. The first hint? Finding himself alone in bed. At least Phoebe didn't vanish on him again. He found her sitting on the grass in the backyard. Her eyes were closed, her pale face lifted toward the sun.

He pulled on his sweatpants and joined her.

In the old days, when Toke Lobo and the Pack were touring, Parker would be getting ready to hit the sack at this hour. Band life meshed well with lycan sleep cycles. He missed those days. Right now, he wanted nothing more than to pull his mate back to the bedroom and grab a few more hours' sleep.

He dropped to the ground next to Phoebe. Closing his eyes, he let the morning sun wash over his face. He didn't question meditation's health benefits. His blood pressure needed to come down, because everything about Phoebe spiked his stress off the charts. Plus, he had an ulterior motive. Deep breathing gave him an excuse to sniff Phoebe. He couldn't get comfortable. Too many lumps in Helga's lawn. Someone down the block smoked a cigarette. A skunk anointed the neighborhood at some point in the night, and the lingering perfume gave him a headache.

He was slipping into a zone when something knocked his shoulder. He cracked open his eyes to discover Ethan standing next to him. He should have heard Ethan approach even if residual skunk juice camouflaged his aroma.

"You didn't answer your summons." Ethan made a face.

Summons could mean only one thing: Restin. Anxiety balled in Parker's stomach.

"My phone is in the house."

Phoebe stirred. "Thanks for disturbing my concentration. Can't you two go elsewhere to have your discussion?"

"Don't blame me." Ethan backed away, both hands in the air, shoulder high, palms facing Phoebe. "Tokarz called me. I'm only the messenger."

Tokarz? Better than Restin and his rebuilding Ulvskog project, but when one's alpha sought out a lobo, things could go either way.

Parker sat on the back stoop to make the call while Phoebe went inside to shower.

Tokarz answered on the first ring. "I expected you back a few days ago."

"Yeah, well, something came up. I've mated."

"I heard. From someone else. Were you planning to tell anyone?"

Ethan has a big mouth. "I'm calling my folks later. We've been busy."

"Who's the female?"

Parker explained Phoebe's origins.

"I didn't know any Limmikin besides the Calhouns survived," Tokarz admitted. "Luke couldn't find any records."

Right. Ethan called the pack's FBI guru.

"Phoebe had it rough. Ugly." Parker scrubbed his face with his free hand. "I'll tell you about it when I get home."

"Limmikin are forest dwellers. Or so I've heard. How's she adapting to town life?"

Dread settled in Parker's stomach. "She's doing fine. She grew up in a town. Ethan's neighbor lady—the older female who helped us with the vampire infestation—broke her leg and took a shine to Phoebe.

She's the reason we haven't come home. Phoebe promised to take care of her."

"Why is Phoebe in Warwick?"

Parker leaned forward and rested his elbows on his knees. He closed his eyes, bracing himself for Tokarz's verbal blow. "I'd prefer not to say on a cell phone."

"Fair enough."

Tokarz's silence lasted so long Parker thought he might have lost the connection.

Still, he listened in case Tokarz intended to impart some wisdom Parker would have no choice but to follow. They had the werewolves-can't-be-doctors-because-the-moon-won't-allow-one-to-do-an-internship-be-satisfied-with-a- lesser-role conversation years ago.

"I hear your mate is in heat." Tokarz startled Parker when he spoke.

"I'm working on it," Parker admitted.

Tokarz chuckled. "Work? Sex is supposed to be pleasant, not work."

"Maybe when it's recreational but getting a mate pregnant can be work."

"Delilah got pregnant as soon as I looked at her," Tokarz boasted.

Parker's memory of Delilah's initiation into the pack didn't match Tokarz's, but a smart lobo didn't contradict his alpha about the past. The present concerned him more.

"I'm giving it everything I've got."

Thank the Ancient Ones for the mating instinct. Without the inherent sex drive, would he be interested enough in Phoebe to fuck her?

A mental cringe accompanied his last thought. *I'm not making love to her, so what else would I call the sex*? If only he were home in Loup Garou. He could bury his disappointment with mating in his studies.

"Maybe she'd be more receptive in a setting more resembling her native habitat. Mountains. Woods."

Scat.

"And you are in Minnesota to help rebuild Ulvskog."

"I thought I came to medically assist the survivors." He was not going back to Restin and Ulvskog.

"Housing them is helping them."

"I'm a healer, not a carpenter."

"And Restin is a fiddle player."

"Restin would be anything, as long as he can be in charge." Parker bit down on his temper. He probably shouldn't have bad-mouthed Tokarz's cousin, but some things needed to be said.

"Ethan and his mate can deal with their neighbor."

"Ethan and Selena ought to be the ones rebuilding their own damn town. They're the ones who want it so badly. Besides, neither one has medical training." Parker's flat tone belied the rage simmering in him. "Helga needs more care than Selena's herbal healing skills can handle. And don't suggest a sapien home aid. Helga is a crone who is more comfortable around lycans than sapiens. She's even claimed kinship with Phoebe."

Parker imagined he could hear the wheels turning in the top lobo's brain. He softened his tone. "The Varulv isn't my pack. Ulvskog isn't my town. I want to come home to Loup Garou. With Phoebe. I want to resume the life this whole mess interrupted. Minnesota is Ethan's mission. I'm here to help with the injured. There were none, only the dead. I'm not ungrateful I stayed for a while, because I found my mate. And now an old woman is injured and needs help, help my mate promised to her. You would order my mate and me to break our promises?"

"The way I understand it—correct me if I'm wrong— the crone is going to need assistance, not medical care."

Parker vowed revenge on Ethan—or more likely Selena—for Tokarz's misconceptions. If they forced him to return to the north woods, he would permanently shift and howl as many hours as his throat could accommodate him.

"The sooner the village is ready for inhabitants, the sooner you can come home."

"There's only me and Restin left," Parker pointed out. Ethan planned to remain with Selena and the Varulv; Dakota and his mate needed to stay because they were persons of interest in an ongoing murder investigation; Hatch wanted to stay a bit longer in the land of his ancestors. Rand wouldn't leave his aging father.

"The Calhoun females have requested their mates return to Loup Garou. I don't like having my pack spread out all over the place. I want you all back in Loup Garou."

Once Parker returned to the mountains, he planned to stay for good. "I want nothing more than to be home, and as soon as we can get Helga safely settled, you're right, Ethan and Selena can take over. But my mate promised to see Helga through this. It sounds as if someone filled you in on what's going on with me, but did they mention a crone raised my mate after Tuttle slaughtered her family?"

"Yes. Ethan also mentioned Senator Tuttle from Tennessee."

"Not so different from Congressman Peters of Minnesota."

"I've asked Luke to dig deeper on Tuttle."

"Thank you." Parker should have expected Tokarz wouldn't let something like the attempted annihilation of another pack go unretaliated. "Did Ethan also mention someone named Dustin? He's on Tuttle's security detail."

"Do you have a last name?"

"I'll get one."

PHOEBE STARED AT THE summer-seared scenery as Parker drove to the hospital for their daily sojourn. She needed to deal with Tuttle and Dustin so she could get on with her life with Parker. Or let Parker get on with his, without her. If meting out her revenge didn't kill her, she could be arrested and incarcerated. Forever. Tuttle's life, according to sapien ways, had more value than his victims did.

Senator Richard Tuttle should be fed to the vermin hiding in Tennessee's mountains. She dreamed of making his death happen. Maybe not the Tennessee part, but based on Parker's blathering about Ulvskog, Minnesota's north woods would make an excellent substitute.

"You didn't ask me what Tokarz wanted." Parker sounded peeved.

Okay, maybe she was slightly self-absorbed, but she had a lot on her mind. She couldn't worry about his stuff, too.

"I assumed you'd tell me if your conversation involved my business."

She couldn't think about his issues. Couldn't deal with his stuff. Could barely deal with her own life.

"He wants me back in Ulvskog."

"For how long?" Maybe she could shake him off her tail so she could do what she needed to do without his constant interference. Except if she wanted his penis she needed to be where he took it.

Maybe she didn't want sex badly enough.

"You're willing to forget Tuttle and hang out in the woods?" Disbelief tainted his tone.

"What? No," she admitted. "I only want to know how long I can expect to be alone."

"Not at all."

She'd been afraid he'd deny her.

"Especially now."

"Why now?" Nothing had changed between them.

"You're mated. Get used to my devotion."

Why couldn't he accept the sooner she moved Tuttle off her plate, the sooner she could be the mate of his dreams—or memories?

Parker rested a hand on her knee. His body heat penetrated the thin fabric of her leggings to her skin, then burrowed deeper until it took up residence in her marrow.

She needed to be done with her business before Parker became any more vulnerable. Before he could be considered an accomplice.

He shouldn't suffer for her exploits.

PHOEBE APPROACHED THE BED where Helga dozed. "Granny?" she whispered.

Helga's mottled, crumpled skin, pale and fragile, brought back memories Phoebe didn't want. Remembering events, people from her before did no one any good. Wallowing in memories of her dead family served only to paralyze her when she needed to do something.

Helga's eyelids fluttered. Her fingers twitched against the blanket's rough weave.

"She's supposed to be your aunt," Parker murmured.

"What?"

"Helga told the administrators you're her niece."

"I know."

Parker said nothing aloud, but the expression on his face confused her.

She needed him gone, if only for a short time. She wanted a private word with Helga before Olivia and Selena arrived. Parker clung like Velcro. "I could use something to drink," she told him.

"There's a water fountain in the hall," he replied.

"You didn't let me finish. I'm hungry, too. I'll bet they have apples in the cafeteria. An apple would be great."

"It's too early in the season for good apples. All they'll have are red delicious, which will be rotting around the core. Besides, you don't like red delicious."

"How would you know what apples I like?"

"You're not ditching me."

"I'm trying to protect you." As much as she wanted to shriek at him, she kept her voice low, barely audible even to a lycan.

"I am protecting you," he countered. "I'm preventing you from doing something foolish on your own when you have a pack poised and ready to assist."

Anger flashed scarlet before fading from her vision.

"You cannot judge me. I don't judge you for..."

"Disobeying my alpha so I can honor my mate?" Sarcasm tainted every word.

"Good morning!" The too-cheery hospital staffer worsened Phoebe's mood. "Your aunt worked hard in physical therapy this morning. I think it wore her out."

"She's fragile," Phoebe said.

"Not so much. She's a tough lady," Parker contradicted.

"The fracture shocked her body," the staffer reminded them. "Sometimes an injury like this marks a turning point." "Good thing she can't hear you trying to make her feeble," Parker muttered.

"I'm not feeble." Helga's voice creaked. "You've got me doped to my hairline."

The staffer shook her head at Phoebe and Parker. Tired," she mouthed.

"Bullshit," Helga mouthed back.

Phoebe hid a snigger. Helga reminded her of Corbie and triggered happy memories of Granny.

"Excuse me a minute." Phoebe grabbed her chance to escape Parker. She slipped from the room before anyone could question her.

She opened her senses and immediately regretted letting in the pain. Agony, despair, and pessimism swirled in an emotional morass. A single thread of arrogance twining with a sense of entitlement led her to Senator Tuttle. His belief the staff should ignore other patients and tend to his needs first dominated everything else. Loathing for the little people. Minnesotans weren't even his constituents.

He should answer to her, one of his home-grown yokels. No one guarded Tuttle's room. Strange, considering Dustin called the local authorities about her.

Phoebe slipped into his room undetected. The senator's florid complexion glowed neon against the white sheets, a stark contrast to poor Helga. A nasty odor lingered in the room.

He was alone.

His shoulders, chest, and arms were bare except for gauze strips glued in place with salve. Wiry gray hair erupted between the white swathes.

He stared at an overhead television, where a news reader droned about the day's happenings, conspicuously slanted toward the network owner's political leanings, which coincidentally happened to match the senator's.

"You're missed in D.C."

Phoebe's soft statement startled Tuttle. The empty cup on the tray table across his lap rattled as he jerked. "What are you doing in here? Where are my guards?"

Phoebe used her quarterstaff to knock the call button from his hand. "I'm a constituent who's concerned about my senator."

"You're stalking me." His hoarse voice confirmed the fear she scented on him. Fear...and something else. Something putrid and yet vaguely familiar.

"Not at all." She swung the call button on its cord like a lasso or a primitive sling shot. "Consider me a...groupie. I was concerned when I learned you'd been hospitalized."

"How did you find me?" He'd recovered enough from his shock to regain his stentorian vocals.

"I overheard your son when you were brought in. I'm visiting my aunt. I'm concerned about you." She lowered her chin and smiled at him. No matter how strongly she wanted to rail at him, she needed to appear cheerful and unafraid. "You know bad things happen to evil politicians in the Minnesota woods. I'm surprised you're tempting fate."

The call button smacked into her palm.

The ruddiness left his cheeks.

"I'm not here to kill you. Yet." She gave him time to absorb the threat. "When I do, you won't be in a hospital where someone can save your life. You're going to die in terror and surprise, the same way you murdered my family." Tuttle made noises, maybe harrumphed a time or two, before he started choking. His pale eyes bulged behind his thick glasses.

"You and your troops made a mistake. You left a survivor. An eyewitness. Dustin Holloway told you all about me, didn't he?" Stomach acid surged into her throat. She dropped the call button on his feet.

"You killed Liam and Connor Peters." Tuttle's hoarse voice betrayed his fear.

"Me?" She didn't have to feign her innocence. "Never laid eyes on them. Wouldn't know them from a hole in the ground. I only arrived in Minnesota a few days ago. On a bus. You can have your minions check it. Besides, dodging your attempts on my life back home kept me too busy to worry about missing politicians in Minnesota."

"You're part of that Scuttle Tuttle deep state group." The senator regained his color. Maybe even collected more. "Let me tell you something, young lady—"

Phoebe rested her quarterstaff a breath above his throat. He swallowed. His Adam's apple brushed the oak. "I'm listening," she assured him.

He must have changed his mind because he didn't speak.

She withdrew the weapon. "I'll see you later. I promise."

"Where have you been?" Parker demanded when Phoebe reappeared. She shouldn't have left him alone with Helga.

"Attending to business." Phoebe scurried into Helga's bathroom as if nothing were amiss.

A minute later she emerged wearing the dark red scrub top he'd lent to her when she first arrived.

"Where did my shirt come from?"

"I bound my breasts with it this morning, thinking it might come in handy. You don't mind, do you?" Her eyes gleamed through her thick lashes as she flirted with him.

"He doesn't mind." Helga didn't sound any happier than she had when they'd first arrived to visit. "You two should be home, taking advantage of Phoebe's condition. I want to be a great-aunt."

"What condition?"

Could Phoebe not realize she was in heat?

Parker considered the possibilities. "We're newly mated," he replied before Helga could interject with the other condition.

"What does being mated have to do with Helga being a great aunt?"

Parker winked at Phoebe, hoping she'd pick up on the hint. "We'll stay until Selena gets here."

"Selena's a nice girl," Helga murmured.

"Selena takes good care of you, bless her heart." Phoebe perched on the edge of Helga's mattress and patted her hand, but she continued to study Parker.

"You look pretty in maroon," Helga rambled.

Parker spent enough time with the old woman to know she didn't say things off the cuff. Maybe they were overmedicating her.

"She looks pretty in black, and in the nude, too," Parker added.

"Excuse me." A uniformed stranger entered the room.

"Who are you?" Helga asked in a querulous voice.

"Hospital security. Someone assaulted a patient. We're trying to locate the assailant." The man's gold-colored badge glinted in the dim fluorescent lighting.

Tuttle. Phoebe had gone after Tuttle. Parker's gut clenched.

Phoebe swung one foot. "What does he look like?"

"A she, not a he," security replied. "Short. Dressed all in black. Carrying a big stick."

Where did she stash Jeeves?

And she wore his dark red scrub top like a dress. She curled her bare legs beneath her bottom to hide their lack of length.

"There's no thug in this room," Helga grumbled. "You shouldn't pick on injured old ladies."

"Sorry for the intrusion." The security officer backed out of the room.

Old Olivia barely sidestepped being trampled. "Or old ladies in general. What's going on?"

"Someone assaulted a patient, and this man is looking for the person who did it," Parker replied.

"That explains why we had such a difficult time getting in." Old Olivia sank into the visitor chair in the corner. "People are so rude."

"Inconsiderate," Phoebe agreed, her eyes wide and guileless.

No one spoke. Parker figured everyone listened to security going door to door, searching for the intruder.

The deep voice finally faded.

Parker stared at Phoebe. "Are you ready to leave?"

"Yes." She hopped off the bed and scurried to the bathroom, where she retrieved Jeeves.

"You're not going to be able to get your stick out of the hospital," he said when she returned.

"Sure I can." She sounded confident.

She irritated him past civility. Her carelessness and arrogance endangered them all. The last female in his life with those traits didn't listen to him and ended up dead. "What are you going to do? Shove it up your ass?"

"You're taller. It would fit better up yours."

"Children, children," Old Olivia chided. Don't you have more important things to do besides bickering with each other?"

"You mean like making a clean getaway? Without the stick every badge in the hospital is looking for?" Parker didn't bother to hide his irritation.

"We'll be fine," Phoebe insisted. "You worry too much."

"You don't worry enough."

"Worrying doesn't change anything. Either a problem can be resolved, or it can't." Phoebe poked Jeeves at Parker. "I prefer to focus on success, not failure."

"Don't you understand there are no do-overs?" He wanted to shout but restrained himself. Shouting might summon the security guard.

Shouting couldn't revive his sister. He'd tried.

"Probably better than you do." Her hands rested on her hips, including the one clasping Jeeves. Her eyes blazed a reddish hue.

"You keep forgetting you're mated now and shouldn't be taking unnecessary risks."

"This conversation doesn't belong here," Old Olivia reminded them. "Go home and have it out."

"Where's Selena?" Helga asked.

"Ethan dropped me off. Selena has things she needs to do before she can visit. I'm serious about those two. Leave."

Phoebe once again feigned a limp and leaned heavily on Jeeves. Parker stuck to her side, hoping his height would overshadow the length of wood.

They made it outside and to his rented vehicle without incident.

Phoebe's lips curved, as if to say, See? I told you.

He chomped back his angry response. Once they got back to Helga's house—

He turned on the radio, which the previous driver set to a news and talk station. Someone who didn't sound old enough to vote interrupted the regularly scheduled national broadcast to hysterically announce an attack on the visiting Senator Richard Tuttle, followed by the usual reminder of Congressman Peters and his missing sons.

Phoebe sat back in her seat and smiled at Parker.

What did he have to do to wipe smugness from her face? Parker waited until he'd closed Helga's front door before turning on Phoebe. "I'm not letting you out of this house again until the full moon."

"You," she said, dropping Jeeves to the floor, "don't get to let or not let me do anything. You can go practice alpha moves on the omegas in your pack. Not on me."

"Wanna bet?" He wadded his fingers into his palms to keep from striking her. The urge itself scared him almost as much as Phoebe did. No one ever struck a female, no matter how much she might require discipline.

Once he banished the impulse, he closed in on her. Invaded her personal space. Backed her through the front room to the kitchen, then against the refrigerator. He figured his size alone would intimidate her. He planted his hands on either side of her head.

He spoke in a low growl. "I get what you're trying to do. I even support it. I plan to help you. But careless arrogance isn't acceptable. You took off on your own and attacked a man in the hospital. The foolish risk you took—"

"I did not attack Tuttle. Even if I did, he deserves to suffer before he dies. I've suffered for fifteen years. Payback's a bitch."

"Maybe you only annoyed him. Like a mosquito."

"I'd like to see him try to swat me." Phoebe lowered her chin.

Why couldn't she get it through her thick skull? "Maybe if he swatted you, other people would be affected."

"Like you?"

"For starters." Most importantly. "Maybe you could learn something from us. Selena, Ethan, Dakota—even Helga. We've been through this. Packs work together. Lone wolf isn't a compliment for a reason."

"You have no right—"

"No right? You let your intended victim see you. You taunted him. Knowing you, you acted as if you were untouchable, when you're as vulnerable as anyone else. The man has a killing machine. He killed your family. Don't you know the most dangerous prey is a cornered animal?"

Phoebe tried to duck beneath his arm, but Parker stopped her. Touched her for a fleeting second, then jerked away. He couldn't touch her right now, not with so much anger in his system.

"Maybe Tokarz is right. Maybe I do need to take you to Ulvskog, at least until after the full moon, so you can get your head on straight. The only thing stopping me is the Peters family's knowledge of Ulvskog. They tried to annihilate it, the same way you claim Tuttle destroyed your family and community. Your arrogance might get us all killed yet."

"Good afternoon, Ms. Rowe. May we come in?"

Phoebe stared at the detective duo who rang Helga's doorbell. Clerkin and Anderson traced her to Helga's house. The sanctuary had been defiled.

Phoebe would have closed the door in their faces, but Parker stopped her. "Sure. Come on in. Have a seat."

The detectives balanced themselves on Helga's old lady furniture. Phoebe wanted to pace, but instead resumed her limp, using her quarterstaff as a cane until Parker nudged her into a wing-back chair.

"We need to know your whereabouts earlier today."

"We were at the hospital visiting Helga," Parker replied. "No secrets there. We signed in. The hospital scanned our ID. Is there a problem?"

Phoebe focused on regulating her breathing. She needed to project calm. She willed her legs not to jitter, her toes not to tap, her fingers to rest ever so lightly on her knees.

"We're investigating an assault on a patient at Warwick General."

"Security came into Aunt Helga's room. Remember?" Phoebe asked Parker before turning to the detectives. "They haven't found the culprit?"

No lies. No misdirection. Questions only.

"We're investigating," the tall cop—Anderson if she recalled correctly—repeated.

"I didn't see anything," Parker said.

"We're learning to care for Aunt Helga when she comes home. She broke her leg, so she's going to need help. She has to stay off it for six weeks," Phoebe babbled.

"You keep calling her Aunt Helga, but we haven't been able to turn up any records of a blood relative." Clerkin, the shorter detective, scrutinized Phoebe.

"It's an honorary title. She's my foster mother's aunt. I came to Warwick to visit her. I thought I explained this the last time you questioned me for no reason. Parker and I found Helga after she'd fallen. I don't know why she claimed I'm her niece. She asked me to look after her house while she's in the hospital. And since my ma...man is an EMT back in Colorado, we offered to stay on to help until she can get on her feet again."

"The victim identified you." The detective's flat tone spoke more than his words.

"Me?" Phoebe's voice squeaked. She gripped the arm of her chair. "I don't know anyone else in the hospital. Oh. Except I heard on the radio Senator Tuttle is in an area hospital. Someone confronted Tuttle? I thought his involvement in the search for some missing politicians made him a local hero."

She stared at Clerkin and Anderson expectantly.

They didn't respond except to return her interest.

She lowered her chin. "I explained all this to you before. I don't know Senator Tuttle. The only connection we have is living in the same city. Oh. And one of his security guards." She widened her eyes as if only now connecting the dots. "Dustin Holloway is on his security team. Dustin is my foster brother. We don't have a cordial relationship. I'll bet he put the senator up to this."

"Why?"

"Dustin and I do not get along." The most accurate understatement she'd ever spoken. She loosened her grip on the arm of the chair and relaxed her fingers. "I have a restraining order filed against him."

The detectives waited. She could outwait them. The time spent hiding in the cave taught her she could outwait anything.

Parker broke first. "What? You never told me he threatened you."

She did not want to tell him about the scene with Dustin. Parker wouldn't be rational, but would go all alpha, which wouldn't be a good thing to do in front of sapien police detectives. "Sure I did."

Parker must have picked up something from her tone, her posture, her hesitation, because his expression darkened. "Then how?"

She didn't have to fake her second sigh. "He tried to... seduce me when we were teenagers. He bears a grudge against me." *And because of him, Corbie cut me out of her life.*

"When you say seduce—"

"You don't need all the details." Phoebe did not want to have this conversation with Parker, much less in front of two strangers who happened to be in law enforcement.

"Yes, I do." Parker's low voice didn't disguise the danger behind the words. "You know I love details."

"He didn't believe me when I said no, so I defended myself." She-wolves were stronger than sapien males. Except on the new moon. But Dustin didn't attack her on the new moon. Silly male.

"I hurt him. And his pride. I'd say he's out to get me."

"We'll discuss this later," Parker muttered.

I don't think so.

"I recognized him at the restaurant the other day, a few hours before you started hunting me." She purposely made her words sound as if the cops were stalking her. "There's no such thing as coincidence."

Neither Clerkin nor Anderson blinked.

"I know the saying goes hell hath no fury like a woman scorned, but a guy wrote the words. My experience has proven the opposite. Dustin is getting back at me for the restraining order. I sicced the cops on him when he tried to force his nasty way with me. Now here you are, on my doorstep."

"His nasty way?" Parker wouldn't stop gnawing the bone, growling when she tried to take it away from him.

"Nothing happened." Time to remind Parker she could growl, too. And snap. "To me. I kicked him in his privates so hard, it took a month for them to descend back in place."

The tall cop couldn't hide his wince.

"Why is it males can get away with harassing females? The more powerful the male, the more they can be jerks and no one retaliates." She gripped the arms of the chair and pushed to her feet. "I'm done here."

At least she remembered to hobble when she left the room.

Chapter 15

THE LONG DRIVE TO Ulvskog didn't lessen Phoebe's fury at Parker's threat to tie her up if he needed to in order to drag her to the local pack's village. She hopped from his vehicle before he could come around and help her out.

Behind her, she heard doors slam as Rand and Hatch, who'd ridden with them, left the SUV.

She drew in a deep breath and immediately calmed.

Sunlight filtered through the green leaves, cool and serene, like her lycan home in Tennessee.

Parker's foolish dislike of Ulvskog could be remedied. She was more comfortable here than she'd been in weeks.

Another sign, she supposed, the Goddess exercised warped humor when making Parker her mate.

The ground beneath Phoebe's feet released the scent of life as she scuffed her way to the new buildings. Parker explained the village's recent history to her on the drive, trying to evoke a response from her. Ulvskog personified the fundamental difference between them. After seeing the village, she understood why Parker hated the place: Ulvskog reflected the place from which she'd come.

If she could stay here forever, she would. Parker might think he could protect her by exiling her to the forest, but the forest gave her strength and freshened her resolve.

Tuttle's Troopers inflicted the same crimes on her Tennessee community as Peters' mercenaries committed here.

"My mate," she heard Parker tell another lobo, one with startlingly blue eyes, "may have put Ulvskog in danger again."

The vividly colored eyes turned in her direction for a moment. "Can't you control your female?"

The lobo asked the question in such a snide tone, Phoebe expected Parker to attack the speaker.

"His mate doesn't need controlling and can speak for herself." Fresh irritation threatened every syllable Phoebe spoke.

"Speaking for herself is the problem," Parker snapped

He needed to get over his snit.

"According to you." Everything she possessed went into sounding serene, when she really wanted to kick Parker's tail into the next county.

"What do you expect from me?" the blue-eyed lobo asked.

"Nothing. We're only here because Tokarz suggested it."

Maybe the lobo couldn't hear the resentment in Parker's voice, but Phoebe could. She tried not to let it bother her. Long-dormant instinct attempted to shred her hard-won self-control. A she-wolf should not be causing this much aggravation to her mate.

"Come here so I can introduce you." Parker's words were more of a command than a request.

She lowered her chin, gripped her quarterstaff, and approached the two males.

"Phoebe McKinn Rowe, this is Restin Zev Garnier, beta of the Loup Garou pack. Restin, my mate, Phoebe."

"McKinn?" Restin asked. "I'm not familiar with the surname."

"It's invented," Phoebe replied. Her chin sank lower until it rested on her chest, and she could barely see Restin no matter how much she raised her eyes. "Short for Limmikin, I'm told."

Parker's lips tightened. She sensed his reaction more than witnessed it.

"Welcome home." Hatch joined them and spoke softly. "You are welcome in these woods."

"You're claiming her?" Restin asked.

"I don't claim anyone. She's Limmikin, and I'm acknowledging it." Hatch sounded annoyed.

Maybe Parker's jealousy over Hatch's immediate acceptance triggered his betrayal when he revealed her secret. "Phoebe came to Minnesota to kill Senator Richard Tuttle."

His disloyalty shocked her speechless. She clutched her quarterstaff so tightly her fingers numbed.

Restin frowned. "Tuttle? The senator from Tennessee? The most powerful man in Washington?"

"Phoebe is from Tennessee, too. And Tuttle is visiting the Peters family. Again." The underlying snide inflection in Parker's tone invited her quarterstaff across his mouth.

Instead, she focused on a coil of blue nylon rope swaying on a peg.

Restin squinted at Parker. "I thought Selena and Ethan took care of the Peters family."

"The daughter, Nola, is engaged to Richard Tuttle, Junior," Parker explained. "We ran into them in a restaurant last week. Dakota's mate met the happy couple a few weeks earlier."

"You forget the old man." Hatch resumed his soft, non-alpha tone. "The father of the one who committed suicide. The one who ordered the Limmikin massacre of my generation. Congressman William Peters."

"He's still alive?" Parker asked.

He had a point. Hatch was an old lobo so the former congressman, if still living, had to be ancient.

"I've looked for his obituary ever since Luke Omega brought a computer and the Internet to Loup Garou." Hatch's expression dared anyone to call him a foolish old lobo.

"None of this is getting the full moon lodge done in time for the Grain Moon. Back to work, everyone." Issuing orders was Restin's element. "Phoebe, you can start painting the walls. Parker, grab a hammer and go with Rand. He'll show you what needs to be done."

"Sturgeon Moon," Hatch muttered. "You're in Minnesota now. Call things by their proper names."

"Phoebe isn't painting. In fact, we're not here to work." Parker kept his tone casual.

"I'm not running a resort and day spa here," Restin snapped. "This is a work site. If you're here, you work."

"Did I mention Tokarz suggested I bring my mate here? Call him if you'd like." Smugness edged Parker's voice.

Restin muttered something, glared at Hatch and Rand, then stalked toward the closest unfinished building.

"I should help," Parker muttered. "The sooner this is off our plates, the sooner we can all go home."

"I'll be fine." Phoebe wanted to be alone as she soaked in half-remembered ambiance. "I'll explore a bit. Thank you for bringing me here."

"This place gives me the creeps. Don't wander too far. Why they insisted on rebuilding in the same spot their families were slaughtered is beyond me."

"To prove they haven't been beaten."

"To show the world the land is ours," Hatch added. "But Parker is right. Don't wander too far. We can't afford to lose you."

"WHY DO YOU THINK your female might have betrayed us?" Restin asked an hour later when he and Parker were alone. They worked on a secret stairwell within a hidden passageway in a small house. Parker admired the beta's ingenuity.

"She confronted and threatened Tuttle."

"She got close enough to a United States senator to threaten him?"

"He's in the same hospital as Selena's neighbor. Phoebe happened to be there when they admitted him."

Restin pounded a nail into a two-by-four with a single blow. "So?"

"He knows she's lycan. According to her, he's behind pack slaughters in Tennessee."

"How would she know about pack slaughters?"

Parker smacked a nail with his hammer. The nail bent. Ancient Ones, he hated carpentry work. The metal screeched as he pulled it from the wood. "Ulvskog was a replay of what happened to her village. She was a kid at the time and witnessed the whole thing."

Another nail vanished into the lumber beneath Restin's hammer. "Does he know there's an eyewitness?"

"Yeah. Long story." Parker planned to teach Dustin-the-foster-brother a few painful lessons. "She called the militia Tuttle's Troopers. Claims the crone who raised her trained her to retaliate. She's stubborn. Headstrong. Knows her own mind. Like Fleur."

Even as the words left his mouth, Parker knew he shouldn't be arming Restin with ammunition to use against him at a later time.

But he needed to talk to someone. Someone who might understand. Restin had been present when Fleur died. Had been a friend and a solid beta-to-be.

"Phoebe keeps going off, half-cocked, like she's an invulnerable ninja warrior goddess." Parker couldn't stop spilling his guts. His heart.

Parker didn't want a ninja, a warrior, or a goddess. He wanted a mate. A plain old regular female lycan. The best creature on earth. Even better than a sister.

"She's going to get hurt. She's already been questioned. Tuttle's people are looking for her. One of them knows she's lycan."

"So you're here to hide your mate."

"Tokarz suggested she might be comfortable in the woods because Limmikin were forest dwellers."

Safer.

"As far as the locals are concerned, Ulvskog is no more. They noticed the fire the day we burned it."

"You don't believe it's safer any more than I do."

"It's a hamlet. A new place. Off the maps. Hidden from politicians and other vampires."

Parker dropped his hammer. "Don't joke about vampires. Phoebe went wandering around the gated community where the Peters family lives and came out stinking like one."

Restin paused mid-strike, his hammer suspended shoulder height. "Yeah?"

Restin made sneering an artform. He brought the hammer down and the nail he aimed for vanished into the wood. The sound echoed around them. "I thought you guys did a vampire purge a couple weeks ago. The reason you all vanished right before the last full moon."

"I don't think we got them all. We never found their source. Selena and Ethan were satisfied because we removed them from their neighborhood." Non-alphas didn't question but did as they were told. How else would he end up in Minnesota with a hard-headed mate?

Restin hooted. "Please. Ethan has mating fever and Selena is female."

Why should Ethan get a pass for mating fever, but not Selena? Parker bristled. Restin's constant negativity caused people to dislike him. Most of the time, Parker didn't like Restin, but Parker knew a side of the beta wolf others seldom, if ever, encountered. Maybe if Restin showed his softer side more often, he wouldn't be universally disliked.

"Selena is still adjusting to her role as alpha," Parker reminded Restin. "And mourning her grandfather. Mourning her home."

"Aren't we rebuilding for her?"

"You're rebuilding for the future of all the packs and their treaties. Peters' mercenaries didn't burn Ulvskog. We did. We destroyed what they'd tried to do to the pack so the Varulv and the Limmikin could start over."

He stopped. Caught his breath. What if Phoebe didn't come to Minnesota hunting Tuttle, but because the Limmikin were instinctively gathering in the land of their ancestors? Gathering for their revenge?

Tokarz sent Ethan to convince Congressman Bryant Peters to continue to honor the treaties protecting the werewolf packs in exchange for services rendered. Peters used lycan services frequently. Hatch and Rand followed Ethan once Hatch learned Ethan's whereabouts. Then Phoebe showed up, allegedly following Senator Tuttle.

Why northern Minnesota?

Parker dropped his hammer, denting the plywood where it landed. "I need to find my mate."

PHOEBE STUMBLED OVER A vine snaking across the path but caught herself before she fell. She hadn't been in deep forest in a long, long time.

The terrain interested her. Ulvskog lay in a wide valley. Paths veered off from the main trail in every direction. Some followed the relatively flat contours of the land; others meandered up mountainsides. Moss and lichens grew everywhere.

Brilliant sunshine broke through the overhead cover in irregular patches, heating the earth. Dense shade provided relief from the heat.

Phoebe hoped hiking would alleviate her unfamiliar anxiety, an itching beneath her skin. If she didn't know better, she would swear her body wanted to shift. The vibrations were similar.

The first time the shift came upon her, the sensations terrified her. Corbie did what she could to prepare Phoebe for her lycan destiny, but not having experienced the shifting, Corbie's advice didn't help.

These new stirrings were different. Her bones seemed to jitter as if trying to poke their way to the surface, and if they did, furious bees would swarm from the hives they'd constructed in the spaces between her skeleton and organs.

Phoebe was so far past her comfort zone she would have consulted with Olivia or even Selena about the manifestation. The buzzing in her body might be a mating side effect.

She needed to keep moving, because if she stopped her body would implode.

She tried to focus on exploring. Ulvskog woods were different from the ones in which she'd spent her first eight years, yet there were enough similarities to trigger a sense of homecoming.

She left the deer trail she'd been following, keeping an eye out for poison ivy, poison oak, or thunderwood. She could always shift to rid her skin of any toxins she might pick up, but avoiding contamination worked best.

Although she trod lightly, undergrowth crunched beneath her feet. A stew of scents simmered in the sultry air.

A partridge, spooked from its nest, burst from the ground cover. Phoebe's startled body rattled in time with the rapid flapping of the bird's wings as it took flight.

Once her heartbeat returned to normal, she resumed her hike.

"Phoebe?"

She paused. The wind ruffling through the treetops and the never-silent insect serenade sounded nothing like her name. Only one person could be looking for her: her mate.

The internal jittering returned. Intensified. At any moment her body would morph into a windchime, bones clacking in the breeze.

Unless she jumped Parker's bones. Yeah. Her female bits voted for bone jumping.

"Right here," she called to him.

A moment later he strode into view.

She propped her quarterstaff against a tree. She didn't need to be coy. She wanted her mate with an intense urgency. Her need might have scared her if getting him out of his clothes and inside her didn't preoccupy her brain. She yanked her shirt over her head, then quickly unbound her breasts.

A single brave and foolish insect landed on her bare arm.

"What are you doing?" Parker asked as he drew within a few feet.

"I'm…overheated." Her breasts grew heavy as her nipples tightened.

An expression she couldn't read flitted across his face. She toed off her tabi boots.

Parker merely stood there like another tree. Maybe his chest rose as his breathing grew heavier.

Her thumbs hooked into the waistband of her leggings. She hesitated, her gaze never leaving Parker. Why did he stare at her as if he'd never before seen her? Were her signals too subtle? She wanted him with an aching intensity. She yearned to be…ravished.

Even thinking the word sounded silly beyond belief, but she couldn't help what she wanted.

She rolled her leggings over her belly, her hips.

"Are you trying to ask me something?" Parker's face, a shifting mosaic of light and shadow from the overhead leaves, betrayed nothing of his thoughts.

A peek below his belt told a different story.

"Are you playing hard to get?" She slipped her right leg from her leggings. "Or playing at being hard?"

THE FEMALE IS MAKING me crazy.

The furious arousal brought on by her awkward attempt at seduction surprised him. Well, she'd succeeded in getting him worked up. Now she could pay the price.

He snatched her off her feet and flung her over his shoulder. Her leggings dangled from one ankle. Her head hit a tree trunk, but not hard enough to do any damage to a normal skull, much less one as thick as hers.

"Ouch."

A half-hearted complaint, it seemed to him. "You're not hurt," he told her, as he continued climbing, searching for privacy.

"Okay," she agreed. "I like it when you get all alpha on me."

"I'm not alpha. I'm your mate. Okay? You provoke the beast in me." He shoved aside a curtain of vines dripping from several close-growing trees. A grotto lay hidden in the shade. He set her on her feet.

She yanked at his shirt, muttering, "I don't know what's wrong with me."

Parker knew but said nothing. On many levels, he enjoyed her frustration.

"Aren't you going to cooperate?" She worked his belt buckle with shaking fingers. "Otherwise, you could get hurt here. Then what good would you do me?"

She made a good point.

He pushed her clumsy hands away from his fly and did the honors himself. He did allow her to help wrest the heavy denim over his butt and down his legs.

Phoebe knelt before him, lingering over the only part of him she ever seemed to want. He turned, more intent on freeing his feet from boots and jeans than whatever idea she nursed about foreplay. They didn't need foreplay.

She fell onto her back, drawing up her knees and spreading her arms in mock welcome as he shed his remaining clothes.

"Oh, no." No silly games. They were werewolves. Homo lupus. He needed to remind her the male dominated a relationship. She answered to him.

He flipped her onto her stomach.

Her respiration increased, and the scent of sex filled the grotto. Her arousal refueled his. Her flirty behavior drove him loco.

Her estrus made them both crazy. Maybe Phoebe didn't realize the hormones driving her to behave so sexy, but once Old Olivia pointed out Phoebe's fertile state, Parker figured after he impregnated her, she would stop being so hardheaded and would settle into motherhood.

Lycan females didn't pose as assassins. They were sexy mates who cherished and nurtured their families. He simply needed to give Phoebe a family.

He grasped her hips and pulled her forward. She didn't resist. She lured him into plundering her. He accepted the invitation, but on his terms.

Phoebe climaxed the moment he plunged into her. Another lobo might assume technique or prowess. Parker knew better. Procreation. The sum of their attraction.

Still, some inherent, maybe prehistoric bit of his brain wanted more. Demanded something beyond what Phoebe had already given. He could have easily followed her into mindless orgasm, but his pride wouldn't let him.

"Again," he growled.

Phoebe muttered something. He told himself her words didn't matter. He didn't want her to be more than a receptacle. Otherwise, he couldn't retain his sanity. She wasn't cooperating. She was getting to him in so many little ways, burrowing under his skin and weakening his resolve.

But she didn't want tenderness from him. She demanded toughness. He didn't know how far he could take playing the alpha you're-my-bitch role, when all he wanted was to cherish her. Her unique aroma drove him guano crazy. Sanity might be overrated. He continued to thrust. Continued to demand another response from her, when another response shouldn't matter. He'd made her happy once. Once should be enough. Yet it was not. Maybe if he kept her happy often enough, she would forget everything else.

"I can't," she moaned.

"Yes, you can," he responded, and bit down on her marking spot. Phoebe screamed and shuddered.

His world exploded into nothingness.

GAMBAYAN, THE OLD TOWN, protected sacred magic. Phoebe couldn't believe Parker's reluctance to spend the night in the low, moss covered dwellings. The boulder-like huts reminded her of...safety. The greenish light faded to gray, not in a bad way but soft and filtered, dissimilar to the harsh and direct sun in Warwick.

"This is nice," she said.

Addy, an extremely pregnant Varulv, smiled. "It's okay. I do miss our house in the village, though."

"Soon enough." Jakob, Addy's mate, caressed Addy's burgeoning belly. "Ours will be the first house finished, after the full moon lodge."

"I would stay here forever." Phoebe continued to scrutinize the layout.

Phoebe and Parker were to bunk with Addy and Jakob.

You have a lot in common, Restin claimed.

"I don't imagine it's as cozy when winter sets in," Parker grumbled.

Phoebe thought it interesting how he studied Jakob's every move, as if seeking guidance on how to behave with a mate. She didn't know how she would handle displays of affection from a male who held no affection for her.

Jealousy rapped at her heart. On the outside again. If he can't love me, why can't he at least respect me and what I need to do? She reminded herself mating was merely a genetic matching in order to create the best possible next generation.

Addy and Jakob fled assassins similar to those who eliminated Phoebe's family. She and Addy each hid from the gunmen, afraid even to breathe. Parker must have shared Phoebe's history with Restin. He shouldn't have.

"When are you due?" Phoebe asked, only to be polite.

"Soon." Addy's tired smile faded in the rapidly vanishing light. "Not soon enough. I went from being excited and happy when not shifting confirmed my pregnancy to weary of being an incubator."

Phoebe yawned. She burrowed deeper into her sleeping bag—the one she shared with Parker because mates shared sleeping bags. She stared at the stone wall, which comforted her with its familiarity.

Parker squirmed in next to her, bringing his body heat with him. She snuggled closer. His arms settled around her, as he spooned himself to her back.

She could sleep like this forever.

"Scat!" Jakob scrambled from his sleeping bag with impressive speed.

Then the stench hit Parker. Once a lycan caught a whiff, he never forgot vampire stink. He, too, abandoned his sleeping bag.

Jakob tossed a stake to Parker, then one to each female.

Why are the Varulv prepared for vampires in their old town?

"What's this for?" Phoebe asked.

Parker clamped his hand over her mouth. "Vampires," he mouthed against her ear.

"It's okay," Jakob explained. "They haven't been able to infest Gambayan yet."

Yet?

Parker couldn't believe his ears. "You have vampires stalking you here?"

Tokarz sent him here with his mate?

"There is old magic protecting Gambayan." Addy's voice quavered, as if she didn't quite believe her own words.

"Then why aren't you settling here where it's safe?"

"Vampires didn't shoot up the town."

"This is what I smelled in Elysian Estates the other night," Phoebe said. "Vampires?"

Parker had told her she reeked of the undead.

He didn't care for her reaction. She, too, freed herself from the sleeping bag. She held her quarterstaff in one hand, the stake in her other. She resembled a comic book female warrior. Except fighting vampires was deadly, not fiction.

Vampires were out there.

"What do they want?" Phoebe asked.

"Me," Addy admitted in a low voice. "My baby. Fetal blood is a vampire champagne or something."

Parker's vision flashed crimson.

"The factotum explained to us the last time vampires were sniffing around here. Right after you burned Ulvskog." Jakob cocked his head, as if listening.

"Factotum?" Parker repeated the unfamiliar word.

"Sapien slave. Maybe the vampires followed you and your mate."

Scat! Jakob might be right. Still, Parker preferred the tested magic of Ash, Oak, and Hawthorn Streets to protect his mate. His possibly gestating mate. He gripped the stake in his hand tighter.

Factotum. Vampires needed sapiens doing their bidding. Thugs barricaded Ethan's block, twenty-four/seven before the last full moon. The vampire stink at night brought tears to the eyes, but once dawn broke, the vamps had been replaced by ordinary males. Factotum.

"I've smelled this someplace else, too. Recently." Phoebe's eyes glittered in the dark. "Senator Tuttle's hospital room."

Chapter 16

Parker paced the length of Ethan's living room. The empty room better suited his need to be furious than Helga's cluttered space or Ulvskog. "How hard can it be to hack a hospital's database?"

He'd left Phoebe across the street, sleeping. They'd stayed awake all night in Gambayan, stakes at the ready. After a quick consultation with Hatch, who, along with his son, opted to remain in the forest, Parker hustled Phoebe into his SUV. For once, Phoebe didn't argue.

"Maybe the senator's records are in a more secure site," Ethan suggested. "Give Luke a minute or two."

The end of Parker's patience loomed. He'd wanted to call Luke right after Phoebe dropped her bombshell. Cell phone service didn't exist in Gambayan and proved spotty at best in Ulvskog itself. Nor did he feel secure. On any level. So he'd driven the serpentine road as fast as he could, cursing the coils of pavement twisting the road toward Warwick and civilization.

Ethan could contact Luke Thibodaux, the pack's computer genius, who also happened to work with the feds fighting kiddie porn. If anyone could find out why a Tennessee senator hid in a northern Minnesota hospital, Luke would be the lobo.

Toke Lobo and the Pack's biggest hit to date blared from Ethan's pocket.

"Really, Ethan?" Parker asked. Everyone associated with the band avoided "Full Moon Lady" if they could.

Ethan lifted his cellphone to his ear. "What do you have for us? I'm going to put you on speaker, so Parker can hear."

Parker stopped pacing to focus on Luke's report.

"Feral cat scratches." Luke's voice sounded tinny. "Infection caused by an unknown pathogen, not responding to broad spectrum antibiotics. Testing to identify the source of the infection continues, while the infection spreads throughout his body. He doesn't appear to be contagious. I'm surprised he hasn't been whisked off to Bethesda or Walter Reed or some other government facility."

"Feral cat scratches? You mean like cat scratch fever?"

Parker could picture Luke's shrug. He knew the younger lobo too well. "Maybe. I'll keep an eye on his chart."

"Thanks, Luke." Ethan signed off. His dark eyes met Parker's. "You know what else has claws?"

"Bears?" There were no lions or tigers wandering loose in northern Minnesota.

"Vampires."

Scat. "Phoebe thought she caught a whiff in Tuttle's hospital room."

"None of this makes any sense." Ethan tucked his phone into his pocket.

"Doesn't it?" Parker resumed his circuit of Ethan's living room. "Let's examine what we know."

He'd been trained to look at symptoms, add them together, and deliver a diagnosis. "There's a movement to end the sanctuary treaties. We know Congressman Peters helped launch the movement."

"Let's write what we know on the white board in the basement. Selena and Britt won't need it any time soon."

As if Parker gave a vampire fart about the herb-based beauty products the two females planned to manufacture and distribute from Ethan's basement. But he followed Ethan down the steep stairs.

Ethan handed Parker a purple marker. "Have at it."

Parker divided the white board into two columns: Known and Surmised.

"Neither Congressman Bryant Peters nor his oldest son were vampires," Ethan reminded him.

The marker squeaked against the board's smooth surface.

Alcohol faintly scented the air.

"Connor Peters became a vampire the night Britt's ex tried to kidnap her. Someone also bit and drained Britt's ex around the same time. Dakota says the Peters mansion didn't stink like vampire the night of the party."

Although Parker hadn't been at the mansion on the night in question, Ethan solicited his aid to rescue Dakota and Britt from inside Elysian Estates. The air reeked of the vampire Britt ashed.

"But vampire involvement starts before then." Ethan pursed his lips. "A vampire attacked Selena less than twelve hours after she went to Congressman Peters' office the day I hit town. Vampires lurked outside Gambayan the night before you arrived. We were also attacked the night Peters blew off half his face."

"The night before your honor guard showed up?"

"The vampires at the ends of the block? Yeah."

Peters equals Vampires, Parker wrote. Then he started a third column. "Who else?"

"A guy named Curtis DiNardo. His uncle works for the Peters family. Greasy guy. Britt went to high school with him." Ethan paused. His eyes seemed to un-focus, as if he were looking into his memories. "Did you see Addy this weekend?"

"Yeah. She mentioned something about—"

"Vampires and fetal blood?"

Blood red rage filmed Parker's vision. A lump ballooned in his throat. "You knew?" He choked on the accusation. If Phoebe were there, he would have snatched Jeeves from her hands and whacked Ethan in the balls. "You knew Phoebe has been in heat and yet you let me go to Ulvskog?"

"Keep your boots on. Phoebe is as safe in Gambayan as she is on Ash Street." Ethan had the audacity to sound amused. "No one has seen vampires in Ulvskog or Gambayan. They've only smelled them. Whereas, well, you helped us rid this neighborhood of the blight a few weeks ago. And you were with me the night we rescued Britt and Dakota from vampires in Elysian Estates."

The red faded from Parker's vision. His throat cleared. "What does fetal blood have to do with this DiNardo guy?" "He's the one who told us someone wanted Addy left alive."

"Who?"

Ethan's lips thinned. "I don't remember."

Something scratched at Parker's memory. "Jakob mentioned a factotum told them about fetal blood."

"Factotum?"

"He said factotums are a vampire's sapien slaves."

"Curtis DiNardo was a vampire slave?" Ethan's voice rose. "I suppose it's not out of the question. You don't need to be smart to work for vampires. He only did what his uncle told him to do."

"Wait a minute." Parker couldn't believe he'd forgotten the aftermath of one-on-ones with vampires. "Selena got sick after being clawed by a vampire. So did Dakota."

Ethan's eyes widened and his jaw dropped. "You think a vampire attacked Tuttle? He's in the hospital for vampire cooties?"

"Vampire cooties." Parker couldn't believe he hadn't considered vampire cooties sooner. He needed to ask Phoebe for details on Tuttle's condition. "We have a sense of how vampire cooties sicken lycans, but sapien symptoms are unknown."

"Luke said cat scratch fever," Ethan muttered. "Tuttle would need to explain his injuries. He's been staying with the Peters family in Elysian Estates."

Ethan turned and headed for the stairs. Then changed direction and stalked back to the white board. He narrowed his eyes as he studied the few words Parker scrawled.

"There's something in Elysian Estates." He plucked a green marker from the tray and savagely stroked the gated community's name across the top of the board.

Parker barely heard the mutter, too busy trying to connect clues on his own. "It can't be centered at the Peters estate. Dakota would have smelled vampires while in the house. Anyone with a nose would have noticed."

"Britt can't smell vampires. Neither can Helga. We need to talk to Dakota." Ethan pulled out his phone.

Parker headed for the stairs. "I'll get Phoebe."

"AND HERE I THOUGHT we would visit Helga," Phoebe grumbled as Parker hustled her across the street to Ethan's house. Parker barely gave her time to wash her face after waking her and dragging her out the door.

"Selena and Old Olivia are there. Don't worry. She's being looked after."

"You're so sympathetic. Great bedside manner, Doc." Her jaw cracked as she yawned.

Logeyness plagued her since returning from Varulv- Limmikin territory. They hadn't slept the night they spent in Gambayan. Parker insisted she nap when they got to Helga's house. Rudely rousing her didn't improve her mood.

"Pack meeting."

"You said Selena was at the hospital." Phoebe stumbled as he steered her through Ethan's front door.

"She is. Don't worry."

"Sexist," Phoebe muttered. "She's the alpha."

"And she's otherwise occupied. You don't know much about packs, remember? Trust me. An alpha doesn't oversee every minute detail of our lives."

He was lying. She could smell the untruth on him.

"Besides, we need to compare notes."

"Notes? I haven't made any notes." She paused at the top of the basement stairs. The last time she'd been in Ethan's basement, she'd lost her virginity. "Where are we going?"

"There's a white board down here we're using to keep track of...clues."

"Clues? Clues to what?" Exhaustion continued to fog her brain.

"We're working on pinpointing a timeline and motivation."

She used her quarterstaff to steady herself as she descended the steep stairs.

Parker led her to a brightly lit area opposite the sleeping area where he'd claimed her. A long table occupied most of the space. A white board decorated with purple and green scribbles dominated one wall.

Phoebe squinted at the writing. Names. Names she'd heard the others mention. Peters-by-the-number. Her own nemesis, Tuttle. "I don't get it."

"Let's wait for Dakota and Britt," Ethan suggested. "And I called Selena. Dakota's stopping by the hospital to collect her and Old Olivia."

So much for Parker's lies.

"What's this confab about?" Phoebe hopped up on the table.

"Let's wait until everyone is here so we only have to go through it once."

She must have dozed, propped against Parker who at some point joined her on the table, because the next thing she knew, he woke her again. Selena, Olivia, Britt, and Dakota were present.

"What's this about?" Selena asked.

"We're trying to figure out what's going on," Ethan replied. "Phoebe, tell us about visiting Senator Tuttle in the hospital."

"He's in the hospital."

Parker nudged her with his elbow. "You visited him. How did he look? Could you see any injuries?"

"Yeah. He had scratches all over his arms and chest. Gouges. Hard to tell how intense, though, because he was swathed in gauze."

"Luke researched the hospital data base. Tuttle is being treated for being attacked by a feral cat."

"Luke?"

"Our FBI contact," Parker reminded her.

FBI? Parker turned her simple assassination goal into a production. What happened to kill Tuttle and get on with her life? Packs, she decided, were ridiculous.

"What did you smell?" Parker asked.

"The same nasty smell I ran into in Elysian Estates. The same stink from Gambayan last night. The one you said was vampire."

"Tuttle has vampire cooties?" Selena's voice squeaked. "Well, scat."

"What are vampire cooties?" Phoebe couldn't be more in the dark if she'd dropped down from the moon.

"A sickness from being clawed by a vampire. Both Selena and Dakota suffered with it," Parker explained. "Was Tuttle asleep when you were in his room?"

"No. He was alert and cranky. Cranky is his usual mood when there's no microphone."

"We don't know how vampire cooties manifests in sapiens," Parker murmured.

"We don't know anything about the sickness in lycans, either." Impatience flowed from Selena. "I remember being exhausted. And I didn't dream while I slept."

"I didn't either." Dakota ceased his pacing when Selena spoke. "I have no memories at all. One minute I'm fighting a vampire. The next, I'm waking up and the cops are questioning Britt."

"You were both weak." Parker's eyes glazed. "You couldn't shift. You were both in four-legged mode. Then, poof."

"Just like adolescence," Selena finished. "No control. Shifting...happened."

"You can bet Tuttle won't have that problem." Phoebe's own restlessness edged toward uncontrollable. A lot of things might...happen. "I think I should visit Tuttle again. Concerned constituent. A face from home."

"You threatened him with Jeeves." Parker spoke as if he'd been in the room instead of her. "He's going to be guarded, now."

"Stop calling my quarterstaff that stupid name. And I know he's going to be guarded."

Probably by Dustin. Whom she knew. Who, being more brawn than brain, would be easy to distract. No one knew his dimwittedness better than she did due to years of practice.

"One of the guards on Tuttle's security detail is my foster brother. Remember? Dustin is not a Rhodes Scholar. Bill Gates can sleep at night. Like most stupid people, he doesn't grasp how lacking he is. Getting past him is not going to challenge anyone in this room."

"What's his weakness?" Britt asked.

She was an attractive blonde who wore tight jeans and a low-cut top. Dustin's type. "You would be."

Britt primped. "I can handle him, then."

"Forget it," Dakota snapped.

"Hey, we all have our strengths. I can't shift, but I can flirt."

"You're not a single female anymore. I forbid it."

"I've met the Senator," Britt reminded Dakota. "Maybe his security detail would remember me."

"I was there, in case it slipped your mind along with your mated status."

"All I'd do is distract the guy with harmless conversation while Phoebe sneaks into the senator's room. It's a no brainer, Dakota." Britt didn't back down. She also practiced her wiles on her mate. She ran her forefinger down his arm. "You can hide around the corner and rescue me if things get out of hand. You'd love me playing damsel in distress."

Dakota's eyes gleamed.

Parker jumped off the table. "This isn't going to happen."

Who died and made you alpha?

"You are all forgetting one key factor here. Phoebe's vendetta."

Parker made her goal a priority?

"You make forgetting sound like a bad thing," Britt said.

"No, Parker is right." Everyone turned to look at Selena. "I'm not saying Phoebe can't avenge her family's deaths, but the hospital isn't the place to do it."

"What if he never gets out?" Phoebe asked.

"Do you sincerely believe the most powerful man in Washington, D.C. is going to die in a backwater hospital in northern Minnesota?" Selena countered. "Worst case scenario for you is his being airlifted out. Anything else gives you time to...react."

Phoebe stared at Selena, who seemed serene as she returned Phoebe's gaze.

"Let's see what else the FBI contact can hack from the medical records," Selena continued. "And try to figure out what we're going to do about the ongoing vampire problem."

"The vampire problem isn't ours," Ethan said.

"When they polluted Gambayan's air, they became our problem," Selena retorted.

Phoebe didn't give a damn about vampires or whose problem they were. Maybe she could approach Britt on her own and the pack outsiders could pay Dustin and Tuttle a visit.

Chapter 17

Parker prayed to the Ancient Ones for patience. The conversation in Ethan's basement rode the same old carousel, circling conflicting opinions and Selena dithering about a decision. In Parker's opinion, Ethan would make a much better alpha than his female.

But who was he to judge? He suffered his own female troubles.

"You need to let me do what I came to do." Phoebe turned on him as soon as he'd closed and locked the door. "Stop interfering."

Her white-knuckled grip on Jeeves betrayed her fury.

Parker summoned every ounce of patience he'd ever held. "I can't let you get yourself killed."

The sound emerging through her nose barely resembled a snort. "Oh, please. You'd like nothing better than to get rid of me."

"Not true." He swallowed the pain that his mate could believe that and vowed to try harder. "I want to find a happy medium. A middle ground. Why can't you work with me to find a place we can both be happy?"

"Because your idea of compromise is to do things your way, and I don't argue about it."

"Sounds fair to me, especially when it comes to your well-being." He braced himself to leap aside in case she started swinging.

"Why can't I do things my way, and you stop interfering?"

"Because you're my mate, and protecting my mate is in my DNA."

"Submission isn't in mine."

No kidding. "Think about what it would do to me if you were killed."

Losing his sister nearly killed him, too. Losing his mate?

He couldn't imagine.

"It's not about you." Phoebe glared as if she had every right in the world to not think about him.

Reality check time. "If you're dead, it is."

"How refreshing to know you have so much faith in my survival skills." She held Jeeves across her chest. "Want to test them?"

Why had he been cursed with hard-headed females?

"You're testing my patience." He fought to lower the

heat on his simmering rage before it boiled over. "I've compromised with you by staying in Warwick for Helga's sake. My alpha told me I could go home. I have paramedic training I want to start. I miss my parents and friends. I need my pack. How much longer, Fleur?"

PHOEBE LOST HER GRIP on her quarterstaff. The clatter of wood meeting the wood floor echoed in the room. "What did you just call me?"

"Now what are you blathering about?" Parker sounded disgusted, as if he had a reason to be annoyed with her, when all the giving in their relationship came from her. Now he called her by another female's name?

"Who's Fleur? An old lover?"

No, she couldn't be, because male lycans didn't, couldn't function with anyone except a mate. Phoebe tried to convince herself being called by another's name didn't hurt.

"Who told you about Fleur?" Parker sounded defensive.

Phoebe resisted the urge to smack him with her quarterstaff. She bent to retrieve it. She tried to defuse the tension humming in the air. "Looks like I dented Helga's floor."

If Parker didn't explain about Fleur, she'd ask Ethan or Dakota. They'd all grown up together in Parker's sacred pack. Except males always stuck together. They wouldn't tell her anything.

"*Who told you about Fleur?*" Parker gripped her arms.

Once more, the quarterstaff fell from her fingers.

"You did." She wrenched free from his grasp. "Just now. Don't ever grab me again unless you want to be a hurting lobo."

Except he already ached. She read it in his smoky quartz eyes. The grief contorting his face before he turned away from her. The way his voice cracked when he asked, "I called you Fleur?"

"Yes." Phoebe focused on his hunched shoulders and bowed head. She retrieved her quarterstaff. "She must have been important to you."

"I'm not discussing her with you."

His words hurt, were as injurious to her as her quarterstaff would be to him. "Fine."

"You're exactly like her," Parker muttered.

So much for not discussing Fleur.

"Hard-headed. Stubborn. Refusing to listen to common sense."

"Sounds like we'll be great friends. Introduce us next time you run into her." Phoebe started toward the kitchen. She wanted to be outside, in the backyard. She wanted to howl. The Goddess chose Parker as her mate, no matter how mismatched they might be. He had no business comparing her to another female. She would never compare him to Dustin. Ever.

And those weren't tears clogging her throat. She never cried. Urban air pollution after breathing Ulvskog's pure air must be irritating her eyes.

"I can't." He spoke as if he carried marbles in his mouth: garbled, but still comprehensible.

Phoebe stopped. Waited.

"She's dead. She didn't listen to me either."

Phoebe tried to swallow around the lump in her throat, but the weight in her chest wouldn't let her. Parker had been mated before? "I'm sorry." She choked on the words, but Corbie taught her manners.

"I don't want to lose you, too."

If he meant to lessen her pain, he suffered an epic fail.

She'd done the good lycan girl thing and didn't let any sapien claim what belonged to her mate. She'd done what she was supposed to do. And once again the Goddess smothered her in shit.

"I told her not to sled down the far trail. She wouldn't be able to steer on the ice buildup."

Phoebe whirled around. Parker still had his back to her, but she glimpsed his reflection in the partially curtained window. His eyes were squeezed shut; his features twisted with an agonizing memory.

"What happened?" Phoebe whispered the question, not wanting to intrude on his grief.

"My sister. My twin." Parker knew he owed Phoebe an explanation. "She died when we were kids. She hopped on her sled and laughed as she pushed off. She laughed even when she hit the ice and lost control. She laughed until she crashed into the tree and broke her neck."

Fleur's mirth ringing over the crunch of snow. Her red snowsuit so still against the white landscape. His mother's sobs. *You're not the boss of me* were the last words his twin ever spoke to him.

"I'm...I'm sorry."

He, too, witnessed a younger sibling die. His memory couldn't be as violent or gruesome as hers. She'd been smart and saved herself. He should have been smart and left Fleur at home.

"She was as stubborn as a rock. Wouldn't listen. A lot like you."

"Why are you the only one who gets to be right? Because you have a penis?"

Irritation flared. Why were females so obsessed with penises? "Because there's such a thing as logic and common sense, something Fleur didn't have, and you don't seem to either."

Phoebe glared. "I have plenty of logic and common sense. Disagreeing with me doesn't invalidate me. You don't get to judge. You are not the Goddess."

"I am your mate," he growled.

"I am your mate," she echoed. "Two halves make a whole, not one overshadowing the other."

"I lost her. I won't lose you, too."

"I'll be lost if I can't make good on my vow to my ancestors. I have to stop Tuttle. Revenge is the reason I survived."

Didn't she understand anything at all? "I'm an EMT. It's my job to save people."

I couldn't save Fleur.

Phoebe tilted her head, scanning his soul. "What if they don't want to be saved?"

"Salvation is up to the Ancient Ones. I'm merely a tool." Why didn't she thunk him on the head with Jeeves? Bury an end in his gut? Thrust it against his balls? Suck the breath from his body until he suffocated? Yeah. Her attitude and actions were stealing his will to live.

No!

He was alive, and he planned to keep Phoebe alive by any and every means possible. Right now, whisking her off to Colorado, away from Tuttle appeared to be the solution. Helga should be released from the hospital at any time.

They could take her with them, if Phoebe insisted on fulfilling her promise to care for the crone. Selena and Ethan could keep an eye on the house. Dakota and Britt could move in. Promise kept.

"We're mated." He chose his words with care and squelched an urge to reach for her. "Mating is forever. In my pack, mated also means keeping each other safe. Your fight is my fight, and mine is yours."

She never blinked. "So you'll support me? You'll help me?"

He turned away from her. Ancient Ones, he needed to shift and run. Even the Ulvskog's forest would be better than standing there on two legs and being asked to risk getting them and their child—she had to be gestating by now— killed. Maybe he could take up jogging until he could get home.

The best solution to every one of his problems involved leaving this place and returning to the Rocky Mountains.

Ethan helped Selena avenge herself against the Peters family. Dakota helped Britt, too.

Parker's conscience refused to keep silent about what other lobos did to facilitate their mates' need for revenge. Besides, Senator Tuttle was different. The most powerful man in Washington, D.C. traveled with a lot more security than Congressman Bryant Peters ever did.

If Parker didn't help Phoebe, his failure would hang over their relationship for the rest of their lives. But helping her also meant risking her.

Chapter 18

Phoebe stood in the middle of Helga's living room, stunned by disbelief.

After being an unabashed jerk, Parker sauntered out the front door and left.

He's not the only one who knows how to use a door.

She could shift, nose around Elysian Estates to get her bearings. While Tuttle might be served up to her on a sterile hospital platter, she ignored the bait. A hospital attack would be sure to end in her death. She didn't want to die; she merely accepted the probability.

Besides, she wanted Tuttle to suffer. To wonder when.

She grasped the doorknob. The doorbell chimed. She sniffed the air. Ethan and Selena.

Phoebe opened the door. "He just left."

"We know." Selena brushed past Phoebe. "He's worried about you."

"He told me about Fleur." Phoebe didn't think his sister's death excused him enough to keep her a prisoner of his whim. Not that her relationship with her mate should concern Selena.

"I was there when Fleur died." Ethan provided perspective. "I ran for help. But I heard about how Restin wrestled him to the ground to keep him from moving Fleur in case she was still alive. He kept saying, I have to help her, I have to help her."

Phoebe wanted to cry but refrained. "It's his nature."

"Not until Fleur died. Fleur's accident changed him. He decided he wanted to be a doctor when he couldn't save her. Tokarz had a reality check with him. Parker settled for EMT."

Details Parker left out. No matter. His sister's death was a tragedy. Phoebe understood tragedy. Now she understood why he'd become an EMT and wanted to continue his education. Why couldn't he understand her need to address her loss? "Did you stop your mate from avenging herself against her rapist?"

"He supported me," Selena admitted, as she settled into a lace-draped wingback chair.

"I helped her." Ethan dropped to the floor at Selena's feet.

Make yourselves at home.

"Everyone helped. Dakota. Ethan's, father and grandfather. Males from my pack."

"No one tried to stop you," Phoebe pointed out.

"Don't be ridiculous. Liam Peters earned his death."

"So did Richard Tuttle."

"No one is saying you're wrong." Selena sounded almost conciliatory. "But your timing could be smarter."

"Let us help you. Let Parker help you." Ethan stretched out his long legs.

"Did you two script this?" Phoebe gave up trying to leave and plopped onto the sofa.

Selena's mouth curled upward. "No. But we've been there, done that. Mates think alike."

"Ha!" If she and Parker ever thought alike, the Goddess herself would be stalking the Tuttles of the world. "Britt offered to help, and you guys jumped all over us."

"Britt doesn't understand strategy," Selena said. "Trust me. She's my best friend, and she's super smart, but there are some things her sapien brain can't grasp. Revenge is right up there on the list."

"You need to be smart about confronting Tuttle. Approaching him in the hospital wasn't smart. Doing it twice is going to scuttle your whole agenda." Ethan sounded so earnest Phoebe wanted to laugh.

"I'd planned on exploring Elysian Estates tonight," she admitted. "I think I found the Peters' house the first time I nosed around."

Ethan leaned forward. "We have Luke, the computer nerd, who has FBI clearance to nose around. We can keep an eye on Tuttle through his hospital records, including finding out when he'll be released."

"Why would he return to the place where a vampire attacked him?" Selena asked.

Selena made a good point.

"He's going to want out of town as fast as a jet plane can take him. Does he have his own plane?"

"He flew commercial to get here," Phoebe admitted. "I saw his arrival on TV at the bus station."

"He'll fly out privately," Ethan mused. "He won't appear weak in public."

"True." Phoebe couldn't imagine a scenario where Tuttle wouldn't be in charge. Even when she'd confronted him in the hospital, he'd postured his superiority.

"Something else for Luke to keep an eye on. Someone should be taking notes." Ethan stared expectantly at Phoebe. Phoebe stared back. He could take his own damn notes.

He might be son of the Limmikin alpha and mated to the Varulv alpha, but where had he or any other Limmikin been when she needed them? Limmikin never came to her aid when the Tennessee pack had been slaughtered. No lycans ever showed up. She'd been rescued by a crone. Her loyalty lay with the ones who helped, even if Corbie was pissed at her.

"Why don't you call Luke and put him on speaker?" Selena suggested with barely concealed annoyance.

Ethan pulled out his cell phone.

"What?" The person who answered the call sounded testy. Children wailed in the background.

"We need your help." Ethan started the conversation without niceties.

"Unless this is about your mission with the Peters, I'm assigned elsewhere."

"It's about my mission with the Peters."

Phoebe exchanged a glance with Selena, who didn't seem perturbed by the falsehood.

"Tuttle—"

"Is not Peters. I've told you everything I could find about his medical condition."

"He's working with the Peters family. We think a vampire mauled him at the Peters' house."

"What?"

Ethan cleared his throat. The background wails turned to shrieks. "How are Abby and the twins?"

"Fine. What did you say about vampires?"

"You said Tuttle claimed a feral cat attacked him."

"It's a long way from a feral cat to vampires," Luke snapped.

"Not especially. Have you ever seen vampire claws? I have. Both my mate and Dakota were clawed by vampires. They got real sick. Does anyone know how vampire cooties affect sapiens?"

"I don't even know what vampire cooties are," Luke retorted.

"Is he always this cranky?" Phoebe whispered to Selena.

"Never met him."

Ethan waved at them, as if to quiet the chattering females. "We don't know what else to call a lycan's reaction to being clawed by a vampire. Do you have a better, scientific name for it?"

Luke snorted. "Scientific? You're joking. Right?"

"No. If Parker were here, I'd let him tell you the symptoms both Selena and Dakota displayed after being clawed."

Listening to everyone dance around the issue irked Phoebe. She tuned out Ethan's stupid conversation with some supposed FBI computer hacker and perused the room. Parker probably sicced Selena and Ethan on her as babysitters, but they were distracted by trying to impress the drummer with past events.

Nothing could change the past, but both now and the future could be reshaped. Unless she fixed things now, while the fixing was good, the future didn't matter. She clutched her quarterstaff at her side and headed toward the kitchen. To a door leading outside.

Parker had issues. Learning what motivated him didn't change anything for her except emphasizing her need to be more cautious.

Relieved to escape Helga's stuffy house, Phoebe let the briskness of the breeze cool her face as she crept through the hedge bordering Helga's lawn. So much lycan energy, trapped by the frou-frou cluttering tiny spaces, quickly heated a room. She sprinted across the back neighbor's yard.

When she and Parker got their own place—

No. She couldn't imagine a future with him until she settled with Tuttle. She'd tag along to Colorado with Parker after mission accomplished. Tuttle's death meant she could live.

Maybe.

THE AUTUMN-SCENTED BREEZE DID nothing to cool Parker's thoughts as he loped toward the neighborhood park. The faintly yellow moon clung to the sky like a blob of melted candle wax, irregular in shape and smeared.

He needed to talk to someone, and Ethan wouldn't be any help. Nor would Dakota. He'd tried with Restin but got nowhere. The pack beta had no wisdom to impart. Nor could he focus on more than one or two things at a time.

Parker needed his alpha. Tokarz.

The park was deserted this time of night. The neighborhood youth were at home being tucked in; vandals had yet to stir from their beds. Parker made his way across the lumpy, dew-laden grass to a gazebo. By moonlight, the structure appeared romantic. Parker had seen it in the sun and knew it made the rest of the neighborhood appear upscale. He circled the octagonal shelter several times before pulling out his phone and dialing Tokarz.

"What?" The alpha sounded testier than usual.

"I need to come home." Parker didn't bother with niceties either. "I need to make my mate break her promise to the crone to guard her house while she's in the hospital."

"Really?" Tokarz tone lost its edge. "You would dishonor your mate by asking her to break her word?"

Scat.

"When it comes to her safety, you better believe it." Parker refused to make excuses.

Smoke from someone's firepit scented the night. Or maybe his temper burned.

"I applaud her vendetta, but not the foolish way she's going about it. She won't listen. She won't accept help. She behaves as if she's on a holy mission." Parker stomped up the soggy wooden stairs to the gazebo's interior.

"You don't think her situation is related to what happened to Hatch's pack or to the Varulv last month?" Tokarz asked.

"Of course it is." Parker kicked a splintering wood strut bracing the inside bench to the wall before resuming his pacing.

"And you don't think your mate has a right, has an obligation to avenge the murder of her family and pack?"

Tokarz made him sound like a self-serving bully.

"I think she's going about it in the wrong way, and what she's doing is going to get her killed. She's in heat. She's not thinking clearly." He fought to conceal his anger from Tokarz.

Tokarz snickered. "If I were you, I wouldn't mention the last part. Blaming anything on hormones could get you in some deep scat."

"I don't think she knows." Parker hated admitting he'd kept such great a secret from his mate.

"Knows what?"

"She's in heat."

"How do you know?"

Valid question. Parker swallowed his guilt before explaining. "One of the grannies in Selena's pack told me. A crone raised Phoebe in a sapien household. The crone might not have understood lycan fertility."

Since most lobos didn't understand their female's fertility, Parker didn't think his theory far-fetched.

"Maybe the old female should have told your mate, not you."

Parker skirted a hole in the floor and rushed to defend himself. "No, it's better for me to know. Phoebe and I aren't getting along, so knowing she's in heat explains why...I still want to fuck her."

"Her being in heat has nothing to do with wanting to fuck her. You want her because she's your mate. The Ancient Ones know what they're doing."

Parker harbored serious doubts the Ancient Ones knew anything. His faith in the old ways crumbled as badly as the gazebo he paced. "I need to come home now," he repeated. "Order us home."

"No."

Parker closed his eyes and clenched his jaw to keep from begging. He still maintained a few shreds of pride.

"You and your mate need to work together to bury her past so you can get on with your future."

Chapter 19

Phoebe paused. Held her breath. Listened. Crickets continued chirping. Other nocturnal insects added to the chorus. A too-loud television polluted the night with the unnatural.

Whoever shuffled behind her also stopped. Her stalker didn't grasp she could hear his heart pumping his blood. Slowly, she released her breath through her mouth, then cautiously inhaled again. She identified stale perspiration and a faint whiff of what Parker called vampire cooties. The aroma meant Parker wasn't the one tracking her.

The vampire cooties concerned her. She ought to head back to Ethan's allegedly magical block.

She readied herself by gripping her quarterstaff with both hands.

Phoebe lifted her face to the moon. In a few more nights, it would be half, meaning Phoebe's inner she-wolf would dominate her personality. Shifting would be easier.

Right now, when she wanted to shift and attack, nothing within her stirred. Too bad the moment came before the half moon could give her lycan strength. She needed to go with her quarterstaff. Good thing Corbie had foreseen enough to make sure Phoebe knew how to fight.

She turned and scanned the sidewalk behind her. This neighborhood didn't boast hedges or other property markers. The cars, huddled at the curb, created shadows. The dense darkness meant nothing. The feeble orange glow from the streetlights didn't penetrate far, but between them, the moon, and the night breeze ruffling the leaves on the scattered trees, the murk hovered only at the edge of the winter-warped sidewalk.

She moved to the umbra, using it as an ally.

Her stalker sighed. The sound carried clearly over the faint rustle of the already dying leaves.

Summoning all the stealth she'd ever practiced, she crept toward the sound, clinging to the darkness as if it were a cloak to conceal her. The stalker's night vision couldn't possibly be as acute as hers.

Unless a vampire stalked her. But vampire cooties residue barely imprinted the air. Dog droppings, grass clippings, and someone getting stoned overwhelmed the vampire stink.

Without warning, the stalker swooped toward her.

She raised her quarterstaff and went on the offensive.

Each blow she landed on her target reverberated through the wood and into her arms. She shoved an end into his stomach, then slammed the sturdy oak against his temple. He dropped to the sidewalk like rabbit poop.

Behind her, someone applauded. "Well done."

She recognized the voice. "Parker, you startled ten years off my life."

"You really do know how to use Jeeves."

That stupid name again. "You doubted me?"

"Never again." Her mate stayed in the moonlight as he approached. "Who's the guy?"

"I don't know."

Parker activated the flashlight function on his cell phone and aimed the beam on the unconscious man's face.

"Dustin?" Phoebe's voice squeaked. She should have recognized his scent. He should have known better than to sneak up on her.

"You know him."

"My foster brother. Corbie's grandson. The one who betrayed my secret to Tuttle."

"Then let's kill him."

"Too much red tape."

"Good point." Parker turned off the light, then made a call. "Selena, we need your cop friends. Someone attempted to mug Phoebe."

"She's fine." Parker assured Selena. "She knows how to use her stick."

He should have been the one to defend Phoebe. He never should have left her alone so she could sneak away.

He studied her face, searching for clues about her mental state. The fight barely winded her.

The assailant groaned. Stirred.

Phoebe placed the tip of Jeeves against the man's exposed throat. "I'd stay down, Dustin."

Her voice—low, deep, and sultry—did things to Parker's body he didn't want to happen.

"We're on Ash, but closer to the park than your place," Parker told Selena. "The guy is starting to come around. She may have to inflict more bodily harm. I want to kill him."

"You can't kill Dustin," Phoebe said. "He's on Senator Tuttle's security team. Too many awkward questions."

Parker hated when Phoebe's thoughts were smarter than his. "He attacked you. You defended yourself."

"True." She seemed to consider his suggestion. "But I think the scandal involving a Tuttle employee being a creep would be more fun."

Just like Fleur. "Life isn't about fun."

He could go for months without remembering his sister, but when Fleur's ghost came around, it tended to stick around.

"You're not the only one who has suffered a loss. I've lived as much misery as anyone. And no, I'm not trying to one-upmanship you. You need to stop lecturing me. Give me some credit for surviving this long."

She used Jeeves to smack the male at her feet across his knees. "Stay down there, Dustin, unless you want me to have another go at your thick skull."

Parker hadn't noticed movement from the would-be attacker. "This is the guy who tried to have sex with you?"

"The same. I owe him a lot." She whacked him again.

"What do you mean?"

"We went steady in high school. Boyfriend and girlfriend."

Jealousy roared out of nowhere. "I remember."

Her nose wrinkled, creating weird shadows on her face. "It was icky. And the rumors. Goddess save me from small- town rumor mills. We lived in the same house, so we must be doing it."

"Doing what?"

"It. The big it."

He had no idea what she meant.

"Sex, Parker. Everyone whispered we were fucking."

The roar between Parker's ears increased. He knew how the rumor started. He was going to rip Dustin's head from his shoulders.

"You know he never touched anything he shouldn't have. I think the moment I broke two of his fingers clarified my differences for him. The whole going away on the full moon thing. My alleged temper. Corbie and I never tried to explain anything to Dustin."

"What do you mean, going away on the full moon?"

"Once I hit adolescence, I couldn't stick around a sapien household when the moon demanded a song."

No, he supposed she couldn't.

"What did you do when you started shifting?"

"Panic."

I imagine she would.

"Corbie told me. Warned me. I don't have memories of seeing my parents shift. I used to spend the night with Granny, as did my brothers and cousins, but I never questioned why. Overnights with Granny were normal. I didn't pay attention to the sky."

"So you don't know—"

"I told you before. I don't know how to be a werewolf. I recognized you as my mate strictly as instinct. Everything lycan about me is hit or miss. Even my instincts are iffy."

He could teach her. They could stop butting heads, he could take her home to Colorado and immerse her in the ancient ways. He could mold her into the mate he wanted. Meek. Supporting his goals. Nurturing their offspring.

If she didn't split open his head like a melon first.

Because she learned to be tough to survive in a sapien world.

Maybe he was finally beginning to comprehend the female the Ancient Ones chose for him.

FOR THE SECOND TIME in her life Phoebe got to witness Dustin Holloway handcuffed and driven away in a patrol car. He'd probably be free by Phoebe's next visit to Helga.

She and Parker headed back to Helga's house. Summer sounds and scents lingered in the night. Crickets chirped, firecrackers whizzed, and someone grilled a late-night burger. Parker remained silent.

Good. Phoebe didn't want to talk about Dustin. She didn't want to think about Corbie's devastation when their relationship imploded.

"Good evening," a soft voice greeted them as they approached Helga's house. Olivia, lurking in the dark.

"Detectives Clerkin and Anderson are here to see you."

Parker muttered a sapien oath so foul Phoebe wanted to laugh. "I know what that means," she told him.

He planted his hand on her lower back to redirect her. "Let's get this over with."

"I'm sorry we don't have coffee to offer you," Selena apologized as Parker and Phoebe entered the house. "How about water? Herbal tea?"

Phoebe considered offering to run across the street and dig Helga's coffee from the freezer. She could borrow Helga's coffeemaker, too.

Selena spied her before she could speak.

"Oh. There you are. The detectives have some questions about what happened tonight."

The detectives sat on folding chairs.

"Good evening, ma'am," Detective Anderson greeted her.

"It was, until someone attacked me," Phoebe retorted. She plopped onto the empty sofa. Parker flopped next to her. "I assume that's why you're here."

"Yes, ma'am."

"I was strolling in the neighborhood when I heard someone following me. He jumped out at me without identifying himself, so I defended myself with my quarterstaff."

"Quarterstaff?" Clerkin asked.

She brandished her weapon.

"Looks like a stick to me."

"One of the many aspects I love about it."

"Someone with a stick accosted Senator Richard Tuttle in the hospital a few days ago." Anderson didn't blink.

Phoebe returned the favor. No sapien cop could outstare a lycan bitch. "Interesting, but not relevant. Turns out the guy stalking me is my ex. From high school. I have a restraining order against him back in Tennessee. I believe I mentioned my problems with him to you the other day."

Anderson blinked. "Holloway claims he works for Senator Tuttle."

"So? Who he works for doesn't give him the right to attack me." No feigning her outrage. "I know politicians believe they are above the law, but I'm not going to meekly resist being assaulted."

"He claims he was on his way to your house to visit you because you're his foster sister."

Parker tensed beside her. She shared a subtle elbow with his ribs, but her discouragement didn't stop him from speaking. "And how would he know where she's staying unless he's stalking her?"

"He couldn't have said, 'Hello, Phoebe?'" she added.

"He insists you planned to meet, then ambushed him."

The saliva in Phoebe's mouth evaporated. "Have I mentioned I have a restraining order on him back in Soddy-Daisy?"

Clerkin repeated the allegation.

"Okay." Her brain raced. "A history lesson for you. Everything I'm about to tell you is verifiable with the Soddy-Daisy authorities. Dustin and I grew up in the same house. We dated in high school. But we fought a lot. We had such a legendary breakup they've written folk songs about it. Ask anyone from our graduating class. I hadn't seen him again until a week or so ago when I ran into him at a local restaurant."

"You guys were at the Steak Out that day, too," Parker interjected.

Phoebe waved him off. "The point is, once he learned I was in Warwick, he started stalking me. How do I go about getting a restraining order in this town? Can I transfer the one I have in Tennessee to Minnesota?"

"You need to register your order of protection here, but if you have a valid one from Tennessee, it's valid anywhere in the U.S.," Anderson explained.

She clenched her quarterstaff hard enough to numb her hand. "In the meantime, you're letting him off, aren't you?"

"You assaulted him. You admit it."

"What does a female have to do to protect herself? Stay locked up in her house on a nice summer night?"

"He attacked her first," Parker said at the same time.

"I didn't know who came at me." Phoebe lowered her chin.

Anderson narrowed his eyes and addressed Parker. "You were with her?"

"We argued." Phoebe thought back to the moment when Parker stalked away from Helga's house and sent Selena and Ethan to babysit her.

"I went for a walk to cool off," Parker admitted. "I was heading home when someone jumped at her."

"You were a witness?" Anderson jotted something in a pocket-sized notebook.

"Yeah. A witness."

"It's true they left the house separately," Selena added. "Parker rushed out, so Ethan and I went to see if Phoebe needed anything."

"Space of my own," Phoebe grumbled, "so I went for a walk, too." Anderson and Clerkin didn't need to know about the phone call to the FBI.

She was tired of defending herself. Tuttle and his minions were the true criminals. "Do you always interrogate victims?"

"This isn't an interrogation." Clerkin sounded weary. "We're trying to piece together what happened. There's a...circumstance because Holloway works for Senator Tuttle."

No shit, Sherlock.

"He'll be out before morning. And because I haven't registered my restraining order here, I'm vulnerable to another attack without consequences." She wanted to howl. She wanted to hit someone in the head with her quarterstaff.

"No. Whether or not there's an order of protection in place, no one has the right to assault anyone else." Anderson's firm tone failed to reassure Phoebe.

Eventually, the detectives left.

"Do you have anything you want to tell us?" Selena asked after several awkward moments.

"I can't think of anything."

"No other surprises?" Ethan's irritation echoed in the nearly empty room.

Why were they so upset? She was the one in danger.

"I don't know why you're surprised. I've been open about my past. Dustin Holloway is my foster brother. He outed me as a werewolf to the man responsible for murdering my family."

"I should have killed him when I had the chance," Parker muttered.

"And I'd be trying to get you out of jail instead of waiting for Dustin to be released," Phoebe snapped. "Did you happen to notice anything else while we were waiting for the cops?"

Parker opened his mouth, shut it, then shook his head.

Phoebe broke the silence. "I thought I smelled what you guys call vampire cooties. But for a change I didn't smell skunk."

Every other individual in the room presented a blank face to her.

"This city, or at least this neighborhood, has to have the highest population of pissed-off skunks in the country. I don't think I've ever been outside at night without smelling one. Except tonight. No skunks. But vampire cooties? Yep."

Ethan seemed perplexed. "I don't follow you."

"Maybe skunks aren't responsible for stinking up the neighborhood."

"Interesting idea," Parker said. "Not that I've been around the neighborhood a lot before now, but Phoebe is right. There's been a lot of skunk lately. But not tonight."

"I didn't smell skunk at Elysian Estates, either." Phoebe slid to the floor. She needed to access something teasing the edges of her brain. "You said you had a vampire problem a few weeks ago?" Her voice rasped against the side of her throat.

"Yes. We battled an infestation," Selena explained. "We killed them all."

"You killed the ones who were here," Phoebe contradicted. "The ones who showed themselves to you. I think they're using skunk juice to mask their odor and to keep the sapiens from investigating their presence too closely."

"Your theory makes no sense," Selena snapped.

"Sure it does." Phoebe refused to let Selena unsettle her. She held her hand out to Parker, who grasped it and pulled her to her feet. "Sapiens purchase skunk juice to use while hunting or trapping to mask their odors."

Selena choked. "Tell me another one."

Phoebe summoned her serenity as she stroked her quarterstaff. "How many sapien hunters or trappers do you know?" When Selena didn't respond, Phoebe continued, "I grew up in a world where every pickup truck has a rifle rack on it. At least half the boys in my high school graduating class were avid hunters. And they bought skunk juice to mask their natural odors."

Parker caught on first. "You think Dustin might have told someone to use skunk juice to hide vampire presence from us?"

Phoebe gifted him with a smile.

"You're implying Tuttle's henchman is in contact with vampires." Selena sounded bewildered.

"He smelled of vampire." Phoebe remained firm. "So did Tuttle when I visited him in the hospital."

"Ash Street between Oak and Hawthorn is protected from vampires," Ethan said.

"I've never smelled skunk spray in Helga's yard. The stink has always come from elsewhere," Phoebe admitted. She stretched to work the kinks from her spine. Rolled her shoulders for the same reason.

Selena pushed off from the doorjamb. "Everything you've mentioned is circumstantial evidence."

"Yes."

"You claim Tuttle is behind the massacre in—" Selena stopped. Looked at Ethan.

"Yeah," Ethan said. "We know Congressman Peters dealt with vampires. We know he placed the honor guard blockading the street."

"Honor guard?" Phoebe asked.

"He's being sarcastic," Parker explained. "Thugs spied on our comings and goings from both ends of this block. Twenty-four-seven."

"If Peters could do it, why not Tuttle?" Ethan's soft voice carried a huge wallop. "Everyone knows what great pals they were. Tuttle is in Minnesota to kickstart the search for the missing Peters brothers."

"His son is engaged to Nola Peters." Phoebe chewed on her lower lip.

"You said Tuttle looked as if he'd been clawed," Parker continued. "Vampires have wicked claws."

"Ain't that the truth," Selena muttered. "If the vampires and Tuttle are on the same side, why would one attack the senator?"

"My theory falls apart there," Phoebe admitted.

"We should sleep on it," Selena declared. "We have a big day tomorrow."

"We do?" Phoebe sounded confused.

"I can't believe you've forgotten," Selena taunted. "Your Aunt Helga is being released from the hospital."

Chapter 20

"I think we've got everything we need." Parker stood, hands on hips, and surveyed the bathroom.

Helga coming home meant one step closer to taking his mate and fleeing this scathole town.

"You've thought of everything," Phoebe assured him. "Except how to keep Selena and Olivia from dosing Helga with their concoctions."

"True. I thought you were raised by a crone. Didn't she practice natural healing?"

"She also had Blue Cross-Blue Shield." Phoebe stood at Parker's side and eyed the bathroom. "Is Helga going to be able to maneuver a walker in here?"

"They've been working with her during physical therapy. They know what they're doing."

Phoebe's scent distracted him, so he turned away and headed for the living room. Helga's recliner waited for her. He'd put fresh batteries in her TV remote. Phoebe replaced all the clutter on the side table next to the chair with tissues and a cordless phone extension. She'd also taped a plastic bag to the table. "Used tissues," she muttered.

Brilliant. He'd have to remember the trick should the need arise again.

"Are you ready to wait hand and foot on her? You're going to need to be available to her twenty-four-seven."

Phoebe shot him a look he couldn't interpret. She nudged the TV remote an inch to the left of the phone. "Selena can spell me. Or Olivia."

"Helga is addicted to television. She kept Ethan and Selena informed. We haven't turned on the TV since we've stayed here. Are you up to listening all day and night?"

Phoebe looked appalled.

Parker couldn't resist digging at her. "What did you think would happen when you agreed to help her rehab at home? Animated woodland animals would come in and take over for you? You're not going to be able to slip off in the middle of the night either."

"You'll be here." Phoebe's voice grew fainter.

"Yes, I'm a medical professional, but females of Helga's age prefer dealing with other females when it comes to the things sapiens consider private. Like bathing. Toileting. You're stuck."

At least caring for Helga meant he couldn't be sent back to Ulvskog until the full moon. The situation also meant he couldn't go home. If forced to suffer, his mate would have to pay the penalty alongside him.

"What about the skunks? Vampires?"

"Helga's house is on the same block as Ethan's. So far the Ash-Oak-Hawthorn triad has held secure."

They were interrupted by the front doorbell. Probably Selena or Old Olivia trying to stick their noses in Phoebe's business.

He yanked open the door and found Detectives Clerkin and Anderson.

Uh-oh.

"Good morning," Parker greeted the visitors. "We're about to head to the hospital. Phoebe's aunt is being released this morning."

"This won't take long," Clerkin said. "Where's your wife?"

Parker sensed Phoebe coming up behind him. "I'm right here."

No way were the cops going to get a direct shot at her. They'd have to go through him first.

"Is there a problem?" Phoebe sounded unconcerned. Her quarterstaff dangled loosely at her side, her grip casual. "Has Dustin confessed to being an asshole?"

"We've confirmed you have an order of protection against him," Clerkin said.

"Did you think she'd lie about something you could easily corroborate?" Parker snapped. He was impressed she'd used sapien laws to protect herself.

"We needed to confirm it." Clerkin sounded disgruntled. "We want to let you know he's out of jail."

"Big surprise. Not. He's one of Tuttle's flunkies." Phoebe sounded matter-of-fact instead of surprised or bitter.

"He claimed you followed him into the Steak Out last week."

"Oh, please. The Steak Out is not the venue Tuttle frequents unless he's on the campaign trail. I don't have insider knowledge of Tuttle's plans. Besides, Parker chose the restaurant, not me."

Senator Tuttle has a contract out on me.

Phoebe's words came back to Parker as clearly as if she'd shrieked them in his ear.

He hired a stupid hit man. I dealt with him.

She'd been so casual, so nonchalant about her accusation, while he'd been ready to follow Tuttle and crew to the parking lot and wreak the havoc only a pissed-off lobo could wreak.

"Thank you for the heads up. Do you think he'll pose any danger to my aunt? She's coming home today."

"He shouldn't. We've notified him we're aware of your order of protection."

"Thank you. I'd hate to have to hurt him again. Although they say the third time is the charm."

Clerkin opened his mouth, then changed his mind. He jerked his head, then retreated, followed by Anderson.

Parker closed the door behind them.

"Did Tuttle hire Holloway as his hitman?" Parker's hoarse voice and grim tone betrayed his agitation.

"Dustin?" She sounded incredulous. "No. Are you ready to leave?"

How could she be so blasé about something like a hitman? His inevitable frustration with her came roaring back. "Why do I get the idea you're leaving out huge chunks? You're not telling me everything."

"I told you Tuttle has a contract out on me. I told you about the hitman. I happened to be smarter than the guy they hired. He ended up in prison." She studied the ceiling as if she'd journaled about the event there. "I think Dustin hired him. I think he found some redneck who wanted to earn some quick cash, not a professional. Dustin tends to be cheap."

"What happened?"

"Oh, there's a list. I caught him tucking a bag filled with rattlesnakes in my laundry basket at the Sudsy-Daisy Coin Laundry." Her voice warbled ever so slightly. "Recorded the whole thing on my phone. And the security cameras at the laundromat caught him, too."

His heart skittered. Rattlesnakes were as deadly to lycans as they were to sapiens. "Let me see the video."

"The cops confiscated my phone."

"Thank goodness you heard the snakes."

"As I said, not the brightest bulb in the chandelier."

"What else?"

Phoebe ticked the items off on her fingers. "He poured ammonia into my half-empty bleach bottle. Hornets—or maybe they were wasps—mysteriously built a nest in the dryer I was using. Goddess, were they pissed when I opened the door. This particular guy focused on the Sudsy-Daisy Coin Laundry."

Parker felt the blood draining from his face with every word she spoke. How could she be so...?

"Why don't you have your FBI buddy run a background check on me? I'm sure the feds have everything. Frankly, I'm surprised you haven't requested a file yet."

Her flippant taunt insulted him. Sort of. In truth, he should have elicited Luke's help to learn more about her.

"I didn't think the Ancient Ones would pair me with a mate who required a background check," he told her. "I still don't think one is necessary."

Her head jerked, as if his admission surprised her.

"Should I be flattered?"

"Honored. I honor you."

"But you don't like me. Except for sex. You do like sticking your penis in me."

The blood rushed back to his head until his cheeks burned from it. "You like the sex, too." Didn't she? She always seemed happy afterward.

One corner of her mouth lifted. "Yes, I like it, too. My body is sore, especially my nipples, but I like the sex too. Do you want to fuck again before we pick up Helga? It might be our last chance to use the kitchen table."

THE HOSPITAL WASN'T READY to discharge Helga. A blizzard of paperwork required shoveling; time needed to be frittered. Helga settled into cranky old lady mode.

Parker, being the most familiar with hospital procedures, got stuck dealing with discharge bureaucracy. Which in any other circumstance would have been fine. He liked the idea of his mate needing him for something other than orgasms on demand. Her mental absence irritated him.

He could predict her mood: she itched to leave Helga's room and confront Tuttle again; she yearned to torture the senator with the knowledge she survived despite his efforts. Not to mention what excuse she could use to escape Helga's room.

"I need to hit the restroom," Phoebe announced.

"You can use Helga's." Parker gestured to the half-open door.

"Oh, not a good idea. This is a small room, if you get my drift. Drift being an important concept."

She believed stinking up the room would bother him. Sometimes females were so silly. Especially since she thought he would fall for something so basic.

He forgot about Helga and her sapien sensibilities.

"Don't be long, and thanks for your consideration," Helga murmured.

Phoebe's lips twitched. "Sometimes these things take time."

Parker wished for something to tie her up so he could toss her in the closet to keep her safe.

Phoebe hefted Jeeves and sauntered out of the room.

Why weren't Selena or Old Olivia around when he needed a female to follow his mate? He'd have to tail her himself. Helga could wait. His mate's safety could not.

"Leave her alone," Helga advised as he headed toward the door. "She's going to be busy enough when I get home. If I ever get released."

"She's in danger. If you understand anything at all about lycan mating, you know I can't let her do whatever it is she thinks she's going to do. My DNA will not allow her to put herself at risk."

Instinct shrieked louder than an ambulance racing toward an Emergency Room entrance. He rushed from the room, following Phoebe's scent through the hall.

He paused at the women's room door. Phoebe left no trace on the push panel.

The elevator doors carried a hint, but faintly, as if many others used the lift since she'd left her scent. She didn't use the elevator to travel to her destination. Yeah, the stairwell door bore a strong scent of Phoebe, and, unlike the elevator, could tell him if she went up or down.

He loped down to the next floor, following her easy trail. He found Phoebe standing in the doorway of an empty room. A freshly made bed betrayed nothing. No sign of occupancy remained.

"They moved him," she said, her voice so low he barely heard her. She lifted her face as if to test the air for Tuttle's scent.

"Maybe he's been released." Parker tapped Phoebe's lower back. "Or he's been moved to an isolation ward. Either way, you can't be seen here, not after everything else."

She turned to face him. "Tuttle is mine. I need to claim his life and soul. They belong to me." Her fierce tone matched the worrisome expression.

"Don't worry. I'm not trying to stop you. I'm only saying here is not the time or place. It's too dangerous."

"I had him. I should have finished him off when I first discovered him here."

"And you'd be in prison right now, which would not be good. Come on. Let's get Helga sprung from this joint."

She shook her head. "I smell him. The stench of corruption and evil is easy to follow. I'm going to track him."

"Not today. Not here." Ancient Ones save me from stubborn females. "If I have to toss you over my shoulder and haul you out of here, you're leaving without laying eyes on the senator."

Chapter 21

Helga weighed nothing in Parker's arms as he carried her into her house. She smelled faintly of hospital disinfectant. Phoebe raced ahead to open the door.

"It's so good to be home." Helga's head lolled against his shoulder. "I can't wait to sleep in my own bed, in the quiet. Who knew hospitals were such noisy places at night?"

"We're glad you're home, too," Parker assured her.

He understood Helga's delight. He wanted to experience a homecoming himself. He counted the days until he could pack Phoebe up and escape to Colorado. Helga at home meant Minnesota could soon be history.

Parker deposited Helga in her recliner.

"We have everything set up for you," Phoebe said. "Parker put new batteries in your remote. All you need is at your fingertips."

Helga closed her eyes. "Oh, this is wonderful."

"Knock, knock, we're coming in."

Old Olivia and Selena arrived. Selena carried a casserole. "I made your favorite hot dish."

The old woman needed something to clog her arteries.

Parker finished his part in Helga's homecoming. Time to escape all the female fussing. Maybe Ethan would be willing to let him vent. Phoebe's disregard for her own safety made Parker crazy. Her similarity to Fleur, convinced of her own invincibility, worried him.

Parker found Ethan in his backyard, cutting up the debris of the mulberry tree growing in the far corner. A lightning strike had split the tree in half, the falling branches killing Britt's father in a freak accident.

The smells of fresh cut wood and male exertion perfumed the air.

"Need some help?" Parker wouldn't mind physical labor, as long as he didn't have to wield a hammer for Restin.

"Sure. We're going to take a load of firewood to Ulvskog for them to use this winter."

"No firepit here?"

Ethan studied his parcel of land. He also owned the empty lot next door. The Varulv dug it up in anticipation of Selena and Britt planting herbs. Too late for gardening now.

"A fire pit isn't a bad idea."

"I'm good for something." Parker couldn't hide his bitterness.

"Let me guess. Female trouble?" Ethan asked.

"Am I that obvious?"

"Mating is an adjustment."

Parker narrowed his eyes, searching for a smirk or any other sign of condescension.

"I get it," Ethan commiserated. "I've suffered my share."

"Phoebe went looking for Tuttle at the hospital today," Parker blurted. "He's been moved or released, thank the Ancient Ones. Phoebe is so intent on her revenge she's not being cautious."

"She didn't grow up in a pack." Ethan hefted the ax then sank the blade into a log. Steel thunked against wood. "Maybe she never learned the subtleties of the hunt."

Since Ethan's latent alpha blood had surfaced, on some levels his insights were better than the ones Tokarz shared.

"She'd better learn quick," Parker muttered.

"Don't get your hackles up, but I asked Luke to run a background check on Phoebe after hearing her version of her relationship with Dustin Holloway." Ethan swung the ax again.

Relief and anger battled as Parker tried to decide how he should react to Ethan's interference. He opted for the former. "I planned to ask if you would. Phoebe's idea." He braced himself for bad news.

Ethan left the ax blade embedded in the log and wiped his forehead with a bandana. Dark splotches circled his armpits. "She's pissed off somebody but good. She could claim she came to Minnesota to escape the attempts on her life."

The world turned red as rage filmed Parker's vision. His head throbbed. "She told me about the rattlesnakes in the laundromat—"

"Maybe you should have a go with the ax," Ethan interrupted.

Parker straightened and squared his shoulders. "I am not an omega."

"But you are a mate."

Whether or not he wanted to be.

He jerked the ax from the log. Lifted it above his head. The blade whooshed as he drove it down. The wood split into ragged edged chunks. "Tell me."

"After the arrest of laundromat guy, her accidents became more sophisticated. Deadlier."

A familiar tickle, a twinge he usually experienced only on the full moon, warned him his body wanted to shift. "How so?" His voice scraped, the emerging sounds closer to howls than words.

"Someone tried to shove her under a bus. Eyewitnesses said they'd never seen anyone move as fast as she did to avoid being struck."

Parker hefted the ax again. "I thought you said more sophisticated."

Whack!

"How about a damaged gas line into her apartment? Fortunately, she smelled it before she went in. The gas company claims if she'd opened the door and flipped the light switch, the whole building would have gone up."

"Good to know her lycan senses are up to par." Parker tried to keep his tone light, but his heavy heart weighed down everything. The ax handle grew slippery in his hands. He left the blade buried in the log and wiped his palms on his jeans. "The killer seems ignorant of basic lycan realities,"

Ethan agreed. "Like how we're immune to most sapien diseases."

Scat. Ethan told him more sophisticated, but Parker never imagined…"What was she exposed to?"

"Don't know. Classified information. Luke doesn't have clearance to access that particular file."

Parker seized on the excuse to take his mind off everything Phoebe neglected to tell him. "Since when has lack of clearance prevented Luke from accessing anything he wants?"

"Since cleaning up his act when he mated with Abigail."

"He must have some clue."

Ethan hesitated. "He did mention a break in at an Army testing facility in Utah."

Oh, scat. "What's missing?" Anthrax? Sarin? Ebola?

"Luke couldn't find out."

Parker's stomach roiled, then tried to escape the rest of his body through his mouth. Breakfast tasted a lot sourer coming up than going down.

"At least you missed the ax and the log," Ethan commented when Parker finished puking. "Good aim."

Parker wiped his mouth with the back of his hand. "You know what they keep in government testing facilities."

"I don't know anything, but I'm good at guessing. Phoebe's lucky she's naturally suspicious."

"Lucky?"

Ethan's lips thinned. "You have every right to be upset. I'm guessing the only reason no one has come after her in Minnesota is because no one knew where she's staying."

"Until we ran into them at the restaurant."

Ethan hadn't finished. "There's one more thing."

Parker braced himself. How could the news be any worse?

"Someone put a flag on Phoebe's file."

"I don't know what a flag means." But he did.

"Clerkin and Anderson tripped it when they dug into her background simultaneously to Luke's inquiry. You need to get her away from Warwick."

"I've been trying since the night I met her."

"They'll track you to Loup Garou."

Clearly Ethan believed Parker needed to rethink his plan. "You're going to hate this, but I think you should hide her in Gambayan."

If he hadn't emptied his stomach a minute ago, Parker would have puked again. "You mean Ulvskog."

"No, I mean Gambayan. The old town is protected by magic."

"From vampires," Parker pointed out.

"I don't know if the magic is limited. Jakob told me he and Addy hid there when the gunmen came to town."

Ethan made the massacre sound like a spaghetti western. Except the spilled blood hadn't been prop blood. The victims couldn't get up and collect a paycheck in the aftermath.

"The Peters family is gone," Ethan continued. "I doubt anyone else even knows about Ulvskog and the old town."

"Except the gunmen themselves. And Nola Peters—who isn't gone—is engaged to Tuttle Junior. Who knows what she knows or how deep into her family's affairs she is."

Parker retrieved the ax. No matter how much she frustrated him, Phoebe was his mate. His maybe pregnant mate.

He raised the ax above his head. *Whoosh. Thunk.*

The Ancient Ones decreed Phoebe belonged to him; DNA bound him to protect her above all else.

PHOEBE SUPPRESSED A YAWN. She'd been trapped with Helga for only an hour and already itched to follow Selena and Olivia out the door. Phoebe had visited the old crone in the hospital with minimal problems; watching Helga channel surf in the discomfort of the overstuffed, overheated parlor fractured Phoebe's patience. For starters, Helga turned up the audio so loud Phoebe expected the windows to begin rattling any second.

She couldn't do this. Helga might be a crone like Corbie, but Corbie would have used the enforced chair time to read or knit or quilt. The TV wouldn't be blasting nonstop. Corbie preferred listening to books on tape or podcasts while she plied her needles. Once she'd discovered podcasts, she'd been as happy as a pig in its wallow.

Corbie knew how much Phoebe loathed TV, especially the news.

Maybe Phoebe could convince Helga leisure time meant more than the peccadilloes of people who ought to know better.

"I'm going out back to meditate," Phoebe shouted over a female crying in a high-pitched tone only dogs would appreciate.

Helga, bless her heart, dozed.

Phoebe crept from the sofa to Helga's chair. Helga's limp hand clutched the remote. Phoebe tried to remove it. Helga twitched, as if sensing someone hovering. Her eyes opened, a vivid blue in her pale face.

"What?" Drool trickled from the corner of her mouth, using her wrinkles as channels in which to flow.

Phoebe pulled a tissue from the box on the side table, then dabbed at the saliva.

"What? What are you doing?" Helga slapped at Phoebe's hand.

"Keeping an eye on you."

"I can blow my own nose." Helga channeled cranky old lady.

"Of course, you can." Phoebe returned to the sofa.

"What time is it?" Helga squinted at the television screen. "Why is this garbage on? It's time for the news."

The TV channel abruptly changed. Bold bright graphics zoomed along the bottom of the screen. A blond female's overly made-up face filled the rest. Helga owned a huge screen. "Top local headlines," the blonde chirped.

Phoebe ignored the temptation to tune out the local news. Reports on Tuttle's condition might be televised because he stayed in the area.

Mind-numbing trivial events littered the airwaves. Phoebe didn't care about the ongoing debate centered on whether or not to cancel the local lutefisk festival. Gardening tips bored her. The story about the ongoing investigation regarding the late Congressman Bryant Peters' missing sons interested her only because Parker and the others kept referring to Liam and Connor. Sometimes, they even alluded to helping the Peters brothers vanish. Their disappearances were the alleged reason Senator Tuttle traveled to Minnesota.

Something flickered at the edge of her vision. She seized her quarterstaff and leapt to her feet, ready to defend Helga and herself. Her heart continued to race for a few seconds after she recognized Parker. The loud TV muffled his return. She lowered the weapon to her side.

Parker raised his eyebrows.

Phoebe lifted a shoulder, then pointed at Helga, who once more dozed.

"How can she sleep through this racket?" Parker asked.

Phoebe read his lips more than heard him.

"We need to talk. Let's go outside," he suggested.

Phoebe didn't bother with an acknowledgement but turned and fled the living room.

Even the backyard didn't escape Helga's television.

Phoebe stuck her pinky fingers in her ears to pop them. "Goddess, it's a miracle Helga isn't deaf."

"Maybe she's trying to stay awake," Parker offered.

"The crap on TV is enough to put a body permanently to sleep."

Parker should have responded. He did not. Her sense of humor probably continued to elude him. She no longer hoped he'd get one himself. He needed to stop looking at her as if she'd sprouted extra heads whenever she made a joke.

"Ethan asked Luke to run a background check on you."

Shit. "Luke? The FBI drummer?" Phoebe lunged at a fly with her quarterstaff. She needed to stretch her muscles.

"Something similar. Do you have anything else you want to tell me, or should I go with the second or thirdhand report?"

Parker had no right to sound peeved.

"I didn't want you to worry." She spoke only the truth. "I don't want you to think I'm weak and can't take care of myself. We met in less than ideal circumstances. I really am capable."

Parker scrubbed his face with his palms. "Ancient Ones, Phoebe, someone is trying to kill you."

"No shit, Sherlock," she snapped. "I am not some mindless, helpless female. I survived a massacre when I was eight years old and staying alive for the past fifteen years hasn't been pure luck."

Her shouts lingered in the air after leaving her mouth. Another insect with a death wish buzzed by her. She took it out with her quarterstaff. Overkill, yes, but kill just the same. Better the bug than her mate. For now.

"Yes," he said after a moment. "Yes. You're right. But you still should have told me, so I can be aware, too. You keep forgetting you're not alone anymore. You and I are supposed to be a team. We can work together to make sure Tuttle doesn't get you."

She froze. His conciliatory tone stunned her.

"How did the feds get involved?"

Phoebe loosened her grip on her quarterstaff. Her voice cracked when she replied. "When I got the mysterious package in the mail. Using the postal service to kill someone is a federal crime."

"Why did you suspect the package was . . . toxic?"

"I didn't," she admitted, "but I hadn't ordered anything so receiving a package after everything else, well, I figured better safe than sorry."

She braced herself, then looked Parker square in the eye. "The police filed a report when someone pushed me in front of a bus. The whole fiasco at the Sudsy-Daisy was on record, too. The power company reported the tampered gas line to my apartment. Too many coincidences for the feds. I'd already filed for the restraining order on Dustin. Adding everything up made people twitchy."

"Twitchy?" he echoed. He came at her so quickly she didn't have time to react.

The quarterstaff dropped from her fingers as he enveloped her in a hug so intense, he squeezed the breath from her lungs. His body temperature burned hotter than when he climaxed during sex.

Sex? Something stirred low in her belly. She battled the urge to tear off her clothes and assume the position. Fortunately, his fierce embrace prevented her from moving. Helga's backyard in broad daylight didn't provide enough privacy to indulge in what her body craved. What his body craved, too, judging by the way his erection pressed into her abdomen. By the way he seemed to vibrate against her.

Parker released her. She felt as if she'd lost a limb or a vital organ. The expression on his face betrayed his dazed state of mind.

She reached for his hand to lead him into the house, where they could barricade themselves in their bedroom and indulge her lust, but at the same time, he dug into his pocket and pulled out his phone.

Oh. The phone vibrated, not Parker.

She turned away so he couldn't see her disappointment.

"What?" he snarled.

Everything else would always come before her. Being mated changed nothing. Parker spoke good words, but his actions were mute.

"What?" Anger morphed to incredulousness. "When?"

Phoebe retrieved her quarterstaff from the ground. When she straightened, Parker gestured for her to join him

"We're stuck here for the time being," he said. "A previous commitment."

Phoebe started toward the house, but Parker grabbed her arm to stop her.

"I'm not letting her out of my sight," he assured the person on the other end. "Tomorrow. Right. We'll figure it out."

He disconnected. "The scat followed you to Minnesota."

"Dustin and the senator? Guess what? I'm shocked, Doc." She yanked her arm from his grasp as the sexy mood fled.

"Oh, not old scat. New scat. In the form of a guy named Mitchell Jasper." Parker sounded grim.

"A famous paid assassin?" Wouldn't more shit be just her luck.

"If only." Grim and bitter. "Then I'd have a good excuse to kill him. But killing the lycanthrope liaison to the government could get tricky."

Chapter 22

PARKER DIDN'T KNOW WHOSE brilliant idea sicced Mitchell Jasper, government stooge, on the Minnesota lycans, but that individual should be tortured for a long, long time. They could start by snapping off his fingers, one joint at a time.

Parker rarely dealt directly with the man. Alphas claimed that privilege. He'd interacted once or twice. Ethan had been deployed to Minnesota on a fool's errand because Jasper convinced Tokarz they could preserve the service for sanctuary treaties by negotiating with prominent politicians, making Jasper indirectly responsible for Parker being stuck there.

The only halfway decent thing to come of Parker's exile was mating with Phoebe, and now Jasper was sticking his nose in that. Tokarz ordered Parker to meet with the sapien goon. Parker couldn't pretend they had a bad phone connection.

"What are you talking about?" Phoebe's eyebrows met over her nose as she scowled at him.

"Tokarz wanted to let me know the government's liaison for lycans is on his way to meet with us."

"Tokarz is your alpha, not mine."

"You are Loup Garou now," Parker reminded her as gently as he could.

"Is Selena Varulv or Limmikin? Doesn't matter. I'm Limmikin. There aren't enough Limmikin left for me to abandon."

A heritage you know nothing about.

The topic was too trivial to debate with Jasper about to descend on them. "You're right."

His phone vibrated in his hand. Ethan, texting him. *Get over here and bring your female.*

He texted back. *Can't leave Helga.*

"We're about to have company," he warned Phoebe. He extended his hand. "Shall we go inside to greet them?"

Phoebe stared at his hand as if she'd never seen one before. She touched her palm to his. He closed his fingers.

Holding her hand felt...nice.

Two minutes later, he opened the front door to Ethan and Selena. "Did you call Tokarz?" he snapped at Ethan.

"Ancient Ones and Creator, no," Ethan snarled. "You mean you didn't call him?"

"Luke is going to die," Parker muttered.

"I'll help." Ethan strode past Parker to the television set and turned it off.

"Hey!" Helga woke from her drowse to protest. She aimed her remote control at the screen.

Selena snatched it from her. "You can have it back in a minute."

"This is my house," Helga reminded them.

"So it is. But your caretakers need to take a meeting, and since you can't be left alone, you're going to have to deal with no TV for a few minutes." Selena spoke firmly. "Unless you turn down the volume. We can meet in the kitchen if you don't turn up the sound to the rattle-the-windows setting."

"Save me from overly sensitive werewolf ears." Maybe Helga thought they couldn't hear her mutter, but Parker caught every word.

Selena pointed the remote at the TV, which blared to life, then muted the volume and turned on the closed captioning. "There you go."

"Hmph," was Helga's only response.

The four lycans went to the kitchen, but no one sat at the table. Parker and Phoebe leaned against the counter while Ethan and Selena resumed their habitual poses against the doorjamb.

"You didn't call Tokarz?" Ethan asked.

Parker resented Ethan not accepting his word the first time. "I told you. No. If you didn't rat me out, then Luke must have. Unless Dakota or Restin are lurking around."

"I don't know what Dakota is up to but Restin wouldn't consult Tokarz."

True.

"Dakota and Britt are painting their living room," Selena added. "Britt bored me with paint samples for two hours yesterday."

As if Parker gave a vampire's fart about Britt's activities.

"Luke," Ethan bit out. "I should have known he'd report back to Tokarz. He's gotten positively tame since mating."

Ethan's assessment of Luke's transformation was pathetically true. When a lycan mated with a sapien the lycan lost his edge. Thank the Ancient Ones both he and Ethan could indulge in their true natures because their mates could handle it.

He grasped Phoebe's hand again. Their fingers twined.

She'd never try to domesticate him.

"Did Tokarz mention why Jasper is heading our way?" he asked.

Ethan waved off the question. "I guess the government doesn't like the way I've handled the mission with Congressman Peters."

As if Ethan were to blame for the congressman's suicide. Besides, if Peters hadn't raped Selena and been threatened by his secret life as a sex pervert being exposed, he wouldn't have been guilty or scared enough to kill himself.

"What does Peters have to do with me?"

"Not Peters in your case. Tuttle."

Scat. "Tuttle? I've never met the man." Ethan focused on Phoebe, as did Selena.

Parker turned to see how Phoebe reacted to the scrutiny.

She stared at Selena and Ethan, her lips barely curved in a smile. "Your Jasper has nothing to do with me."

"Yeah, he does," Ethan contradicted. "He's in charge of the treaties between the packs and the government."

"I'm Limmikin. I am bound by no treaty. Ask your grandfather if you need to be reminded." Her hard tone rivaled the concrete steps leading to the back yard.

Ethan crossed his arms over his chest.

Parker squeezed Phoebe's hand. "She has a point." He might not agree with her, but she claimed nothing invalid.

"But I am bound. So is Parker, so we have to listen to what he has to say."

Phoebe's chin lowered. "You do. I don't. The only reason I'm in Minnesota is to—"

Helga's television blared to life, effectively drowning out Phoebe's statement.

"She's not deaf," Selena mouthed. "I don't get this new obsession with cranking the audio. She never played her TV this loud in the hospital."

Phoebe headed toward the living room. She needed to pass through the portal of Selena and Ethan, but neither one tried to stop her. What did Phoebe think she would do? Take the remote away from an old lady who couldn't defend herself?

Parker followed. He found Phoebe and Helga playing tug of war with the remote. "Factotum," Helga said, the word barely discernable above the booming TV.

"Why do you keep saying that?" Phoebe asked.

Parker recalled where he'd heard the word before.

Factotum described the sapiens who assisted vampires.

"Why are you worried about factotums?" he asked Helga.

Her sharp blue eyes fixed on him. "The vampires can't come onto this block because it's protected by strong magic. But their factotum can. Do."

"How do you know?" Selena followed Parker.

"How do you not know?" Helga countered. "They still don't have what they want."

"Do they want Senator Tuttle?" Phoebe asked.

"What?" Selena sounded incredulous. "Tuttle doesn't frequent this neighborhood."

Or did he? Parker's gaze met Phoebe's. No, the senator himself wouldn't go slumming, but if anyone knew how well Tuttle could use flunkies, Parker would put Phoebe at the top of the list.

Tuttle used flunkies to go after Phoebe in Tennessee. Flunkies were still stalking Phoebe. Who then, hunted the senator?

The wounds Phoebe described on Tuttle matched his experience treating clawed-by-vampire victims.

Why would vampires go after Tuttle?

Phoebe's thoughts must have followed the same labyrinth. "I'm going back to Elysian Estates," she said in the quiet following her silencing Helga's TV. "Tonight. The answers must be there, at the Peters' house."

No! Parker wanted to howl from the rooftop, the treetops, the tops of the clouds scudding across the sky. He didn't want her trying to shift. If she were pregnant, he couldn't smell it—stupid pervasive skunk juice—but he didn't want her to risk harming the possible baby by attempting to change. Shifting constituted the only way she could get into Elysian Estates.

He shot a silent plea at Selena, who pretended not to know what he wanted her to do. Surely Ethan or Old Olivia shared Phoebe's condition with her.

Someone leaned on the doorbell, interrupting his thoughts. After a flurry of pointed looks and shrugs, Selena and Ethan took up their standard stances at the door. Phoebe dropped the remote on the side table next to Helga, then stood behind Parker, Jeeves clutched in both hands.

Parker peered through the peephole before opening the door. "I thought you two were painting your apartment today."

Britt stomped into the house, followed by Dakota. "What is going on?" Britt's hostile tone heated the air.

"Why don't you tell us why you came storming in here?" Selena's cool rebuttal contrasted Britt's anger.

"Clerkin and Anderson and Curtis DiNardo," Britt snapped.

"You're the one who went to high school with them," Selena reminded her.

"Curtis is—"

Helga's TV blasted away the rest of Britt's words.

Ethan marched over to Helga and snatched the remote from her hand. After lowering the volume, he pried off the back and removed the batteries.

"You're mean to an old lady," Helga whined. "Or do you want the factotum to know what you're saying?"

HELGA'S WORDS CLICKED WITH Phoebe. "White noise. Helga has been providing us with white noise."

Parker's jaw dropped. Selena's eyes popped as wide as Parker's gaping mouth.

Phoebe knelt next to Helga's chair. "How do you know about the factotum?" She kept her voice low.

"You know a crone doesn't reveal her secrets."

Corbie would have told Phoebe the same thing. She patted Helga's thigh, then stood. "I believe her."

"Curtis DiNardo paid you a visit?" Selena asked Britt. She held herself so rigidly, Phoebe though she might snap.

"No. But Tom Anderson and Mickey Clerkin did." Britt hadn't cooled off at all.

"You're a person of interest in Connor Peters' disappearance," Selena reminded her.

"They didn't question me about Connor. Curtis's Uncle Tony was with them. You know, handyman to the Peters dynasty. Nobody has seen Curtis since Liam Peters vanished." Britt stared hard at Selena and Ethan.

Parker's palm on her lower back warned Phoebe to say nothing.

"Maybe they went fishing," Parker offered. "I've never seen so many avid fishermen as I have since coming to Warwick."

Britt narrowed her eyes at Parker, who subtly shook his head.

Everyone here knew something Phoebe didn't. If she had to guess, she'd say this Curtis character's vanishing act and the missing Peters brothers were connected.

"You can't tell what you don't know," Selena pointed out.

"Exactly what I've told them. Repeatedly." Britt spoke through clenched teeth.

What did Britt expect Selena and the others to do? Confess?

Phoebe hoped this Curtis guy died screaming.

"I vaguely remember him," Selena admitted. "He showed up to replace the windows in the house I rented when I met Ethan. A few fries short of a Kiddie Kafeteria."

Again, Phoebe sensed a subtext she couldn't read. If Parker ever planned on getting in her pants again, he needed to dish.

"For all I know, Curtis ran off to escape Uncle Tony, who is one scary dude." Britt shuddered. "Have you ever met him?"

"Once. When I rented the house on Pine from him."

"Didn't Curtis spend time in prison?" Parker's innocent tone didn't fool Phoebe for a second. "Maybe he ran off to start over. It happens."

"Uncle Tony is worried," Britt repeated. "I would not want to have him worried about me."

"Worrying about you is my responsibility." Dakota draped an arm across her shoulders.

"Didn't you say this Tony DiNardo works for the Peters?" Phoebe asked.

"Yeah."

Something wanted to click for Phoebe, but there were too many brainwaves disrupting hers. She needed to return to Elysian Estates.

"Can I have my batteries back?" Helga demanded. "It's time for *Wheel of Fortune* and *Jeopardy,* then the news. Don't you want to hear the news?"

Chapter 23

Phoebe dragged Parker outside after begging Olivia to stay with Helga for an hour. She needed to get away from the chaos in the house on Ash or go mad.

"I'm going," she told her mate when he balked. "You can come with me, or I can go by myself, but I am leaving this house for some fresh air, peace, and quiet. Unless you tie me up and toss me into a closet. Sounds like a sex game we can play when we get back."

The priceless expression on Parker's face amused her.

But he accompanied her into the night.

She paused on the corner of Ash and Oak to test the air. Marshmallows burned on a campfire; someone nearby enjoyed a vanilla cigar; a distant rainstorm headed toward them; the inevitable skunk. No vampire stink.

"Do you smell vampire?" Parker used a low rumble for his question.

"Skunk."

"Do we dare venture off the block?"

Phoebe raised her quarterstaff.

"Then let's go." Parker cupped her elbow and steered her toward Mooney's Diner.

No one tailed them. She figured Parker listened to the night as intently as she did. Movement and the cooler air banished the lethargy caused by Helga's stuffy house. The clutter prevented air from circulating. Phoebe ought to do the crone a favor and clear out the obstacles to make maneuvering a wheelchair and walker easier.

"We need to go to Elysian Estates." She timed her words with their footfalls.

"No. Not until after we meet with Jasper."

Always an obstruction in the world according to Parker.

"What does he have to do with anything?"

"He's the one who will have our backs if the situation here turns to scat."

A gloomy obstruction.

"He won't have my back. He doesn't even know about me."

"Oh, I'll bet he knows more than even Luke could uncover about you."

"Sounds like a jolly guy." Phoebe scanned a looming shadow and concluded the wind in the tree created the movement she sensed. "We can play *Jeopardy* with him. I'll take useless crap about Phoebe the Foundling for six hundred. He'll win, and we can all whine about rigged games."

Parker barked a laugh.

"I made you laugh?" Her shock colored her voice.

"I do have a sense of humor and sometimes you're amusing."

"I'm amusing all the time, and we don't define humor the same way."

She paused, yanking on his hand to stop him. She jerked her head toward the shadows, which might have changed shape during their conversation.

Parker twitched his head toward the street.

Maybe they were getting in sync with each other.

Parker steered her across the street. If something lurked in the shadows, waiting for them, they'd thwarted it.

Sapiens never understood how lycan senses worked. Corbie never grasped how Phoebe could hear conversations without eavesdropping. Could locate missing items without searching. Could run fast enough to avoid being flattened by a bus or could smell a gas leak seeping beneath an ill-fitting door.

She didn't hear a heartbeat or the soft bellow of lungs. Maybe nothing skulked in the shadows but taking chances had been scared out of her. Parker seemed to agree.

Once they gained the other side, his hand left her back and found her elbow again, as if he couldn't bear not to touch her. A few days ago, his need for constant contact might have irritated her. Tonight, she welcomed his attention.

With Parker now knowing everything, he might stop threatening to lock her away in some gilded tower as if she were too precious for the big bad world. Maybe he even respected her.

"What do you think you saw?" Parker steered her around a corner onto an unfamiliar street.

"No idea, but my hackles reacted to the shadow. I trust my hackles."

"You have amazing hackles. I admire them greatly."

She giggled. Phoebe couldn't remember the last time she'd giggled. "You made a joke, Doc. I'm impressed. Maybe I'll let you play with my hackles later."

"I would love to play with your hackles." His low, throaty voice sounded sexy in the night.

Desire stabbed her female bits. "Maybe you could show me your hackles later," she suggested.

"How much further are we going?"

She loved his impatience. "Until we get back to Helga's. Do you have your own place in Loup Garou?"

She knew nothing about him. What a self-absorbed she- wolf she'd been.

"Yeah. Private. My folks live a couple miles down the mountain."

"No siblings?"

He didn't answer, and she remembered what he'd told her about his younger sister who died in an accident when they were children. "I'm sorry," she apologized. "I didn't mean to bring up bad memories."

The playfulness left his voice. "It's okay. You remind me of my sister. A lot. We were twins. She always thought she knew better than anyone. Stubbornness killed her."

"I'm not your sister."

"I know that. You only inspire the same frustrations. But I have no other siblings. For some reason, the Loup Garou don't have big families. The number of offspring born each year is shrinking. And there has been a spate of mixed matings, which concerns some of the elders."

Phoebe lifted her face to the stars salting the night sky. A breeze toyed with the wisps of hair surrounding her face. "If the matings weren't meant to be, they wouldn't happen. The Goddess doesn't make errors."

"I know. But I'm still glad you're lycan. I tend to forget your heritage. Everyone I hang out with in Loup Garou is mated to a sapien, so the females need to be coddled."

Phoebe stopped. She turned to look at him. The light from the streetlights turned his complexion slightly orange. "That explains a lot."

"I only realized it myself." His smoky quartz eyes glittered brighter than the stars. "Today, while Ethan filled me in on your FBI file."

She really had an FBI file? She'd joked with Parker about having one, but—

All these years she thought she'd been living off the grid, and the FBI compiled a file on her. *Shit.*

"I never meant to insult you," he continued.

"I know that now."

"If you weren't a capable lycan, despite your upbringing, you would be dead."

She hated thinking about how differently her many escapes could have turned out. Sometimes the memories crept into her dreams. Sometimes, she opened the mystery package and...woke up. No one ever told her what the package contained, but the government suits and uniforms thrust her into isolation for fourteen days. Did Parker know about the quarantine?

No moping. Refusing to dwell was how she'd managed so far. She'd work toward getting to the root of her troubles and eliminating it or would die trying. "So, do you want to shift and head over to Elysian Estates?"

"No!" The refusal exploded from his mouth.

Needing a good reason to explain rebuffing her suggestion, Parker suppressed a guilty ping. He ought to explain she was either in heat or gestating. Growing up, isolated from a pack, excused her ignorance.

"There are protocols about shifting," he lied.

If he told her she might be pregnant, maybe she would stop putting herself in danger. Even capable she-wolves were mortal. His DNA demanded he keep her safe. He ought to tell her. He had no reason not to instruct her on lycan procreation.

The words couldn't leave his mouth. Scathole behavior, no question. He assumed the Ancient Ones contemplated their revenge on him. He still couldn't tell her.

"Protocols? Such as?" Phoebe prompted.

Oh, Ancient Ones, his silence would ruin their tentative compatibility. They'd been getting along. They'd found common ground besides sex.

His secret surpassed hers because his involved her. If Tokarz were around, he'd probably cuff Parker upside the head the way they'd all smacked Luke around before he'd turned respectable.

"We rarely shift at will." He nudged her forward. Her slender spine reinforced his sense of her fragility.

"Why ever not, when we can?"

"Because shifting depletes our energy reserves." True. "If we use up all our energy, we might not be able to shift when we need to."

"Sounds like a load of crap to me."

"Think about it," he insisted. "Lycans have lunar batteries. A few weeks ago Britt reminded us lunar light is nothing more than reflected solar light, so it's weaker."

Phoebe stopped again and glared at him. "Load of crap," she repeated. "What about the full moon? We can't stop from shifting then."

"Because lunar power is strongest on the full moon."

He knew his theory made sense, even if he did invent it as he spoke.

"You know gestating females can't shift, right?" He approached the topic cautiously, afraid to give too much away. "Because they need their energy to grow the baby."

She stiffened, then retreated several inches. "You're lying."

"You should talk to Selena and Old Olivia. They can tell you more about the perils of female shifting. Gestating is outside my expertise."

He needed to elicit the other females' support before Phoebe spoke to them.

Old Olivia and Helga were drinking tea in front of the TV when Parker and Phoebe returned. Parker explained his dilemma to Old Olivia while Phoebe used the bathroom.

The flushing toilet started a countdown.

Old Olivia placed her teacup firmly on the coffee table.

"She's not pregnant. You've got a nose."

"I don't see how that's possible. I'm on her constantly since you told me she's in heat." Parker opened a window. The room desperately needed fresh air.

"She is." Old Olivia didn't expound because Phoebe rejoined them. She looked at Old Olivia, him, then Helga. "What's going on?"

"I'm trying to listen to the news, but these two are chattering up a storm," Helga groused. "And close the window. I'm not paying to heat the outdoors. I'm not going to get any peace and quiet while I recover, am I?"

Parker closed the window.

"Probably not." Old Olivia sounded positively cheerful. She picked up her tea and sipped. "There's a lot going on. If you didn't want to be involved, you shouldn't have bought a house on this block."

"I lived here first." Helga plucked at the blanket covering her legs.

"True, but you had to know the magic would draw others."

"The people across the street before Selena and Ethan didn't last long. Maybe you won't either. We never experienced a vampires or factotum problem until werewolves moved in."

Tea blew out Old Olivia's nose. "There is no we. There's only you, and you are a survivor. You know the lycan will protect you. You helped us with the vampires a few weeks ago. We won't forget the favor. Aren't we taking care of you now?"

"Are you saying I'm a factotum to werewolves? Don't insult me."

Helga's whining grated on Parker's nerves.

"Maybe Parker knows some widower back in Loup Garou he could fix you up with." Old Olivia teased relentlessly. "Then you would be part of his pack."

Parker hoped Old Olivia merely teased.

Helga slammed her teacup onto the side table. "As if I would ever get married again. It took me too long to get rid of the first one. My daughter's father."

Old Olivia sobered. "The daughter Congressman Peters fucked to death."

"Yes." Helga pointed her remote at the television. The sound blasted into the room. Phoebe and Old Olivia covered their ears.

"The Peters family are all evil. Going way back, ever since I can remember." Helga addressed the TV.

Hatch, Parker recalled, claimed the same thing.

"As long as even one is alive, anyone who isn't a white Christian sapien is in danger. Including everyone in this room." Helga's bright blue gaze landed on each of them. "So I guess I am a factotum to a werewolf pack. I'll do anything to rid the world of the Peters dynasty."

Phoebe fidgeted throughout the exchange. "I don't care about the Peters," she blurted. "They were only taking orders from Tuttle."

"Then why did Tuttle end up in the hospital while visiting the Peters?"

"Nola Peters is engaged to Junior Tuttle," Phoebe reminded them. "She's one of Helga's factotum."

Helga rolled her eyes. "The old man is still alive. Bryant's father. William."

"Hatch says he's been looking for the old man's obit ever since Luke showed him the Internet." Parker sensed they were missing something else. Something important.

"You're missing the point," Phoebe insisted. "Tuttle is the true villain."

"Tuttle never fucked my daughter." Helga shuddered. "Why is it so cold in here? Did you close the window?"

Sweat trickled down the sides of Parker's face. Beads of perspiration dotted Phoebe's forehead and nose. Even Old Olivia appeared to be wilting. Helga hunched under a pile of blankets. "Yes, I closed the window."

"I want to go to bed."

The night was early by lycan standards, but Parker lived to serve, thanks to Phoebe's promise to the crone.

Phoebe knelt at Helga's side. "Do you want Parker to carry you or do you want to try what they taught you in the hospital?"

"Parker can be my backup plan. I don't want to depend on anyone."

"WHAT ARE YOU UP to?" Phoebe stretched out next to Parker on their bed, aiming for maximum exposure of her naked body to the night air sifting through the screen in their wide-open bedroom window. Parker closed the heat register when they'd fled to their room shortly after settling Helga for the night.

"Easier to control the climate in our room than the entire house," he'd muttered.

Phoebe indulged in a cold shower.

Now they were trying to sleep in a house prepared for the winter solstice above the Arctic Circle when in fact they were wasting a lovely late August evening.

"What makes you think I'm up to anything?"

"Your penis prodding my hindquarters?"

"Oh. That." He sounded amused.

"Is there something else?"

"Nope." His answer came too quickly. "Unless this isn't enough for you."

"It's perfect for me, and you know it. Let's go outside and test its perfection."

"I prefer a bed to Helga's lumpy lawn. Now, when I get you home, I have a few spots on the mountain in mind for us to christen."

She opened her thighs. Parker pushed into her. He grasped her hip with one hand, while the other toyed with a nipple.

After Dustin's fumbling attempts to cop a feel, who knew how much she'd enjoy having her breasts touched by the right male?

A few thrusts later she climaxed. Parker followed suit.

"What were you and Olivia discussing when I went to the bathroom?" she asked. Post coital languor seeped into her every pore.

"I asked her to explain shifting protocols to you, female to female." He didn't hesitate. Didn't indicate in any way he might be lying. "I know your foster mother did the best she could by you, but there are lycan secrets I'm sure your granny didn't divulge, even to her best friend."

"Thank you."

Something wonderful had happened in her relationship with Parker. She caught glimpses of what a good mating might be. Knowing what could await her after she finished with Tuttle urged her to approach her task with more caution. "Do you want offspring?"

She forced out the question, battling her shyness and insecurity. "I don't even know my status. Maybe I'm an omega female."

Even she understood the lowest of the low.

"Why do you ask?" His voice held an edge.

"You mentioned gestating females and shifting earlier."

"Oh." His hand slid off her breast, where it had created a puddle of perspiration. "Yes. I want offspring more than anything, even more than getting my paramedic license."

Wow. He really did want offspring.

"Offspring with you will be perfect because we are both lycan. Tokarz's son or Luke Thibodaux aren't imperfect, but they lack full access to our particular reptilian brain."

Wow again. He'd given offspring a lot of thought.

Reptilian brain. Someone in her high school biology class asked about reptile brain and gotten shut down for mentioning the evils of evolution. Phoebe researched the term on the Internet. Lycans possessed active reptilian brains, the knowledge stored therein crucial to their everyday lives. Major distinctions between sapien and lupine brains existed because their bodies functioned so differently.

"Sounds like you've thought about offspring a lot."

"Since meeting you. I never understood before when my elders told me mate and offspring above all else. The concept can only be fully appreciated once one is mated. Offspring follow mating." His voice faded.

A moment later, a soft snuffling snore betrayed his slumber.

She'd wanted to ask him about this Jasper guy, but the talk of offspring sidetracked her.

She wouldn't allow any government goon to dictate to her. Her pack signed no treaty with the government when the senator gunned them down. The Limmikin were in North America before the self-important Europeans showed up.

She eased away from Parker whose body gave off as much heat as Helga's furnace. The sheets were limp and damp from their sweat. The night threatened to be long.

Chapter 24

"You need to stay with Helga," Parker told Old Olivia and Selena. He'd pounded on Ethan's door when no one answered a phone. "Phoebe and I have to meet Mitchell Jasper at the federal building downtown at nine o'clock."

Old Olivia squawked. She sported a serious case of bedhead, and the skin on her face sagged more than usual. Her gray robe did nothing to compliment her skin tone. "Helga wants you and her niece. You're the EMT and Phoebe is her family."

Parker ignored the twinge the flattery evoked. "Hey, we don't want to meet with the government agent. I'm a lowly rho and Phoebe doesn't even know what she is. We shouldn't be the ones being called on the carpet."

"You're assuming you're being called on the carpet." This came from Ethan, who stood in the doorway to his bedroom and scratched his bare belly. Navy shorts, hanging low on his hips, kept him from being naked.

"Minnesota is your gig. Has been from day one." All Parker's old resentments boiled to the surface.

"Maybe the meeting isn't about you. Phoebe is a person of interest." Ethan sounded smug.

"Jasper didn't say." And Parker didn't ask the man when he'd called Parker's phone at daybreak. He'd been too stunned by the direct contact to think clearly.

Besides, Phoebe smelled wonderful, which distracted him. The memory still distracted him. They'd have time for a quickie before they needed to shower if he could get it through someone's head Helga needed another body on premise for a couple hours.

Maybe he and Phoebe shouldn't shower at all but let the funk of werewolf sex perfume their meeting with Jasper. The effluvia might teach the sapien not to schedule early morning meetings with nocturnal creatures.

"Selena's number is programmed into Helga's speed dial," Old Olivia muttered.

"Then why didn't Helga call Selena when she first fell?"

Parker snapped in response.

"She doesn't carry her phone with her all the time." Old Olivia sounded grim. "Between the heat and the TV volume, she's turned into a demon. Can't the government suit meet you here?"

"No. The government has its own agenda." Ethan's gaze never left Parker.

"We're leaving here at eight-thirty to give us enough time to find the place. Someone should be in Helga's living room by then." Parker stomped away from Ethan's house.

"THEY WON'T LET YOU into the federal building with Jeeves," Parker told Phoebe.

Phoebe wore her inevitable black ensemble and carried Jeeves. "You said the same thing about the hospital. I'll take my chances." Her voice quavered.

"Don't be nervous."

"I'm not. I'm angry. Your government treaties have no bearing on me at all."

He'd explained how mating and packs worked several times, but Phoebe refused to accept mating bound her in numerous ways.

Stubborn female.

The federal building lot charged Parker to leave his car, which annoyed him. He paid his taxes every year, and some years when Toke Lobo and the Pack were gaining success on the road, he'd made substantial payments. Why the scat did he have to pay to park, too?

Phoebe got away with bringing Jeeves into the building by using it as a one hundred percent wooden cane, verified by the x-ray machine.

They were crossing the lobby, his boot heels echoing loudly on the marble floor, when he spotted a familiar figure standing in front of the elevators.

Pale yellow hair, skim milk complexion, barely blue eyes: Mitchell Jasper.

Tokarz claimed Jasper smelled so bad, even a vampire would reject him. Parker sniffed. Yep. The guy smelled as if he were rotting from the inside out.

Parker greeted Jasper. "I'm Parker Rowe and this is my mate, Phoebe."

Jasper looked him up and down, then shifted his gaze to Phoebe. She resembled nothing so much as a waif, with her petite frame, her short, ragged haircut, and enormous wide eyes telling lies about her innocence.

Phoebe stared back at Jasper, but Parker noticed her knuckles whiten on Jeeves.

Jasper jabbed the already-lighted elevator call button.

Three of the four elevators bore Out of Order signs.

My tax money continuing to work. Like Jasper's paycheck.

Parker tried again. "We've met before. In Loup Garou."

"We shouldn't be having a conversation in a public space." Jasper's lips barely moved.

"Gee, honey," Phoebe quipped. "You didn't mention his sparkling personality."

The elevator doors stuttered open as the car jerked to a stop.

Parker held no particular fondness for elevators, but he'd been instructed to report to the twenty-third floor.

Jasper punched the button for the top floor, Parker noted.

The car shuddered into motion.

Phoebe grinned and waved at the security camera mounted in the corner, before turning her attention to Jasper. "I suppose you read my FBI file, so you know I am the victim here."

The overhead cables whined. An oily, hot metal stench filled the car.

"I don't know anything about you." Jasper's eyes didn't flicker from the digital numbers over the door. "You don't exist according to the census."

"Because I'm Limmikin. One of the untreatied."

"The Limmikin vanished a generation ago." Jasper spoke as if by rote. "Then suddenly, here you are, attacking a United States Senator while he's in the hospital. Senator Tuttle is a major proponent of the service for sanctuary treaties in Congress."

"He uses Limmikin for target practice. I'm a witness."

"Wait until we get to the interview room," Jasper snapped. He set his briefcase next to his feet.

The elevator car lurched.

"I won't attack you here," Phoebe assured Jasper. "The security camera protects you."

"Phoebe," Parker warned. Her belligerence would only make the upcoming interview more difficult. Maybe Jasper only planned to congratulate her on her survival.

Yeah. Right. And Parker would turn into a vampire on the next full moon.

Parker stared at the digital numbers marking their ascent. Something felt...off. The elevator moved too slowly, with too much groaning and rattling. The whirring sound overhead concerned him. He wanted off. He didn't care if there were a hundred and twenty-three floors, he would arrive by stair.

He pressed the button for the tenth floor. The button lit, but the elevator continued its upward journey.

Jasper glared at Parker and pulled out his cell phone. Parker pressed every button for every floor between where they were and their original destination. The car persisted with its lurching ascent.

Pressing the emergency stop button did nothing.

He tried the emergency phone. The cord dangled, unattached.

Parker called Ethan with his cell phone. Someone needed to know what was going on. Better a recorded message than a long, drawn-out conversation going nowhere. "There's an elevator issue," he told Ethan's voice mail.

Jasper turned his back on Parker and Phoebe, hunched his shoulders, and muttered into his phone, "The elevator needs maintenance."

Maintenance? Too late for repairs. Parker knew what could happen to the human body—homo sapien or homo lupus—if an elevator cable snapped. They needed something to cushion the landing.

Parker made a decision. "Jasper. Get on the floor. In the center. Flat. Spread eagle. Except cover your head with your arms."

Phoebe's enormous eyes widened more. "What? What's happening?"

"Something is wrong with this elevator." He checked the red numbers over the door. The fifteenth floor. "If the cable breaks, the only chance a sapien has for survival is to distribute the force of impact."

The elevator jolted. Swayed.

Jasper complied without arguing. His anemic complexion turned ashen as he hit the floor.

"What about us?" Phoebe's voice squeaked.

"Remember what I told you last night? About preserving our lunar energy to shift only when we really need to? Well, we're really going to need to."

He had a theory. Only a theory.

"If the car starts to fall, shift. Keep shifting. As quickly as you can. Without a corporeal body, we might be able to survive."

And thank the Ancient Ones she wasn't gestating.

The elevator continued its rocking rise. Jasper resumed his phone conversations, as if being a government agent allowed him to defy the laws of physics.

Parker clutched Phoebe's hand. He could be wrong. He could be overreacting. If so, why didn't the elevator stop at any of the floors to let them off? Even on an express elevator, the emergency stop button should have functioned. The phone cord had been cut.

Terrifying spasms shaking the car accompanied each foot gained.

At the twentieth floor, the ride smoothed. The elevator glided upward.

Jasper unwrapped his arms from his head and peered at Parker, who waggled a finger at him. "Remember I tried to save your life."

Jasper climbed to his feet and brushed at the debris on his suit. "Or purposely tried to scare me to death."

Yeah, the elevator floor was nasty.

The tension in Parker's chest eased. He released Phoebe's hand.

Twenty-one.

Twenty-two.

Twenty-three.

The elevator stopped. The tension in Parker's chest eased. The doors slid open...

And something overhead boomed.

Phoebe screamed.

The car hurtled down the shaft.

"Resume your position!" Parker shouted at Jasper.

Phoebe started her shift. The leather of Parker's boots burst as he did the same.

Wolf. Man. Wolf. Man. Parker didn't try to count the times he reversed the process. He focused entirely on shifting and prayed to the Ancient Ones Phoebe did the same.

Chapter 25

"WAKE UP!" HELGA SHOUTED.

Olivia snored on the sofa. Some guard dog she turned out to be. She wasn't even good company nowadays. Or maybe they were getting sick of each other. But what did the ancient she-wolf have left to do? She'd fostered Selena after her mother died and taught her the old ways of healing, but with Selena mated, Olivia had no purpose.

Helga picked up the tissue box and tossed it at her companion. The cardboard bounced off the wrinkled forehead.

"Wha...?" Olivia blinked awake. "Why did you throw the tissues at me?"

"You need to get Selena and Ethan. Now." Helga's anxiety prevented her from putting her thoughts into words. "Accident. Need Selena and Ethan."

"You had an accident?" Olivia lifted her nose as if testing the air.

"Not me." Helga's frustration mounted. "On the news. Accident at the federal building."

Olivia finally understood. "Call Selena's cell phone. Now."

Helga should have thought of phoning, but she didn't like talking on the phone, especially when the person she wanted to speak with lived across the street. Phones made a body lazy. Besides, you couldn't read body language or facial expressions on a phone, unless you used one of those new-fangled cell phones she'd heard caused brain cancer.

But Phoebe, ever so thoughtful, placed a cordless phone extension on the side table next to Helga's recliner. Helga lifted the phone from its base and pressed the button Phoebe programmed to dial Selena's cell phone.

Olivia stared at the TV, where a curvy blond reporter in a tight red suit tried to look solemn as she stood outside the federal building in downtown Warwick.

"I'm Alicia Dain reporting from outside the Warwick Federal Building, where we've learned an elevator cable snapped while carrying passengers to the top floor of this twenty-three-story building."

"Gods of our Elders," Olivia whispered. "Parker. Phoebe."

"Maybe they weren't on the elevator." But Helga knew better. Every cell in her body shrieked a confirmation of her fear.

"Hello?" Selena sounded sleepy. Languid. As if she and Ethan were having as much sex as possible while they had the house to themselves.

Helga would never understand lycan obsession with sex. "You have to come over here. Quick. There's been an accident. On the news." Helga disconnected. Her disjointed message conveyed enough info to get Selena in front of the TV so she could hear for herself without going through the filter of a tired old crone.

Three minutes later, Olivia opened the door for Selena and Ethan. "It's bad," she told them.

Selena wore leggings and her inevitable flannel shirt.

Ethan wore nothing but navy shorts, riding low on his hips. Okay, maybe Selena had a reason to be sex obsessed.

The couple blocked Helga's view of her TV. She didn't mind. She'd seen enough.

Besides, Ethan wasn't bad to look at from behind, either.

"Ancient Ones. Creator." Ethan summoned his deities in a voice barely audible over Alicia Dain's blathering.

Conjecture, not true reporting.

"A broken elevator cable doesn't mean anything." Selena sounded as if she tried to convince herself more than the others.

Ethan's grim response sent shivers through Helga. "You know what Phoebe's FBI file contained."

"The elevator plummeted twenty-three floors," Alicia Dain reminded her viewers. Ambulances and police cars filled the screen behind her. "A passenger surviving such a fall would be a miracle."

"We need to get downtown," Ethan said.

"Why?" Helga asked. "You can't shift the dead back to life."

"What if Phoebe and Parker weren't on the elevator? Ethan, call Parker to check on him." Selena went alpha mode.

Ethan pulled his phone from his pocket.

Oh. That explained his intriguing bulge. Except his bulge didn't diminish. His shorts were positively indecent.

He frowned at the screen. "I have a voice mail. From Parker." He put the phone on speaker before playing back the message.

"There's an elevator issue."

"Scat," the three lycan cursed, while Helga added her own, "Damn."

Ethan dialed Parker's number. The call kicked to voice mail. "If you get this, call me."

"We need to be there." Selena's voice quavered.

"You can't do anything," Helga insisted.

"We can hear better than sapiens," Selena explained.

Okay, Selena made a good point, as much as Helga hated to admit it. "You're not going to be able to get close enough to hear anything."

"Pack clean clothes for them," Olivia suggested.

The dead didn't need clean clothes, but Helga knew better than to argue with grieving werewolves.

ETHAN SPOTTED PARKER'S RENTED SUV in the parking lot right away. Its presence meant nothing. A bevy of emergency vehicles blocked access to the lot and the building.

Helga had been right about one thing: the officials on the scene weren't letting anyone approach the building. Ethan tried claiming next-of-kin-status to a person on the elevator, but his story went nowhere.

Selena called Anderson and Clerkin.

"You read Phoebe's FBI file," she reminded them in a low, menacing tone. "Now there's an elevator accident when someone summoned her to the Federal building? I don't believe in coincidence."

She disconnected and glared at Ethan.

"Good job." He meant every syllable.

"Call your Luke guy," Selena suggested. "See if he can find blueprints for the building. There might be a way we can get closer without alerting the authorities."

Sometimes Ethan loved his mate so much he thought his heart would burst.

It took Luke half an hour to find the blueprints. Another fifteen minutes passed as he studied them. Ethan paced the sidewalk outside the barricades.

"Got it," Luke said. "There's a tunnel for transporting prisoners from the jail to the courthouse, located on the first floor of the federal building."

For the first time since Helga's phone call, Ethan experienced a spark of hope.

"Hold on. There's more."

Ethan heard incessant tapping as Luke worked his computer keyboard as well as he played his drums. The same tapping drove him crazy when they'd roomed together on tour with Toke Lobo and the Pack. Now Luke wasn't fast enough.

"No one ever breaks into jail," Luke muttered. "There has to be a way...air vents. You need to locate the air vents to the tunnels. They'll look like ordinary storm grates street side. It'll be a tight fit. You might want to shift before trying."

Ethan started scanning the neighborhood, looking for the jail. "Thanks," he said. "Oh, and you might want to warn Parker's parents."

Luke cursed, but Ethan disconnected before Luke could argue.

Selena elbowed his ribs and pointed toward the crowd gathered outside the barrier. "Who's that?"

"Who?" Ethan studied the faces; no one looked familiar.

"In the chambray work shirt and jeans. Wearing a red baseball cap. Looks like he has grease on his hands. I've seen him before."

The brim of the cap cast a deep shadow on the man's face, but Selena recognized him anyway. "Tony DiNardo. Curtis DiNardo's uncle."

"The one who is a handyman for the Peters family?"

"So I've heard."

Ethan remembered Curtis DiNardo well. Ethan would never rid his mouth of the taste of Curtis and his death. "Why is he hanging around here? Congressman Peters' office isn't in this building."

Selena pursed her lips. "Grease-stained hands on a handyman makes sense."

"We can't prove anything." Unfortunate but true.

"To borrow a word from Helga—factotum. An employee who does all kinds of work. A utility player."

"A handyman." Ethan grabbed Selena's arm and twirled her around. "I don't want to deal with him right now. We have to find Parker and Phoebe before it's too late."

THE AIR VENTS LUKE mentioned were easier to locate than a place for Ethan and Selena to stash their clothes and shift. They had to remain two legged, two armed in order to remove the protective grating, then shift and hope no one fell into the hole in the street. Selena borrowed a pylon from a nearby parking lot to caution pedestrians.

They managed to coordinate everything. The hardest part proved to be discreetly stuffing two wolves into a narrow hole barely wider than a stovepipe.

Ethan hated being in such a tight spot, but he managed to wiggle free and drop into the tunnel.

"Gods of our Elders, could we have squeezed any tighter?" Selena morphed from four to two legs. The heat from the energy of their shifts bounced off the tunnel walls.

Ethan took a moment to acclimate himself. Blood and scat stench carried on the damp air. "That way." He pointed left.

"It doesn't smell promising."

He refused to accept Selena's pessimism. If he didn't admit it, he wouldn't jinx Parker and Phoebe's luck. Because only lucky lycans could have survived the accident.

Despite the damp air and the sound of condensation dripping in the distance, the tunnel remained dry. Their bare feet slapped against cool, rough concrete. The evenly spaced vents provided only enough illumination for them to see where they were going. The reek of death increased with each foot they gained.

"Wait." Selena grabbed Ethan's arm. "Do you hear that?"

He strained his ears. He heard Selena's heart and lungs and the irregular drip, drip, drip of moisture. "Hear what?"

"It's a pattern. Three rapid, three long, three rapid," Selena whispered.

Not water. Morse code. SOS. Someone was alive.

Chapter 26

The car stopped with a jarring thud. The structure collapsed. If Parker had been in corporeal form at impact, his teeth would have shattered. Dead or alive, his teeth would be fragments.

But he was alive. Weak, but breathing.

The emergency light illuminated the destruction within the car.

Blood spattered Phoebe's naked body. She lay half buried by debris, panting as if she'd run a marathon.

"Phoebe." He crawled toward her. His palm landed in something . . . wet. Gooey.

Jasper.

Jasper was...a mess. A dead mess.

The roaring in Parker's ears faded.

"Are you all right?" Phoebe's voice warbled. "Goddess, you're covered with blood. Are you all right? Damn you, answer me."

Parker's voice wasn't much stronger than hers. "The blood is Jasper's."

Hadn't the man resumed the safety position as Parker told him?

Parker would never know. In the end, what Jasper did or didn't do wouldn't matter. He was dead. Parker and Phoebe were not.

When Parker reached Phoebe, he cupped her tiny, fragile face in his hands and lowered his mouth to hers.

Shocks and aftershocks sparked through him. Her lips were soft. She tasted of good memories. Her mouth opened in an invitation he couldn't refuse. His tongue brushed against hers. She made a funny noise, exciting and calming him at the same time. She was alive. Not being pregnant kept her alive. If he could swallow her whole to protect her, he would.

He released her face and wrapped his arms around her, never breaking the fusion of their mouths. He needed to stay connected to her.

She broke off the contact. "That's the first time you've kissed me." Her voice sounded insubstantial.

His first kiss. Ever. He should have kissed her when he first met her. He should have kissed her every morning of their lives together, and again each night.

"How did I do?" He fought jealousy, knowing she'd kissed other males in her life.

"The best kiss of my life."

He could breathe again.

Parker searched for his cell phone but located only bits and pieces, some of which were embedded in...Jasper.

At least he and Jasper made phone calls before the accident.

If the crash was an accident.

"Can we try to get out?" Phoebe whispered, as if afraid vibrations from her voice might knock something loose.

"Better to wait for help. There are going to be questions because we survived when Jasper didn't."

Not that he retained any strength to do more than hold Phoebe. A gaping hole in the floor, in front of where the doors should have been, worried him. The doors themselves were twisted and off their tracks. No, he'd used up his energy reserves.

"I'm naked. So are you."

Shifting shredded their clothes, a common occurrence among adolescent lycans.

He couldn't identify her response as a giggle or verging on hysteria. "We can blame g-forces or something. It happens a lot in airplane crashes."

So did random survivors. Experts were still studying why some people made it and others didn't.

"I've never been on an airplane."

"Neither have I." Then Parker added, "Tokarz has. He hated it."

"So we would hate it too?"

"Probably. Tokarz is a wise alpha. He once got drunk on Moonsinger Beer and didn't shift on the full moon."

"I thought alcohol poisoned our kind."

"Not shifting on the full moon could drive a werewolf mad, so legend has it. But he believed his mate betrayed him. He craved madness."

Parker—and the others—survived the terrible night.

He would survive this day, too.

"If I were a doctor, I could have helped him."

"You're smart enough to be a doctor. You saved us by suggesting we shift. You tried to save...him." She gestured at what remained of Jasper.

"I wasn't smart enough to save my sister." He couldn't believe he'd confessed his deepest regret aloud.

"You were a kid. You tried to stop her, just like you try to stop me all the time." Phoebe snuggled closer.

The wreckage groaned.

Parker stilled. Waited. Listened.

"No one could have survived this."

Parker's imagination didn't conjure the distant voice. Help had arrived. He didn't dare move and feared even shouting would destabilize their situation.

Phoebe's eyes widened. "Should we tap out an SOS?"

He was at a loss. If the elevator rested at the bottom of its shaft, they'd be okay shouting and tapping. But if they were stuck between floors or something else equally as unstable, anything they did could have dire consequences.

The stop had been sudden. Hard. The car itself hadn't moved since stopping. The creaking and groaning could be the structure making its hurts known.

"Tap." They needed to save their remaining strength, because who knew how long it would take rescuers to find them.

He found a metal strip which may have held the ceiling tiles in place. He snapped it in two and handed one piece to Phoebe.

She refused his offering and with a flourish, producing an unscathed Jeeves. "Have at it."

Chapter 27

PARKER WORRIED THEY WOULD run out of air before being rescued. Jasper polluted what oxygen they did have. Parker did not mention his concern to Phoebe.

They took turns tapping on every available surface. Jasper's stench increased by the hour. Granted, he'd smelled bad enough alive. Dead, he was revolting.

The emergency light seemed to be fading. Or maybe Parker's consciousness dimmed.

Phoebe let Jeeves fall from her fingers.

"Don't give up." Parker could hear the rescue workers talking. "There are emergency workers out there."

"I know. I hear them, too. Kiss me again."

The request startled him. But...okay. He brushed his lips against hers. Her mouth opened beneath his, her tongue searching for his.

How could this bliss have been his for the past several weeks, and he not know it? He blamed the scarcity of mating advice: don't hurt her and make sure she's happy. Which about covered conventional wisdom. Elders should instruct a lobo about kissing.

He wrapped his arms around Phoebe. The elevator car grew warmer. Their bodies were sticky with perspiration and Jasper's body fluids. Despite everything, his penis grew hard and rose until it rested between their bellies.

"Fuck me," she whispered against his ear as she spread her thighs.

"No." This might be the last time they would be together. "I'm going to make love to you."

PARKER ROLLED OFF PHOEBE. Something jabbed him in the back.

"You thrust SOS." Phoebe tapped the pattern on his chest with her forefinger.

"You shouldn't have noticed," he replied. If true, not a conscious thing.

Her smile confused him, as always. "I only noticed because my climax is still pulsing the same pattern."

A foreign sound interrupted Parker's chuckle.

"Hello?" The tinny voice sounded distant.

Parker sat up. "Hello!" he shouted.

"Dear God, someone's alive. Are you hurt?"

He exchanged a look with Phoebe before answering. His deeper pitched voice would carry better. "My wife and I are shaken but uninjured. Someone else on the elevator didn't make it."

Phoebe brought her hand to her mouth and gnawed on her knuckle. "Ask if the car is secure."

They should have considered stability before making love, but he did as she requested.

"You're at the bottom of the shaft. Car isn't going anywhere," came the reassuring answer.

Phoebe lowered her head, as if praying.

"The doors are jammed," Parker explained. "There's also a big hole in front of where the doors should be, and the edges look…unsafe."

"Thanks for the heads up," the deep voice responded.

"Hold on a second," another male said. "That looks like blood."

Parker swallowed. Hard. "The other person in the elevator with us was...is...he's dead, and there's a lot of blood involved."

"This isn't from inside the elevator."

Light fragments played along the twisted seams.

"Holy Jesus Christ."

A chorus of sapien curses followed.

Phoebe stared at Parker, the dimming light glinting off her eyes.

"How many folks were in the elevator?" the first voice asked.

"Only the three. My wife and I, and a...another man." Parker didn't know how else to refer to Mitchell Jasper.

"And all three of you are there?"

What was he supposed to do? Inventory body parts?

"It's difficult to tell, but yeah, I think so. What's going on?"

More cursing punctuated by the screech of metal. The elevator car shifted. Phoebe clutched Parker's arm.

Selena's blood abandoned her brain, making her giddy. "They're safe."

They'd crept closer to the accident site. The racket being made by the rescue squad concealed any sound the duo might inadvertently make. They could even carry on a whispered conversation.

Selena swallowed hard. Parker and Phoebe were alive. Maybe not as okay as Parker claimed, but they'd survived. Their lycan metabolisms would heal them from any superficial injuries.

"I wonder who the poor sucker beneath the elevator car is."

Selena shook her head, trying to clear her hearing. She thought she heard Ethan say a fourth victim lay under the elevator. "I don't follow."

"The rescue team is so upset because there's a body under the car."

THREE HOURS LATER, PHOEBE and Parker, strapped to gurneys, emerged from the dark elevator car into the brilliant afternoon sun. Phoebe started to argue about being restrained, but Parker told her to let the EMTs do their jobs.

She capitulated, except about her quarterstaff. She pitched enough of a fit, they let her keep it.

Phoebe squinted against the bright light, intensified by TV cameras attempting to get in her face. Rescue workers rushed her into a waiting ambulance. They loaded Parker into another.

She needed to be x-rayed. X-rays shouldn't reveal anything except maybe a weakness in her bones from the shifting marathon. If she hadn't believed Parker before about conserving energy, she did now. But the insurance company for the building would demand proof they weren't injured.

Especially since two sapiens didn't survive the alleged accident.

She heard Parker recycle his tale of airline crashes and the randomness of survival. The excuse for their shredded clothes. No one seemed to question his claim.

"Phoebe!"

The crowd discombobulated her for several moments, but she recognized Selena's voice. Phoebe turned her head but couldn't spot the other she-wolf in the crowd.

"We have clothes for you. We'll meet you at the hospital."

Phoebe didn't need to see Selena to get the message. She wouldn't be returned to Helga's wearing a hospital gown.

The inevitable wait at the hospital didn't bother her. She had the option. Mitchell Jasper did not.

The interminable questioning didn't annoy her, either. Telling the truth—until the time she and Parker started their shift—covered everything but their survival. Parker instructed Jasper to stay flat on the floor. No, I didn't see what he did or didn't do. From the moment the cable snapped until the car hit bottom, I closed my eyes and prayed.

Because praying was what sapiens did in desperate moments, the answer appeased the authorities.

She left out parts of what happened after the landing, too.

They let Selena stay once Phoebe filled out the forms.

She usually resisted pack ways, but Selena's presence reassured her.

"Has anyone told Helga?" Phoebe asked in a lull in the action.

"She's the one who caught the accident on the news," Selena admitted. "Ethan and I got there as quickly as we could."

Something in Selena's tone told Phoebe not to ask more questions, so she replied, "Thank you."

Every muscle in her body ached. Her bones complained. She wanted Parker. When she woke from dozing, she murmured his name first.

"He's fine. He's asking about you, too," Selena assured her.

"Where's my quarterstaff?"

"You have it next to you. I told them it's your version of a security blanket."

Phoebe's fingers found the familiar, worn wood. She relaxed.

More questions from inspectors; more prodding from the medical community.

"You don't need my blood. I don't have the bends." No way would she surrender a sample of her non-sapien blood. After several hours spent mostly refusing medical treatment and answering the same questions rephrased a dozen different ways, Phoebe sat up. "I'm out of here," she told Selena. "Where are my clothes?"

"Against medical advice," the latest tech, sent to harass her, intoned.

"If people have new questions, they can find me at my aunt's house. No one is sticking a needle in me."

"Phoebe is checking out," Ethan told Parker, as he slipped his phone into his pocket.

"Good." Parker wore his civvies. "Let's meet the females in the lobby."

Phoebe rested her head on Parker's shoulder as Ethan drove them to Ash Street. Who knew such a simple gesture could hold so much meaning?

"We'll pick up your vehicle in the morning," Ethan said.

"Okay." As far as Parker was concerned, the rental company could retrieve the car.

"How did you—"

"Later. Please."

Of course, Ethan wanted to know what happened.

Everyone wanted to know.

Parker had never been closer to dying in his life. Yeah, a couple years ago he'd been trapped in a barn fire in Montana— or maybe

Wyoming—with snipers outside waiting to pick off anything that moved. Parker had a fighting chance then. Not this time.

As soon as he could arrange it, he and Phoebe were boarding an airplane, and getting the human hell out of Minnesota. Fuck fear of flying. If Tokarz could fly to save his mate, Parker could do no less.

He kissed the top of Phoebe's head. Her hair smelled of fear and perspiration. He imagined he didn't smell much better. The hospital stay didn't include spa treatments.

First priority: showers all around.

He needed a new phone. Sapiens used smart phones to make flight arrangements, so how difficult could it be?

The Varulv honored Helga for her assistance in the fight against vampires, the Varulv could shoulder the responsibility of caring for her.

He and his mate were getting out of Dodge.

Chapter 28

Detectives Clerkin and Anderson waited for them in Helga's living room.

"Sorry," Olivia muttered when Selena shot her a dirty look. "They wouldn't let me call you."

Phoebe tightened her grip on her quarterstaff as she perched on the sofa. Parker sat next to her and put his arm around her. She rested her head against his shoulder, as she'd done on the ride to Helga's, but the detectives' presence prevented her from appreciating the strength Parker shared.

"Any guesses about who might be at the bottom of the elevator shaft?" Clerkin asked.

"Me. Phoebe. The remains of Federal Agent Mitchell Jasper," Parker replied.

Phoebe thought he'd answered brilliantly.

"Under the car," Clerkin amended. "You do know they found another body beneath the car."

Phoebe held herself as still as she could.

"What an interesting question," Selena interjected.

Selena hadn't been in the elevator. She hadn't been spattered with the remains of a stranger. What gave her the right to speak now?

"Because I noticed someone hanging around while we were trying to find out what happened to Phoebe and Parker," Selena continued.

Oh.

"Tony DiNardo."

Clerkin and Anderson both reacted.

"How do you know Tony DiNardo?" Clerkin asked.

"He was my landlord before I moved in with Ethan. I met his slimy nephew a couple times, too. The nephew did odd handyman jobs for his uncle. Maybe there's a connection."

If Phoebe didn't know better, she would swear Selena told the truth.

Anderson made a note in the spiral pad he'd pulled from his pocket.

"Why are you here?" Phoebe ended her silence. She didn't bother trying to hide her bitterness. "Because I'm accident prone?"

"We don't think you are accident prone, ma'am. The preliminary investigation indicates something severed the cable. Clean cut. Little to no fraying." Clerkin remained expressionless.

"The other elevators had Out of Order signs taped to the doors." Parker's voice and face mirrored Clerkin's. "We were purposely directed to the damaged car."

"Any thoughts?" Clerkin persisted. "Taking the stairs is better for the heart."

A corner of Anderson's mouth twitched.

Phoebe closed her eyes. She wanted nothing more than to crawl into bed next to Parker and sleep for the next year.

After a long, hot shower.

Seemed as if neither would happen any time soon. "Have you checked Dustin Holloway's whereabouts?"

Clerkin and Anderson exchanged a look.

"What?" Parker asked.

"We're still trying to locate Mr. Holloway. We're taking your order of protection seriously."

As if being taken seriously was a gift.

"I don't know if you're aware," Parker said, "but I'm a licensed EMT in Colorado. As a medical professional, I'm putting a stop to this questioning. My wife and I have been through severe physical trauma and—"

"Left the hospital against medical advice," Anderson interrupted.

Phoebe lowered her chin. "I don't trust public places. Everyone in town who turns on the news or reads the paper is going to know who was in that elevator and is going to believe I'm in the hospital. I'm nobody's sitting duck."

Fifteen more minutes of going-nowhere questioning got wasted before the detectives left.

The tension knotting Phoebe's shoulders left with them. Even Parker's arm and shoulder melted to slush. She couldn't figure out whether he had the shakes or she did.

"Helga, white noise please," Ethan requested.

Helga turned on her TV and jacked the volume.

Phoebe winced.

"How did you survive?" Ethan didn't beat around the bush.

"We shifted," Parker explained. "Look, can we get into this later? I'm wiped. Phoebe's wiped. We're still wearing Jasper's blood and guts. We shifted and weren't in either corporeal form when the elevator stopped. I'll explain later."

"Tokarz and your parents are blowing up my phone," Ethan said.

"My parents? Tokarz? How would they know?"

Pink tinged Ethan's cheeks. "I called Luke...I had him tell your folks. I'll explain in the morning."

"Give me your phone." Parker disengaged from Phoebe and extended his hand. "Mine didn't survive."

Ethan complied.

Parker punched in a phone number, then a text message. *Parker here. No phone. We survived. Will call in morning. Love you both.*

Hurt and loneliness gathered in Phoebe's throat, making it difficult to swallow. Love you both.

She had no one to text. Corbie? Corbie warned Phoebe the last time they spoke: *Dustin is my blood. Don't make me chose. You will lose.*

Corbie would never admit Dustin forced the choice.

Phoebe's circle sat in this room, and not one person there, except maybe Parker, even liked her.

True, Selena and Ethan rushed to the accident site but their concern focused on Parker, not her. Selena stood by her at the hospital because her alpha role made Phoebe her responsibility, not her friend, much less her loved one.

And Parker? The Goddess stuck them together. He liked the sex but if she'd died today, he might not have noticed.

His sister's young death shaped him the same as Phoebe's childhood trauma molded her. Nothing about Phoebe could alter Parker's essence. She didn't want to, but it would be nice to think she impacted his life. Or helped him find a sense of humor.

The only reason she survived the elevator fiasco was Parker's doing. Otherwise, Tuttle would have won. She remained in the game, but Tuttle lost a minion. A factotum.

She hoped Dustin had been far away. Because if Dustin died, even while trying to kill Phoebe, Corbie would never forgive her.

Parker awoke with an agenda. First on the list was a new phone.

He'd have to ask Ethan or Dakota for a ride to pick up his vehicle from the federal building lot or take him to a mall. Then he needed to call his folks and reassure them he and his mate were safe. Maybe they could talk to Phoebe. A phone conversation wouldn't reveal her strength and honor, but their relationship needed to start somewhere.

Then he'd deal with Tokarz. He didn't see how his alpha could blame him for Mitchell Jasper's death, but there were still going to be questions.

And the authorities probably weren't through with them yet. He needed to escape with his mate. He had to hide her.

PARKER ENTERED THEIR BEDROOM from using the bathroom when Phoebe blindsided him.

"Here." She handed him a phone. A no-frills cell phone. The kind one could purchase at discount chain stores. A pay- as-you-go phone. Disposable.

"Where did you get this?" When he thought she couldn't do anything else to surprise him, she pulled a burner phone from her backpack.

She didn't react. She didn't retract her hand either. "I thought you might want to speak to your parents as soon as possible."

He took the phone. "Thank you." He couldn't think of anything else to say.

"I'll give you some privacy." She'd slung her backpack over her shoulder.

"Where are you going?"

"To shower and give you privacy to speak to your parents."

"They'll want to talk to you."

"Whatever for? They don't know me."

"Yet."

She reacted as if he'd slapped her.

He grabbed her wrist, keeping his fingers loose as they circled the tiny bone, and pulled her closer. "You're their daughter-in-law, as the sapiens say. The mother of their future grandbabies. They'll want to know you. You don't have to be afraid."

Because her fear perfumed the room. Fear and sadness.

When he kissed the tip of her nose, her reluctance filled his head with its dark aroma and bitter flavor.

"Objects don't need to be known, only utilized." She pulled free from his grasp.

"You think I'm using you?" Parker didn't know whether to be pissed or hurt. He went with pissed. Phoebe could understand pissed.

"Not intentionally. But you described me as their daughter-in-law. The mother of their grandchildren. You never mentioned Phoebe the assassin."

"Because you're not an assassin." He required a sharp tone to cut through the scat spewing from her mouth. "I've killed more people than you have."

"Someday either Tuttle or I will succeed. Either way, you and your family are better off keeping me as a figurehead." She rubbed her wrist, even though he'd barely grazed her skin.

"Don't insult me," he snapped.

Her head jerked. "What insult?"

"You're saying I can't protect my mate, when protecting my mate and offspring is the only priority a lobo has."

Her bottom lip quivered. She laid her palms on his chest, as if to push him away, but exerted no effort. "You have a good life planned.

You're going to take your medical training as far as you can with the limitations placed on you. I wish I could be the mate you deserve. The Goddess must have eaten bad shrimp when she put us together."

"The Ancient Ones don't make mistakes." He'd learned that from observing other lobos adjust to sapien mates.

Her fingers wadded into fists and she knocked against his heart. "You could have been killed yesterday because of me. Shall I inform your parents, who already lost one child, I could prove fatal to you?"

How dare she use Fleur against him? This discussion needed to stop now before he said something he couldn't take back.

"Take your shower."

"YOU CAN'T COME HERE." Tokarz's flat tone brooked no argument.

Parker knew better than to question his alpha. He also didn't need an explanation, but Tokarz provided one anyway.

"A federal agent is dead."

As if Parker hadn't been spattered with Mitchell Jasper's blood. Hadn't been trapped in a hot, dark box with a dead body giving off stinks Parker still couldn't banish from his mouth, no matter how many times he brushed his teeth, hit the antiseptic mouthwash bottle, or kissed his mate.

He swallowed his sarcastic retort.

"Ethan came to Minnesota for the sole purpose of convincing a congressman to continue to stand behind the service for sanctuary treaties. Instead, the place is a clusterfuck. I don't even know what clusterfuck means, but it sounds better than goat fuck."

Don't laugh. Don't laugh.

"Mitchell Jasper's death is only the latest fuck up."

"We had nothing to do with his death." Parker could no longer contain himself. "My mate and I were on that elevator, too. My mate could have been gestating."

"Is she?"

"If she were, she and the embryo would be as big a splat as Jasper." He explained how they'd spent the entire plunge shifting.

"What made you think to shift?" Tokarz asked.

Parker gritted his teeth. "It's the only thing I could think of. It's like a car accident, only with more velocity. The body and internal organs keep moving even after the vehicle stops. The result is...messy. I hoped not having bodies with organs would save us."

"Good call," Tokarz replied after a long pause.

"If I can't come home, what am I supposed to do?" Parker asked. "My mate isn't safe here."

"You need a safe house."

Parker clamped down on the urge to howl. Even if there were such a place, Phoebe's noncompliance created a whole other kind of SNAFU...Situation Normal, All Fucked Up.

A tap on the closed bedroom door prevented him from attempting to word-flay his alpha.

"Parker? There are federal agents here to see you," Old Olivia warned him.

"Phoebe is in the shower. We'll be out shortly."

"What?" Tokarz asked.

Parker explained, then added, "All we can do is tell them the truth. Luke filled you in on Phoebe's FBI file. This isn't the first attempt on her life. I told you about what happened when she was eight years old. It's all tied in together, and Senator Richard Tuttle is involved. The man is on my short list."

"You have to be able to prove he's behind everything."

"I don't have to prove scat if it involves my mate's safety, and you know it."

Parker disconnected before he talked himself into a deeper hole. Meeting with the feds could be a disaster if he couldn't control his temper. The Ancient Ones knew he couldn't control his mate.

Phoebe burst into the room wearing her standard black ninja costume. Water flew from her wet hair. Old Olivia must have warned her.

"What are we going to do?" Phoebe whispered.

"Wing it."

Chapter 29

Special Agents Grant Foster and Ray Benz were cookie cutter as-seen-on-TV federal agents: short hair; dark suits; white shirts; conservative neckties; polished-and-buffed-to-a-gleam shoes. Only Benz's constant sniffing and throat- clearing differentiated them.

"We need to speak to the two of you privately," Agent Benz said, after a not-so-discreet cough into his elbow.

"Not happening," Parker growled.

"Are you insurance agents?" Phoebe played for time to figure out how to avoid this conversation.

"I checked their IDs," Olivia grumbled from the corner where she huddled.

"They're G-men," Helga added.

"G-men?" Phoebe didn't care if they were X-Y-Z-men. She'd put up with all the crap she could take. No more.

"Government agents from the State department. I called Selena." Olivia's expression could scare a ghost.

Foster and Benz exchanged a look. Benz cleared his throat. "We need to speak to Mr. and Mrs. Rowe privately."

"What part of not happening don't you understand?" Parker bared his teeth.

"Do we need a lawyer?" Phoebe worked to get the agents off task; shift the burden of making sense to them. "We were practically killed by a faulty elevator in the federal building yesterday. Are you here to keep us from suing? Because we can sue, you know. We'll probably win a big settlement, too."

"We have no record of you, Mrs. Rowe." Special Agent Foster cut through her nonsense.

"Because I don't hold any insurance policies."

Foster ignored her. "The earliest records we can find on you are when you were eight and enrolled in the Soddy-Daisy Public School system by one Corbie Holloway. Before that, you don't seem to exist."

"Maybe my parents never insured me. I was only a kid, so I couldn't say."

"Where were you before you were eight?"

Her soul cringed; she wrestled with memories to keep them hidden. "I don't remember."

Foster and Benz clearly didn't believe her.

"What?" She didn't have to fake her outrage. "I don't remember. I was eight."

"So you woke up one morning living with Corbie Holloway?"

"Pretty much." Phoebe decided to give them something. A hint. She wrinkled her brow. "I remember trees. Lots of tall trees."

And blood. Shooting. The taste of gunpowder on my tongue. Screams.

She blanked her brain. If she didn't think, thoughts couldn't betray her.

"There are a lot of trees in Tennessee," Benz replied in a dry tone. "Why didn't Ms. Holloway turn you over to child protective services?"

"You'd have to ask her. CPS is not something an eight- year-old would know about."

The agents exchanged another look. They weren't subtle. "You don't know?"

"About CPS? No. I was eight." Maybe if she repeated her age often enough, they'd get a clue.

"About Mrs. Holloway." Foster hesitated. "She was killed in a home invasion two weeks ago."

Foster's revelation impacted Phoebe the same as if someone jammed her quarterstaff into her gut. Or smacked both temples with the solid oak. Or pressed the length of wood against her throat, cutting off her oxygen.

Corbie can't be dead. Not like Mama. Not like Granny. Not like everyone except me.

Parker shoved her head between her knees and held it there. "Breathe slowly and deeply."

Who's that man on TV?

He shot my mama. That man shot my mama!

The roaring in her ears gradually subsided.

"You could have broken the news more gently," Helga scolded. "It's not as if we get Tennessee news in Minnesota. Phoebe considered Corbie her mother."

But Corbie banished Phoebe. Cut her off. Maybe Corbie's death was why Dustin violated the restraining order. Maybe he wanted to tell her Corbie was dead.

Corbie is dead. There could never be another chance to attempt a reconciliation.

On the other hand, now she could kill Dustin without guilt.

One could always discover a bright side if one looked.

"I think this interview is over." Parker's voice was as hard as her oak quarterstaff.

She pushed away Parker's hands and sat upright, needing control. The news blindsided her, but she owed it to Corbie's memory to maintain control. Too bad she couldn't keep her voice from warbling. "So I'm a beneficiary of her life insurance policy?"

"For the last time, we are not insurance agents." Foster spoke between clenched teeth. "We're federal agents investigating the sabotage of an elevator in the federal building yesterday."

Would they follow through if Phoebe suggested they interview Senator Richard Tuttle?

"We have reason to believe you weren't the intended victims. The rigged elevator was meant to kill someone else." Benz sounded grim but destroyed the illusion by sniffing.

"This time?" Phoebe wanted to stick her pinky fingers in her ears to clear them.

"We have your FBI file, Ms. Rowe. Ms. McKinn. Whatever alias you're using these days. You've led an interesting life the past year or so. I hope your husband has taken out a good life insurance policy on you."

PARKER RESISTED THE URGE to shift and lunge for the funny guy. Ripping out a throat speaking such a terrible insinuation might appease his rage. Or not.

Then again, having no throat might cure Benz of whatever ailed him.

Instead, Parker questioned Selena's absence. She'd had more than enough time to cross the street.

"If not us, then who?" Phoebe asked.

"Mitchell Jasper."

"What?" Parker didn't believe it for a minute. "He's one of you."

Until he remembered Jasper's job: Liaison between the government and the werewolves.

Neither special agent reacted. Parker's gut screamed he'd made a tactical error. Phoebe went rigid.

"You knew Mitchell Jasper?" Benz dabbed at his nose with a tissue.

Maybe Parker could recover.

"We were at the federal building. He wore a suit. He didn't do well at taking suggestions. I assumed he worked for the government. What's that saying about assuming making an ass out of you and me? Call me an ass."

Even Helga looked at him as if he'd lost his mind.

Foster ignored his words. "The video from the camera shows you both conversing with the deceased."

Scat. How could Parker have forgotten the video camera?

"We were discussing how slow and unstable the elevator seemed." Phoebe's cool tone reassured Parker she'd gathered her wits and resumed her ninja mode.

"Does the camera show me trying to stop the elevator and get off?" Parker mimicked Phoebe's icy manner.

"If so, we want a copy. We can use the footage as evidence in our lawsuit," Phoebe added.

"It does show Mr. Rowe pressing buttons," Foster admitted. "It also shows Jasper spread-eagle on the elevator floor. It doesn't show either of you assuming the position."

"I was paralyzed with fear." Phoebe's expression dared them to contradict her.

"Then we see Jasper standing again."

"The elevator stopped jerking us around," Parker explained. *Unlike you.* "We were getting ready to get off on the twenty-third floor."

Benz cleared his throat again. Hacked. "Where you three were scheduled to meet."

"Are you sure you're not insurance agents trying to scare us out of a lawsuit?" Parker tried Phoebe's diversionary tactic.

"Then what do you see on the video?" Phoebe's face still lacked color after learning her foster mother was dead.

Where the human hell is Selena? Or Ethan?

"Nothing," Foster said. "The camera malfunctioned."

The heat generated by two lycans, serial shifting in a closed space, could fry electronics. Low-tech equipment couldn't capture energy. Either way, his and Phoebe's secret remained safe.

"Look." Benz sniffed. Dabbed his watering eyes with a white handkerchief. "We know Mitchell Jasper scheduled a meeting with members of...your community."

"Are you all right?" Old Olivia asked. "I can make you some herbal tea for your cold."

"I don't have a cold," Benz admitted. "I'm allergic to animal dander."

PHOEBE CONTINUED LAUGHING AS Selena stalked through Helga's front door, Ethan at her heels. "Then you'd better request reassignment." Selena sounded pissed. "Exposure to dander is an unfortunate side effect of your new position."

She strode across the room, then struck her habitual stance against the doorjamb leading to the kitchen. Ethan mirrored the pose on the opposite side.

"I was delayed because when the government wants to discuss the new treaty liaisons, you have to take the call. I'm Selena Wolfe Calhoun, by the way. I'm alpha of the Varulv, which is the local pack of werewolves. Alpha, in case they didn't include the word in your orientation, means I'm in charge. I'm offended you didn't contact me before hassling the Rowes. I'll excuse your rudeness this time, but there are protocols to be observed, and I expect you to follow them."

Phoebe loved Selena's nasty smile.

"If Foster and Benz are replacing Mitchell Jasper," Selena said, since she and Ethan were the only ones with any clue what she meant, "we can cooperate with them."

"I preferred them as insurance agents," Phoebe muttered. She still refused to tell them anything. Her secrets were hers until either she or Tuttle were dead.

She glared at Ethan for not speaking up. His role of heir apparent-to-be Limmikin alpha should make him a player. Selena had him so whipped, he merely stood like one of the tall trees witnessing the slaughter of her pack.

Time to remind these arrogant lycans of a few unpleasant truths. "Not all packs have treaties. Your government liaisons have nothing to do with me."

"Wrong." Selena didn't sound sorry at all. "If someone is trying to kill you in my territory, it's my problem. I will work with the liaisons. You don't have to like it, but you will follow my directives."

Phoebe opened her mouth to argue, but Selena spoke over her. "That includes you, Parker."

"What? I'm not Varulv."

Ethan added, "Selena neglected to mention we also called Tokarz. Does the name ring a bell? The alpha you hung up on last night?"

Parker crossed his arms over his chest. "I want to go home. We'll be safe enough in Colorado."

"Don't you think the first place they're going to look for Phoebe is your home? You would risk your parents and your pack because you're homesick?"

"I have plans!" Parker's rage burst from him like a volley of poorly aimed arrows. "My classes start—"

"Yes, we know all about how you want your paramedic training, but you and your mate need to go into hiding."

"Double standard!"

"You forget your rank, Rho." Ethan's icy tone should have chilled the heat of Parker's frustration.

"The difference between Phoebe and me is no one targeted me for death." The thin line of Selena's lips belied her sensible statement.

"I told you who has a contract out on me," Phoebe reminded the werewolves in the room.

"A contract?" Foster asked. "Someone contracted to have you killed?"

Oops. Phoebe needed this conversation without government handlers trying to run interference, so she ignored them. "I take it you have a safe house in mind."

"Gambayan." Selena lifted her chin.

"No fucking way." Parker pounded the sofa arm so hard it fell off. "Your family, your pack was massacred there not three months ago. If you think I'm taking my mate—"

"Massacre?" Foster asked. "Hold on a second and—"

"She said Gambayan, not Ulvskog," Ethan interrupted in a steely voice. "And I will thank you not to address my mate in that tone."

"Same fucking place." Parker's tone didn't change. "Tombstones growing moss and mold in the woods."

"Wait a minute." Foster again. "Back up. What massacre?"

Selena's eyes sparked, but she held on to her temper. "There is old magic protecting Gambayan. Old magic may be the only thing to keep your mate safe."

Phoebe needed more to be impressed or convinced. "Killing my enemy will keep me safe," she retorted. "I can't kill him if I'm hiding."

"Hold on." Benz hadn't cleared his throat recently, and it affected his voice.

"If you're going to be working with lycans, get used to the idea of killing," Selena snapped. "The problem with this case is her enemy is too well protected."

"Either he or I have to die!" Phoebe banged her quarterstaff on the floor.

"Let's back up to massacre." Foster's voice cut through the cacophony.

"Oh, you don't want to go there," Olivia advised from her corner. "You'll only stir everything up again."

Parker refused to give an inch. "We could be in Loup Garou if—"

"Don't you dare blame me." Phoebe whirled on Parker and got in his face. She thought they'd finished with this particular topic. She'd thought the elevator accident moved them to a new place in their relationship. Wrong again. "I'm the victim, not you."

"Your excuses are getting old," Selena countered. "How about you explain it?"

"Let's talk about the massacre," Foster tried again.

"Which one?" Phoebe snapped. "Your political friends have been secretly wiping out packs for years."

"Can you prove it?" Foster acted as if he retained control.

"My mate was killed in a massacre fifty years ago," Olivia offered. "I would have been killed, too, if not for visiting my birth pack. Ethan's grandfather survived, but he's not here right now. He's helping rebuild Ulvskog."

"I found my grandfather cut in half by automatic weapons a few months ago. Only a dozen or so local pack members managed to escape," Selena added.

Old news.

"And you want to send us back there!" Parker shouted.

Phoebe had nothing to add.

Corbie didn't believe Phoebe at first when she told her what she'd witnessed. Corbie warned her to never speak of that night again.

But Phoebe knew what she'd seen. Corbie knew. And Dustin. He'd been lurking about his grandmother's house.

Which reminded her…"Who else was killed by the elevator accident?"

Foster hesitated. "We haven't confirmed an identity or notified next of kin," he admitted.

"I don't suppose there's enough intact for a visual ID." A runaway elevator car squashing you to death might be quick, but messy. Still, if she could confirm someone's identity…

"We've rushed DNA identification. But thanks for the offer."

Time to be less subtle. "Have you found Dustin Holloway yet?"

"Not yet."

"Do you think he's your John Doe?"

Foster eyed her as if he could read her mind before admitting, "He and Curtis DiNardo are both possibilities."

Phoebe weighed each word before she spoke. "I was eight years old when gunfire woke me. I didn't know at the time what the sound meant."

The popping had sounded like fireworks to her young ears.

"My grandmother shoved me out the back door and told me to hide. So I climbed my favorite tree."

Blood. Gunshots. The taste of gunpowder on my tongue. My mama's screams.

Dustin had been present the day Phoebe freaked out when she'd seen the man on the TV news. The man who shot her mother.

Who's that man on TV?

Senator Tuttle. He just reelected again.

He shot my mama. That man shot my mama!

Chapter 30

Parker hefted his duffel and glared at Ulvskog's partially constructed buildings. The scent of fresh cut lumber couldn't mask the lingering traces of smoke or the reek of violent death haunting the air. A coil of blue nylon rope, hanging from a spike, swayed in the breeze.

Ethan drove Parker and Phoebe to Ulvskog after returning Parker's vehicle to the rental agency. Selena cut off every chance Parker or Phoebe could escape. They would be prisoners in Ulvskog and Gambayan.

Or, as Tokarz called it, a safe house.

"Ulvskog isn't so bad." Phoebe stood beside him, clutching her backpack. "It reminds me of where my family lived."

"And where Tuttle slaughtered your family," Parker snapped. "You should be more pissed than I am."

"I am."

Phoebe didn't sound pissed. She should be, and part of her anger should be aimed at him.

He'd been a vampire's asshole about wanting to return to Colorado. Selena shouldn't have bewitched Tokarz into thinking Gambayan, not far as the buzzard flies from Ulvskog, would be secure. Maybe from vampires. But the ones after his mate weren't vampires.

Tokarz stashed Parker's parents somewhere but wouldn't say where. Safer, Parker hoped, than Gambayan.

Because Tuttle now knew an eyewitness survived, anyone even remotely connected to Phoebe was at risk. Such as her foster mother had been.

Tuttle's minions' aptitudes would eventually catch up with Phoebe's survival instincts. Parker wanted something safer than vague "old magic" to protect his female.

His gestating female.

Old Olivia told him to use his nose, and she'd been right.

Phoebe smelled...delicious.

She must have conceived on the elevator. Parker hadn't touched her since the screaming match with the federal agents.

He also wondered if she had a clue about the pregnancy. Probably not. Her foster mother wouldn't have known about lycan gestation any more than she did about mating.

No one acknowledged their arrival in Ulvskog. *To human hell with Restin, Hatch, Rand, and the rest.*

Parker grabbed Phoebe's arm. "Come on. Do you remember the way to the old town?"

"Yes." Phoebe seemed unsure. "Don't we have to check in or something?"

"I don't care. What is Restin going to do if we don't? Exile us?"

Phoebe stared at him as if she couldn't believe the words came from his mouth. Then her lips curved upward, creating dimples in her cheeks. Her eyes shone brighter than any star.

At that moment, his mate's beauty shamed the moon.

"Damn straight." She raised her hand for a high five. "I'm a bad influence on you."

PARKER NEEDED TO GET over his snit so they could figure out how to get back to locating Senator Tuttle and exacting their revenge. Their revenge. Ever since the elevator, Phoebe knew she and Parker were on the same side.

She located the path to the old town. Her reptilian brain had trod the trail a thousand times. Instinct directed her toward the grove of ash, oak, and hawthorn hiding Gambayan's stone huts.

Corbie explained old magic came from females who created it to protect them against marauding males bent on pillage and rape. The charms were effective until someone shared the knowledge with males. Corbie theorized the traitor had been coerced—tortured—into betraying the spells.

The more time Phoebe spent with other shifters, the more her instincts sharpened as if she absorbed the lore by osmosis.

Corbie had told her so much more than Phoebe realized. Phoebe hadn't yet found the time to mourn her foster mother. She'd been too busy trying to keep her mate alive.

The living always took precedence because nothing could be done for the dead.

Old growth trees cooled the day. Moss carpeted the ground. Phoebe sniffed the air to see if she could scent Gambayan, but she caught only the early stages of decay as summer waned toward autumn, and the trace of a buck looking for trouble.

Parker didn't tread as lightly as she did; the earth quaked beneath his footfalls. Marauder. Maybe she could work with him on his stealth.

He could probably benefit from learning how to use a quarterstaff, too.

She stopped and turned to face him. Parker stopped short to keep from running into her. "We don't have to stay here."

"What?"

"We can shift and walk away. Not having a vehicle never stopped our ancestors."

His smoky quartz eyes gleamed for a second or two before the light faded. He offered the weakest excuse she'd ever heard. "Where would we go?"

"The nearest bus station. There's more to the world than Loup Garou, Soddy-Daisy, and Warwick."

"I've seen plenty of this country, on tour with Toke Lobo and the Pack."

Right. She'd forgotten his history consisted of more than his thwarted desire to become a medical doctor.

"Besides, Tokarz has a network. I think there is an alpha hotline or something. We'd be sent somewhere else. Better the devil we know."

"You think we're incarcerated?" Blue patches of sky visible between the fading green of leaves hinted otherwise. The moon, barely past half, floated in the sky like a promise of liberty. No devils, no demons.

"What would you call it?"

"Isolation. We don't have to break out to leave. We keep going. Past Gambayan, past whatever. Eventually we'd end up somewhere."

"They'd only track us."

So much for thinking she'd influenced him.

She'd have to leave on her own.

Gambayan remained as loathsome as Parker remembered. The moss and lichen-covered lumps the Varulv called dwellings looked like tombs to him. Or oversized molding toadstools. The place reeked of mildew. Even the air tasted of rot.

Jakob waited for them. He lifted his nose, nostrils flaring when he scented Phoebe.

Parker shook his head when Jakob opened his mouth.

Jakob's brows rushed together but altered his greeting. "Addy will be glad to see you. We're looking forward to having you as neighbors. And Restin is looking forward to more hands. We're behind on completing the full moon lodge." Jakob scooped up a few pebbles, then tossed them at a rock. "Addy hates spending the full moon here, but until the lodge is done, Gambayan is the safest place for her."

Ethan had shared what he'd seen in the Varulv lodge the morning after the massacre: Shot like fish in a barrel. Did impending fatherhood erase Jakob's memory?

Even more worrisome, would Parker get stupid and careless, too?

"I know you don't want to work with Restin," Phoebe said after Jakob departed. Her voice echoed in their cramped, dark quarters.

"Understatement," Parker grumbled, as he ducked through the low door to return to the outside. As much as he didn't like the trees, they were better than being trapped in a sarcophagus.

"I have an idea." Phoebe followed him outside. She didn't have to stoop to use the door.

Great. He hated her ideas. She spouted horrible ideas. If he thought about it, he could probably trace this banishment to one of her ideas. "What?"

"You don't need to sound so excited. Do you want to get off carpentry detail or not?"

She'd hooked him. She would always be able to hook him. "What do you have in mind?"

"You need to learn quarterstaff weaponry fundamentals."

"You're crazy." He'd seen her take out her foster brother and swat mosquitoes out of the air, but in a true battle? Give him his fangs. His speed. His lycan strength. His pack.

"Don't snap at me. Teaching you would give us both something useful to do. Who knows? Maybe you'll like it."

Not likely.

Three hours later, Parker stood in a clearing stripping a length of ash with a borrowed knife. "The only reason I'm doing this is to keep us away from Restin," he repeated for the umpteenth time.

"Thank you. He's even nastier than Selena." Phoebe lunged toward nothing, brandishing Jeeves. "I don't have the patience to paint, anyway. I think he suggested it only because I'm female."

Restin backed off his suggestion because he'd gotten a good whiff of Phoebe. He knew a pregnant female when he smelled one. Gestating and paint fumes didn't mix well.

"If your mate doesn't want to paint, she can keep Addy company," Restin suggested.

"I'm giving Parker lessons on how to fight with a quarterstaff," Phoebe replied. "It helps to be armed on the new moon. Maybe Addy would like to join us."

"Phoebe is not leaving my sight." Parker refused to be flexible. "We're here because someone is trying to kill her, and Selena brainwashed Tokarz into thinking this scathole is safe. Nope. Phoebe goes nowhere without me."

Restin's pissiness changed nothing. Gestating females were protected at all times.

So here Parker stood, stripping a stick he'd pretended had spoken to him. "How did you choose Jeeves?" he asked.

"Stop calling my quarterstaff that stupid name. I picked it up in the woods on my way to the cave the day my family...died."

Parker stopped peeling the bark. "You've carried that exact stick for fifteen years? It hasn't broken?"

"It's oak. Sturdy. And I take care of it."

"Why did you pick up a stick?" He would have gone for a rock himself.

"Snakes. My father taught me always to poke ahead in the woods as a snake alert. Good thing I grabbed a stick because I ran into a copperhead. I think it was a copperhead."

How many different ways could he have lost this female before she ever made it into the same city as him?

"Jeeves is oak. Are you sure ash will work?" He didn't want some inferior wood if she went at him with oak.

"Oak, ash, or hawthorn are the best woods to use."

"Figures," he muttered.

Phoebe twirled Jeeves then jammed it into the soft dirt at her feet. "You know, if the same themes keep repeating themselves, they probably contain a truth or two."

"I never heard of this so-called sacred triad until Ethan bought his house." Parker hacked at a particularly difficult knot. "Then they were all blathering about how magic protected the block of Ash Street between Oak and Hawthorn, creating a sanctuary."

Something becoming more and more difficult to find.

"The three woods belong to ancient female magic. Magic is why they're strong, why males chose them for weaponry." Phoebe continued her fluid dance using Jeeves as her partner.

Parker admired her grace.

He couldn't picture her petite frame heavy with child. The EMT-trained part of him worried. He knew females went through natural hormone therapy to prepare for childbirth, but unless their child grew only to its mother's proportions, he wished Phoebe could give birth in a sapien hospital. Not possible.

What did the Ancient Ones have planned for her?

THE MONOTONY OF HER days drove Phoebe stir crazy. She couldn't shake her lethargy, no matter how strenuously she trained with Parker, who turned out to have some natural skill with his quarterstaff. Why didn't she rebound as quickly as Parker from their elevator ordeal?

The stale and fetid air in their cramped hut added to her bad mood. Her breasts continued to hurt. Binding them each morning helped, but she regretted not tracking down some lanolin before being exiled. At least Parker didn't go at them all the time anymore. In fact, Parker developed a total disinterest in sex.

Maybe her request to fuck her in the elevator disgusted him. Or his anger about not returning to Colorado affected his penis. He didn't touch her if he could avoid it. She'd lost her twenty-four/seven urge to seduce him.

The daily reports from Selena to Restin only added to Phoebe's depression. Tuttle had been released from the hospital. Ethan and Dakota nosed around Elysian Estates a night or two, trying to pick up traces of the senator, but weren't having any luck.

The Varulv clearly didn't know what they were doing, despite their bragging. She'd stick around Gambayan until after the full moon, postponing her departure only because once in her life she wanted to experience the shift with a pack.

Once would have to be enough.

Chapter 31

All the Varulv in Ulvskog gathered to greet their alpha mere hours before moonrise. Phoebe joined the crowd, barely able to contain her excitement at spending the full moon with a pack.

Selena hopped from the cab of Ethan's red truck. "Old Olivia is staying in Warwick to help an injured ally."

"Who will stay with Addy?" Jakob wanted to know.

Addy placed her hand on his arm. The gesture didn't stop his irritation.

"Addy will be fine." Selena busied herself unloading logs from the truck bed.

"It's not right. Grannies always stay with the babes and the gestating ones on the full moon," Jakob argued.

"It can't be helped." Selena dropped the logs. "Addy will be safe in Gambayan."

"Since when do sapien needs outweigh the pack's?" Jakob muttered.

"Since the sapien is an elder who risked her life to help this pack," Selena snapped. "Would you like to question your alpha some more?"

Jakob and Addy exchanged a look, but neither spoke.

Selena cast an eye at the cloud-heavy sky. "Sunset isn't far off. We should probably get ready."

Phoebe had never spent a full moon with her own kind before. Her expectations probably exceeded reality. She prepared to leave once the moon set. She didn't mention her plans to Parker because he would try to stop her.

Parker led her into the woods. "This looks like a good spot to shift." He lifted his nose. "I smell rain. Good thing I have plastic bags for my clothes."

"Why don't we leave our clothes in the hut?"

Parker started to toe off his boots. He acted weird. "I was taught the whole process to honor the moon needs to take place where she can witness."

"How does this work?"

His empty boot dropped to the ground. "How does what work?"

Her face heated. "Shifting as a pack."

He paused. Stared at her as if he'd never seen her before. "Ancient Ones. You've never spent the full moon in a pack."

As if she'd never told him. His listening skills sucked.

"What did you do?"

She shrugged. "What matters is, what do I do tonight? I'm depending on you to teach me."

He hesitated, as if unsure what to say. "We strip off our clothes and hide them in a safe place, a spot we'll remember so we can get dressed after moonset."

Nothing different from what she did on her own. "Okay."

He plopped onto a boulder so he could remove his other boot. He seemed...cautious, as if he thought she might embarrass him in front of the others.

She chose a smaller boulder not too far from his as her staging site. Her tabi boots came off more easily than his leathers. "When I was alone, I would moon sing for a while, maybe chase a few rabbits for sport. Sometimes I would study the sky through my wolf eyes. But I was always alone."

His expression softened. "Your instincts are dead on. Singing is more fun in the pack. I like the stars, too. The sky is so...vast. Puts the day-to-day problems in perspective."

Phoebe never considered the humbleness she'd always experienced in quite the same context. She started to pull her shirt over her head.

"There is one thing." Parker sounded uncertain. No, cautious.

"What?" She swatted a mosquito who dared land on her exposed belly.

"If for some reason you can't or don't shift—" His shirt fell to the ground.

"What?" She did not want to spend her last hours with him being pissed off at him, but he thwarted her with his weirdness.

"Hear me out. If you don't shift, promise me you'll join Addy in Gambayan."

Irritation at him mounted. He knew damn well she could shift. "Why wouldn't I shift?"

He unsnapped the waist of his jeans as nonchalantly as he mentioned the rain. He should have given her a storm warning. "I think you're gestating."

Shock clogged her throat.

His eyes avoided her. "Old Olivia mentioned you might be in heat, so I did everything I could to get you pregnant."

His jeans joined his shirt and boots.

In a minute, so would his head. And his penis. She could flip a coin to determine which to rip off first.

She forced a response from her fury. "How dare –"

"It's my duty to get you pregnant. It's not my fault you're ignorant of your fertility."

All the times she wanted him physically, even when she didn't want him emotionally or rationally, was her body betraying her?

"You smell pregnant. That's why Restin agreed you didn't have to paint. Because of the fumes."

Fumes? She would show him fumes.

Parker stood. Stretched. He was a fine-looking lobo. For now. After she finished with him would be a different vision. The pressure in the air around them changed. Something strange happened in her head. Her sinuses. Her ears. Heat shimmered around Parker. Enveloped her. Caressed her. A moment later Parker stood before her, a magnificent black wolf.

And she—she still wore her leggings. Her turtleneck. Only her feet were bare. The full moon peeked between the tall trees and mocked her.

"No!" she shrieked. Her lunar batteries must not have recharged after being depleted in the elevator.

Parker growled his response. He stared at her with smoky quartz eyes.

"I will never forgive you." Her voice quavered.

He nudged her with his nose. His lower lip fluttered, revealing his canines. He nudged again, harder.

She tried to finish removing her top.

Parker snapped at her.

"Stop it!" She raised her quarterstaff. She could, she should beat him bloody.

He growled again.

She had no choice. His DNA wouldn't allow her to do anything to harm the child he believed she carried.

She backed away, stumbling on a tree root and nearly losing her footing. Her bare feet inventoried every pebble, twig, and bit of debris strewn on the path.

Parker brought her boots to her in his mouth. She brushed off her soles, then pulled on the tabi with shaking hands. Parker stood next to her, guarding her. He was going to make sure she went to Gambayan like a good little gestating she-wolf and sit out the full moon with the grannies, the pregnant ones, and the children.

She could take off now. Tuttle had left town. Nothing held her in Minnesota.

She looked Parker in the eye. "You are not the boss of me."

Except she found Addy waiting for her in Gambayan.

She was hunched alone in her hut. A single lantern provided feeble light and polluted the air with kerosene fumes.

"Phoebe? I wondered where you were."

PARKER WATCHED HIS MATE stalk down the hill toward Gambayan. At least she did as she'd been told. Phoebe didn't take instruction well.

He turned and trotted toward the mountaintop where he could join the other wolves singing their praises to the full moon. His prayers of thanks to the Ancient Ones filled his heart.

The scent of rain intensified. Being in wolf form amplified all of a lycan's senses.

He stopped to lift his nose to test the air. The breeze ruffled his pelt. Ozone preceded the rain. Distant thunder threatened his sensitive ears. A thunderstorm blew its way toward Ulvskog.

The steadily falling barometric pressure played havoc with his lycan sinuses. He hated thunderstorms. Most lycans did.

He'd been so focused on the weather, he nearly missed another scent lurking on the ground, unfamiliar and apparently wanting to stay hidden.

He ignored a frisson of concern, labeling it his fear Big Foot planned to join the songfest.

Chapter 32

"Congratulations!" Addy, who'd known Phoebe only a few weeks, threw her arms around Phoebe and hugged her so tight, Phoebe thought her ribs would break.

Her quarterstaff thudded to the floor. "Where are the others?"

Addy released her. "I thought someone told you. Everyone else was killed in a massacre two full moons ago. Only fifteen Varulv survived. Old Olivia should be here tonight, except for a friend in town needing her."

Helga. Addy was talking about Helga.

"At least we have each other. Isn't being pregnant wonderful?"

No! Phoebe wanted to howl. *Pregnancy is inconvenient. I have work to do!*

"I've been envying your energy since you've been here," Addy babbled on, as if Phoebe were participating. "My first few months of pregnancy were dreadful. Your breasts don't hurt?"

I bind them. Besides, Parker's been at them constantly. Before the elevator.

"Your stomach is okay?"

No, my stomach isn't okay. Stress is nauseating me.

"You aren't exhausted all the time?"

Serial shifting is debilitating. My lunar batteries were depleted. I'm still trying to recoup.

"Old Olivia explained how our bodies get tired because it's busy making babies. Parker must be over the moon." Addy babbled as if they were holding a conversation.

Parker is out of his mind. Especially after I separate his head from his body.

"He's probably lurking outside with Jakob, guarding us." Addy winced, her hands splayed over her enormous belly.

"Are you all right?" Phoebe asked, more from politeness than concern.

"Yeah. When we found out Old Olivia couldn't be here, Jakob wanted me to go to Warwick. But we didn't have enough time to find a ride and make the trip. Besides, I don't want to risk being away when I go into labor. Our babe will be the first born in the new village. The first of a new generation. A stronger generation because we're merging with the Limmikin."

"But you're not Limmikin." Phoebe's census counted only four full-blooded survivors plus Ethan.

Addy flinched at Phoebe's harsh tone. "No, but Ethan is. His and Selena's offspring will be raised with mine. And yours. We're guaranteeing the lycan future."

Phoebe swallowed a shriek of denial. She didn't even know what to do on the full moon. How could she grow a werewolf baby?

Addy winced. Her fingers curled as she stroked her belly.

Phoebe didn't like Addy's action at all.

"Twinges." Addy pasted on a smile. "Pregnancy is great for several months, but toward the end, when the baby is so big, lugging around the weight is uncomfortable."

"You're not going to have that baby tonight, are you?"

Do not panic. Do not run howling into the night.

"Don't be silly. Babies are never born on the full moon." Addy punctuated her statement with a gasp.

A sharp ammonia-like scent filled the space, overwhelming the odors of damp mossy stone, mold, and kerosene. A dark stain spread on the worn floor at Addy's feet.

"Did you piss yourself?"

"My water broke."

"What are you talking about?"

"My water. The amniotic fluid in the sac around the baby. The sac breaks when the baby is getting ready to be born."

"Tell it to stop." Phoebe thought she hid her panic well.

"I can't."

"Try! You're the parent!"

The moon wouldn't set for hours. Phoebe couldn't be alone with a female about to give birth. Assassins, even novice ones, weren't qualified to deliver babies. Besides, everyone's preoccupation with the full moon provided her with a chance to escape.

"Childbirth doesn't work according to what the mother wants. Don't you know anything?" Addy's calmness only further irritated Phoebe.

"No." If Addy possessed any sense she would be panicking, too. "I didn't grow up in a pack."

"We need to start getting ready, although it may be hours before the babe is born. Jakob and I did some studying, and Old Olivia coached us in case she couldn't be here." Addy's cheerful expression faded. "We thought the other females would be around. Jana's birthed a couple children. Amelia, too."

Addy's butterscotch-colored eyes met Phoebe's. "It's the two of us until moon set."

"Tell the baby to stop," Phoebe repeated.

"The baby doesn't understand words yet."

"Hasn't it been listening all this time?"

Addy ignored her. "We'll need water. Hot water."

"Why? Because you broke yours?"

"Don't be silly. Maybe to keep us busy." Addy's voice sounded shaky. "Water from the sacred spring would be best."

"What sacred spring?" Phoebe could pretend to go for water and not return.

"You really don't know anything? Every sacred grove has a sacred spring. Gambayan is in a sacred grove."

Okay. Corbie rambled on about sacred springs. Phoebe wished she'd paid more attention. "Where do I find the one here?"

Addy closed her eyes and breathed through her teeth. The whistling air mimicked the rising wind.

When she didn't answer Phoebe's question, Phoebe figured the child's timing horrified Addy as much as it horrified her. Until Addy said, "We will need a knife."

"I am not cutting you open." What if she missed and cut off the baby's ear or arm? She carried a quarterstaff, not a blade.

"No, silly. For cutting the umbilical cord."

"Can't you give birth in your lycan form and eat the placenta?" Sounded disgusting but would solve so many problems.

"If we're going to be friends, I'm going to forget you suggested that. Until it's your turn to give birth."

Who mentioned friendship? The double threat appalled her. Addy's experiences meant nothing to Phoebe. Parker's male ego misinterpreted any signs. The damn moon had to be wrong.

"You need a midwife. A doctor. An EMT. Parker is an EMT. He can help you birth the baby. Tell the baby to wait until after moon set. Parker can take care of everything." *Damn his traitorous soul.*

Addy's gleaming face paled. "Or Selena. She's been trained in midwifery."

Such a paragon of lycan virtues, that Selena. Alpha, vampire slayer, hot dish chef, and midwife. No wonder she carried a boulder on her shoulder.

Bless her heart.

"Okay. Selena."

Parker would be a better choice. He represented the new age of lycanthropy and modern medicine.

Phoebe tried to settle her mind. She spied several rolled up sleeping bags in the corner, protected from the natural damp by clear plastic. Two brightly colored buckets rested on their sides. The sleeping bags would help, but Addy might need more to keep warm. And, Goddess forbid, they would need something in which to wrap the baby. If Addy couldn't stop her labor.

"I'm going to run out for a bit." Phoebe needed the night breathing down her neck instead of Addy. She could fetch the water for Addy, then make her getaway.

"Don't leave me." Addy grabbed Phoebe's arm.

"Water from the sacred spring. Remember? Why don't you roll out the sleeping bags?" Phoebe disengaged Addy's hand and snatched up the buckets. "I'll be gone for a couple minutes tops."

The trip took closer to half an hour. She found the spring easily enough. Filling the buckets took time, as did hauling the water back to the hut.

"It's going to storm," she told Addy when she returned. "The clouds are piling up. I couldn't see the moon at all. Listen to the wind."

"It stormed on the last full moon, too." Addy paced the hut, fingers of both hands entwined and supporting the bottom of her belly.

The constant motion drove Phoebe crazy. Maybe she could teach Addy to meditate. "Don't you want to lie down?"

"Old Olivia told me to walk as long as I could." Addy slowly released her breath. "Walking keeps the baby's head down, toward the floor. Gravity to help labor."

Phoebe couldn't argue with logic. "Fine. Keep walking."

Addy glared at her. "Thanks, Doc."

"I'm not Doc. Parker is Doc."

Parker. Maybe she should try to find him before she abandoned Addy. Even in four-legged form, he might be able to assist.

The wind dashed through the surrounding trees, as loud as a beast crashing through brush. The lantern flickered. Thunder clapped in the distance.

"Parker is an amazing EMT." As if she knew anything about his skills beyond what she'd observed with Helga. But she could lie. "He's so good, Colorado wants to make him a paramedic, which is a higher classification than EMT. Why don't I try to find him?"

"He can't help if he can't talk and doesn't have hands." Addy turned and headed toward Phoebe again. "I prefer Selena. Jakob won't like another male looking at...me."

The idea of Parker getting that up close and personal with another female didn't sit well with Phoebe, either, even after she decapitated him. "We need help."

"What's this we scat?" Addy grew testier.

"You're right. You're doing all the labor. Ha, ha. I made a joke. How are you doing with the walking?"

"I'm not an invalid," Addy snapped. Her good nature had vanished.

"I didn't say you were," Phoebe snarled in response. "I was going to offer you my quarterstaff to use as a cane to lean on, but if you're going to be a bitch about it—"

"I am a bitch!" Addie shrieked as she bent over, clutching her gut.

"Breathe. Fill your lungs." Phoebe half-remembered Corbie saying the same words when Phoebe hurt herself. The pain had been enough to make her vomit. *Breathe your way through the pain. Let the oxygen carry you to the other side.*

"I am breathing."

"Sounds more like gasping to me. Stop talking and focus on inhaling, then exhaling."

Addy straightened and planted her palms on the rough walls. The porous stone crumbled beneath her clutching fingers.

Her short, choppy respiration bothered Phoebe. "Suck in the air all the way to the bottom of your lungs."

"I am! My lungs are cramped by the baby."

"Try harder."

"How would you like me to take that stick of yours and smack you across your boobs?"

"I'd like to see you try. Now, shut up and keep breathing."

STORM CLOUDS VEILED THE moon. Parker, a lowly rho, huddled at the rear of the gathering atop the mountain where Selena preferred to spend full moons. Tonight, though, even the higher ranked lycans couldn't see the moon. Tonight marked the second month running where the weather conspired against the werewolves.

He'd have to tell Phoebe she'd missed nothing.

She wouldn't be appeased. The female could hold a grudge. Okay, Tuttle and Holloway deserved her wrath, but not at risk to her safety.

He'd heard Ethan let Selena take the lead when it came to dealing with her rapists. Dakota had described the scene to Parker in detail. Even now, Parker had to squash the urge to protect his privates.

The wind gusted, battering those gathered, whistling like a crazy stalker. Chilly fingers of rain tapped on Parker's pelt. He shivered and wondered how the females were faring in their cramped stone huts.

He mistook the first crack for a tree limb breaking. Not a lightning strike, because the full storm hadn't yet arrived. The howls alerted him to the danger.

He flattened himself in the mud and scanned the area. Part of the cliff had fallen away—always a danger when rain soaked the ground. But it hadn't rained in at least two weeks. The ground couldn't possibly be saturated to the point of collapse.

Selena! Ethan!

Their voices weren't audible in the cacophony of howls. Others, like him, dropped to their bellies. They crawled through the mud to the crumbling edge where the ledge once jutted into the sky. Rubble the exposed roots couldn't contain continued to drip from the raw wound. The scent of freshly opened earth filled his head. Something else lingered, too, something—

Yelps of confusion and agony interrupted his thoughts. They came from below. Selena for sure. Maybe Ethan. Restin. Others. He yipped a question, hoping one of them could hear and respond.

Selena. *Ledge maybe twenty feet down. Ethan maybe broken leg, ribs. Restin quiet and still.*

Parker didn't know the Varulv well enough to identify who else might be missing.

Hatch, Rand, below us. Somewhere.

Ancient Ones. The alphas and alphas to be. The sole beta. The three packs were without leadership on the full moon.

Chapter 33

Phoebe needed to get unpregnant. Fast.

Pregnant meant family. Families were slaughtered. She couldn't bring a child into the world when the world didn't want her kind.

Some herbs could do the trick. Corbie often counseled females with unwanted pregnancies. But Corbie was dead. Neither Selena nor Olivia would help her. Maybe Helga knew something.

Fists of wind pummeled the hut.

"I hope this place is sturdier than it looks," Phoebe muttered.

"If you were out there in four-legged form, you wouldn't even think about it. Gambayan is invincible. My granny told me the gods of our elders created this haven with old magic." Addy resumed her waddling.

"Maybe if I'd been raised in a pack, I'd have a clue about your blathering, but my pack was massacred fifteen years ago. I'm the sole survivor, raised by a crone friend of my granny."

Addy stopped her pacing. "Seriously?"

"My instincts are suspect at best," Phoebe confessed.

"No, they're not. You came home to Minnesota."

"Home?" The pain must have addled Addy. "No. I'm from Tennessee."

"But you're Limmikin, and the Limmikin are originally from here. These woods."

Addy may as well have punched her with a labor pain. "I...I'd forgotten."

According to her granny's tales, Hache-Hi's miracle survival happened in this forest, where he would one day emerge in triumph from hiding.

Phoebe couldn't possibly be fulfilling the legend. Not pregnant with her mission unfulfilled. Why did she have to be pregnant now? Revenge was what mattered. She had a senator to torture. Truth to be wrung from his dying lips.

Her ancestors cheered for her to win. Political ambition also victimized them.

Phoebe paused to stare at Addy. The lantern cast exaggerated shadows across the other female's face. Did she not understand what happened in Ulvskog wasn't an isolated incident?

The world didn't deserve their offspring.

Phoebe found herself cradling the mythical child who prevented her from shifting this full moon. A child she wasn't ready for.

Addy's soft words annoyed Phoebe. "You'll get used to your condition." Then her breath whistled between her teeth, and she doubled over.

Jakob growled as he nosed around. *Check this out.*

Parker and Dakota put their noses to the ground. The unfamiliar scent again. The one Parker tried to identify. Big Foot? Familiar—not vampire familiar—but one he'd encountered before, although less intense than tonight. Rain always refreshed the smell of the world.

Jakob growled again, lowering his face and patting a spot with his paw. *Here. What does this look like to you?*

Rain dripped from Parker's brow into his eyes, but he focused on the exposed earth capturing Jakob's attention.

Smooth and even in contrast to the rest of the edge. The ragged, shredded edge. To Parker's inexpert eye, the earth looked as if someone slid a shovel into the ground to weaken the ledge. Deliberate sabotage of the spot werewolves traditionally gathered on the full moon.

Had the saboteur known the alphas and betas positioned themselves closest to the moon when paying homage?

A leader needed to emerge and a rescue plan developed, even when rescue wouldn't be possible until moonset.

Things could be done before then. Rope could be fetched from Ulvskog. Not easily but it could be done. Someone could scout a way to the ledge where the injured lay. Again, not a simple task, maybe even dangerous, especially considering the weather, but one that might save time when time again became an ally.

No one seemed motivated. No one took the initiative.

Parker exchanged a glance with Dakota. Loup Garou lycans weren't afraid to overstep their status if something needed to be accomplished. What was wrong with these Varulv?

Ulvskog wasn't Loup Garou territory. The longer the Varulv waited, the more time wasted. Parker hated wasting time, especially when there were injured to tend.

You! He barked at a dithering female. *We're going to need rope. Is there any in the village?*

Everything in the village burned a couple months ago, she replied.

Foolish female, a male snapped. *We've been using rope to hoist rafters.*

Is it accessible now? Could you and the female fetch it and bring it here?

Why do we need rope?

Parker wanted to howl his frustration. *To rescue your alpha come moonset.*

Comprehension dawned on the lobo's face.

Before you go, who is the most sure-footed in your pack?

WHY WOULDN'T THE MOON set?

Phoebe fretted at the open door and surveyed the night. She tried to judge the time, but she couldn't track the moon's progress crawling across the sky; the storm blindfolded the world.

Parker needed to stand on two legs, not four, because he needed to deliver Addy's baby. She needed his medical knowledge and his skills.

Or Selena. Selena could be alpha bitch and midwife to Addy when she whelped the next generation of Varulv.

Phoebe wasn't going to stick around. As soon as Parker showed up or Addy gave birth, whichever came first, Phoebe was history.

The heat inside the hut threatened to drown her. She refilled her lungs with air smelling faintly of ozone.

Phoebe closed the door and faced the immediate future. Humidity cloaked the hut's interior, a heavy, sweltering blanket clinging to her with cobweb tenacity.

Sweat pearled on Addy's forehead, amber beads strung on beams from the lantern. Her movements slowed and grew more laborious.

Goddess, Phoebe had to help Addy deliver her baby. So much for escaping.

"Talk to me," Addy moaned. "Distract me. Tell me about your pack."

"I have no stories about my pack other than what I've told you. I'm the massacre's sole survivor." *Unlike you and your fifteen.*

"Was it politically motivated, like here?" Addy paused, moved her hands to her lower back, and stretched.

"I don't know. I was only eight."

"Everyone says Congressman Peters ordered the shootings here, but no one can prove it except by hearsay. Hatch says the congressman's father wiped out most of the Limmikin." Addy resumed her pacing. "Gods of our Elders, I wish I could walk outside."

Phoebe opened the door again. The wind had intensified until it keened around the contours of the building. Thunder sent up a litany of constant complaints. Lightning flashed, illuminating the world in strobes of lavender light. Rain slashed through the opening, briefly cooling Phoebe. "Probably not a good idea."

"Probably not." Addy wiped her brow. "How did you manage without a pack?"

"I lived with a coven. The crone who took me in and my granny were friends, so she knew some lycan ways." *But not enough to tell me how to prevent pregnancy.* "I couldn't miss what I didn't know."

ELECTRICITY CRACKLED IN THE air. Thunder beat on the darkness. Selena moaned as Parker sniffed at her. Ethan wasn't the only one with broken bones.

It's me. Parker Rowe. I'm an emergency medical technician. Try not to move. We'll get you to safety once the moon sets.

Mud covered Parker. He and a Varulv lobo discovered a way down to the ledge where Selena, Ethan, and Restin landed. The Varulv continued searching for Hatch and Rand.

I'm not senile. Selena was conscious. *In some pain, but my brain is still functional. Too bad we couldn't use your shifting trick as we fell.*

Too bad, he agreed. *Here's your status. The ledge you're on is wide enough for the three of you to shift two legged at moonset. The full moon should speed the repair of any broken bones. Internal injuries are a different problem. So are head injuries. I've sent lobos to Ulvskog for rope to assist everyone getting back to the top.*

He waited for her reprimand for assigning tasks to her pack.

Instead, she complimented him. *Good idea. What else?*

Thank you, Ancient Ones for Selena's leadership.

We're looking for Hatch and Rand.

What aren't you telling me? Is anyone else hurt?

Scat. The female read his mind.

He shared Jakob's discovery with Selena, the smooth- sided cut in the earth indicating sabotage.

Selena's long silence worried him. He checked her consciousness before she said, *Someone is out for my pack.*

Or out to get Phoebe, Parker reminded her. *She would have been here if she weren't pregnant.*

Scat. He needed to warn his mate. He lifted his muzzle to the sky in the direction he thought the moon might lie and let loose a lament. He hoped his voice contained the strength to slice through the storm and make its way to Gambayan and Phoebe. He cautioned her to stay put, that evil lurked in the night.

Do you want to go to her?

Duh? Selena needed him more.

My mate will be fine. She can defend herself with the stick she carries. She taught me a few tricks since we've been here, and she's good. She's strong, like Gambayan magic is strong.

Something nudged his leg. A Varulv lobo. *We found Rand and Hatch. It's not good.*

THE STORM CONTINUED TO torture the corner of the world where the two pregnant women were trapped. The blustering weather gagged even the occasional thread of a howl woven into the night. Phoebe missed the reminder she wasn't alone.

"I'm going to lie down now," Addy announced. "My legs hurt too much to keep going."

Phoebe assisted Addy as she lowered her bulky body to the pallet. Addy clutched Phoebe's hand so tightly, Phoebe feared her fingers being crushed. Once she'd freed herself, she flexed them to encourage blood flow.

"Are you close?" Phoebe used the corner of a sleeping bag to wipe Addy's brow before offering her water from the sacred spring.

"How would I know? I've never given birth before."

"Good point."

Lightning crackled. The wind shrieked. Addy howled.

No answering howl of reassurance, only the thunder clapping its agreement. Addy reached for Phoebe's hands again.

Phoebe extended her quarterstaff. "You're going to break my fingers. Use my staff to squeeze next time you have a pain."

Addy's eyes glinted orange fire. "Maybe I'll club you with it."

"Me?" Phoebe exaggerated her reaction. "Club your mate. He's responsible for your condition."

Just as Parker was responsible for hers.

Her dream, ever since she learned she could shift, involved killing Tuttle in her wolf form. She wanted to taste his terror, his blood, his pain. Her quarterstaff would work, she supposed, but her inner wolf mocked the wimpy weapon. Besides, two-legged vulnerability made her easy prey.

If the senator learned of her pregnancy, he could use the condition against her.

Her pregnancy couldn't have come at a worse time.

Phoebe resumed pacing.

"Why now?" Addy moaned, mirroring Phoebe's sentiments. "Why couldn't the baby wait?"

Both babies. "Look on the bright side. It will be known as the child born on the August full moon. Maybe they'll add The Chosen's Moon to its many names."

Addy grunted. "You're so funny."

Thirty steps to circle the room. Clockwise. Counterclockwise. Diagonally. Tic-tac-toe.

"I'm having this baby," Addy announced. As if there were any question. "I'm having this baby now!"

"You don't need to scream."

"You wait. You'll be screaming, too." The sentence ended on a shriek.

Phoebe froze. "You mean right now." "Did you put the water on to boil?"

"With what? This isn't the best fire-starting weather."

The rain Morse-coded its agreement on the roof.

Thunder applauded, followed by a loud snap. In the hut. "What was that?" Phoebe stared at the door.

Addy broke off panting to say, "I think I broke it."

A chill clutched Phoebe's heart, despite the steaminess of the room. "Broke what? You already broke your water."

"Your stick. The one you gave me to grip."

Her quarterstaff. Addy broke her quarterstaff?

Phoebe's lungs seized. She couldn't breathe. Dizzy. Her head felt light enough to float, the low ceiling the only thing keeping her from flying away.

Her quarterstaff. Her weapon. She'd learned to fight with the stick. The strong wood could withstand as well as deliver killing blows.

Not five minutes ago she insulted it by thinking it a wimpy weapon. Now she would give anything to have it in one piece again.

The staff had been her constant companion since the morning after the massacre. She picked it up from the ground when she crept from her hiding place in the tree and fled the bloodied corpses of her grandmother, her parents, neighbors, and friends. She used the stick to hobble through the woods, looking for someone, anyone alive. Except for the snake she cold-cocked. Slashed her way through brush and briers with it. The stout oak acted as her lifeline. The wood withstood death.

How could the threat of new life fracture it?

Everything she believed about herself was gone.

OVER THERE. SEE THE knob to the left and up a bit?

Parker peered through the silver slashes of rain in the direction the Varulv lobo indicated. Lightning strobed. The purple-blue light glinted off something.

What is it? Selena asked.

Something shiny. You know these woods. Is there anything that would reflect lightning?

Only owl eyes. Can someone investigate?

The rain pounding in his ears interfered with his hearing, but he thought Selena breathed easier. The full moon's power couldn't be diminished by a summer storm.

Ethan moaned. *Who beat the scat out of me?*

The ledge where you were singing collapsed. You fell about twenty feet.

Shouldn't we be dead? Restin chimed in, his tone snide; a sure sign Restin would be okay.

It takes more than a tumble to take out a lycan on the full moon. Selena reclaimed her role as alpha. *How's everybody healing?*

Ethan responded first. *I'm getting there.*

Getting there wouldn't help Rand or Hatch. Parker filled the leaders in with what he knew.

How much farther down are they? Selena asked.

Maybe ten yards. They're not responding. I'm heading down now.

The rain limited his vision and turned traversing the mountain into a treacherous excursion.

The blessing of rain intensified scent, the moisture refreshing aroma. The wind carried the odors across gullies and bridged ravines. Scents mingled in a stew of the rain itself, ozone, raw earth, gunpowder, the coming autumn—

Gunpowder?

He paused his descent and lifted his muzzle. Tested the air. Got a nostril full of water he had to blow out before trying again.

Gunpowder. Could the scent be related to the flash on the opposite knob? He didn't know much about guns but what if someone attached a scope to a rifle? Or maybe the lightning glinted off the barrel.

What reflected didn't matter. Fresh gunpowder did.

He finished making his way to the narrow outcropping where Hatch and Rand lay. The Ancient Ones still provided miracles. The shelf barely contained space for the two lobos who'd landed there. Parker doubted he'd be able to get close enough to one to sniff their injuries.

Both lobos still breathed. Hatch's age concerned Parker. His bones were frailer than his son's. Rand's ear, his only visible wound, was a bloody mess.

Parker sniffed.

Gunpowder again.

Rand had been hot.

"Gods of our Elders, will this child ever be born?" Addy's shout echoed off the low ceiling. The lantern flame flickered.

"Would you like more magic elixir?" Phoebe doubted the spring water contained any medicinal or healing properties, but Addy believed. Corbie claimed the only thing a person could control was attitude. If Addy believed, then her attitude would help with the pain.

"No." Addy turned her face from Phoebe.

Why would anyone willingly go through this?

"I wish Olivia or Selena were here to help you." Phoebe knew she sounded lame. "Or Parker. He knows all about stuff like this."

"My baby is not stuff like this. It's the first new member of a pack someone tried to exterminate." Pride overshadowed Addy's pain. "Yours will be the same."

The power of Addy's statement, each word as precise as a master archer's arrow, pierced Phoebe's soul. Not merely her heart, but deeper, more elemental. The agony surpassed even her ever-simmering rage.

The first new member of a pack someone tried to exterminate.

Addy continued philosophizing. "Hache-Hi procreated with his mate when they escaped. Their son mated to produce Ethan, half Limmikin. Now he's mated with the surviving alpha of the Varulv. They're creating a new pack by mingling elements of the old. We're proving our resilience to the Washington politicians who think they can kill us off."

Chapter 34

Parker found shelter beneath a tree, where he lay panting for a moment. He needed to catch his breath. Climbing from the shelf where Rand and Hatch lay consumed most of his energy. Mud caked his claws, reducing his traction. He slid backward two feet for every three he gained.

Learning the nature of Rand's wound infuriated Selena.

What should we do now? A Varulv lobo interrupted his rest.

Couldn't any Varulv lycan think for himself? How any of them managed to avoid being shot during the massacre constituted a miracle. No wonder Selena micromanaged. Her pack needed everything done for them.

He resisted the temptation to send the lobo down to Selena to get his orders directly from his alpha. Instead, Parker summoned his reserve of patience.

We're going to need to haul everyone up with the ropes once the moon sets.

Selena and Restin would need the rope only as a fail-safe. Ethan might need more. Self-healing would be in progress. The injured could assist with their rescue.

Like hauling rafters into place? The Varulv lobo seemed confused.

Parker closed his eyes. This night seemed endless.

Almost.

Parker's eyes popped open.

Restin stood next to him. He should have expected Restin to do whatever he could so he could be in charge. Restin had experience in rafter hauling.

The beta formed other plans. *Since you're the EMT, you should oversee the rescue. I'm trotting over to where you saw the glint. Trace the source of gunpowder.* He bared his teeth. *Maybe maul a sniper.*

ADDY WRITHED AS IF possessed.

Oh. Wait. She is.

Phoebe grabbed Addy's clammy-skinned wrist and found her pulse. Not that she knew what a healthy pulse of a female in labor should be, but she could confirm Addy's heart still pumped. The harsh rasp of breath verified Addy's lungs continued to bellow.

The humidity in the room turned her own body into the headwater for a new tropical river. Her clothes adhered to her, increasing her discomfort. As much as she longed to run into the rain to rinse away the miasma clinging to her, she couldn't abandon Addy.

The birth of Addy's child meant something important.

"I can't do this," Addy moaned.

"Don't you think it's a tad too late?"

"Nobody warned me birthing would hurt like this." The tears oozing from the corners of Addy's tightly screwed eyes mingled with the sweat sheeting her face.

"Maybe drinking more water from the sacred spring will help."

Ice chips. Parker gave Helga ice chips in the hospital. Oh, what Phoebe wouldn't have done for some ice chips.

She helped Addy sit up so she could sip.

Phoebe blanked her mind of everything unrelated to getting through this night. *What would Parker do?*

"I'm dying, aren't I?" Addy asked.

As if Phoebe would know. "You're having a baby. Females do it all the time."

"Lots of females die in childbirth."

"Do you sincerely think the Goddess would let you survive a massacre so you could die in childbirth? You escaped for a reason."

Addy twisted. "Only to give birth. The baby is what matters."

"A motherless child is a burden on the pack. If the Goddess or gods of your elders or whatever wants your child, the whatever wants you, and not merely as an incubator for the Chosen, but to teach it."

"Oh, please. Chosen?" Addy made a face, which Phoebe took as a good sign.

"You're the one who said it. By giving birth and surviving, you're not letting Washington win."

"Neither of us is letting Washington win."

Oh, Washington was going to lose its most powerful senator as soon as Phoebe could get close enough again. She should have killed him in the hospital when she confronted him.

Except Parker, Helga, and the others might have been implicated. She couldn't endanger them. She needed to be the lone assassin. No matter how much the others claimed they would help her, she couldn't accept their help.

She'd survived the massacre for a reason.

PARKER CONSIDERED RESTIN'S IDEA. *Mauling a sniper would work. What if we lulled him into complacency?*

Restin's head jerked. *What do you mean?*

Moonset isn't far off. What if we send a false message? Our leaders are dead, mourn with us. We are lost souls in the storm.

No one is dead.

Maybe Rand, possibly Hatch. Parker shoved away the thought. *False message,* Parker repeated.

A sapien won't understand our lies.

Restin would never go along with an idea he didn't generate.

Let's run it by Selena, Dakota suggested. *She's the alpha.*

Where did you come from? Restin's annoyance came through as clear as a howl.

But Dakota vanished as unobtrusively as he arrived.

Parker and Restin stared at each other. The rain seemed sparser. Lightning no longer crackled overhead. Thunder lingered as a distant distraction. The wind whimpered as it weakened.

A few moments later, Selena's sob rose in the air. *Follow my lead,* she instructed her pack. *Lament my death with all the sorrow you can put into your song. The moon will forgive our lies.*

Parker's heart thudded four times as the Varulv digested Selena's odd directive. One female joined Selena in a dirge duet. One lobo, then another, more females–the night reverberated with the song of a pack whose leader died.

Jakob remained silent. He stared at Restin until he snared his attention. *I know these woods better than you do. I'm going with you.*

Addy's shriek crashed Phoebe's pity party. "It's not going to wait for Parker or Selena. It wants out now."

Phoebe squatted next to Addy. The other she-wolf shed her underwear. Phoebe helped hike her skirt to her waist. Addy lay fully exposed. The bulge undulated.

It's living. It's been growing inside her, taking what it needs from her body in order to survive.

Phoebe shut down the thinking part of her brain, so the parts that acted and reacted could focus on getting Addy's baby born. *Females gave birth all the time. Every day. Hundreds of times a day. Addy could do this. She could probably give birth without help. Other creatures did. Insurance companies probably invented the need for medical intervention. Tap into your cynicism.*

Cynicism wouldn't bring Addy's baby into the world. As much as she wanted someone else, anyone else there, Phoebe acknowledged she and Addy were on their own.

"I have to look," Phoebe warned Addy.

Addy growled.

Phoebe took her reaction as assent and crawled to where she could get a good look at the baby's progress. Additional light would have been helpful. Better yet, if she could shift, her lycan night vision would make a major difference. The lantern glow barely penetrated the corners of the room. She needed to bring it closer to where Addy reclined.

The kerosene fumes irritated Phoebe's eyes. The baby didn't need its first breath filled with poison, but Phoebe saw no other way to provide even half-assed illumination. She'd worry about the consequences later.

The potential for too many consequences increased with every passing moment.

A loud crack accompanied by another scream distracted Phoebe from her woe-is-me moment. Addy snapped a piece of the quarterstaff in two.

Phoebe peered into the gap between Addy's legs. Something bulged. Something she thought might be a baby's head. Or else she'd misinterpreted her own private parts all these years.

"I think you should try to squat again." Phoebe believed in gravity. Gravity would help the baby emerge.

"I don't think so." Addy writhed and groaned again. "I think I'm supposed to breathe or something."

"Of course, you're supposed to breathe."

"Old Olivia told me to pant instead of pushing. I need to push." Addy proceeded to sound as if she'd run a marathon in the high summer heat.

"If you squat the baby might fall out on its own."

"And land on its head? I don't think that's such a great idea."

Phoebe swallowed hard. "I'll catch it. Let the laws of the earth assist you."

She made her way behind Addy. "I'm going to help you up." Phoebe hooked her arms under Addy's.

"You're too puny to lift me."

Phoebe squelched a flare of anger. "I'm stronger than I look." She jerked on Addy's arms to make her point. "There you go."

"That's better," Addy admitted after a long moan.

This would work better with a bed. But Phoebe planted herself in front of Addy.

Addy's moans turned to howls.

The door crashed inward.

Addy shrieked.

Chapter 35

THE MESSAGE FROM JAKOB and Restin came sooner than Parker anticipated. Jakob's knowledge of the land led the scouting party.

Two, Restin yipped into the night. *With guns.*

The lamentations ceased, so everyone heard Jakob's furious addendum.

They want gestating females. Our mates.

"THERE ARE TWO PREGNANT bitches?" Shock turned into a chuckle. "Well, well. Isn't this interesting."

Phoebe's mouth gaped as the most powerful man in Washington, D.C. dripped his way into the hut. She reached for her quarterstaff, but—

"Two?"

A second person, smaller but just as wet, followed Senator Richard Tuttle out of the storm. Female, judging by the scent. A familiar scent.

Addy moaned.

"You!" The lantern light reflected off Tuttle's glasses.

"We might be too late." The unknown female pushed past Phoebe to stand over Addy. "Is it still a fetus?"

Shit. Phoebe recognized the voice even though she'd heard it only once or twice.

"Is it still a werewolf fetus?" Nola Peters' commanding tone only served to piss off Phoebe.

"No. It's a baby."

"Help me!" Addy moaned. "I have to push."

"Don't push," Nola ordered Addy. "My grandfather needs a fetus, not a newborn."

Phoebe turned to protect Addy and her baby, but Tuttle grabbed her arm.

"We've got another incubating right here, Nola. Let's get going."

Nola stared at Phoebe's skinny body. "What are you talking about? That one isn't pregnant."

"Yes, she is. She's a werewolf, it's the full moon, and she hasn't shifted. According to my werewolf specialist, breeding females can't shift. That's why tonight is the best night to snatch as many breeders as we can."

Phoebe jumped on his words. "Werewolf specialist? You must be talking about Dustin Holloway. The only thing he's a specialist on is his dick. He lied to you because he's pissed at me."

"Is the fetus big enough to help my grandfather?" Nola asked.

"Wait a minute." Maybe Phoebe wasn't ready for motherhood, but that didn't mean someone could simply steal her baby. Unless they had a death wish. Maybe she couldn't shift on the full moon, but a she-wolf didn't lose her strength because she walked on two legs instead of four.

She wrenched free of Tuttle's grasp.

He backhanded her.

She didn't expect his maneuver and went flying to the floor. Something hard poked her ribs.

"Don't you touch my baby!" Addy swung something at Nola. Connected.

Nola staggered from the blow. "You bitch!"

"Don't you forget it." Addy's voice went from a piercing high-pitched squeal to a lower growl any lobo would be proud to produce.

Phoebe groped for whatever jabbed her. A splintered stick. Her quarterstaff. A piece of it. She wrapped her fingers around the familiar wood with the strange new contours.

She rolled away in time to avoid Tuttle's kick.

"I thought old magic protected this place from vampires." Phoebe hopped to her feet. Muscle memory molded her stance, with a slight adjustment for the shorter quarterstaff.

"It is. Use your nose, she-wolf," Addy managed between pants. Another soft moan. "My baby is coming."

"Not if I cut it out of you first." Nola lunged toward Addy. A blade flashed orange in the lantern light.

Phoebe whirled and used her shortened staff to strike Nola in the temple.

Nola dropped like a swatted mosquito.

Phoebe pried a French chef's knife from Nola's grip.

"Addy! Nola brought the knife. Wasn't that nice of her?"

Tuttle snorted. "There's not a nice bone in Nola Peterson's body. She's a stone-cold cunt. Attacking the bitch lying in the corner is the most passionate I've ever seen her."

At least he didn't call Nola a bitch. Maybe I'll go easier on him for that. Ha!

"Rick says fucking her is like fucking a corpse," Tuttle continued, "so he probably won't notice you killed her."

Phoebe knelt next to Nola. Her heart still beat. Her lungs continued to suck in oxygen. "She's not dead."

"Yet," Addy grunted.

"Too bad for your son." Phoebe stood, her gaze never leaving Tuttle. "Does he fuck corpses on a regular basis?"

He seemed taken aback by her saying fuck, as if only sapien males were allowed to use the word. "Cute. Nola will have her revenge on you. She's vicious and vindictive, especially when it comes to her grandfather, and you thwarted her."

"I fucked with her." Phoebe trod on Nola's chest as she approached Tuttle. "Don't push, yet, Addy. I need to take out the trash before we can deliver your baby."

She bared her teeth at Tuttle. "What about Nola's grandfather? What was she babbling about?"

"He's a vampire. Sun allergies forced him to retire from congress. He needs periodic infusions of fetal shifter blood to maintain his status."

Phoebe's gorge rose. She swallowed hard to keep from spewing all over him. The hut smelled bad enough as it was, in part because Tuttle reeked of vampire, although not as strongly as he had in the hospital. "Are you a vampire? You stink like one."

"Don't be ridiculous. How could I be in the senate if I can't be in the sunlight?"

Phoebe could think of lots of ways.

With Addy sprawled behind her and Nola crumpled in an inconvenient spot, Phoebe found no room to circle behind Tuttle. She continued to inch into a better fighting position. *Keep him talking. Distract him.*

"How did a good ol' boy like you end up with Minnesota vampires?"

"William and I formed an alliance between the House and the Senate during my first term. He had power, and I used his power to boost myself get to where I am today— more powerful than he ever was."

"Some power, since you're about to die in a hut in northern Minnesota. You pissed off the wrong people." If only she could shift. She could rip out his throat.

"You're not people, and I'm not going to die. Neither are you. Yet. William is going to want a go at you. He loves pregnant werewolf bitches, and it's been a long time."

"Fifteen years?"

Tuttle's head jerked. "What are you talking about?"

"I was there. I saw you." Maybe she could distract him. "Tennessee, about fifteen years ago. You and your troopers murdered my family. Wiped out a whole village of shifters."

"Dustin Holloway mentioned a story like that going around."

"I watched you."

Tuttle smirked. "I don't think so."

"I climbed a tree. I saw you shoot my mother." Images in black and white darted through her memory. She wanted to close her eyes, squeeze them shut to wring the flickering pictures away, but didn't dare take her eyes off Tuttle. "Life's a bitch, you said, so kill one. Bang. You shot her. The night of the new moon. No one could shift to protect themselves. You didn't use automatic weapons, though. You used my family for target practice. Skeet."

The shadow of Tuttle's larynx wobbled in the wavering light.

"Aaahhh," Addy moaned.

Phoebe managed to keep her tone conversational as she continued to maneuver into position to pounce. Fragments of memory demanded her attention. "One guy with you called you Senator Bullfrog."

There. A balk.

Phoebe swooped at the lantern and extinguished the flame. Darkness swallowed the room. Her lycan eyes quickly adjusted.

Tuttle coughed at the onslaught of heavy kerosene fumes.

Even if she were blindfolded, Phoebe could locate Tuttle by the wet rattle of his breathing.

"I'm glad I don't have to track you down," Phoebe growled. "I can kill you here and now. Leave your body in the woods for the scavengers to feast on."

"Like you did with Liam and Connor Peters?"

Phoebe! Keep Jeeves handy!

Phoebe flinched. She never expected Parker to communicate with her. How did he know Nola Peters and Senator Tuttle had shown up, unless—

"What is that?" Tuttle whispered.

"What is what?"

"The howling. The werewolves are supposed to be—"

"Supposed to be what?" Her broken quarterstaff's lighter weight concerned her. She hoped the myth that sapien eyesight wasn't as keen as lycan was true. There could be no do-overs.

"Nothing."

"You're the one who dies this time," Phoebe assured Tuttle as she focused on the sounds and scents in the room.

Tuttle's wet breathing. Addy's grunting and panting. An aroma mingled with blood related to the imminent arrival of Addy's baby. The change in Nola's respiration as she regained consciousness.

"What's Nola's grandpa's problem, anyway?"

"Who knows how a vampire's mind works?" Tuttle played for the same stakes as Phoebe: time.

I'm on my way. The wolves' howls drew closer.

Tuttle recoiled again.

"Why do you hate the Limmikin so much? You at least owe me an answer."

"I don't owe you anything."

"I'm your constituent. I voted against you in the last election, but my taxes still pay your salary."

Appealing to the politician worked.

"The Limmikin refused to sign a service for sanctuary treaty." He spoke the words as if she should have known.

Which she did because Corbie told her. Corbie made sure Phoebe knew every scrap Phoebe's granny shared with her over the course of their friendship. "The Limmikin don't need sanctuary in their own home."

"We can't have vicious shifters running amok." Tuttle spoke slowly, as if he were trying to mask the sounds of Nola stirring and rising to her feet.

Funny. Phoebe didn't remember her family as being vicious or running around without purpose.

"And we can't have arrogant politicians deciding who gets to live and who gets to die," Phoebe countered as she whirled around and jammed her quarterstaff into Nola's stomach, then smacked her in the face. Blood spurted from her broken nose.

The woman resumed her crumpled state on the floor.

"Why did Grandpa Peters attack you?" Phoebe guessed Peters caused Tuttle's "cat scratch fever."

"A flare up of an old disagreement over the value of the Limmikin."

"What?" His answer surprised her.

"Congressman Peters used the Limmikin to get his fix of fetal blood. Like cows or goats. He considered them his herd. They serviced him without their consent. He was livid when I eliminated the local pack a while ago."

"You failed. There were survivors." Phoebe smiled as she thought of the legendary Hache-Hi and the reality of Hatch Calhoun.

"Really? I suppose like you they hid in trees?"

"I don't know. All I know is the alpha lives. And when he learns you were behind his pack's massacre, he's going to want a piece of you." She lowered her voice. "But there won't be any pieces left. I don't share."

Tuttle lunged. Phoebe easily sidestepped his attack. Tuttle stumbled over Nola and went sprawling. Phoebe tested his skull's thickness with her quarterstaff.

"Phoebe?" Addy's weak voice fractured Phoebe's focus. "I think I need your help now."

Chapter 36

THE RAIN SLOWED TO a drizzle. The wind whined like a tired toddler. Parker heard Jakob and Restin as clearly as if they were standing next to him.

Two sapien males, Jakob shared. *The younger one carried a gun and sniveled because the air pressure messed with his aim. They smell like skunks.*

We're following them to Ulvskog, Restin added. *Meet us there. Take care. Moonset is in about half an hour.*

I'm going to Gambayan. Jakob dared contradict a higher ranked lobo. *My mate is there. These two weren't vampires, the old magic might not keep them out.*

Phoebe and Jeeves didn't stand a chance against a gun.

Selena didn't hesitate. *Leave me two lobos. Harry. Ed. Take everyone else with you. Between us, we should be able to get Ethan, Rand, and Hatch off the mountain. I'm a healer. Maybe not an EMT with sapien tricks, but a healer regardless. I will care for the injured. You care for your gestating mate.*

Parker took off before Selena finished.

PARKER DECIDED THE STENCH coming from Restin's newly constructed full moon lodge won the Worst Smell I've Ever Encountered Award, paws down. Even the night they'd ashed the dozen or more vampires lurking on the edges of Ethan's neighborhood had not reeked this bad.

Parker's eyes weren't the only ones watering from whatever lurked behind the walls. A Varulv female started coughing.

So much for a sneak attack.

"Who's there?" The old, creaky voice carried an undertone of authority. A tone used to being obeyed or risk the consequences.

Parker knew he should wait for Restin. The Varulv needed a figurehead. He couldn't stay. Rescuing his mate trumped Restin's bruised ego.

Go! Dakota jerked his head. *I'll hold down the fort. Lodge. Whatever.*

Parker didn't need to be told twice.

ADDY'S SCREAM SHATTERED THE predawn stillness. Jakob, who arrived in Gambayan at the same time as Parker, wanted to burst into the hut where the females isolated themselves. Parker blocked the entrance. Something didn't smell right.

Yes, he scented Phoebe inside. She'd done as he asked. She didn't abandon him. But—

"I see the baby's head," he heard Phoebe say. Jakob froze.

"I have to push!" Addy shrieked.

"Okay, okay." Phoebe sounded as frantic as Addy.

The moon set.

Jakob didn't wait for his transformation to finish before shoving Parker aside and rushing into the hut. "You weren't supposed to give birth without me," he chided. "What the—"

A thunk. A thud.

"I swear to your god I will skewer you and gut you like a deer if you come any closer to me." Phoebe's icy tone chilled Parker.

"You? Hah." The unfamiliar male voice froze Parker's balls. Judging by the smell, not a vampire, but something close. Maybe one of Helga's factotum creatures.

Jakob moaned.

"Don't tempt fate, Senator." Phoebe sounded distracted.

Senator? Parker could think of only one man claiming the honorarium. Then it hit him. *Phoebe knows I'm here.*

Parker stood on two legs. His pelt vanished. Rain slid down his bare skin in silken streams. He listened as his mate fed him information.

"I've got Nola's knife and all my werewolf tricks. What do you have?"

Nola? Nola Peters? Why was she in Gambayan?

"Push, Addy. Let's get your baby born."

"Not if I stop her. Congressman Peters needs a fetus, not a newborn."

"I remind you again. I am holding a big, sharp knife."

Parker slipped into the hut as unobtrusively as he could.

The darkness aided him. The space smelled of kerosene, blood, and birth. He stumbled over Jakob's sprawled body. Parker blinked to adjust his vision.

The senator, focused on Phoebe and Addy, didn't react to Parker's appearance. Phoebe acknowledged his arrival by turning her attention to Addy, half-lying, half propped, legs spread.

"The baby," Addy gasped.

"I've got it." Phoebe laid the knife at her side and reached into the shadow between Addy's spraddled legs. "Let's get the first baby of the new Varulv generation born."

"They can't keep us down," Addy replied on a moan. Tuttle lunged toward the females.

"I don't think so, Senator." Parker tackled him.

Tuttle swung something at him. Connected with his jaw.

Agony burst from the impact point.

Tuttle swung again.

"You're doing fine," Phoebe crooned.

Parker grabbed Tuttle's arm and snapped it. Tuttle screamed as Parker twisted.

"He hit me," Phoebe tattled. "Tried to kick me, too. Okay, the head is out."

"Shoulders next," Parker called out, twisting Tuttle's arm in the opposite direction. "Shoulders are the tough part. All downhill from there."

He dropped Tuttle's now-useless arm. "You struck my mate?"

"And tried to kick me," Phoebe reminded him.

Tuttle used his good arm to cradle the broken one against his chest. "You'll pay for this," he threatened. "You don't know who I am or what—"

Parker's fist landed squarely on the senator's mouth. Tuttle's head snapped back. Teeth crunched. Blood welled. "Why don't you explain it to me?"

Addy grunted.

"Push!" Phoebe urged. "I've got the shoulders."

"The hard part is over." Parker grabbed Tuttle by the throat and lifted him from the floor. "Baby should pop out practically on its own."

He flung Tuttle against the stone wall. The crack of his skull overrode Addy's loud grunt as she finished squeezing her baby into the world. The senator slid to the floor like thick, oozing slime.

Jakob stirred. Groaned.

The newborn whimpered.

"How do I cut the cord?" Phoebe asked.

"Cut the cord?" Jakob's voice rasped from howling all night.

"Do you really have a knife?" Parker picked Tuttle up by his coat lapels and slammed him against the wall again. Bones crunched.

"Your daughter," Phoebe explained to Jakob. "Come meet the next generation of Varulv."

Jakob crawled to his mate's side. "What do I do?" he asked, as Phoebe handed him the knife.

Jakob's awe squeezed Parker's heart. *Someday...*

"I don't want to hurt them."

Parker figured he'd better act as an advisor. "Has the cord stopped pulsing?"

"I don't think so." Jakob's voice strengthened.

"Phoebe, do you have something to tie off the cord? Maybe your breast bindings?"

Phoebe stood. Stretched. Whipped off her shirt.

Parker didn't expect her to bare herself to the world. She could have removed the cloth band without removing her shirt.

But there she stood, bare-breasted and unconscious about it. She tore the fabric into narrow strips. "What do I do?"

Parker crossed the room. "Here, I'll do it."

There is nothing like the miracle of birth, he thought as he tied off two spots on the umbilical cord. "The baby and Addy can't feel this," he told Jakob. "Go ahead. Cut between the two ties."

The next several moments were peaceful. Gentle, even. Parker checked out the baby the best he could in the dark. Everything seemed okay. Addy delivered the placenta with no problem. The child's wail signaled all was right in the world.

"No!"

The female shriek startled him.

"It shouldn't have been born! Grandfather needs a fetus, not a newborn."

"Nola, shut up before I rip out your tongue." Phoebe sounded weary. She'd put on her shirt. Her breasts bobbed with every movement.

"What's she talking about?" Parker asked.

"Her grandfather is a vampire who is addicted to lycan fetal blood or some such bullshit. He used the Limmikin as his own private suppliers until Tuttle started killing them off for not signing service for sanctuary treaties." Phoebe fumbled in the dark as she spoke.

"It's not bullshit." Nola sounded frantic. "He's gone too long without an infusion."

"I'm going to solve Grandpa's problem once and for all." Phoebe waved something. Too short to be Jeeves. The knife glinted on the sleeping bag next to Jakob, Addy, and their baby.

Phoebe swung. Her weapon connected with Nola's jaw. She dropped to the floor. "There. That ought to shut her up. We can kill her when we off Gramps. Come on, Parker. There's still work to do. Grab Tuttle, I'll take the girl. Apparently Gramps is in Ulvskog awaiting his elixir. We need to get to him before he goes to ground at sunrise."

Ulvskog. Scat. How could he have forgotten? Rand. Hatch. Ethan.

Phoebe hoisted Nola's inert body over her shoulder. Being taller than Phoebe, Nola's feet dragged on the ground. "I'll take them both," Parker offered. They couldn't leave either of the intruders with the new family. Maybe they could be used as bargaining chips.

Phoebe looked odd as she handed over Nola. Something seemed...different. Yes, her breasts weren't bound. The glow of pregnancy barely flickered in her. But something else...something missing...

"Where's Jeeves?"

Phoebe never stirred without her quarterstaff. She scooped two pieces of kindling from the floor. "Broken."

Nothing in her tone, nothing on her face betrayed her significant, maybe even traumatic loss. Someday he would get her to tell him what happened.

"Do I have time to grab some clothes?"

Phoebe looked him up and down. "I like you like this, but I don't want Nola to get any ideas. Hurry."

Chapter 37

Phoebe's stomach couldn't handle the stench emanating from Ulvskog's newly built full moon lodge. She dropped the quarterstaff pieces and vomited into a cluster of bushes. Random raindrops tickled her nape.

"Are you okay?" Parker asked. He dumped Nola and Tuttle next to a rain-pocked puddle, then rubbed Phoebe's back.

"I heard this is normal," she muttered as she straightened. Bad stomach was on Addy's symptoms punch list. She could have used some water from the sacred spring to rinse her mouth. She picked up the remnants of her weapon.

Fog wrapped the clearing in a gray blanket. The number of naked Varulv surrounding the lodge surprised Phoebe. She didn't know everyone by sight, but she figured the entire pack clustered around the building.

"So glad you could join us," Restin sneered.

Phoebe didn't like his tone. He had no right to speak to Parker with such contempt. She concentrated on keeping her eyes on his face. Maybe the Varulv and Loup Garou were used to running around buck naked, but the sight embarrassed Phoebe.

"Other business occupied us, as you well know." Parker's cool tone contrasted against Restin's sarcasm. He jerked his head toward Tuttle and Nola Peters. "What's your progress?"

Restin glared, then blinked as rain dripped into his eyes. "Selena and her team are en route with the injured ones. She ordered us to wait until she arrived."

"Injured ones?" Phoebe looked from Restin to Parker.

"Didn't you tell your mate anything?" Restin's contempt rivaled the stench from the full moon lodge. "Ethan, Rand, and Hatch accidentally fell off the mountain."

Three Limmikin.

Phoebe's hand crept to her belly. "Accidentally?"

"Sabotage." Parker sounded grim. "We were busy delivering Addy's baby and dealing with intruders. Did Selena say anything about the injuries?"

"Not important." Phoebe couldn't believe the male posturing when a more pressing matter needed to be addressed. They could continue their pissing match later. "There's a vampire in the full moon lodge. He has to be dealt with before sunrise."

"Selena ordered us to wait," Restin repeated.

Phoebe clutched her bits of quarterstaff. "Well, Selena isn't the boss of me."

"Phoebe."

Parker frustrated the hell out of her when he tried to hold her back.

"She's not. I have no pack. Hatch, if anyone, is my alpha, and according to Restin, he's injured. As are his successors. I'm the only Limmikin still standing." She gripped her sticks tighter to keep from touching her belly. We're it, kiddo.

"She's not my alpha, either." Restin sided with Phoebe.

"We need to act before sunrise," she repeated.

"What about the ones you followed?" Parker asked. "The snipers."

Clearly Parker failed to share everything with her.

"Disarmed and secured. Waiting for Selena." Restin sounded annoyed by Parker's questions. "Not that I report to you."

"I didn't say you did. I wanted to know. Guns scare me." Parker didn't blink. "And they're traumatic for my mate. Thank the Ancient Ones they were lousy shots or Rand's injury could have been a lot worse."

Phoebe wanted to shriek, *What injury?* Her questions could wait, though. The vampire in the full moon lodge could not. Instead, she appealed to their innate lobo as she studied the building. "You guys have experience. What kills a vampire?"

"Staking its heart." Parker didn't hesitate. "Tearing its heart out of its chest. Maybe fire. We could check with Luke."

"You're not burning down my new full moon lodge," Restin growled.

Parker tried logic. "What if the stink won't come out?"

"You two can debate this later," Phoebe reminded them. We're wasting the predawn hour. We need to kill the vampire."

"Wouldn't it be easier if we attack after sunrise? He's going to need to find a daylight safe place." Parker checked the sky. "Which means he needs to come out. We should block all the exits and entrances."

"Front door, back door." Restin counted off the many escape routes. "Windows."

"What about the secret passage?" Parker's sharp tone betrayed his frustration. "Where does it come out?"

Restin glowered at Parker. "The crew worked on digging a tunnel to Gambayan. I'm not sure how far along they are."

Phoebe's stomach dropped. *Secret passage?* "They what?" If they could have innate lobo, she could have innate bitch.

"A tunnel to the old town," Restin repeated.

"Oh shit!" She turned and ran toward the old town. Toward Addy and her baby. The old magic might keep vampires from entering through the woods, but a tunnel could bypass the charms protecting the place. Stupid male mentality. Phoebe might have been raised sapien, but even she understood what could go wrong.

"What is it?" Parker dogged her heels.

"The vampire wants fetal blood. A tunnel will bypass the magical forcefield protecting Gambayan."

Parker didn't question her conclusion. Instead, he grabbed her arm, then spun her so they faced each other. "No. Not you. Me. You're carrying the only thing close to a fetus here. Addy's baby is a newborn. Her blood system is now independent of Addy's."

His smoky quartz eyes bore into hers.

She understood. His DNA couldn't allow him to do anything else. Mate and offspring above all else.

"Take this." She thrust one splinter-ended quarterstaff piece at him. "Do you remember what I taught you?"

"Yes." He hefted the mini weapon. "Go back to Ulvskog. Stay with the pack."

She swallowed her ire. Revising the mindset of a lifetime needed more than half an hour. She brushed the tips of her fingers against his cheek, mimicking the soft kiss of the gradually tapering rain.

He crushed her fingers in his hand and dragged her closer for a kiss. When he released her, she couldn't tell if mist or steam shrouded his body. Her female bits tingled.

She tested the air. No sign of vampire, thank the Goddess. Only rich earth, lingering ozone from the lightning, and skunk.

She hadn't smelled skunk since leaving Warwick.

Someone emerged from the trees into the path. She froze. Time creased the tall male's face into a perpetual scowl.

Scrapes and red patches maturing into bruises marred his complexion. Something in his eyes haunted her.

"There you are."

She knew that voice. Not in a good way.

Parker! She knew they weren't psychically connected, but her brain called for her mate anyway.

"Here I am," she agreed. Her voice remained steady.

Whatever the stranger wanted couldn't be good. Her fingers gripped the fractured quarterstaff. "Clever to use skunk juice to disguise your scent."

"I learned it from Junior. Hunting tips are about the only thing Senator Bullfrog and his tadpole are good for."

Senator Bullfrog.

She swallowed hard and tried to blink away a rush of dizziness. The last time she'd heard Tuttle called Senator Bullfrog came from this man's mouth. She'd been cowering in a tree while the tall stranger aimed his gun at her grandfather's head. *This isn't much sport, Senator Bullfrog. My boss wants pregnant ones. You promised me you could provide them.*

Tuttle had given this man a dirty look. She'd never before seen pure loathing on another being's face.

Then bang! Grandpa's head exploded, and he collapsed.

Where the wolf women at? Then the stranger laughed.

The tree bark bit into her cheek, leaving a pattern that didn't fade for a week.

"You're the one they say is an eyewitness to a hunting trip Bullfrog arranged ten, fifteen years ago. Good hunting in Tennessee, he claimed. He lied." The skunky stranger leered at her.

Phoebe didn't move. Barely breathed. The stranger breathed heavily enough for both of them. He grimaced with each step toward her.

Restin and the others might have confiscated this man's gun and beaten him into submission, but they hadn't disarmed him.

"I'm afraid we haven't been introduced," she worked up the courage to say. "Are you on Senator Tuttle's staff?"

"I work for Congressman Peters, not that hillbilly."

"Congressman Peters? Didn't I read he committed suicide and his sons ran away?"

The stranger's face morphed from scowl to sneer. "The congressman's pervert son committed suicide, and his grandsons vanished, along with my nephew."

"Your nephew? Then you must be Tony DiNardo." Phoebe kept her tone conversational. "I heard one of your former tenants mention your name."

"What's your name, little girl?"

"Phoebe the Factotum Hunter."

DiNardo's laugh turned into a wince. "Yeah. How did you know what the congressman likes to call me? I don't know what it means, but he says he's ordering business cards for me."

"It means gofer. Flunky. Handyman. It's a skill. Not everyone could sabotage an elevator and kill an annoyance at the same time. I assume you trapped Dustin Holloway at the bottom of the shaft."

"Dustin mentioned you were a quick study." DiNardo inched closer. "He claimed to be a werewolf expert. Bullfrog bought into it. Any idea why?"

She did her best to look confused. "Nope."

"He told Tuttle he grew up with a female werewolf."

"Dustin possessed a wild imagination. I thought you ran into a pack of werewolves and were…subdued."

DiNardo guffawed. "Werewolves are stupid creatures. I never met one who could do more than beg and whine."

"You sabotaged the full moon gathering place. Shot a couple of werewolves."

"We hit some?" DiNardo hawked and spat into the bushes. "Damn air pressure fucks up a bullet's trajectory."

"The werewolves ate your nephew." Phoebe spoke without emotion.

"What?" DiNardo faltered.

"I personally didn't participate, nor do I have a taste for sapien flesh." She'd never eaten sapien but feigning a shudder seemed like the right thing to do. "I heard Selena bit off Liam Peters' penis before those begging, whining werewolves went to town on someone named Curtis. Your nephew?"

DiNardo blanched. The contusions on his face stood out like mildew on a toilet.

"You could check the Warwick sewage treatment plant for DNA traces, but werewolves also shit in the woods. Why don't you run around and gather scat samples and send them to a lab? Using your congressman's name might get your request prioritized. Oh. Except your congressman is about to be staked."

Phoebe showed her teeth. "Vampires taste nasty. Rotten. Worse than they smell, or so I'm told. And yours will be especially revolting because he's so old. So it will be oak to the chest, then poof."

That's what Helga told her. *Vampires go poof when they explode.*

"Not once he drinks the fetal werewolf blood." DiNardo sounded sure of himself.

"No fetuses in the werewolf population around here. Your congressman's son ordered them exterminated."

"Yet here you stand."

"I'm not from around here, remember? Eyewitness to Tuttle and you in Tennessee. Well, Tuttle got his. You're next."

She leapt at him, the stub of her quarterstaff raised.

DiNardo tried to sidestep her attack, but his age and the beating by Restin's posse made him clumsy.

She jammed the end of her quarterstaff into his throat. The breakage of tissue and muscle reverberated through the wood and up her arm. DiNardo gurgled. He clasped his hands around the stake and yanked it free.

Phoebe ducked to the side so she wouldn't be spattered by the spray of blood. He staggered toward her, blood- drenched hands extended. Reaching.

She swooped behind him, scooped up the gore-covered quarterstaff piece, and swung it at his head. Oak connected with bone with a satisfying thunk. He dropped. The ground quaked.

The rain stopped, but the wind dried the leaves the way a dog shook off a swimming hole.

"Nicely done."

Phoebe whirled to find Richard Tuttle, Junior aiming a gun at her. No lycan could outmaneuver a speeding bullet.

What happened to Restin, Dakota, and the others who were supposed to be guarding the snipers? How did the tadpole get his hands on the gun?

"You killed my father and my fiancé."

Nola died? No loss.

Phoebe fought for control. "Your father killed my entire family. Your fiancé tried to steal babies to feed her vampire grandfather." *My baby.* "Now it's your turn to hurt."

The wind continued to rustle the leaves; the collected rain plunked to the ground. Not even the scent of fresh blood could mask the skunk juice with which Tony DiNardo doused himself.

Another smell, one she now recognized as vampire, overrode everything else.

An old man hobbled up to Junior. His fangs flashed in the gray light. "Grab her."

"Aren't you risking a lot to be here?" Junior asked the old vamp.

"She's pregnant. She has what I need." The old man's voice didn't creak. "I heard the others talking. Don't shoot her, subdue her, so I can—"

He staggered. Tried to turn. He hissed. Grabbed for Phoebe with disgusting curved claws.

The end of a stake protruded through the old man's chest right before...poof.

Cold ash blew into the air and mingled with the recycled rain.

"Son of a bitch," Tuttle, Junior muttered right before a petite wolf ripped out his throat.

Selena sang her victory to the dying night, blood dripping from her jaws. She darted through the trees toward Ulvskog. Phoebe sank to the wet ground. A moment later Parker emerged from the same trees Selena used and joined Phoebe. "I'm sorry. I know you wanted to be the one to kill them, but I couldn't risk you."

Her. Not just the baby.

"It's okay. I wanted revenge." She took his hand and placed it on her belly. "This is revenge. The next generation of a pack they tried to exterminate."

Chapter 38

Parker tossed Junior Tuttle and Tony DiNardo's bodies over his shoulder. The two males weighed more than his earlier load but was nothing he couldn't handle. The ordeal might be over, but until the loose ends were resolved, he couldn't celebrate the way his soul longed to. "Let's finish this."

Phoebe shivered in her wet clothes. "I want to know what happened."

"I have gaps, too." He started toward Ulvskog.

"I feel naked without my quarterstaff."

"I know you do." He'd find her another one as soon as they got to Colorado. Their offspring would be taught the skill as soon as they could grasp one.

They found the Varulv milling around a half-built house on the edge of town. The sun tried to dispel the rainclouds with touches of gold. The clouds were winning.

"The full moon lodge must stink too much," Parker murmured. "Old Man Peters holed up in there."

He dumped Junior and DiNardo next to Tuttle and Nola Peters.

"Good night for hunting," Restin observed.

"What's happening?" Parker straightened, then rolled his shoulders.

"Selena and Ethan want Phoebe."

Parker and Phoebe exchanged a look, then hurried toward the half-built structure.

Ethan looked pale, but he stood upright. Rand sat, holding a piece of what looked like a flannel shirt against his ear. Both were caked with mud.

Parker vowed to examine them at his first chance.

Hatch was a different story.

"Oh no." Phoebe left Parker's side and knelt next to Hatch, stretched out on the bare plank floor. She took his gnarled hand in hers. "Hache-Hi."

The old lobo's eyes flickered open. Rested on Phoebe. The corners of his mouth twitched.

His dreadful color and rattling breath told Parker the Limmikin alpha wouldn't last the morning.

Tears dripped down Phoebe's cheeks and formed runnels in the mud on Hatch's hand.

"Revenge," Hatch whispered. "You understand?"

Phoebe blinked away her tears. "Yes."

"Good." He closed his eyes.

Ethan and Rand joined Phoebe at Hatch's side. Rand swayed, but Ethan braced him.

Outside, scattered howling shattered dawn's stillness.

The Varulv mourned the passing of another pack's alpha.

Phoebe couldn't appreciate the ritual. No one mourned her family, her pack. Parker stood behind her, hands on her shoulders. She didn't belong to Hatch's family, but she as a Limmikin female could substitute for Hatch and Rand's mates. After all, she was the only other known Limmikin in the world.

Selena, who stood behind Ethan, stared straight ahead.

Selena, too, never said goodbye to her grandfather.

Their vigil didn't last long.

Phoebe released Hatch's hand. Rand crossed his father's arms over his chest. One shuddering breath. Another. Then...nothing.

"We thank the Gods of our Elders for Hache-Hi, Hatch Calhoun's life," Selena prayed.

"We thank the Ancient Ones for my father's life," Rand intoned.

"Thank the Goddess for Hache-Hi." Phoebe whispered her benediction.

"And the Creator," Ethan added. "My grandfather's deity."

Outside, the werewolves sang a eulogy to the old man they'd come to know.

The rain-weakened sun found its way through gaps in the partial walls. A finger of gold brushed Hatch's face as though in blessing.

Phoebe's shoulders quivered beneath Parker's hands.

The lycan lamentations gradually ceased.

Eventually Selena spoke. "Goodbye, grandfather of my mate."

Ethan climbed to his feet, then helped his father stand.

Parker squeezed Phoebe's shoulders. "Are you ready?" he whispered in her ear.

Her head jerked an assent.

He helped her rise. "Will you be okay if I check on Rand?"

She nodded, a smoother action this time, but her breathing remained shaky. Tears stained her cheeks. She needed comfort. "Go. He needs you most."

"WHAT DO WE DO now?" Phoebe's brain had turned to mush. So much happened. So much to process.

The hours after Hache-Hi's passing were spent caring for the living. Washing away mud. Tending wounds. Phoebe tried to patch together the conversation scraps she overheard but large pieces were missing.

Then sleep. Selena ordered everyone to nap.

Daylight faded toward night. Clouds continued to smother the sun. Someone built a campfire in the center of the main road. Orange sparks shot into the sky like stars flying home.

The smell of burning wood dredged memories for Phoebe. Memories of the good times with her family. Of her grandparents telling stories. Of laughing and singing, hugs and kisses.

The campfire smell also hid the aroma of ripening sapien corpses.

Selena stood by the fire, her body a dark shadow against the brilliance of the flames. "We have things we need to do. We have decisions to make."

"Decisions are your job," a Varulv muttered.

"Not without council," Selena snapped. A burning log popped. "We're in this together. I need to hear your thoughts."

The Varulvs' reluctance to share with Selena irritated Phoebe.

"The world has changed." Ethan sat on a stump directly behind Selena. "More of our kind are mating with sapiens. The service for sanctuary treaties protecting us are being rescinded. We can't stop our enemies. We're on our own."

If Phoebe were a fanciful she-wolf, she would have sworn she felt a collective shudder.

"The first thing we need to discuss is what we're going to do about the bodies."

Four dead sapiens. Parker confirmed Nola's death. The corpses had lain around for hours, ripening by the moment.

"Burn them."

"Shove them in the secret passage and burn the full moon lodge. It stinks now, anyway."

"Bury them."

Some Varulv lobos did have brains.

"Find the cars they arrived in, toss in the bodies, and drive them back to Warwick," Dakota suggested. "Leave them someplace not easily found, but also not too hidden. We need the bodies to be found and identified. Otherwise, the limbo of Liam and Connor Peters' status continues."

"How would we explain the wounds?" Selena asked.

"We don't." Dakota sounded amused. "Explanations are the cops' problem, not ours. We're not connected in any way. Why would we be asked? We load them up, scour the tires so there are no soil samples, run the vehicle through a car wash, then abandon it somewhere not too populated, but not here. There's enough summer left for the bodies to cook real nice in a closed up car."

Phoebe thought it should bother her that these lobos were so...cavalier about the dead, but it didn't. Maybe she was learning how to be a real werewolf.

"Let's talk about what happened!" someone in back shouted. "We were up on the ledge singing, like we do every full moon, and then the alphas and betas vanished."

"Parker, tell us what you found," Selena instructed.

Phoebe stared at her mate as he related his story. Her jaw dropped with every other sentence. The traditional ledge sabotaged, the rain weakening the ground, the collapse. Five werewolves, every alpha and beta, washed down the mountain. How Jakob found shovel marks, and someone else noticed lightning reflecting off something that shouldn't be there. Discovering Rand had been shot.

"We know the rest." Selena glossed over rescuing Ethan, Rand, and Hatch. "What happened in Gambayan?"

Phoebe's face heated as everyone turned to her.

"I went into labor." Addy spoke softly as her daughter quietly nursed. "And Phoebe found out she's pregnant."

Everyone in Ulvskog knew about her condition before she did.

"It's all fuzzy for me," Addy admitted.

"Childbirth fuzzes the brain," a she-wolf confirmed.

"Otherwise, we'd never let our mates near us again." Female snickers cut the tension.

Phoebe continued her tale. "Then Senator Tuttle and Congressman Peters' daughter showed up. They wanted Addy's baby before it was born. I couldn't let them steal her baby."

"Fetal blood for a vampire," Addy added.

Low growls broke the silence following Addy's revelation.

The simple words belied the long, tense hours in the hut. "Then Parker and Jakob showed up. Parker dealt with Tuttle and Nola Peters while I helped Addy." Phoebe licked her lips. She wished for a sip of water.

"After the baby was born is a blur. I know we came here and learned the vampire might have escaped through a secret tunnel to Gambayan. After all the work I did to bring Addy's baby into the world, I couldn't let anyone harm her."

"He didn't use the secret passageway," Parker said. "False trail."

Restin took over the telling, spitting into the fire before speaking. "Wiley old vampire. I always thought the whole vampires hypnotizing victims was a myth. Maybe he didn't use hypnosis, but he did something to the lobos guarding Tuttle Junior and the factotum. Freed the prisoners and pointed them toward the old town."

Phoebe picked up the thread. "Where they ran into me. They isolated me. They knew about my condition and planned to substitute my fetus for Addy's."

"Wouldn't they be surprised when they learned Otis is still an embryo." Parker patted her belly.

"Otis? You come up with the stupidest names."

"I'll explain later. An embryo doesn't become a fetus until about ten weeks."

She couldn't possibly be ten weeks pregnant.

"I recognized the first sapien because he referred to Tuttle as 'Senator Bullfrog.' One of the gunmen called Tuttle that the night they slaughtered my pack. I still had part of my quarterstaff, so I defended myself."

"Only part?" Selena's sarcasm set Phoebe's teeth on edge.

"I broke her quarterstaff," Addy confessed.

"Enough to slam into his throat." The shock on his face. The way he yanked the wood from his throat. The gush of blood.

"Tony DiNardo." Selena looked around at the assembled wolves. "I killed his nephew the same night we dealt with Liam Peters. And I killed Tuttle's son while he held a gun on Phoebe."

"Good."

"Of course you did."

"You had another choice?"

Not one voice condemned Selena.

"Then Old Man Peters himself arrived." Phoebe would never forget his stench. "He tempted daybreak to get his fix of fetal blood."

She closed her eyes. The movie of the night her world came to a bloody end played out on the screens of her eyelids. "I recognized him, too. From the night my village was slaughtered. I'd forgotten so much about that night, but seeing his face, smelling his stench, brought it all back."

She opened her eyes and swallowed hard. Parker's arm tightened across her shoulders.

"I hid in a tree," she explained. "I saw everything. My mother was pregnant. I forgot. She was going to have another baby, and I hoped so hard for a sister. My brothers were pains in the ass, but I figured a sister would be on my side."

Parker's arm, his whole body tensed. It seemed everyone around the campfire held their breath, even though they knew the ending. She needed to speak the words. She needed to rid her mind of the poison.

"Congressman Peters knocked my mother down. Tore open her belly with his claws and buried his face in the gash he'd made. My mother screamed the whole time he fed. Until Tuttle shot her in the head. 'Life's a bitch, so kill one,' he said."

"Are you okay?" Parker didn't like the sing-song manner in which Phoebe related her horrible memory. The telling had to be therapeutic, but her stillness worried him. Scared him. He thought she should be trembling either from the hideousness of her experience or fury. With Phoebe, he'd bet on fury.

She had every reason in the world to be furious.

Yet if not for the thud of her heart or her controlled breathing, he wouldn't know she lived.

"Never been better."

She spoke the truth. He would have smelled a lie. There was a boneless quality to her body that surpassed even her post-coital relaxation, as if the memory of that long-ago Tennessee night was the only thing that had held her together. That, and the dearly departed Jeeves.

She rested her head against his shoulder. "It's over. Everything. So many years I dreamed about killing Tuttle. I always figured I would die trying. But here I sit, and he's about to simmer in a car turned slow-cooker."

The others were dispersing. Selena sent two lobos to search for any vehicles in which the invaders arrived. Addy and Jakob headed back to their hut in Gambayan. Restin sat across the fire from Parker and Phoebe and stared at the all- but-finished full moon lodge. The building reeked so bad no other lycan would approach it.

They'd probably have to burn it and start over.

Ethan and Dakota stood to one side, gesturing at the structure. They were stuck here in Minnesota.

Ethan bore the double whammy of being mated to the local pack alpha, and still needing to negotiate the continuation of the service for sanctuary treaties with whoever filled the area's congressional seat. Maybe not such a tough task now that both Tuttle and the elder Peters were out of the picture.

Dakota would forever remain a potential suspect in a missing person case where the missing person ended up a staked vampire. Rebuilding Ulvskog would give the lobos something to do until Selena finally admitted Ulvskog could be no more.

Phoebe seemed content to sit and stare at the campfire's dying flames. The moon hung low in the sky, one edge barely worn away. Anyone but a werewolf might think a full moon beamed down on them.

"I wonder how Olivia and Britt are dealing with Helga."

Oh yes. Helga and Warwick. Parker hadn't spared them a thought in days. Something in his chest tightened. "We'll find out tomorrow, if Selena will let us go."

"I bet they're doing fine. If Selena and Ethan stay on Ash Street instead of moving back here, Helga will be more than looked after. Didn't Selena do a great job with the injured last night?"

Parker didn't think he'd ever engaged in small talk with Phoebe before. His breath hitched. "She did."

"You're not needed here. You don't need Selena's permission to leave because you already have your alpha's blessing to go home."

Maybe not such small talk after all.

She sighed and seemed to snuggle closer to him.

He hadn't touched her sexually since the elevator. All his pent-up desire rushed to his groin. He shifted on the log, trying to ease the pressure behind his fly.

"My brain is mush. It's as if I don't know what to think about. Killing Tuttle consumed my thoughts for so many years. Good thing I don't have to come up with something to replace my obsession." Phoebe took Parker's hand and held it against her belly, on the surface of the place the embryo they'd created rested. "You did that for me. Thank you."

He twined his fingers with hers. "The pleasure was all mine." His voice came out rough from scraping the sides of his throat.

"No, not all yours. I was there, too." Her fingers tightened on his.

"I remember."

"Do you? Because I barely do."

Was she hinting that she wanted to have sex?

"Maybe I should remind you."

"I do have a terrible memory."

As if he didn't know she had a memory like a steel trap.

"For instance, I've forgotten what it's like to live in a family unit within a pack. You know. Mother. Father. Children. Grandparents down the road."

Colorado. She's talking about Loup Garou and my family.

"You definitely have your work cut out reminding me of those things." She lifted her chin. "In addition to your paramedic classes."

My agenda. The tightness in his chest broke, the ends snapping at his ribs.

She sparkled in the moonlight, the silver beams glinting off the fine hairs on her face.

"You know, you did a great job with Addy's baby last night. Maybe I could give you lessons in playing doctor."

She laughed, and it was the most beautiful sound he'd ever heard. "You're developing a sense of humor, Doc. No wonder I love you."

She loves me. "We have a lot to teach each other, being in love with each other and all."

There. He'd admitted it aloud.

"It's a good thing we have the rest of our lives to practice." Phoebe released his hand and cupped his cheek. "Why don't we start with a lesson in kissing and see where it takes us?"

I HOPE YOU ENJOYED Parker and Phoebe's story.

Sign up for my newsletter, where subscribers are always the first to learn my news: titles, covers, release dates, sneak peeks of my works in progress, and occasional bonus material for subscribers only. When you sign up, you will receive a FREE short "origin" story about Toke Lobo & the Pack.

So why wait to subscribe? Go to my website (www.mjcompton.com) for the form.

Also By MJ Compton

Pinch of Spice, Justice Served

COLUMBIA GEMS BASEBALL ROMANCES
PARANORMAL ROMANTIC SUSPENSE (Shifters)
THE WRITE PLACE RETREAT ROMANCES

About the Author

MJ Compton grew up near Cardiff, New York, a place best known for its giant—a hoax so successful, P.T. Barnum duplicated it. The tale of the "petrified man" convinced MJ that inventing stories could be a career.

Although her 30 years working in local television included such highlights as being bitten by a lion, preempting a US President for a college basketball game, giving a three-time world champion boxer a few black eyes, and meeting her husband, MJ never lost her dream of creating her own stories.

MJ still lives in upstate New York with her husband. Music and cooking are two of her passions, and she enjoys baseball, college basketball, and sitting on her patio on summer nights to count lightning bugs, but she's primarily focused on writing.

www.ingramcontent.com/pod-product-compliance
Lightning Source LLC
Chambersburg PA
CBHW030738310726
48969CB00005B/1254